# HEAVEN SENT

**Alan Carter** was born in Sunderland, UK. In 1991, he immigrated to Australia and now lives in splendid semi-rural semi-isolation south of Hobart, Tasmania. In his spare time he follows the black line up and down the local swimming pool or drags on his wetsuit and braves the icy waters of the D'Entrecasteaux Channel. He is the author of seven previous novels: the Fremantle-set DS Cato Kwong series *Prime Cut* (winner of the Ned Kelly Award for Best First Fiction), *Getting Warmer*, *Bad Seed*, *Heaven Sent* and *Crocodile Tears*. His New Zealand–based *Marlborough Man*, featuring Sergeant Nick Chester, won the Ngaio Marsh Award for Best Novel. Its sequel is *Doom Creek*.

# ALAN CARTER
# HEAVEN SENT

 FREMANTLE PRESS

*For Norman*

# PROLOGUE

*I can see him from here. Talking to himself like always, arguing with his demons. It's another one of those balmy days in Fremantle, midmorning sun climbing into an electric blue sky. Any workers are at their jobs by this time. Now it's just the mums and babies, the pensioners, the hippies and the losers. The breeze caresses the hairs on my arms. Birds dart between the trees outside the church. The servant has brought me my coffee and told me to enjoy it. As usual it's a thick layer of lukewarm froth, looks nice and creamy but tastes bitter as hell. The old man wouldn't put up with this, he'd go in there and wipe the floor with them. Don't let them take you for granted, he always said.*

*He's got his hand out again. Pinching pennies from the warm-hearted suckers. Gives them his pathetic smile of gratitude. Now they've gone, he gets his tin and empties it into that pocket where he keeps his iPhone. Repositions his scrawled cardboard sign.*

***Homeless, Please Help, God Bless***

*What a fuck-up. That's the problem with this country right there. Bludgers and parasites. Like the old man says, they've turned the 'fair go' into the 'free ride'. Me? I'm like my dad. We're both self-made. Self. Made. Man, you can't get any closer to God than that, can you?*

*I'll take a walk. Ditch the shitty coffee and the alfresco cafe and the airy-fairies bleating about the government. Feel the sun on my face, the jingle of coins in my pocket, the breakfast in my belly. Feel my muscles bursting to be free. Think about the babe at the gym with the slick thighs and the sweat between her breasts. The tattoo on the back of her neck, some swirly writing — To Thine Own Self Be True. Hell yeah.*

*The dead kid has seen me coming. Shakes his head briefly like he's trying to expel a gatecrasher. He's wondering whether I'm worth the* bother. Decides I am. He looks up at me. A flicker of recognition: does he know me, or just think he does?

'Morning, mate,' he says. 'Got a dollar?'

I chuck him two and wish him a good day. After all, it's his last.

# 1

'It's your turn.'

Cato opened one eye. Surely it had only been five minutes since the last time? He switched over to automatic pilot, swung his legs out of bed and sat up. He padded across the room and lifted Ella out of her cot, held her close and softly patted her back, breathing in that luscious sweet-sour milky scent. She was bawling and there was only one remedy. He carried her back to their bed. Sharon was sitting up, breast at the ready. Cato handed the baby over.

'Thanks,' said Sharon, eyes still closed as Ella latched on and went quiet.

'Tea?' Cato yawned.

'Mmmm.'

He stood and watched them for a moment. Drank it in: this good fortune, this miracle.

'What?' Sharon opened an eye. 'What are you smiling at?'

'Nothing,' said Cato. 'Toast?'

'No, no carbs allowed. I'm trying to be a yummy mummy.'

'You're not doing too bad.'

'Is that your idea of a compliment?'

Cato ducked away. 'Tea. Coming right up.'

He fumbled for the light switch in the kitchen. Took a moment to remember it was on the other side from where he was used to. New house, new wife, new baby. The last two years or so had been a mad, glorious whirlwind since Sharon Wang had entered his life. Every so often he would catch himself looking at her, at them, and that old fear would creep in. Fear that he was somehow not worthy, not deserving, and that it would all be taken away from him. Sharon would sometimes catch him then too.

'What?' she'd say.

'Nothing. All good.' Fantastic in fact.

He could hear murmuring from the bedroom as the kettle began to bubble. He filled two mugs and headed back down the hall, aware of the brightening grey outside and the rising twitter of birds. Ella snorted and Sharon smiled down on her. Then Cato's mobile went. It was DC Deb Hassan.

'Yep?' he said.

'There's been another one.'

The old chill returned. Cato got the details and closed the call. Sharon was looking up at him, drowsily sipping from her mug, Ella asleep on her breast.

'What?' she said.

Hassan handed Cato a coffee, a mask, a spacesuit and a pair of blue paper booties as he bent under the perimeter tape. The sun peeked over the eastern skyline and a breeze snaked through the Norfolk pines. Crows aarked. A white tent had been erected behind the old Carriage Cafe in Esplanade Park. The forensic team had rigged up lights and were already laying a trail of orange specimen markers, measuring, filming and commenting along the way. Cato suited up.

'The body was found by a jogger. That's her over there, with Thornton.'

DC Chris Thornton was sitting on a park bench, unprofessionally close to a young woman in leggings and a sports bra, pen in his hand and hanging on to her every word.

Hassan held the flap of the tent open for him. 'Sleep well?' she enquired. Cato's new parenthood in his mid forties was the subject of much mirth around the office.

'Like a baby.' Cato swallowed the remainder of his lukewarm coffee and gave her the cup.

The deceased was a middle-aged man, to judge by the tufts of grey around his temples. He had been kicked and stomped, his face obliterated, his head and chest a sticky mass of dark blood.

'Workboots,' said Hassan. 'Steel-capped, we assume.'

The clothes, blood aside, were in reasonable condition. The man's trainers were relatively clean and unscuffed. The head and hands had been bagged to preserve trace evidence. Cato crouched down and took a closer look at the hands through the transparent plastic. If you disregarded the defence injuries, they were well-kept with clean and trimmed nails.

'He's definitely one of ours?' said Cato.

Duncan Goldflam stooped into the tent. The forensic guru waved an evidence bag in Cato's face with a blood-smeared playing card inside. 'Jack of Clubs.'

It was the same signature as the previous two: the jack, placed on the body, easy to find. The killer was working his way through the suits. Maybe once he'd done diamonds he would stop. 'Do we have a name?'

Goldflam shook his head. 'I'm running his DNA and fingerprints to see if he's known to us. Keep you posted.'

'Cameras?' Cato asked Hassan.

'The Italian Club car park, two over the road at the Esplanade Hotel, a couple at the skate park. We're on it.'

They stepped out of the tent, Cato taking one last look at the man on the ground, wondering how he fitted the pattern. A dark blue Commodore pulled up and disgorged its occupants: two women and two men in sunnies and suits.

'The Reservoir Dogs,' said Hassan.

Major Crime. This case was theirs, since day one. The older woman gave him a smile. 'DS Kwong, another early start.'

'Boss,' said Cato.

DI Sandra Pavlou ran Major Crime. A year ahead of Cato at the Academy, her career had zoomed while his had coughed and sputtered after a jump-start. She'd tried to recruit him to her team a couple of years earlier but he'd resisted temptation, citing creative differences. Cato filled her in on the story so far, while her entourage made calls, played with iPads and checked themselves in reflective surfaces. The sun was well and truly up now, and early commuters slowed to take a gander. A couple of news crews were also poking around. Pavlou dispatched a minion to keep them at bay until she was ready.

'Jack of Clubs, you say?'

'That's right.'

'This one could run and run, couldn't it?' She sounded wistful.

'Yes,' said Cato. 'If we don't stop him.'


By 8.00 a.m., the Major Incident Room was crackling with anticipation. Another body. Another chance for the killer to reveal more of himself. Cato checked out the assembled faces, more and more of them unfamiliar. More and more of them seeming so much younger these days.

'Listen up, boys and girls.'

DI Mick Hutchens had to clear his throat loudly and tap a spoon on his mug before they paid attention. He was a shadow of his former self — fifteen kilos lighter, hair thinner and greyer, loose skin around the neck and a slight sag at the left corner of his mouth where some nerve endings had stopped working. The commanding foul-mouthed baritone was now an easy-to-ignore throaty rasp. His purposeful stride had become a contemplative stroll that was heading towards an aimless shuffle. Even Cato was inclining to the wider view that maybe the bloke should have taken the early retirement and compo after that savage beating he copped. But no, two years past his use-by date, Hutchens' knuckles were still gripping the door jamb.

'Number three.' Hutchens lifted a finger to the photo of the dead man on the whiteboard. The face was destroyed and unrecognisable. 'Found this morning behind the cafe down at the Esplanade. The usual calling card, Clubs this time. Our friend is taking the piss. Leaving us messages like he's "Son of Sam" or something.'

Sandra Pavlou stepped forward. She'd allowed Hutchens his moment of respect as the local office head honcho but really it was time to get down to business. Fremantle Detectives, after all, were the gophers: a bit of spare shoe leather and doorknocking capacity in the suburbs. 'Latest, Duncan?'

The forensics OIC lifted his head. 'No hits so far on the fingerprints or DNA. He has no previous.' Goldflam addressed his answers to a vacant spot somewhere between Pavlou and Hutchens. 'We're doing a print lift from the right cheek to get the make on the boots. It's looking like Steel Blue, size tens. Otherwise, still sifting. We'll probably be able to wind the scene down by the end of tomorrow, or the day after, at least narrow the perimeter.'

'Post-mortem?'

'This afternoon,' said Hutchens. 'Two o'clock. The Professor's expecting you.'

'Double-booked. Do you fancy it, Mick?'

Hutchens shook his head. 'Double-booked. I'll let Sergeant Kwong do it.'

Pavlou looked at Cato. 'Sure. Maybe take Trimboli with you. Okay?'

Amy Trimboli was Pavlou's new golden girl. 'Fine,' said Cato. 'Where is she?'

A blonde head bobbed out from behind a couple of tall male shoulders. Booky specs and endearing dimples. 'Right here, Sarge.'

Pavlou turned back to Hutchens. 'Mick, local council elections are coming up soon, right?'

'Yep, across the state.'

'Well, things might get a bit heated here in Freo. We don't want these killings to become somebody's bandwagon.'

'Can't see how we can stop it, if that's what they want to do.'

'Maybe some hearts and minds, talk to the incumbent and his rival. Get them on side. We've got enough to think about without them whipping up a media circus.'

'Good point.' Hutchens caught Cato's eye. It looked like he was going to do some more delegating.

Pavlou dished out the rest of the jobs and the meeting broke up. Hutchens nudged Cato and lifted his chin in the direction of Trimboli. 'Watch her.'

'Why? She seems harmless enough.'

'Don't be fooled by the golly-gosh student act. She's aiming for the top.'

Like it was a crime. Such qualities would be deemed admirable, if perhaps slightly distasteful, in a male. In a woman it was downright dangerous — Australia in the twenty-first century. 'I'm surprised she's on your radar.'

Hutchens tapped his nose. 'Mark my words. She's being groomed.'

Cato changed the subject. 'How's Mrs Hutchens?'

'What's it to you?'

Retirement, thought Cato, definitely. Hutchens was losing it. 'I'll let you know how the P-M went. When are you back from your meeting?'

'What meeting?'

'The one this afternoon that's keeping you from the mortuary?'

'Fuck that. Didn't want Pavlou to think she's the only busy bee around here.' A grin, twisting down at that munted corner of his mouth. 'It keeps you in the centre of things too.'

'And that's a good thing, right?' said Cato.

'Not wrong. Not above a bit of grooming myself.'

Groomed by DI Hutchens. Cato shuddered.

Hutchens clapped him on the shoulder. 'And can I leave the pollie wrangling to you too?'


Norman Lip had been watching everything from the room on the third floor. He'd woken in the early hours, needing to piss. Too many single malts in the Norfolk dungeon and that woman in town for the pharmaceuticals conference, coaxing him back to her hotel room for a right royal fuck. The wonder of Tinder. She was snoring softly on the bed behind him now, older than he'd first realised but, on balance, not a bad result for a few swipes of the thumb. Stumbling back after his slash, he'd seen the coloured lights flashing through the curtains and sneaked a peek. He'd been transfixed ever since. It was clearly a murder: he'd watched the tent go up around the back of the cafe. The forensics people ghosting about in their jumpsuits. The detectives with their phones, tablets and clipboards. The tape being wound around the trees. This was what he'd been waiting for: his chance to prove himself.

There was a rustle of bedsheets as she stirred behind him.

'You're still here. Come back to bed, gorgeous boy.'

'My name is Norman,' he said.

'Fuck me, Norman. One more time before breakfast.'

He did as he was told. Wondering idly about that figure he'd seen also watching events from the darkness of a car angle-parked in Essex Street. A face glimpsed briefly by the light of a passing police vehicle. The figure sliding down into the seat, intent on not being seen. Norman saw it as a joining of destinies, as casual and powerful as the swipe of a thumb on Tinder.

Once he'd dispatched his team to follow up on CCTV and local doorknocks, Cato bought a strong flat white from the cafe over the road to help keep the sleep deprivation at bay. Eight months old, and Ella had taken over his life. As, for that matter, had Sharon Wang. They'd consummated their relationship within about ninety minutes of her getting off the plane from China. Approximately the time it took to clear customs and drive back to Cato's house beside the beach in South Fremantle. After overstepping the mark to help Cato out on his Shanghai murder enquiry, Sharon had been transferred from her job as liaison in the Australian Federal Police outpost in Beijing. It was meant to be a punishment, hands up the bums of drug mules and escorting drunk passengers off the inbounds from Bali. Some punishment. It had been life-changing for both of them, instant soulmates. And so, for Cato, one became two. It was about six months into the new job that Sharon learned she was pregnant. The South Fremantle cottage, way too small for a family, was rented out and they moved into a bigger place in White Gum Valley a few kilometres inland. And then Ella arrived and two became three: all-consuming and gloriously so. Along the way a snap wedding with a celebrant and a few friends down at the South Beach pagoda. Colleagues were commenting on the new-model Cato, a smile that never strayed far from his face and a bounce in the step, even after a broken night.

Cato found himself staring at the murder board. At the photos of the victims one, two and now, three. At the lines, arrows, circles, and lists of names. The question marks. Victim one: Dean Anthony Pearson, aged twenty-two, no fixed address. Found six weeks ago near the B Shed down at the wharf. Tracking his mobile phone usage, they'd retraced his steps over previous days: a depressing and repetitive circuit of the port city underclass hangouts — the fast-food joints, the train station, the parks. If he'd been wearing a Fitbit he'd have well and truly covered his ten thousand steps a day but none of his movements provided any solid clues to his demise. He'd been stabbed twelve times in the chest and stomach. The tears in his sleeping bag, the angle of the wounds, the blood pattern, all suggested he'd been asleep when the blade first struck. Knife blade eighteen centimetres, serrated, and never found. The Jack of Spades on display, tucked into the zipper of his blood-soaked jeans. At the time they'd assumed a drug or alcohol connection. Significant traces of both had been found in his system. The playing card didn't make sense but was put down to gangsterish melodrama on the part of the perp.

Then came number two: Maureen Bryant, aged forty-seven, occasional resident at managed short-term accommodation off Hampton Road, the busy north–south artery running into Fremantle. According to the accommodation manager, Maureen was a refugee from a violent marriage and she had developed an addiction to prescription painkillers and tranquillisers. The painkillers were for her shoulder, dislocated by her husband a few years earlier and never right since. She regularly went off the rails, disappearing for days at a time and often ending up either at the hospital or in police custody in a confused state and sometimes injured. No mobile phone to help the investigators retrace her steps. Maureen had been discovered a fortnight ago in a bus shelter on Marine Terrace beside the sailing club, with a ligature of nylon washing line tight around her neck. The rope was new, made in China, and available in most DIY outlets. As yet, untraceable. A half-empty goonie of sauvignon blanc with hers and other, as yet untraced, DNA on it. The wine had been traced back to Liquorland in South Fremantle, paid for in cash by a medium-height, muscular, youngish man whose face was shielded from CCTV by the peak of a baseball cap. The Jack of Hearts was wedged under the noose around Maureen's throat. The playing cards were among the secrets being held back by the police and, as far as the media knew, the first two murders weren't linked. But Cato had the feeling that now, with number three, the lid was about to come off.

'So what's your thinking, maestro?' Hutchens pulled up a chair and eased himself into it, like he was hurting somewhere.

'I think he's been watching too many bad films. It's all a bit staged and ostentatious, like he's been reading *Murder for Dummies*.'

'Prefer your serial killers a bit more subtle do you?'

'Something like that,' said Cato.

'But for all that, he's good at covering his tracks. So far anyway.'

'Maybe the P-M will throw something up.'

Hutchens drummed his knuckles on the desktop. 'You know the Velvet Hammer's up at HQ talking media?' The Velvet Hammer was the widely held nickname for DI Pavlou. It suited her: a soft voice and demure presentation backed up by a killer finish. Underestimate her at your peril. 'They're going to up the ante in time for the evening news.'

'No surprise,' said Cato. 'Might even be a good idea. Somebody somewhere is missing victim number three. And somebody must know who's doing this.'

'Funny, these days I seem to care less and less.'

Cato thought he saw a tremble in Hutchens' bottom lip. 'Boss?'

'Do you know what occupies my time these days?'

Cato had a pretty good idea. The Commissioner was rolling out a new policing model: a social media initiative bringing communities into more direct contact with their local police team. Part PR spin, part public safety and domestic security advice, part shortcut for dobbers. It improved the stats but was yet another administrative headache for already over-burdened middle managers like Hutchens.

'Frontline 2020?' guessed Cato.

'They've put me on fucking Twitter,' muttered Hutchens. 'Tweeting in the treetops all day long.' He crossed his eyes and mimed pressing a keypad. 'LOL, just bagged another crim. Hashtag *sleepeasyFreo*.' Hutchens put a steadying hand on Cato's shoulder and stood up. 'Yeah, I know. Time to give it away.'

Cato rose from his chair, patting his pockets for car keys. 'I'd better get off to the P-M.'

'Enjoy,' said Hutchens as he drifted down the corridor.


'No tattoos, birthmarks, scars or interesting blemishes.' Professor McKenzie pushed her spectacles up her nose with the back of her rubber-gloved hand. Her Glaswegian accent was as steely and sharp as the scalpel she held.

'X-rays? Teeth?' said Cato.

'Aye, we've done those.' Her assistant, a surfie named Tim, finished photographing and measuring the wounds. 'We're running the teeth through the database but, to be honest, there wasn't much left after the going over with the steel toecaps. The X-rays don't show any old wounds, injuries or broken bones.' She breathed out through her face mask. 'Plenty of new ones though.'

'Any other first impressions?' Detective Constable Amy Trimboli was taking notes directly into her iPad. There was a sheen of perspiration on her upper lip even though it was relatively cool in the bowels of Charlie Gairdner Hospital, and her gaze kept sliding to Tim the Surfie. So far, Cato had found Amy relatively inoffensive and easygoing. She'd been respectful without being obsequious, intelligent without being smart-arsed. You really couldn't ask for much more from a colleague in Major Crime.

'I'd put him at around fifty. Well-nourished. Non-smoker, not a heavy drinker. And, as far as I can see, not an obvious drug abuser, although that might change once we open him up properly. Reasonable muscle tone, he kept himself in pretty good shape.' She rested a hand on his abdomen. 'What a waste,' she murmured.

'Doesn't sound like your average homeless person,' said Cato.

'What makes you think he's homeless?' The Professor reached for the rib secateurs.

'That's who the killer seems to be targeting, so far.'

Tim the Surfie raised an eyebrow while he adjusted the drainage flow.

The Professor shrugged. 'Aye, not typical, but we're seeing all sorts on the slab these days. Lawyers and bankers with the insides of a street meth addict.' She tested the snippers, waving them in the direction of the deceased. 'What you see is not always what you get.'

## 2

DI Sandra Pavlou's afternoon media conference went down a storm. Nobody was using the term 'serial killer' officially, just 'possibly connected crimes', but the newshounds weren't so coy. An e-fit photograph of victim number three, an educated guess based on what was left of the face, had been distributed to traditional news outlets and on social media and had already prompted some response: he looks like the noisy bloke in the unit upstairs; he works in a mine out Boddington way; he was hanging around the kids playground last week, et cetera. But so far the fingerprints, DNA and dental records had elicited zilch. Pavlou wanted a word with Cato and Trimboli.

'We need a name for victim three.'

'We're on the case,' said Cato.

'According to the Professor's prelim he doesn't fit the usual profile, is that right?'

Cato nodded. 'Good shape and health, no outward or inward signs of illicit drugs or alcohol abuse. Although there are traces of some sort of medication there, still to be confirmed but possibly an antidepressant. Otherwise clean.'

'Maybe our killer got the wrong man?'

'Maybe,' said Cato.

'It would help.'

Amy Trimboli glanced up from her iPad. 'So everybody should be worried, not just deros?'

Pavlou allowed herself the ghost of a smile. 'Easy on the pedal, Amy. Words can wound.'

'Sorry, boss.'

Pavlou looked at Cato. 'So, Philip, a name and a story for number three would be good. Can you make that your priority?'

'Sure.'

'Excellent. Maybe you could keep Amy with you on this. Take her under your wing?'

Amy gazed at him through her round red frames.

'Sure,' said Cato.

'It's looking like another late one.'

'Thought it might be. So what time do you reckon?' Sharon sounded half asleep. Maybe that accounted for the distance in her voice. Cato remembered that same dull flatness from his marriage to Jane. Then it had evoked guilt and irritation in equal measure. Now, the guilt was still there but there was something else. Fear. He really didn't want this one to fail.

'Mid to late evening?' He changed tack. 'What's Ella been up to?'

'Oh, she's walking and talking and already got her eye on the boy up the road.'

'That's my girl.'

There was a muffled wail. 'I have to go, she's woken up. Tits out. Catch you later.'

'Something funny?' Amy Trimboli was sitting at an adjacent desk, expectant and, it seemed to Cato, a little impatient.

'What?'

'You've got a strange smile on your face.'

'Married bliss.'

Amy looked puzzled. A foreign concept, obviously. 'Why do they call you Cato?'

'I don't want to talk about it. It's too painful.'

'Oh, sorry.'

'Joke. It was a nickname they gave me at the Academy. Generic for Asian sidekick.'

'Does it bother you?'

'Not any more.'

'Okay,' she said, not entirely convinced. 'So. Victim three?'

Deb Hassan dropped by, leaned against the doorframe.

'Anything from doorknocks yet?' asked Cato.

'Nothing. Everyone was tucked up in bed when matey died.'

'What about Chris Thornton?' Their colleague in local enquiries.

'Still neck-deep in CCTV as far as I know.'

'Can you call him, find out where he's at?'

'Sure.' Hassan glanced at Trimboli then back at Cato. 'Any developments from your end?'

'The P-M suggests a possible mistaken identity. Maybe our killer got the wrong man. The DI wants us to follow it up.'

'You and Amy?'

'Yep.'

'I'll leave you to it then,' said Hassan. 'Get back to doorknocking.'

'Regroup at six, here. Okay?'

'Okay.' Hassan pursed her lips and made herself scarce.

'I don't think she likes me,' said Trimboli.

'Nothing personal. There's not many people she does like.'

'What should we do now?' A grumpy tap on her iPad. 'Sarge?'

'Maybe we need to educate ourselves.'


'We've been expecting you. Pity you're six weeks late.'

Not a good start, thought Cato. Sonya Allegretta from St Mary's Community Support Centre had an orange and blue butterfly tattooed on the inside of her left wrist. She ran one of the organisations operating at the sharp end of the homelessness crisis in Fremantle. And she had a point: this meeting was way overdue. True, the first victim was officially No Fixed Abode but because he was on the police system for prior offences he was known to them, and his family were tracked down quickly. Dean Pearson, just twenty-two, stabbed repeatedly. His homelessness was seen as a factor of his high-risk lifestyle, not as a motive for murder. Until victim two, a month later, it was still regarded as some kind of drugs or alcohol thing. So perhaps they were only two weeks late, not six, if that made it any better.

'We're here to listen and learn,' Cato said.

'Deano dropped in here most days for a feed,' said Sonya. 'He was no angel but he didn't deserve what happened to him.'

'Nobody does,' said Cato. On the whole, he meant it.

'He'd been on the streets for about three years. Dropped out of uni in his second year. Put on anti-anxiety medication. Couch-surfed for a few months but it doesn't take long before you've used up your favours and overstayed your welcome.'

'Family didn't help?' Cato had met some of them in the early days of the investigation. They'd been suitably shocked and sad yet, to Cato's mind, also unsurprised and possibly even relieved. Still, he wanted Sonya's take on them.

'Mother died of cancer when he was in his early teens. Father remarried and focused on his new brood. He ran out of patience when Deano dropped out of ECU. Turned the tap off.'

Cato got to thinking about his own son, Jake. Now sixteen and building up a collection of infringement letters from John Curtin Senior High. Both his parents moving on with new families, new kids. No contact now for at least a month and Cato had let it fly by.

'You seem to know a lot about Dean.' Amy Trimboli pushed her glasses back up her nose.

'It's my job,' said Allegretta.

'So how did he get by?'

'A bit of begging, some benefits, picking up a feed from groups like ours.'

'Anything else?' asked Amy, already knowing the answer.

'Such as?'

'Crime or prostitution? Drugs?'

Allegretta scratched her nose. 'Not to my knowledge.'

Amy didn't let up. 'Shoplifting, burglaries, drug dealing, assignations with strangers. All risk-taking behaviour isn't it?'

'So he had it coming?'

'Just wondering if you knew any of that dangerous company he kept.'

'No. I only know the non-dangerous ones.'

'Where did he usually sleep?' asked Cato.

'Here and there, depending on the time of year and the weather. Summer you could usually find him down at South Beach. Winter we might get him some temporary shelter or he'd be in the Woolstores, or a multistorey car park, abandoned building, shop doorway. Take your pick.'

'The place he was found, down by the wharf. That was a favourite spot of his?'

'Yes. You know it was, your blokes asked around at the time.'

'Do many people know about that spot?'

Allegretta shrugged. 'Enough. They talk, they share.'

'How about Maureen Bryant?' said Cato. 'Did you deal with her?'

A shake of the head. 'She was with the Salvos or the Anglicans wasn't she? Try them.' Allegretta fixed her gaze on Cato. 'So what brings you here, now?'

'The third victim, discovered overnight. He doesn't seem to fit the profile.'

'Yeah? How come?'

Cato told her.

'So he doesn't seem to have been a drug or alcohol abuser and he kept himself in reasonable shape?'

'Yes.'

'And you're figuring or hoping he's not really homeless,' said Allegretta. 'Maybe you're starting to care now? Maybe everybody out there will start caring now, if they think they might be next?'

Cato didn't want to get into an argument. 'Just wondering, really, if you had any thoughts about who he might be.'

'Take a drive along the coast any night anywhere from Hillarys down to Rockingham. You'll find most beach car parks have somebody living in their car or van and fitting your description. You don't have to be a junkie or a fuck-up to find yourself homeless in WA. Mortgages and rents the way they are at the moment there's a lot of people just two pay cheques away from the street. Fall ill, get evicted because your landlord wants to redevelop or up the rent even further, leave your abusive violent partner and click' — she snapped her fingers — 'you're one of the invisible.'

'So we shouldn't make any assumptions?' said Cato.

'Fucking right,' said Allegretta.


As a result of DI Pavlou's afternoon at HQ, the enquiry into the murders of Dean Pearson, Maureen Bryant and Person Unknown had been upgraded and given a new name: Task Force Hermes. The operational names often seemed random, plucked from the air, or maybe from the job description of one of the spare Assistant Commissioners.

So, wondered Cato, is our killer some emissary of the gods? He was reminded of Dieudonne, the Congolese former child soldier and assassin who'd wreaked havoc in Fremantle a few years earlier. His name translated roughly into 'gift from God'. Last time Cato checked, Dieudonne was carving out his fiefdom as one of the Lords of Casuarina Prison. But it wouldn't harm to double-check he was still there.

DI Sandra Pavlou had gathered the Hermes management team for a brainstorming session: DI Hutchens, Cato, Chris Thornton and Duncan Goldflam representing Fremantle; Pavlou, a bald and morose detective sergeant called McMahon, and DC Amy Trimboli flying the flag for Major Crime. Pavlou had brought in an extra whiteboard, there were three plungers of coffee on the table, and pizza had been ordered. She meant business. It was just after 8.00 p.m. and Cato was fading. The media conference and the evening news had lit up the phones. The subsequent new avenues of enquiry would quadruple the workload. Unfortunately the team strength hadn't been quadrupled in response. It would be at least another two or three hours before Cato would be able to go home.

'So three bodies, three different ways of killing. Why?' Pavlou dunked an Anzac in her coffee.

'He bores easily?' said Hutchens. It raised a few sniggers but nobody was really in the mood.

'It's real "look at me" stuff, isn't it?' Cato ventured.

'Go on,' said Pavlou.

'The calling cards, the different modus for each one, the locations. Very stagey.'

'So he's got our attention. His deeds are on the telly.' Pavlou rescued a soggy piece of Anzac from her cup. 'What do we glean from the methods? Duncan?'

'According to the P-M, the stabbing on victim one was frenzied and deep, striking bone at times, the strangulation with number two required strength and determination, and the stomping on number three needed stamina.' Goldflam smothered a yawn, he'd been up and about even earlier than Cato. 'All in all we can probably assume a younger, stronger person. Most likely male but you can never be sure these days, there's some scary women doing CrossFit.'

The pizzas arrived, boxes were opened, arms reaching across the table. Pavlou summed up the work-in-progress. 'So we're looking at a fit, strong male under forty, like our mate from the Liquorland CCTV.'

'Try the local gyms,' said Hutchens.

'With something to say about the underclass?' added Cato.

'What do you think that message is?' said Pavlou.

Trimboli dabbed her lips with a napkin. 'They're not wanted?'

'As in, they're not wanted because they're an eyesore or a burden?' said Cato, dwelling on his afternoon meeting at St Mary's. 'Or society is unfair and so they shouldn't exist?'

'A warped crusader.' Pavlou liked that and wrote it on the whiteboard. 'What about the playing cards. Any ideas?'

'From a jack to a king,' said morose McMahon.

'Loneliness to a wedding ring,' added Hutchens with a faraway look.

'Jack, as in lowest form of nobility, or knave as in servant, or trickster, or person without moral code.' Chris Thornton looked up from his phone and waggled it. 'Wikipedia,' he said. Thornton had developed a reputation for being a details man and was once again in charge of collating the tsunami of information gathered during an investigation and giving it some preliminary shape.

Pavlou wrote that down too. 'How's it going with the trawl on similar crimes?'

Thornton read from notes on his iPad. 'About nine months ago three homeless died in a fire in an abandoned storage warehouse up in Perth, near City West station. Looked like an insurance job as the site was marked for redevelopment. No arrests, case still open.'

'I remember it,' said Pavlou. 'It went back to local enquiries after a while, judged the deaths were by accident rather than design. But I think Gangs had an interest too. Primary motive, money.' She asked Thornton to review it, talk to the investigators. 'Anything else?'

'Around the country there's been a handful of cases of rough sleepers being killed in mainly one-offs either by strangers or friends but nothing as sustained as this. Targeted. Serial. Nearly all of those cases have produced a culprit and a conviction pretty quickly.'

'Find out if any of those convicted culprits have been released and moved to WA recently.'

There was a knock and Deb Hassan stuck her head around the door. She looked first at Cato then at Pavlou. Decided this was for Pavlou. 'The phone-in, boss. We might have a name for number three.'

Cato left the office a little before midnight. En route, along South Terrace, lights still glowed in the cafes and pubs. Last drinks. Staff sweeping and hosing down the footpaths, clearing away chairs and tables. Those with homes to go to said their farewells. Those without, waited in the shadows for a favourite spot they could claim as theirs for the rest of the night. The wind was up and there was a salty bite to it. At home Sharon was sitting up in bed with Ella on her breast.

'Is this all there is to life?' she said, opening one eye and mustering a smile.

'I hope so.' Cato yawned and leaned in to kiss her. The baby complained at the space invasion but suckled on determinedly.

Both Sharon's eyes were open now. The look was both troubled and troubling. 'We're stuffed.'

'Yep.'

'Something's got to give.'

The script was sounding familiar. Cato absent-mindedly brushed a finger against the baby's cheek. Ella's little hand lifted, as if trying to swat him away. 'I know, but ...'

'Yeah, I don't have any ideas either.' Sharon switched the baby to the other side. 'How's it going out in the real world?'

Real world, thought Cato. A sociopath cutting a swathe through the most vulnerable people in the city. Fear stalking the backstreets. The invisible only becoming visible through sensational headlines. Cato looked at his wife and baby daughter bathed in the soft glow of the bedside lamp and breathed their warm musky smell. 'Slowly,' he said. 'I think after the news tonight there'll be a few less people sleeping soundly in their beds.'

Ella had finished and gave off her little snores. 'Speaking of which ...' said Sharon. She handed Cato the baby and slid down under the covers.

Cato settled Ella and found himself waking up again. He went into the kitchen, checked the mail on the table and binned it. He drank a glass of water then rinsed it under the tap. Out the kitchen window the breeze rustled the olive and lemon trees in the back yard. At the edge of his vision there was a smudge of movement as if a shadow had broken from its background. Cato frowned out into the darkness. He really needed to sleep.

# 3

Cato pushed the victim's e-fit photo across the desk. 'You're sure it's him?'

The woman had hit the road before dawn and driven up from Mount Barker, in the state's south, a four or five hour drive. She was in her early forties and had that stocky, weather-burnished look of those who have grown up on a farm. She'd been offered coffee but preferred tea, strong with milk and one sugar. Her name was Denise Anderson née White.

'As sure as I'll ever be. I haven't heard from him in nearly ten years but I'd swear that's Chris.'

There was hardly enough of the face left to make that kind of call. The e-fit was a guess, a sketch from the computer's imagination. Maybe she just wanted it to be so, thought Cato. 'What makes you think it's him?'

'It's him. Sometimes you just know, don't you?'

'But you haven't seen your brother in, what, ten, eleven years?'

'Heard from him. Haven't seen him in nearly fourteen. He was heading off to Iraq. Two thousand and three.'

The Second Gulf War, thought Cato. The one where they couldn't find any of those weapons of mass destruction. 'Your brother was in the military?'

She nodded. 'Special forces. Some kind of commando, hush-hush. If I tell you, I'll have to kill you, kind of thing.' She rummaged around in her bag and pulled out a photo. 'That's him back then.'

A man in a beret and khaki, clean-shaven, uncertain smile. Plain background. The kind of photo they show on the news at the funeral of a homecoming hero. If the man on the slab was indeed Christopher White, then the killer had proved himself capable of besting an ex-Special Forces commando. What were they dealing with here?

'Excuse my saying this,' said Trimboli, 'but you don't seem very upset.'

Denise Anderson sat up straighter and took a drink of tea. 'Expecting me to bawl, are you? Not sad enough, like Lindy Chamberlain?'

Trimboli held her ground. 'So *are* you upset? Or not?'

'He was nearly ten years older than me. He'd been away in the army most of the time I was growing up. I never really knew him as a person, just a photo on the mantlepiece. Besides,' she sipped some more tea, 'we still haven't confirmed it's him yet, have we?'

'And that's it?' said Trimboli.

'Yep. That's it.'

That wasn't it, she was holding something back. Cato let it go for the time being. They'd arrange for a viewing at the morgue later that morning, and comparison blood and DNA tests. Denise Anderson could be back on the road to Mount Barker after lunch.

'He was on antidepressants.' Cato checked the update from the lab. 'Celica, or citalopram. Know anything about that? Why he was depressed?'

A shrug. 'War veteran. Par for the course I imagine.'

'Thanks for coming in,' said Cato. They shook hands and she turned to leave.

'Was it a bad death?'

Kicked and stomped into oblivion. 'Yes, I'm afraid so,' said Cato.

Denise nodded and walked out.


'Christopher John White, aged fifty-one, ex-military.' The comparison DNA tests had confirmed it. Now DI Pavlou would have the delicate and probably frustrating task of liaising with the Defence Department to get access to White's army service record to see if that held any clues to his murder. 'Was at the sharp end in Afghanistan and Iraq. Another angle to pursue, maybe?'

'You reckon some jihadi's got it in for him?' DI Hutchens wasn't convinced.

'As always, Mick, I'm keeping an open mind.' Pavlou was also struggling to keep her patience. Cato could sympathise. These were long hours and tough times and Hutchens' unremitting negativity wasn't helping anybody. 'Look at the news most nights. The zealots from both sides have brought the war home to everyone everywhere.'

It was true enough. Cato recalled the horrifying TV news images from the UK of a soldier hacked to death in broad daylight on a busy London thoroughfare, massacres in Paris, elsewhere. This was the age of the lone wolf, unpredictable, resourceful and all the more terrifying for it.

Hutchens persisted. 'What about victims one and two? Where do they fit into your new theory?'

'I don't have a theory, Mick. I just want to see the bloke's army record to show due diligence. All right?'

She set Morose McMahon the task of preliminary contact with Defence. Cato reiterated his thoughts on the killer and Pavlou concurred: anyone who could bring down an ex-commando wasn't to be taken lightly. Then again, nobody *had* been taking this bloke lightly. So far neither CCTV nor doorknocks had elicited any sightings or hearings of suspicious activity around Esplanade Park before, during, or after White's murder. As with the first two victims, the killer had ghosted in and out leaving no trace. Except the bodies of course.

'Duncan?' Pavlou wanted a forensics update.

'As with the previous ones, the blood perimeter stops about five metres away. Our man must have changed out of his killing clothes and boots and gone on his way. Lots of detritus to work through. We'll keep at it and let you know.'

Pavlou turned to Cato and Trimboli. 'So we now have a name for number three, but still no indication of whether he was homeless, or whether he was mistakenly targeted. Thoughts?'

'The lady from St Mary's reckons you get all sorts on the streets these days,' said Trimboli. 'Not just junkies and fuck-ups, as she put it.'

'If it was a mistaken encounter,' said Cato, 'what was Mr White doing hanging around the park at that time of night?'

'Looking for company?' offered Amy.

'Well, there's another line of enquiry for you,' admitted Hutchens.

'Sober, drug and alcohol free, and in reasonable physical shape.

Ex-military hard man. You'd have to catch somebody like White unawares if you're going to come off best,' mused Cato. 'That suggests to me that he *was* sleeping rough and didn't see it coming.'

'Yet nobody from St Mary's, or the other agencies, or the rough-sleeper community seems to have known of him,' said Trimboli.

'But once again,' pointed out Pavlou, 'our killer knew exactly where to find White as he did with numbers one and two.'

'It wouldn't be hard to wander around and find a victim at random,' said Hutchens. 'Their sleeping spots aren't a secret.'

Duncan Goldflam lifted a finger. 'Somebody this neat isn't acting impulsively or randomly. This requires patience and planning.'

'Like a croc at a waterhole. Matey knows this terrain,' said Cato. 'Intimately.'

Pavlou was back on the whiteboard, marker at the ready. 'He's homeless?'

'Or used to be,' said Chris Thornton. 'Or knows someone who is, or has been.'

'Or works with the homeless,' said Cato. 'Or used to.'

'Social worker, medic, cop,' said Hutchens. 'Do-gooder.'

'Ranger,' pointed out Thornton. 'The council's diverting them from locking up stray dogs to moving the beggars on.' He was a veritable font.

It didn't really narrow things down but it would help focus their minds.


Sharon strapped Ella into the stroller, adjusted the sun shade so the bub would keep on sleeping, put on a hat and snicked the door behind her. It would be about a twenty to thirty minute hike down to the South Beach walk track, another twenty to the old Coogee Power station, stop off at the kiosk on the way back for a cappuccino, and then home. Keep it brisk and it could be an hour and a half's worth of meaningful exercise, albeit ruined by a cuppa. But better than nothing and she'd be having a coffee anyway, there or at home, just to stay awake for a few more hours. Ella's unpredictable sleeping patterns ruled Sharon's life: motherhood — exhilarating and exhausting.

Passing the bistro at South Beach, Sharon looked out across a glass-flat, azure ocean. She was still in awe of the kind of days Fremantle could conjure up. After three years in Beijing, she'd come to see pollution and congestion as pretty much normal. Places and days like this had been remote, unreal, the stuff of fantasies or photoshopped pics in magazines. Middle-aged cyclists, hipsters with dogs, jogging mums with grunty off-road strollers — all seemed to have the time and inclination for a quick smile or hello in passing. On past the South Beach apartment blocks and the sudden quiet as buildings gave way to bush on one side and shimmering water on the other. Among the bushes, a few splashes of blue. Tents. Freedom campers? Homeless? Ahead, a few metres out into the ocean, the statue of C.Y. O'Connor and his horse. Phil had given her the history: it was a monument to a man who took failure personally, riding into the sea to kill himself, unaware that his feat of engineering brilliance would prove successful after all. Taking failure personally: it could be Australia's motto — you're not allowed to be unlucky in the Lucky Country.

Approaching the old Robb Jetty cattle rails, a jogger who had passed her in the same direction earlier was on his way back now. A gym junkie by the looks of it. That powerful concoction of workouts, steroids and self-belief you could see in any gym, any courtroom, or any prison yard, any day of the week. A face so sculpted it could have been plastic. He slowed and gave her a nice smile. Maybe she was too quick and too harsh in her judgement.

'Beautiful day,' he said, coming to a stop. A deep, mellifluous voice. He'd be nice to listen to on the radio or the phone.

She nodded. 'Glorious.'

He crouched down for a look into the stroller. 'Boy or girl?'

Mr Muscles was only young, twenty maybe. He probably thought he was just being friendly. Unaware that he'd already crossed a line and encroached on her space.

'Girl,' she said.

He peered into the gloom of the shaded stroller. 'Lovely.'

'Well, I need to be going,' said Sharon.

'Haven't seen you down here before?'

'No,' she said.

He straightened up. 'Bye, then.'

'Yeah, bye,' said Sharon.

He jogged away. Nice arse.

Sharon chastised herself for thinking uncharitable thoughts.


Lunchtime. Cato decided he needed some fresh air and time on his own. He headed towards the food hall beside the old markets with seafood pad thai and a psycho on his mind. He turned the corner into a bustling Market Street and nearly bowled someone over.

'Fuckin' hell!' said the man.

'Sorry, mate,' said Cato, reaching out a steadying hand. 'You okay?'

'What's your name?' the man said, putting down his shopping bag, taking out a notepad and licking a stubby pencil. He was short and middle-aged with yellow boardies, thongs and a Metallica T-shirt. At his feet, a grimy IGA shopping bag stuffed with official-looking papers. He didn't seem like he was the full quid.

'Philip.' Cato smiled, aiming for a quick resolution and onward to lunch.

'What's your proper name?' he said, pointing to Cato's lanyard and ID.

'Sergeant Philip Kwong. That better?'

'Barry.' The man stuck out his hand and Cato shook it.

'Where you off to today, Barry?'

He pointed ahead of him. 'Station. Joondalup. Court.'

'Court? What for?'

'Swearing. Not allowed to swear on the train, it says so here on the restraining order.' He started rummaging around in his bag among the reams of papers. Thrust one in Cato's face. 'See.'

Cato held up a hand. 'Okay, I believe you. It's not nice, swearing, shouldn't do that, mate.'

Barry nodded sourly as he ran his finger down the crumpled pages, squinting and reading with his mouth open. 'Not allowed to say "fuck" on the train.'

Cato felt a twinge of sympathy for Barry if he was obliged to travel regularly on the Joondalup Line. Best not to encourage him though. 'Right, I should think so too.'

'Or cunt.'

'I get the picture, Barry.'

'Or shit even. Not on the bus either. Or the ferry.'

Barry waved down a bus even though it was only one stop to the train station. He climbed aboard. As the bus doors closed, Cato saw Barry sit down, mime zipping up his rude mouth, and stick up his middle finger at his fellow passengers.

At the food hall Cato took a table outside in the sun and waited for his noodles to arrive. He unfolded a *West* he'd found in the kitchen at work. The headline was all about the rough-sleeper murders — FEAR STALKS FREO — with one pic of DI Pavlou looking determined against a Crimestoppers backdrop and another of the early morning Esplanade Park crime scene with a blurry Cato caught on long lens. Inside, more photographs of the victims and sketchy backstory on each of their lives, except of course Christopher John White who, at the time of printing, remained a person unknown. Interviews, vox pops with scared residents, and reminders of other notable WA serial killings. They managed to fill four pages with it. Rumblings about the mayoral election: the challenger accusing the incumbent of letting the city go to the dogs, the incumbent trying to stay nice and reasonable. It reminded Cato he still needed to do that bit of pollie-wrangling. Further inside, joy of joys, the cryptic was untouched. *Herald angels, haven't seen anything like it* — six and four. The pad thai arrived and Cato dug in, spearing a piece of squid on his chopstick. He glanced at his fellow diners as they ate and chatted and enjoyed the midday sun. He wondered if the killer might be among them and, if so, whether he'd be distinguishable from the crowd. No, of course he wouldn't. He was a phantom, drifting in and out of people's lives, leaving no trace of himself except the stench of death. *Herald angels, haven't seen anything like it.* Six and four. Cato put down his chopsticks and picked up his biro. An anagram, *haven't seen* — Heaven Sent.

His phone burbled. It was Chris Thornton.

'The CCTV's thrown up something worth a look.'

'Yep?'

'The same car in the vicinity of murders two and three during the time frame. Holden muscle ute. Silver.'

'ID?'

'Wayne Joseph Bradley. Lives in Palmyra. He's got form for violence.'

Cato chased a bean sprout around his plate. 'Do we know where he is right now?'

'At home. He's FIFO, it's his week off. He flies out tomorrow.'

'Quick work. Have you told Pavlou?'

'Her phone's off.'

'DI Hutchens?'

'He says, quote, "Do what the fuck you like."'

# 4

Wayne Joseph Bradley did indeed have a record for violence. He was nasty enough to warrant the Tactical Response Group: in the last four years he'd glassed a stranger in a club in Rockingham, put his de facto in hospital with a broken jaw and headbutted a taxi driver who had the temerity to ask for the fare. He'd served some time for the glassing but had managed to keep it to fines and good behaviour bonds for the rest. Last, but by no means least, there was a firearms licence in the name of his de facto — and somewhere in that house there was an Adler A110 repeater shotgun, the spree killer's friend. The mine Bradley was working at was one of the smaller operators in the Pilbara with few resources to check on their employees' characters and little option but to take the scrapings from the big boys' table. Bradley had the Southern Cross and the Eureka Stockade flags flapping in his front yard and a massive rottie on a chain on the front verandah. It was going berko and a few plant pots had already gone flying. With the paths on either side of the house blocked off by a rusty corrugated iron fence topped by barbed wire, the only way in was past the dog. The neighbours at the side and back were a possibility for access and negotiations were ongoing.

The TRG squad leader was a bloke called Dave whom Cato had had dealings with on several occasions. 'You still here?' he said. 'I thought they had a rotation policy to avoid burnout.'

'They lifted the retirement age for key personnel,' Dave hissed from under his Darth Vader helmet. 'I'm here until I'm seventy.'

Chris Thornton wiggled his mobile. 'Bradley's not answering.'

'But the ute's in the driveway and the neighbours haven't seen him leave,' said Cato.

It was midafternoon and warm enough for Cato to be sweating

under his Kevlar vest. Bradley lived in Aurelian Street. It was a quiet and pleasant enough suburban street, dog notwithstanding, except now a news helicopter was approaching. 'He couldn't still be sleeping through that racket?'

'So are we going in, or what?' said TRG Dave.

Cato shrugged. 'Okay.'

'The dog?'

'Anyone on the way for that?'

'RSPCA's stuck in traffic on the freeway,' said Thornton. 'And the council bloke's on a sickie.' He squinted at a point past Cato's left shoulder. 'Is that smoke?'

It was. Billowing from a window down the side of the house.

'Get in there,' said Cato. And to Thornton. 'Fire brigade. Now.'

'The dog?' said TRG Dave, again.

'That's an operational matter for you.'

Dave waved his squad into place and they advanced. The rottie's chain was taut and the fencepost securing it looked old and weak. The dog was going bananas. Dave had his taser at the ready, he aimed and fired. The rottie got even more riled as the darts sent a charge through him. The fencepost snapped and the dog flew at TRG Dave, knocking him to the ground, snapping at his head and gloved arms. The dog's front paws were on Dave's chest, its head lowering, teeth bared and drool dripping.

'Get this fucker off me,' Dave yelled.

A colleague obliged with a burst of his AR-15. The rottie disintegrated in a splatter of fur, blood and bone. Sirens heralded the approach of the fireys. There was a creak and groan and Wayne Bradley's verandah began to collapse in on itself, leaning with a sad sigh and a dry crack into the front yard. On cue, the front door opened and Bradley himself poked a sleepy, unshaven and distinctly hungover face through the gap. He looked like a tasered koala.

'What?' he grumbled.

They all agreed the pictures on the evening news would be worth rushing home for. DI Pavlou had already given Cato a blast over the phone and he could expect more in person later that day. It turned out Wayne

Joseph Bradley was as deaf as a doornail as well as partially disabled from some birth defect. The result was a left leg that didn't work too well. The chances of him kicking and stomping an ex-commando to death were remote. The house smoke was from burnt toast and he wasn't happy about the verandah. Or the dog. Bradley had been allowed to put his hearing aid in after being arrested.

'What'd you have to kill Scottie for?' he whined.

'Self-defence,' said Cato. 'We need to talk about your whereabouts on a couple of dates.'

'Got any Panadol?' Bradley said. 'Got a bastard of a headache.' Chris Thornton put a call through to a minion to organise it. 'And a cuppa tea? Throat on me like a dead dingo's dick.'

'Make it two,' said Cato to Thornton. 'Milk and none.' Thornton added a third for himself. Back to Bradley. 'You're happy to waive the right to a lawyer?'

'Done nuthin'. Who gives?'

'What's your opinion of homeless people?'

'They need a haircut and a proper job.'

Cato slid a CCTV still image across the table. 'Is that your car?'

'Yep. Flash, eh?'

He pointed to a frozen blurry face behind the wheel. 'Is that you driving it?'

'Don't let no other cunt drive me ute.'

Cato pointed to the date and time imprint. 'Wednesday, twenty-third of August. Eleven forty-six p.m.' The location. 'Marine Terrace, South Fremantle, just outside Sealanes fish factory.'

'And?' said Bradley. His Panadol and water had arrived and Thornton passed around the tea. The uniformed constable retreated with that look of bored contempt common to many Fremantle waitpersons.

Cato slid a second photo across the table. 'Thursday, seventh of September. One-thirty a.m. Give or take. That's you again, isn't it?'

Bradley spun the photo absent-mindedly on the tip of his finger. 'Like I say. My ute, so it'll be me, won't it?'

'Corner of Marine and Essex by the Esplanade Hotel,' said Cato.

'Yeah. So?'

'So within about a hundred metres of those locations, at around the time you're passing by, two people have been murdered.'

Bradley shook his head. 'Aw, fuck off, mate. No way.'

'So explain your presence. The Sealanes one first.'

'I'll need me phone. Check me diary and that.' Under close supervision from Thornton he was allowed to do so. A few finger flicks and a nod. 'I was halfway through a five off. Kaz was on nights at the hospital.'

Thornton was making notes, all of this would be checked.

'That night?' pressed Cato.

Another glance at the phone. A shrug. 'Nothing special. Can't remember.'

'It was near midnight. Where had you been? Where were you going? According to the camera you're heading north, towards the city centre.'

'Drink maybe?'

'You tell me,' said Cato.

A shake of the head. 'Fucked if I know.'

'How about this one, then?' Cato prodded the second photo. 'That's just the night before last. You should be able to remember that.'

'Yep, Kaz was on nightshift again.'

'And?' prompted Cato.

A smirk. 'I'd been for a few down at the Orient and over at Little Creatures and I was headed for Ada Rose.' A brothel on South Terrace.

'What time did you get there?'

'About five or ten minutes after that photo I reckon.'

'What time did you leave?'

'An hour or so later. I like to get my money's worth.'

'Who were you with?'

'Dunno, wasn't interested in her name.'

'Describe her,' said Thornton. Wayne did, in salacious detail. It could and would be checked. 'Kaz might not be too pleased.'

'Good try, mate, but we have an open and trusting relationship. Kaz acknowledges that I'm a man with extraordinary needs and she's usually too tired after her shift.'

That would be Kaz, the understanding de facto with the gun licence.

'What's with the firepower? The Adler?' Cato asked. TRG had found and confiscated it — covetously it seemed to Cato at the time.

'Cool, isn't it?'

'They're supposed to be banned.'

'We ... she got in early, before it came into effect.'

'What do you use it for?'

'Not me. Kaz. It's her licence, her gun. She's a farm girl.' A smile. 'Gun club. At the range. No law against it. Second amendment right, mate. Or fifth. Whatever.'

'Wrong country,' said Cato. 'Is it okay if we take fingerprints and DNA samples from you?'

Bradley hawked some phlegm into his plastic cup and passed it over. 'Help yourself.'


It was late afternoon by the time Cato got the promised face-to-face bollocking from DI Pavlou.

'A blameless citizen. Drunk, deaf and disabled, dog dead, and house demolished. Having a good day, Philip?'

'We've managed to eliminate him from our enquiries,' said Cato, as brightly as he could. 'And he did have a record of violence. And a firearm. A nasty one.'

'I wasn't aware there were any nice ones. So what does he do on the mines anyway?'

'Chef.'

'He can drive a ute with his gammy leg?'

'Seems so. It's an automatic.'

'The news hyenas are going to love this.'

Cato shrugged. 'It shows we're being proactive in the hunt for a serial killer.'

Pavlou shifted position to signify she was moving on. Cato was beginning to appreciate that about her: she wasn't a grudge-bearer like Hutchens. Or himself for that matter. 'Paddy McMahon's managed to set up a meeting with Defence about Christopher White. I'd like you to sit in with him.'

'Sure.'

'They're sending somebody out from Campbell Barracks. The meeting's tomorrow at ten, here.'

'Yep.'

'And you might want to look at this.' She slid a sheet of paper across the desk.

It was a formal request from Pavlou to have Cato seconded to Major

Crime for the duration of the investigation. 'What's the point?' said Cato. 'I'm already on the case.'

'But this means you're on my team and wholly under my command.'

'Again, I take that as read, anyway.'

'It's a subtly shaded detail, Philip. One that could make all the difference.'

Uh-oh, he thought. 'What does DI Hutchens say?'

She tapped a ticked box and a set of initials at the bottom of the form. 'He says yes.'


Norman had finally persuaded the editor to let him run with it. The media frenzy around the serial killer revelation earlier in the week had tipped the scales. But *New WAve* was an oily-rag online news site, set up as a tax break by Betsy's over-indulgent daddy. Betsy was a minnow with ambitions to be a piranha.

'Newspapers are dying a slow, gangrenous death, limb by limb,' she'd said at the job interview. 'We're the future, sweetie. Niche, targeted, hungry, influential. Think *Crikey*, think *New Matilda*, think *Mamamia*, think ...'

'*Breitbart*?' offered Norman.

'Who?'

'Never mind.'

She'd been loathe to play futile catch-up with the media barons and wanted a different angle, more depth, more ... she'd searched for the words and failed — more *je ne sais quoi*. Betsy never bothered to hide her lack of confidence in him. She had him down as a gigs and movies guy, indie stuff, maybe food and bars — hipster shit. News was for the Curtin ex-grads who fawned at her feet. He was only from lowly ECU. They all found that funny or really cool, like he was brave, or maybe disabled.

'How about a hotline to the killer?' mused Norman. 'Seeing things from his perspective?'

'Pander to the freaks, you mean? We're not skanky clickbaiters at *New WAve*.'

My arse you're not. 'The election's next month: Funky Freo versus Prosperous Port, and serial killers making things a bit less predictable. I see it more as tapping into the zeitgeist?'

Zeitgeist. That got her attention, she didn't expect words like that from him. Try that for *je ne sais* fucking *quoi*. He'd explained what he saw from the hotel bedroom window. Betsy, flushed, had high-fived him when he told her what he was doing in that hotel in the first place. Made some comment about checking out Tinder herself. Good luck with that, he thought. Now she wanted detail. How precisely would he make contact? What were the legal implications of what they were proposing?

'Legals? Who gives a toss? Did Woodward and Bernstein care about the legals when they played footsy with Deep Throat?'

'Bad boy,' she chided him. 'Still, maybe you could come up with a road map? Then I can sign off on Monday.'

So how would he make contact? Norman stared at his iPad, willing the plan into existence. He had three new notifications waiting on Tinder. Destiny at the swipe of a thumb. That gave him an idea.

# 5

Cato allowed himself the luxury of an extra hour in bed. It almost made up for the three or four lost during the night. Ella's demands for a feed accounted for one of the hours. Sharon deciding she felt horny as a hoot owl took care of another. And in the shifting pre-dawn shadows Cato had snapped awake again and lay fretting about a killer worming his way under the skin. He'd been dreaming: he was climbing a staircase, dark and creaking, black viscous fluid under his feet. The stairs went up and up, endless. The smell of rotten roadkill in his nostrils. The sound of a low, throaty, childish chuckle. The scrape and click of a door opening. Then he'd awoken. The old knife scar on his lower abdomen, itchy. That door sound had seemed so real and so near.

Cato could hear Ella babbling away in the kitchen, the sound of running water and pots and pans colliding. He could smell coffee and he headed for it. Sunlight streamed through the kitchen window, silhouetting Sharon's outline beneath the light cotton shirt. On the floor Ella was rolling back and forth and chewing on a plastic hammer.

Sharon turned at the sound of his approach. 'Dada!' She turned off the taps and kissed him, lasciviously. 'Morning, gorgeous. Coffee?'

Cato helped himself. Ella was too absorbed in the hammer to pay him much attention but he did warrant a lip bubble and a grin when he crouched down to kiss her.

'What time do you have to go in?' Sharon was back at the washing-up.

'Meeting at ten. Hoping it won't go too long. Might be able to get away with a half day.'

She gave him a look that was sympathetic, but unconvinced. 'Don't make promises you can't keep, Phil. The Job's the Job.'

'What about you?' he said, dropping some bread into the toaster.

'Ella's got a Skype teleconference at midday with grandad, they can gurgle at each other, then I've pencilled her in for a feed, an afternoon nap, followed by another feed. I think we've got a window mid to late arvo for some time with Dada if you're around. Otherwise we might go for a walk.'

Cato smeared some Vegemite on his toast. He wondered if he should say sorry but he recalled that used to infuriate his ex-wife Jane even more. His phone buzzed. It was Jake, a text.

**You around today?**

He tapped back, **tonight after 6 ok? eat here**

Then he thought better of it and tried to ring instead. He was put straight through to his son's messagebank and told to leave his number.

'Work?' said Sharon.

'Jake. Wanting something.'

'Maybe he just wants to catch up with his dad?'

'Maybe,' said Cato, putting on a brave face. In his recent experience, contact with Jake, voluntary or otherwise, often came with a sting in the tail.

They chatted for a while, he lay on the floor with Ella and made some funny noises, then it was time to shower and get ready for work. He and Sharon kissed on the front doorstep and Cato turned to leave, an unsettling tightness in his chest which he put down to lack of sleep and Jake's text. That's when he noticed the side gate propped open. It was on the other side of the wall from where he lay sleeping. The gate was usually bolted.


'Corporal White left the army just over eight years ago.'

'Eight years!' said DS Paddy McMahon, last night's Jim Beam still seeping from his pores. 'Where's he been since then? He's not on the record anywhere.'

The captain gave an amicable shrug. He was an affable bloke in a suit, forty-ish, not quite as fit as he perhaps used to be. His business card said he was Captain William Fletcher from Public Affairs. Call me Will, he'd insisted. According to him, Corporal Christopher White was a highly regarded soldier with a number of commendations to his name and had earned the respect of his peers and his superiors. A tough man and a good bloke to have beside you in a tight spot. He'd served in Iraq and Afghanistan a number of times, as well as East Timor. Stuff they knew already from his sister.

'What were the circumstances of his departure from the Army?' asked Cato.

'Circumstances?'

'Why did he leave?'

'Pastures new, I expect.'

'What does the record say?'

'Nothing much,' said Captain Will apologetically. 'Just gives a date.'

Cato noted it. 'And there's been no contact between him and the Army since then?'

'Not to my knowledge.'

'A Special Forces commando leaves after nearly twenty years service, some of it in war zones and other highly stressful environments, and there's no pastoral care? No follow-up?'

'These are tough men, Sergeant. They know what they're signing up for. I expect it's not so different for police officers, right? A few beers and some war stories among old comrades usually goes a long way.'

Condescending prick, but he had a point. If the army was anything like the police, then it was not improbable that once White left, that was it. He was pretty much on his own.

'Is there anything on White's medical record that may be helpful to us?'

'As with the exact details of his military service, his medical record also has to remain confidential I'm afraid.'

'So all you can tell us is that he was a good bloke. That right?' grumbled McMahon.

'Exceptional,' said Will.

'Could you imagine somebody getting the better of him and kicking him to death?' asked Cato.

'Only with the element of complete surprise, a great deal of luck, and perhaps even better training and experience than he had.'

McMahon leaned forward. 'And can you offer any explanation as to why a man of this calibre and service to our great nation might be sleeping rough in Fremantle in the twenty-first century?'

'None at all. Sorry.'

They all shook hands and Will left.

'Smug bastard.' McMahon crushed his cardboard coffee cup and binned it.

'Cagey,' agreed Cato.

'Maybe we should try the RSL.' McMahon softly belched some Jim Beam into the atmosphere. 'Or one of those veterans associations. See if anybody knew him. Shared some war stories and a beer, as Captain Weasel suggested.'

It wasn't a bad idea. They put it on the TO DO list.

'I hear you've come over to the Dark Side,' said McMahon, eyes on a distant spot high on the wall.

'What?' said Cato.

'DI Pavlou tells me you're in the fold.'

'Yeah,' said Cato. 'We're colleagues now, you and me.'

McMahon shook his head. 'Nah, I'm taking your desk in the local office as from Monday.' He pulled a grey-white handkerchief out of his pocket and snorted into it. Checking the contents, he folded and returned it. 'Trading places. If you work out what that mad bitch is up to, can you let me in on it?'


Norman Lip was running late. Head buried in his writing, he'd lost track of time and only remembered when an angry text came through.

**Where r u duckdace!!! :(**

Was that one of her jokes or was she losing her motor control even quicker than he realised? On arrival he gave the receptionist one of his cute smoulders and raced down the corridor. The door was open and there she was, cigarettes in her lap and fury in her eyes.

'Duck you. Fuckface.' He laughed and so did she. 'Get me out of here, I'm dying for a smoke.'

She prodded her wheelchair into action and they whirred down the corridor. The receptionist looked up from her computer screen as they passed. 'See you, Naomi. Bye, Norman.' A return smoulder. Maybe he should follow it up someday. 'Make sure you bring her back in time for dinner.'

'Shit yeah,' said Naomi under her breath. 'Wouldn't want to miss my gruel, would I?'

They left the River View Residential Care Centre, the river view denied to anyone living their lives at wheelchair or bed height, and rolled down the hill to a riverside cafe where they grabbed an outside table. Norman carried it a few extra metres away from the other patrons so Naomi could light up. The place was nearly empty, she was a regular and the staff knew about the muscular dystrophy so they felt sorry for her and pretended they didn't mind the smoking. Norman placed the order and pulled up a chair beside his sister.

'Whatcha been doin'?' she wanted to know.

'Writing.'

'Yeah, yeah. Writing what?'

Should he tell her? Of course he should. She was his muse, his nagging, snarky muse. 'I'm putting together a piece about this bloke that's killing the homeless down in Freo.'

'Opinion piece? News story? What?'

'Kind of opinion piece but trying to start up a conversation too.'

'Who with? The punters?'

His coffee arrived plus a Coke for her. He popped the can, put a straw in it and handed it over. 'Yeah, them too, but mainly him.'

'Him? Fucking hell.' She sucked on her straw. 'Interview with the Vampire?'

'What?'

'Anne Rice. Get it on your Kindle and educate yourself. You're such a disappointment to me, Normie.'

Her pet name for her little brother. She knew he hated it. Cow.

'Okay, I will,' he said. 'So what do you think?'

'What's the point?'

'Like I said, start a conversation.'

'With a psycho? Why?'

Why didn't she get it? She was meant to be the smartest in the family. 'Find out what makes him tick. Hear his side of the story.'

She crossed her eyes and raised her good hand in dagger fashion. 'I like killing people. I'm a sick fuck. End of story.'

'People lap it up though, don't they? Chuck your girlfriend off a high-rise hotel balcony and get acquitted, and you get interviewed on telly and fifty grand in your bank account. Get caught smuggling drugs overseas and as long as you're a photogenic Aussie, crime pays.'

She grinned. 'You're coming along, Normie. Let's hope your killer fits the bill.' A seagull hopped close to them and Naomi hissed at it. 'Assume you're right, what's in it for you?'

'Notoriety, infamy, a chance to make waves.'

'Spoken like the true son of Anthony Lip, OAM.' She sucked on her straw. 'I'll watch this space.'

He changed the subject. 'What you been doing this week?'

'*Métro, boulot, do-do.*'

'What?'

'Usual shit plus I'm learning French online. Duolingo. Passes the time while they change my nappy.' She looked over at a bunch of people taking paddleboard lessons by the shoreline. Wobbling. Falling off. 'Ever wished you could do that?'

Norman glanced over. 'Life's too short.'

'It is for me. I'm meant to be dead in another six years, at most.'

'Sorry.'

'Relax. You need to learn to take a joke.'

'Yours are so black I need a headtorch to see them.'

She smiled. 'So the writing's coming along. Metaphors, similes, all that?'

'Fuck off.'

'Started your book yet?'

'Not yet. Still playing with some ideas.'

She lit up a new cigarette. 'Playing with yourself more like.'

'You sound like Dad.'

A sombre face, furrowed brow. 'I only want the best for you, son. Success is ten per cent talent and ninety per cent effort. Do the hard yakka and you'll win a Walkley, just like me.' A bout of coughing. Respiratory complications of MD or just too many coffin nails? 'Least I won't be around long enough to get lung cancer like him.'

Norman snorted. 'Miserable bastard only got his Walkley because he was mates with the premier and wrote whatever the premier wanted him to. Some devious bastard's mouthpiece, that's all.'

'And here you are looking to do the same.'

'Duck off.'

Cato called it a day at lunchtime and spent the afternoon gardening, gurgling with Ella and canoodling with Sharon. Before he left work he'd remembered the unlatched side gate and the creepy dream he'd had. Bringing up the local crime stats on the desktop he'd spotted reports of three break-ins in his street in the last week plus two more around the corner and down the block. Somebody could have been prowling for an opportunity but the Kwong–Wang household had little worth stealing. Was it worth a padlock on that side gate? He didn't want to set off down the path of shutting the world out, it did strange and unhealthy things to the mind. But now he had a family to consider maybe he needed to be more diligent.

Jake showed up while they were preparing dinner and Ella was testing her lung capacity with some ear-splitting bellows.

'Dad!' He gave Cato a hug on the doorstep. Jake was as tall as Cato now and he had some fuzz on his upper lip and around his chin. The pale pink scar on his cheek, a close encounter with a madman and a nail gun several years ago, added a certain panache. He was dressed in standard teen gear of shorts, T-shirt and skate shoes. He had filled out a little, his jaw seemed firmer and squarer and there was a muscled hardness to his hug. 'How's it going?'

'Good.' Cato squeezed his son's upper arm. 'Been working out?'

'Mum got me a membership at the gym.' He grinned. 'Thinks it might keep me out of mischief.'

They went through to the kitchen. Jake gave Sharon a hug and tickled Ella which made her stop yelling, and giggle. Cato poured them all a cup of tea and threw some Tim Tams on a plate.

'So what's new?' said Jake, taking control of the conversation. He was bright, energetic, grown-up. Cato hadn't seen the like in his son for many months. It was great.

'This and that,' said Cato. He pointed to a few unfinished jobs around the kitchen and lounge area. 'And Ella's a project all by herself.' Cato's hand rested on Sharon's shoulder. 'But most of that falls to Shaz.'

Cato would reflect later on that frozen snapshot. He, Sharon and Ella on one side of the table, happy families, and Jake on his own on the other.

'Staying for dinner?' enquired Cato.

'Sure. Thanks Dad.'

It was Cato's standard offering of pesto and pasta. Jake chatted amiably about his life. School. 'Yeah, I need to pull my finger out. I'm onto it.' Home. 'Mum and Simon seem really happy and the twins are great.' Hobbies and pastimes. 'Spending a fair bit of time at the gym. There's some cool guys down there.' The future. 'Yeah, it's out there, isn't it? Waiting.'

Cato had been on edge all day wondering what Jake had wanted when he texted that morning. It turned out he just wanted to catch up and say hello.

More hugs at the end of the evening. 'See you soon, mate.' Cato smiled and gave his son a last squeeze, a surge of unexpected emotion in his chest. He felt a sudden tension in his son's embrace. 'Everything okay?'

'Yeah.' Jake looked down at his shoes, scuffed them a little on the path. Lifted his chin towards the side gate. 'That granny flat you've got out the back. Do you use it?'

'It's full of gear right now. Sharon's and my stuff, waiting to come out of removals boxes. Never seem to find the time to get round to it. Why?'

Jake shrugged. 'I don't know. Sometimes I feel like a spare part at Mum's. The new family, kids squalling. All that.'

'I thought you said it was all fine?'

'Yeah, well.' His eyes seemed to film over. 'And you've got your own family now, too.'

Cato thought about Dean Pearson. Bloody and lifeless. Abandoned. 'Maybe we can look at something, I'll talk it through with Sharon. And with your mum.'

'Great,' said Jake, backing down the path with a little wave. 'No worries.'

# 6

Monday, 11<sup>th</sup> September.

Cato set out for the office feeling rested and refreshed. No more nightmares, some long-neglected domestic jobs ticked off, and Sharon open to the idea of offering the granny flat to Jake.

'It's a compliment, really, isn't it?'

'I suppose so,' said Cato. 'It'd be nice to spend some solid time with him. We kind of missed out, those early years. The Job, you know?'

She'd nodded. 'It happens.' And a look that said it better not happen again.

'I'll call Jane later, sound her out.'

But he'd forgotten to. He added it to his mental TO DO list for today. Cato parked down near the Round House for the walk back up High Street to the old bank building that now housed Fremantle Police. These premises might well be flasher than the old limestone, asbestos-riddled nick but car parking was a pain in the butt. He picked up a takeaway coffee at Cafe 55 and, coming out, noticed a familiar face selling the *Big Issue* on the corner.

'Barry, g'day.' He fished a ten dollar note out of his wallet and took a copy of the magazine.

'Morning, Sergeant Kwong.' Barry slipped the money into his bag and rummaged around for change.

'Don't worry about it,' said Cato. 'How'd you go in court?'

Barry frowned. 'Fined. Hundred bucks for a single "fuck" at Carine Station. Shoulda got me money's worth. Arseholes.'

'Careful,' said Cato spotting an approaching council ranger. 'Or you'll be another hundred bucks poorer.'

The ranger was late twenties maybe or early thirties and built like the proverbial brick outhouse. He gave Barry a stare then turned to Cato. 'Everything okay here, sir?'

'Yep,' said Cato. 'No problem.'

The ranger turned back to Barry. 'You know there's an agreed precinct, mate, up the street and around the corner.'

'That's for beggars,' said Barry. He pointed to his official seller's ID lanyard and uniform shirt. 'Not begging. Working.'

'All the same.' The ranger smiled and reached for Barry's elbow in a shepherding manner.

Barry shook him off. 'Have I introduced you to my friend, Sergeant Kwong? He's a policeman.'

Cato stuck out a hand. 'G'day. And you are?'

'John.' They shook and John clapped a paw on Barry's shoulder. Gave it a squeeze. 'No worries, Barry. Have a good day. See you around, yeah?' He gave a final nod to Cato and left.

'You two seem well acquainted,' said Cato.

'Jackboot John knows all our names.' Barry's gaze followed the man up the street. 'I'd love to swear right now but I better not, eh?'


When Cato got to his desk, he found Paddy McMahon sitting at it.

'Morning,' said McMahon. 'What can I do for you?'

Cato murmured a return greeting and went in to see DI Hutchens. 'What's the score?' He thumbed over his shoulder at McMahon, now clipping his fingernails into Cato's rubbish bin.

'Take a seat,' said Hutchens, squinting at his laptop. 'Just finishing a tweet about the weekend arrests. Hashtag *dontdrinkandtalk*.'

Catching a middle-aged man mid-tweet somehow deprived him of any residual dignity, reflected Cato. This former warrior of the streets, sunk so low. Would this be Dirty Harry in the twenty-first century? Hashtag *feelluckypunk*?

'You signed a form agreeing to send me over to Major Crime and having McMahon take my job here.'

'That's right.'

'Why?'

'You're needed at the sharp end, mate. Somebody's got to catch this nutter and if anybody can do it, it's you.'

'Not with Pavlou scrutinising my every move.'

'I suspect you'll find she's more flexible than you think. She's had her eye on you for yonks, mate. It's time to show her what you're really made of.'

'And you're dropping me, just like that? No consultation, nothing?'

Hutchens lifted his gaze from the screen. 'Trust me on this one, mate. It's for the best.'

Cato shook his head. 'So what, I hop on the train up to Perth now?'

'No, not at all. You're based just along the corridor here.' Hutchens nodded in the general direction. 'Special outpost of Task Force Hermes. You're their permanent Major Crime man on the ground. Different budget allocation, too. You get your own coffee plunger and a gopher.' He closed the laptop. 'Young Amy's waiting for you with breathless anticipation. Catch you around the water cooler sometime.'

On the way to his new office Cato received looks from Deb Hassan and Chris Thornton carrying those same elements of bewilderment, hurt and betrayal that he too was feeling.

'We make him come to us.' Norman concluded his pitch to Betsy.

'What if he doesn't read us?' She laid a hand on his, mock-concerned. 'It's possible, you know.'

'We write something provocative enough to enrage the mainstream rags and draw his attention to us via them. And we add a coded invitation within our piece.'

Her dark brows knitted in a frown. 'How provocative?'

Norman handed his iPad over. 'Try that.' He'd sweated over it the whole weekend. Wrote, rewrote, cut, pasted, deleted. Stayed in. Ignored Tinder. She had to love it. Had to.

A smile on the bright red lips. 'This is good.' Like it was a fucking surprise. Her hand went to her mouth and she stifled a laugh. 'You're bad. You bad, bad boy.'

*Dig deep for the homeless. About six feet should do it. Yes, the homeless are now part of the funky Freo story. And paying the price, in spades. Geddit? It's taken three murders for the cops to pull their fingers out and admit there's something funny going on.*

*Maybe if the victims had been upstanding members of the Fremantle Sailing Club, or lived in a big house by the beach, the killer would be behind bars by now. But they're not. They're the people you avoid in the street. They're the people you wish would go away. And now your wishes are coming true.*

And further down:

*So what's your message, Mystery Man? Sick of bludgers tugging your sleeve, saying buddy can you spare a dime? Maybe you're the Caped Crusader, cleaning up the streets and making them safe for the white middle-class cappuccinistas? Or maybe you're just a sad bastard who got bullied at school and rejected by the pretty girls. What's it all about, Alfie?* New WAve *would love to know.*

Norman had included his name, a dedicated mobile and email contacts at the end. He'd signed off with the words *Don't. Be. Shy.*

'How do you separate the wheat from the chaff? A whole bunch of weirdos and time-wasters are going to take up your invitation.'

'I'll turn it into another story: My Life as a Freak Magnet. Call it research if you like but I'll know when the One True Lord reveals himself to me.'

'Run it,' said Betsy, shaking her head and chuckling. 'Live from tomorrow. This is going to be fun.' She summoned a flunkey. 'Martin, sweetie, I need you to rev up the advertisers.'

'All good?'

DI Pavlou was on her way down the freeway and had called a squad meeting for an hour hence. She'd phoned ahead to check on the 'new boy'.

'Yes,' said Cato.

'Amy looking after you?'

'Yep, got her following up a few things.'

'Great,' said Pavlou, brightly.

'Might be an idea, after the squad brief, if you, Paddy and me get together to talk about this job swap.'

'Sure,' she said. 'No worries.'

And that worried Cato even more.

Amy Trimboli stepped in to hand Cato a printout. It was a spreadsheet of organisations and names of people working with the homeless in Fremantle. It was, to Cato's eye, a surprisingly long list. Chris Thornton was running the names to see if any of them had previously come to the attention of the police for any reason. Cato was interested in Barry's reference to the council ranger as 'Jackboot John'. There were two council rangers called John. Over the coming days Cato intended to introduce himself to both of them. There was a tentative rap on his door. Chris Thornton.

'Sarge?' He handed over his copy of the same spreadsheet with a handful of names highlighted in different colours. 'Still more to come in but three of those so far have records for violence, one for drugs and one for unpaid fines.' Thornton traced a finger down the page. 'Blue is for biffo.'

Cato studied them. A volunteer on one of the soup runs had a restraining order out against him for repeatedly bashing his wife. A community outreach worker for one of the NGOs had been arrested twelve years earlier for assaulting a police officer at a demo in Perth. And a ranger employed by the council had a conviction for assault but at the lower end of the scale. There'd been a minor ruckus in a late-night taxi queue eighteen months previously. Cato smiled grimly. Judging by the age and first name of the offender, it looked like it was Jackboot John.


'So let's take stock.'

DI Pavlou had gathered the whole team in the big room. There were half-a-dozen extra civilian data wranglers on board, a few more detective foot soldiers poached from other districts, and bonus uniforms on call as needed. The briefing room that morning reminded Cato of his brief experience of the Shanghai underground at rush hour — if everyone cooperated they'd all still be breathing at the end of the day.

First up, Duncan Goldflam with a forensics update. He brought an image up on the wall-mounted screen. 'We've confirmed the make of boots, they are indeed Steel Blue, and there's a couple of telltale nicks in the tread according to the impression we took from the victim's face.' He then showed pictures of other detritus collected from the scene: lolly wrappings, cigarette butts, chewing gum and so on and so forth. As yet, no identified relevance.

Next it was Deb Hassan with a summary of the doorknocks and other local enquiries. She confirmed that she had phoned the victim's sister in Mount Barker and, to her knowledge, Christopher White didn't leave behind any childhood enemies with burning grudges. All the same, the local Mount Barker cops would do some nosing around. She went on. 'All of the staff from the Esplanade Hotel have been interviewed and we're working our way through the guest list from that night. So far nobody saw or heard anything of consequence out on the street or in the park.' She scrolled through her iPad. 'We're following up on some calls from the phone-in of people who say they were in the vicinity that night and we'll be inputting the results of that as it becomes available. But so far, again, nothing jumps out.'

Chris Thornton's CCTV trawl had, of course, netted them Wayne Joseph Bradley and his rottie, and when Chris stood up to do his bit there were a couple of woofs from the back of the room. He took it in good humour. 'Nothing to report on CCTV at this stage. The focus at the moment is on collating names associated with the homeless industry and running them through the system.' He nodded towards his trusty team of civilian data wranglers. 'That's ongoing.' He looked over at Cato. 'A couple of names have come up already.'

Pavlou looked interested. 'Philip?'

'Some violence convictions,' said Cato. 'Relatively low-level compared to what our perp is doing, but it's a start and may be helpful with some arm-twisting.'

Pavlou then explained the job swap between Cato and McMahon, which was met with little more than bemused or blank faces. She looked over at DI Hutchens. 'Mick? This works for you?'

'Paddy's going to be a real asset to Frontline 2020 and we're glad to have him on board.' Hutchens kept his eyes on Cato the whole time he was talking. Cato had seen that lying glint before.

'Great,' said Pavlou. 'And Paddy, I believe you and Sergeant Kwong met with Defence over the weekend?'

'Yeah,' said McMahon. 'Captain Fletcher. Nothing to say but he was very nice about it.'

'Follow-up?' said Pavlou.

'Unless you have access further up the food chain I don't think they're going to give us anything. But Captain Fletcher did suggest talking to the veterans associations to see if they knew Chris White. I'm onto it.'

'Bravo,' said Pavlou.

The meeting broke up and Pavlou asked Hutchens, McMahon and Cato to stay behind.

'Problem?' said Hutchens when the room had cleared.

'Au contraire,' said Pavlou. 'Just dotting some t's.' The seating arrangements said it all: Cato had taken a place on Hutchens' side of the table while McMahon joined Pavlou on the other. She seemed to find it amusing. 'My apologies for the short notice on the job swap, guys.'

McMahon looked like he'd rather not be there. He probably didn't do conflict and confrontation well unless it was the easy stuff involving cops and crims and a bit of honest biff. He was a behind-the-scenes mutterer but never took it any further.

'An unusual step,' conceded Cato. 'Normally it's a more consultative process. What's your rationale?'

'Frontline 2020: optimising our resources to meet our primary targets — happy customers and unhappy criminals.' She paused to allow McMahon a moment to finish snorting into his handkerchief. 'The timing of these murders isn't good, just as the Commissioner is launching another one of his restructures. So Task Force Hermes is under a great deal of scrutiny both internally and externally.'

A nod from McMahon like that all made perfect sense.

'And rearranging the deckchairs optimises those resources?' asked Cato.

An icy smile from Pavlou, a Velvet Hammer special. 'I see it more as a reprioritising and retargetting of available skills and assets.'

Cato remained unconvinced. Was there some other agenda at work here? Testing Cato? Booting McMahon? He wished these people would just play a straight bat now and again.

Hutchens shifted in his seat. 'I'm with DI Pavlou on this one. Cato, you're a kick-arse investigator and left-field thinker and Hermes needs you out there chasing after this maniac.' He turned his attention to McMahon. 'Paddy, on the other hand, is a small-minded, clock-watching waste of space fit only for the drudge of piss-easy volume crime. Perfect for the local office.'

Paddy twisted his head. 'Bit harsh, mate.'

'The truth is my sword,' said Hutchens.


Cato and Amy dropped by the town hall to have a chat with the head of the council ranger team, a statuesque woman with an open face and a relaxed manner. Her name was Courtney. Cato didn't catch the surname but he was glad Amy wrote it down.

'I've been expecting you,' said Courtney.

Hasn't everybody, thought Cato. He wanted to know how the rangers dealt with Fremantle's homeless and whether any of Courtney's team had noticed anything or anyone unusual in recent weeks.

'Not as such, this is still a relatively new area for us. Until about nine months ago our focus was on barking dogs and noise complaints. The council has only recently become interested in homelessness and begging and begun to formulate policies and strategies.'

'What prompted the change?'

'A rise in numbers of homeless generally but also increased visibility over the summer months; the nice weather brings out the tourists, the citizens and the beggars all at the same time. A consequent rise in complaints.'

'About what?' asked Amy.

'Take your pick: blocking the footpaths and shop doorways, scaring customers, harassment, vandalism, being unsightly, making people feel guilty or sad.' She glugged from a water bottle. 'The citizens of Fremantle don't like being made to feel guilty or sad.'

Cato was beginning to like Courtney. 'So what is the policy?'

'Our first step was to fund the various agencies operating in the city to do an audit, count their clients if you like, so we had a better idea of the numbers we're dealing with. We can't be waiting until the next census before we act. Then we formulated our strategy. The council calls its approach "holistic".' She accompanied the last word with finger quotes. 'Very Freo. We don't want to be seen as hostile to an already downtrodden and vulnerable section of society. We leave that to our neighbours up in Perth.' A wry grin. 'Did you know some councils in the UK have even installed anti-homeless spikes in shop doorways? Retractable — tucked away in the day and spring out at night, like a flick-knife. Try sleeping there and it's like one of those beds of nails the cartoon fakirs sleep on. Poms, eh? Nothing they're not capable of when they put their minds to it.'

'Holistic?' prompted Cato.

'Yeah, right. So we recognise there are genuine homeless people in need and that there are genuine concerned citizens who want to be able to help those in need.' Her mobile buzzed on the desk but she did a good job of ignoring it. 'As opposed to pro beggars.'

'Pro beggars?' said Amy.

'The same faces turn up in several shopping precincts across the CBD. They're really professionals, sometimes operating in gangs or at least loose associations, supplementing their income with begging.'

Cato frowned. 'And the rangers tell you this?'

'Actually, we call them community safety officers. They have a chat with the beggars about who they are, where they're from. We also talk to our colleagues from other municipalities. Share intelligence if you like. It's clear there's a hard core that give the genuine homeless a bad name.'

Cato wasn't aware that the homeless, genuine or otherwise, had ever had a good name. He didn't buy it, gangs of pro beggars, this sounded like spin, nonsense. Dickens meets *Mad Max*. 'So once you've talked to them and decided which category they're in, what next?'

'We've allocated agreed begging precincts in Adelaide and William Streets, to keep them from cluttering up the mall. We know the local, genuine ones and they're registered with us. We pretty much leave them alone as long as they behave. We encourage the pro beggars to move on.'

Cato recalled Barry's interaction with the ranger that morning. *Yeah, Jackboot John knows all our names.*

'How do you move them on?'

'Ask them nicely, at first. If that doesn't work we hang around, crowd their space, stand right next to them if we have to, and that usually discourages donations so they get the message. If all else fails we might ask for help from your good selves.'

'Would it be okay if we have a chat with your team to see if they've heard or seen anything unusual?'

'Sure,' said Courtney.

'And I probably need to talk to the mayor. We don't want this to become an election issue.'

A wry smile and a lifted hand. 'I'm just a bureaucrat, you can take that up with him.' Her phone buzzed again. 'Sorry, do you mind if I take this?'

Cato shrugged and smiled.

'Fuck,' said Courtney after a few seconds.

When her eyes found Cato's, he realised this might involve him too.

# 7

The fracas was just across the street outside Culley's Tea Rooms in the mall. When Cato and Amy arrived, there were already a couple of uniforms on the scene plus Courtney who had rushed ahead to deal with the emergency while Cato and Amy were escorted out of the town hall by a staffer. Somebody was on the ground being attended by a paramedic team. There was a ranger there, standing with his head back, dabbing at a bloody nose with a handkerchief. It was Jackboot John and Courtney was talking to him.

'What happened?' said Cato to a police uniform. His name badge said Oliver, they'd nodded a few times passing in the corridors of the cop shop.

'The ranger had a run in with a dero. Asked him to move on. Bit of push and shove apparently, then the bloke punched him.'

'The bloke on the ground?'

'Yeah.'

'And how did he end up there?'

'The ranger punched him back, harder.'

'Witnesses?'

'Heaps. The main one is the guy who runs the souvenir shop. He'd apparently made the original complaint to the ranger. There's also the woman from the travel agent, the busker over there and half-a-dozen punters having their lunch outside Culley's.' Smart phones were raised for selfies while sausage rolls cooled. Oliver squinted at his crackling radio piece. 'Wouldn't have thought something like this would interest you? We're happy to deal with it.'

'Just passing,' said Cato. He directed Amy to talk to the souvenir shop man.

At that moment the ambulance officers parted as they helped their patient to a sitting position. It was Barry, shaking his head groggily. 'Fucking bastards.'

Cato crouched down for a chat. 'You okay there, Barry?'

'Sergeant Kwong!' He no longer had his *Big Issue* magazines or his seller's uniform and ID. He was back in civvies: thongs, cargo pants and an NWA T-shirt. His IGA shopping bag lay a few metres away. Barry pointed at Jackboot John. 'Arrest that man.'

Courtney joined them. 'Barry, mate. You okay?'

'What's it to you?'

She repeated the question to the ambos who seemed to think there was no major damage but they'd take him across to Fiona Stanley A&E for a check-up.

She gave Barry a smile. 'You landed a corker on John there. You can look after yourself, can't you?'

Barry lifted his chin proudly. 'Fucking right.'

'Fucking right,' she agreed. 'Look, I've had a word with John and he's happy to not press charges. Just call it quits. What do you reckon?'

'He started it.'

Another smile. 'And you finished it, didn't you, champ?'

Not exactly true but Barry was open to flattery. 'Yeah, that's right.' 'So?'

Barry gave it some thought. 'Just keep him away from me, that's all.'

Courtney looked at Cato. 'What do you reckon? Save us all a bit of paperwork?'

He thumbed over his shoulder at the uniforms. 'Their call, they're the attending officers.'

After some discussion it was agreed to issue both combatants with a caution and leave it at that. Cato and Amy left them to it. But not before he noticed a wink pass between John and the souvenir shop owner, and relief ghost across Courtney's face.


'Why Fremantle?'

Cato was ruminating on the meeting with Courtney the Boss Ranger and her comments on 'pro beggars' moving from suburb to suburb, donor shopping.

'What?' said Amy Trimboli, emerging from Subway with a big sandwich.

'If our killer is carrying a grudge or wanting to send a message about the homeless, why Freo? Why not Perth or somewhere else?'

'Familiar territory? He lives or works here or has some connection with it?'

It was a good, if obvious, point and Cato acknowledged it with a nod. 'If Perth is cracking down maybe he wants to discourage the refugees heading to Freo.'

'Stop the Tramps?' said Amy.

'Be nice.'

As they headed back to the cop shop, Cato put in a call to set up a meeting with the mayor. The PA promised to get back to him asap. Cato thanked her and pocketed his phone. All around them old Fremantle landmarks, some ugly and some not, were being demolished to make way for the vision of a new, more vibrant glass and steel Freo. The billboards called it 'Freo 2020'. Cato wondered how many marketing and policy strategies out there were tied in to that year and the notion that everything would become clearer by then. The 2020 vision looked to Cato like the same high-rise high-density model that had dissolved what heart and soul there had been in other Perth suburbs and turned them into anywheresville. Would such developments offer any relief to the homeless? If so, Cato suspected it would be a very slow and very small trickle down. Then again, housing and caring for the homeless was primarily the remit of the state and federal governments. Councils empty bins, police pets and strays, create development opportunities, oil the cogs of commerce and community. Set off fireworks on Australia Day — or decide that Australia Day should not, in fact, be celebrated. Yes, more than that. A council, a good one, tapped into what it believed was the soul of a city. Was that what the killer also believed he was doing? Tapping into the dark heart?

Amy seemed to read his thoughts. 'Chicken or egg? Is he responding to a mood out there, or aiming to shape it?'

'Or are we crediting him with more depth than he warrants?'

'Prob'ly.'

They crossed at the Market Street lights, dodging a cyclist running the red, and headed along High Street past the refurbished National

Hotel. Cato remembered it as a dingy, old man's pub before economics and arson left it a neglected shell for many years. Now it was back, boasting black-suited bouncers with headsets, boutique beers and a clientele with a healthy disposable income. The National was a microcosm of the transition from old Fremantle to new. Those old blokes with their working clothes and middies wouldn't last two minutes in there.

They swiped themselves through the cop shop security doors and climbed the stairs. The question still floated in front of Cato, unanswered. Why Fremantle? In the office Amy unwrapped her sandwich and Cato dug a tupperware box of leftovers out of the fridge.

'So what did the souvenir shop man have to say?' he said, picking through last night's chicken stir-fry.

'Neil Foster. He doesn't think much of the council, or the mayor, he's sick of the beggars and he thinks the buskers are crap.'

'What did he have to say about this particular incident?'

Amy finished chewing on a section of her demi-sub. 'He said the beggar, the bloke the ranger decked ...'

'Barry.'

'Right. Him. He was hanging around the shop doorway and swearing at customers. The ranger was called and the fight led from that.'

'Was the ranger nearby or did Mr Foster call the council?'

'I'll check.'

Cato thought about the wink that passed between the men. 'I think Foster and Jackboot John might be acquainted. I wouldn't be surprised if they have each other's mobiles.'

'Jackboot John?'

'Barry's name for him.' Cato explained the recent history.

'Sounds like he warrants closer attention,' agreed Amy. 'As does Foster.'

Chris Thornton stuck his head around the door. 'Sarge? DI Hutchens reckoned I should bring this to you.'

'Yep?'

'The nerds examined Wayne Bradley's GPS from his car.'

Wayne and Scottie the Rottie already seemed so long ago. 'And?'

'His account of visiting the brothel on the night of victim three's murder stacks up. 'Shanelle' from Maddington gave him an alibi. Plus the GPS shows his car was where he says it was at the time and the only stops he made were the car park outside Little Creatures, Ada Street round the corner from the knocking shop, and home.'

'So we can eliminate him from our enquiries?'

A sly grin materialised. 'But on the night of victim two, Maureen Bryant, the car makes a stop for six minutes just fifty metres from where she was found and within an hour of the likely time of death according to the P-M report.'

'That's the night he failed to account for properly.'

'Another chat?' asked Thornton.

Cato still didn't see Bradley as being physically capable of stomping Chris White to death but the question needed an answer if only for due diligence. Besides, he might have seen something useful. Either way, the man was already milking his victim status on a handful of news outlets and they couldn't afford another PR disaster. 'Send it through to DI Pavlou,' said Cato. 'That decision's above my pay grade.'

Jackboot John's real name turned out to be John Jason Jenkins.

'Triple J,' said Amy. 'Cool.'

They'd been given a meeting room at the town hall and Courtney, less friendly and a lot more wary since that morning's biff, had offered to sit in.

'I think we'll manage fine, thanks,' said Cato.

John Jenkins dabbed a tissue at his nose. It was red and swollen and he still looked mightily pissed off. Whether that was from the run-in with Barry, or from a chastening chat with his boss, Cato wasn't sure. Jenkins was thirty-two and had joined the rangers department nine months earlier.

'What does your job entail?' asked Cato.

'This and that. Until about six months ago I'd run around in the van, telling people off for letting their dogs go where they shouldn't, or pay a call on somebody with a yapper and ask them nicely to do something about it. Rock and a hard place in Freo, they're nuts about their dogs here and won't have a word said against them.'

'What about enforcing the council's policy on beggars?'

'That's the main gig now. Much easier to deal with than dogs and their owners.'

'So have you heard or seen anything unusual over the last couple of months in that aspect of your job?'

'Like what?'

'People behaving suspiciously, stuff like that.' A shake of the head. 'What about your ... clients?'

'Clients?'

'The beggars you move on,' said Amy.

'What about them?'

'Have they mentioned anything unusual? Have any of them changed their behaviour recently?'

'Nah, same as ever.'

'What was the fight about, Mr Jenkins?'

'Fight?'

'This morning with Barry,' said Cato.

'I thought that was all settled? Isn't this about your murder enquiry and whether I've seen or heard anything that might help you?'

'You don't seem to have anything to offer on that score. How would you describe your relationship with your clients?'

'Professional.'

'In what sense?'

'In every sense. I have a job to do and I do it.'

'You don't like them very much, do you?'

'It's not in the job description.'

'We're trying to stop a murderer, Mr Jenkins. Your help would be appreciated.'

'We finished here?'

'For now.' Cato handed him a business card. 'If you think of anything, or see or hear anything, call me. My mobile's on the back.'

Jenkins examined the card for a moment. 'Sure, mate, no wucks.'

'Just one more thing,' said Trimboli. Jenkins turned. 'What size shoe are you?'

'Ten. Same as my dick.'

As the door closed behind him, Amy Trimboli took a set of tweezers from her bag, retrieved Jenkins' bloody tissues from the rubbish bin and dropped them into an evidence bag. 'Same as your IQ as well.'

'Naughty,' said Cato.

'If we get a match I'll ask him nicely for an official sample.'

That was fine by Cato. He checked his phone. The mayor's PA hadn't been back in touch, so he decided to take the initiative and drop in.

'We were just passing,' Cato told the PA as she looked up from her computer screen. He nodded towards her ID lanyard. 'Jess?' He introduced himself and Amy.

'Steven's still out.' She tapped her keyboard. 'He's available first thing tomorrow. How about meeting him for coffee? He likes Little Lefroy. Eight-thirty okay for you?'

'Make it eight,' said Cato. 'Mine's a strong flat white. No froth.'

Next a visit to Neil Foster at the souvenir shop over the road. A face pinched and lined from too much frowning. Neil was from somewhere in Wales originally. They had the chat in a cramped back room while Neil's equally pinched wife kept watch over a shop full of koalas, placemats, tea towels and postcards. The thing was, the more Cato listened to Neil the more he felt for the poor bugger: absentee landlords charging crippling rents, online competition undercutting his meagre profits, ratbags smashing the windows, pissing in the doorway, stealing merchandise, harassing customers. And now the council's development plans which, during the construction phase, would disrupt business for the next eighteen months or more.

'And no, I don't buy the idea that soulless concrete towers can be karmically offset by buskers and murals and an old brickwall facade.' A man after Cato's own heart, but he hadn't finished his rant. 'Fucking tower blocks in the centre of Freo? Tacky shite.'

That wasn't entirely fair coming from a man who sold plastic platypus keyrings. Having heard him out, it was time to get to the point. 'The antisocial behaviour. That's been a major bugbear for you, hasn't it?'

'Scum and deadshit, the lot of them.'

'The ranger, Jenkins, do you know him?'

'I think his correct title is Community Safety Officer.'

'All the same, do you?'

'Yes, our paths have crossed.'

Amy brought up a spreadsheet on her iPad. 'An average of three calls a week to the local police for the six months up to last February. After that, nothing. No problems since then?'

'The cops were useless, overstretched, whatever. Other priorities. The council officers are able to expedite matters.'

Cato had a memory of the municipal security officers in Shanghai, the *chengguan*, and their ruthless ability to 'expedite matters'. Breaking spines, chucking people off rooftops. 'Fair enough, but the council phone log also shows that you stopped calling their hotline sometime in March. Did the problems suddenly go away?'

'No.'

'So?'

A sigh. 'I've known Johnny's family from way back when I lived down in Albany. He gave me his mobile, said he could deal with things quicker that way.'

'Johnny. Personal service,' said Amy. 'Nice.'

'If you like. What's this all about, anyway? It was just a scuffle between him and that *Big Issue* loser. I thought that was all over? Lot of fuss over nothing if you ask me.'

'Just trying to build a clearer picture,' said Cato, taking out his business card. 'Thanks for your time.'

# 8

*I was happy enough just to pass the time. Pass through their lives and leave my mark on them. Enjoy the sport and the chase then rub them out like they were never there.*

*Then a chance encounter. A ghost from the past. But not a ghost. And I see there was a meaning after all.*

*I remember this one night my old man took me out shooting in the bush. I was nine. It was the middle of winter and there was a gale and driving rain ripping our faces off. We had the ute windows down and the spotlight pointed off to the side and there must have been twenty roos sitting in this paddock waiting to die.*

*'Take your time,' my dad said. 'Pick your target, stay steady, let out a slow breath and squeeze. Make sure it's a proper kill.' He waved a thumb at the rain. 'We don't want to be getting out in this shit just to put down a winged roo.'*

*I did take my time, picked my target, stayed steady, and squeezed.*

*And I didn't kill it.*

*My dad lit up a smoke and sat with the engine running. 'Go and finish it then.'*

*The rain ran down my neck and my clothes were soaked. I was shivering and miserable out there in the middle of the paddock. The wind gusts nearly blowing me over.*

*'Left, about ten steps,' Dad yelled from the ute.*

*I found it, a female. The bullet had gone through the side of her neck. She was still moving, dragging herself along the ground, making this terrible screeching and wheezing noise. The spotlight from behind showed shiny blood pumping down her body.*

*'Kill it, then,' Dad shouted.*

*I put the twenty-two barrel to her eye and pulled the trigger. The head exploded. Then I noticed the joey. Its ears were poking up out of the pouch and its eyes were big and round and scared.*

*'There's a baby,' I called back, trying not to cry.*

*'Finish it off.'*

*But I couldn't.*

*I shook my head. Started blubbing.*

*Dad swore and got out of the ute. He took my arm with the rifle in it, and placing my finger back on the trigger, squeezed it. 'Like this.' No more joey.*

*It wasn't so hard, after that.*

*Like this, Dad said.*

*Take your time, pick your target, stay steady, let out a slow breath and squeeze.*

# 9

Cato was shaken awake by Sharon. It must be his turn again. He opened his eyes to darkness and readied himself to go and fetch the baby. But something wasn't right. It was silent. Ella wasn't crying.

'There's somebody down the side path,' Sharon whispered.

Then he heard it too. The soft scrape of shoes on the concrete paving slabs. And another noise. A hiss: intermittent, irregular. Rattling, like peas in a tin. A spray can. 'Little bastards.' Cato threw back the covers, pulled on some daks and headed for the front door.

'Leave it, Phil. You don't know how many are out there. Call it in.'

She was right but he was pissed off and sleep deprived and somebody had to pay. He flicked on the porch light and unlatched the security door. Listened again. No running footsteps, the light hadn't scared them off. The hissing still there. They were still spray-painting.

'Hey!' he called, stepping out on to the verandah.

A chuckle. Low. Relaxed. Unafraid.

Cato went down the few steps into the front yard and edged towards the side path. Clouds scudded across a half moon and wind blew through the gum trees. Somewhere a dog barked. He shivered, looked around for something to defend himself with. Saw only an old teapot with a geranium cutting in it. He bent to pick it up. The quality of the air and light around him changed a second before he felt the blow. A kick to the side of his head. Then another and another. He rolled himself tight, bracing for more. A hawking sound and a gob of phlegm on his face, then the sound of retreating running steps.

When he opened his eyes again, it was quiet and still as if it had never happened.

'You can't do shit like that now, sweetie.'

Sharon dabbed at his grazes with a Betadine-soaked cotton ball. The two kicks and a stomp had left him sore yet remarkably blood-free. On balance it could have been a lot worse. Maybe he shouldn't have washed the spit off his face, saved it for DNA testing. No, too disgusting to contemplate.

'Yeah, sorry.'

He had been stupid, venturing out in the middle of the night clad only in his daks and with a geranium-filled teapot for a weapon. He'd been easily overcome and, it didn't bear thinking about, he had left his wife and child vulnerable. They should have kept everything locked and called the cops as she suggested.

Sharon finished dabbing a scrape on his cheek and pressed her lips to it. 'There, there. All better.' She chucked the cotton ball in the bin. 'We'll check the vandalism in the morning. It'll wait.'

On cue Ella woke ready for a feed. 'No rest for the wicked,' said Cato.

Sharon mustered a semi-vixen look. 'Too stuffed to be wicked right now. Maybe later?'

Cato climbed back into bed, thinking about how close he'd possibly come to putting his loved ones in danger. He chastised himself to sleep.

Mayor Steve Pinder favoured a tweedy jacket and autumnal colours, and his hair was neatly parted around an angular goatee-bearded face. If he came to your door you'd be forgiven for thinking uni lecturer or self-published poet. He slid a mug towards Cato. 'Strong flat white, no froth.'

The cafe was full of locals supercharging their day ahead. Pinder acknowledged passing nods and greetings. 'Thanks for taking the time to meet me,' said Cato, handing him a business card.

'My pleasure.' A look of concern at Cato's injuries. 'Been in the wars?'

'Nothing serious.' He sipped some coffee. 'How's the election going?'

'Early days.'

'Confident?'

'Hopeful. I try not to take anything for granted.'

'You're aware, of course, of these recent homeless killings.'

'Yes. Terrible. Any progress?'

'Early days.'

The mayor's ham and cheese croissant arrived. He took a bite and brushed the crumbs off his chest. 'I'm still not sure what this is about?' He gestured at the space between them. 'Why the meeting?'

Cato wasn't so sure himself. 'My boss wants reassurance that these killings won't become an election issue. She fears external pressures would distract us from our primary aim.'

Pinder frowned. 'I'm sure she's right and I wouldn't dream of adding to your burden. That would be an appalling thing to do.'

Cato nodded. 'Much appreciated.'

'I'm almost offended that you felt the need to bring it up with me.'

A shrug. 'Only obeying orders.'

'Yes. Right. Of course.' Another bite of croissant. 'How does your boss see this as a potential election issue?' A smile. 'Not looking for tips or anything. Just out of interest.'

Cato pulled his legs in so a couple could get by with their pram and three dogs on leads and keep checking their phones at the same time. 'Homelessness has become more of a problem in Freo the last year or so. I talked to Courtney in the town hall. The new policies, rangers, beggars, all that.'

Pinder didn't reply. Waited for more.

'A candidate might use this as an opportunity to, for instance, stir up public fear, or antipathy towards the homeless, or criticise the police?'

'They'd have to be pretty despicable and desperate.'

'What about the opposition?'

'I can't speak for him.'

'Aren't there several people standing?'

'Yes, but few of them are contenders.'

'So by "him" you mean ...?' Cato checked notes on his phone.

'Brian Knight,' Pinder broke in with a grin. 'Dark Knight I call him. He's been a councillor in City Ward since the Stone Age. Now he thinks his time has come.'

'Do you have a mobile number?'

'Sure.' He gave it to Cato. 'Good luck.'

'How's parenthood?' enquired Hutchens, casting a glance over Cato's injuries.

'Hectic but, on balance, a blessing.'

'Marriage still on track?'

Cato gave in and explained his wounds.

They were in the office kitchen and Hutchens had made himself a tea. 'Water's just boiled,' he said helpfully. 'Did you report it?'

'Hardly seems worth it. I'll live. And the graffiti amounted to a big white letter "Y" on the weatherboards. We were going to get the outside repainted anyway.'

'A big Y?'

Cato shrugged. It hurt. 'Maybe they were interrupted writing "you suck". Maybe it's a form of existential street art. I've seen other "Y" graffiti around the burbs from this year's bad boys, Yardies they call themselves.'

Hutchens nodded. 'I did a tweet about them a few weeks ago. Hashtag *hardertheycomehardertheyfall*. They sometimes hang out down at the "Youth Plaza".' Hutchens did finger quotes for the last two words. He was talking about the Esplanade skate park: a few hundred square metres of useless grass concreted over in the name of civic progress. 'An excellent council initiative,' said Hutchens. 'Now we just need to put a fence around it and a couple of guards and we'll always know where to find the little bastards.'

'You're a dark-hearted cynic, sir,' said Cato, squeezing his teabag out.

'Either way, intelligence, mate. Every statistic counts.' He tapped his nose. 'Hashtag *biggerpicturepolicing*.'

'You seem to be growing into the new role.'

'Old dogs, new tricks. Maybe I can be some kind of viral sensation after I retire.' Hutchens lifted his mug at Cato. 'Anyway, zap it through to the local police team so they can file it away.' A wink. 'Look after yourself, okay?'

Amy Trimboli was waiting for him in their Major Crime outpost two doors down from the toilets. 'Ouch, what happened to you?'

Cato explained himself again. It looked like being one of those days.

She tutted in sympathy and passed a spreadsheet his way. 'Chris Thornton's update on names of those connected with the homeless industry, cross-referenced with the national crime-tracking system.' If any names on that list had been in trouble anywhere in Australia it would be available on the national database.

Cato scanned the list: a Perth food-bank volunteer who had a restraining order out against him in Queensland; a Rockingham paramedic who'd spent time in the military had copped a fine for his involvement in a brawl between US and Australian servicemen on exercises in Darwin six years earlier. Maybe he was worth pursuing in case he had any previous connection to victim three, the ex-commando Chris White. Cato put it on the action list for Deb Hassan's outside enquiries team, along with a general follow-up on all the names, highlighted or not, to see if they'd heard or seen anything of interest lately.

Amy handed him another summary sheet. 'And these are new calls from the Crimestoppers phone-in, filtered for irrelevance and nutcases.'

Cato took a sip of tea and squinted at the log, a headache squeezing his eyeballs. 'Any Panadol around?'

'Coming right up.' Amy wandered off to organise it.

The phone log, even in filtered form, remained a haven for dobbers and score-settlers and all the lonely people. But one name did stand out.


Jake loved this time of day at the gym. He had a double free on Tuesday mornings, not that there was much point going to school anyway. The pre-work crowd had thinned and he could count on a solid hour of space, peace and concentration before the mums and oldies rocked up and ruined it. This was his sanctuary away from the twins, away from bloody Simon and his disapproval, and from Mum and her constant worry and disappointment.

'Jake, mate, give us a hand?'

It was Lance. Over the past week or two they'd progressed from exchanging nods to sharing jokes at the expense of the weak fatties and helping each other out on the big lifts. Jake still didn't know much about Lance though, except he came from somewhere out bush and was built like a tank.

'Early today, but?' said Jake, sliding another plate onto the bar as Lance settled himself for the bench press.

'On nights. Can't fuckin' sleep when I finish. Too pumped.' He expelled some air and took the strain. Jake was ready to ease the load if it went wrong. Lance did five lifts, face beetroot red, veins bulging on the forehead and neck, utter focus and concentration. He hissed on the last lift and Jake helped guide the bar back onto the rack. 'Your turn, Jakey-boy?'

'No way. That's forty over my usual.'

A grin. 'Gotta be in it to win it. Come on, give it a go.' He sat up and patted the bench beside him. 'You know you want to.'

Jake caught a look in Lance's eye. Trust me, it said. I'm with you. He lay down and slid into place. Looked up, seeking reassurance, and found it.

Lance stroked the bar. 'Don't worry, I've got it.'

Jake gripped, flexed his fingers, tested it. This was suicide. He nodded his readiness. And took the weight.

'Easy now, easy,' said Lance.

Jake lowered it for the push up. He felt his eyes were going to explode. It was hot. Fucking insane. He felt Lance's fingertips lightly brush his biceps, a tingle.

'You're better than you think, Jakey-boy. You can do this.'

Jake snorted and roared. Pushing. Straining.

'Show those bastards, Jakey. Use that rage.'

And there was plenty there to draw from. He felt a new power he hadn't known he possessed. And the bar was moving. He had it. Just the one drop and lift but it was forty over and he'd done it.


The call to the Crimestoppers hotline had been anonymous but once again the name had come up. John Jenkins. Jackboot John. Cato listened to the recording of the call again.

*Check out Jackboot John, the council ranger, he's always bashing them. He's a fucking hater. Jackboot Johnny Jenkins. Got it?*

It was a woman's voice, so that ruled out a vendetta by Sweary Barry. Unless she was a friend of his. The voice was familiar. 'Them, not us,' said Cato.

'Yeah?' Amy was organising for a copy of the recording to be downloaded.

'The caller says he's always bashing "them" not "us". So she's an outsider, of sorts. Not actually a victim herself.'

'Defender of the weak,' said Amy, as they replayed it. 'Sonya Allegretta?'

Cato nodded.


When they arrived at St Mary's, they were told she was in the canteen. They found Sonya helping out, wiping down tables.

'G'day,' she said. 'You're back.' She flicked her dishrag at a stubborn crumb. 'Give us a moment, had the mayor in here today, and the newspaper. Never been so popular. He wants to reassure everybody that he loves hobos. Must be election time.'

Cato smiled to himself. He and Amy took the cuppas offered and slid into some chairs on the other side of the hall while Sonya finished up. Eventually she joined them, bringing a cup of her own.

'So what now?' she said.

'Perhaps we could go to your office?' said Cato.

'Nah, here's good.'

Cato shrugged and signalled to Amy to press play on her iPad. It was the Crimestoppers recording, volume turned down for discretion but Cato still noticed a few heads turn their way.

'That's you, isn't it?'

A slight flushing. 'Can you prove that?'

'If we get the techs in, yes we probably can.'

'So?'

'So tell me about Jackboot John.'

'His name's Jenkins, he's a ranger for the council.'

'Yes,' said Cato. 'We know.'

Sonya gave him a grim smile. 'So he's already on your radar. That's good.'

'Why's he on yours?'

'We started getting complaints about six months ago, just when they brought the new policies in.'

'Go on.'

'At first it was assumed somebody from outside was doing it. Gear getting nicked, sleeping bags and stuff, or getting trashed, pissed on. Then came the harassment and verbal abuse.'

'In what way?' said Amy.

'In what way?' mimicked Sonya. She really didn't like Amy very much. 'Imagine you've got two bags full of shopping and you've been on your feet all morning and you just fancy a sit-down somewhere for a few minutes. How would you feel if, as soon as you took the weight off your feet, some tosspot gets in your face and orders you to keep moving?'

'Mmmm,' said Amy.

'Mmmm. And he's holding his nose and looking at you like you stink. Saying things under his breath: loser, scum, slag, bitch. Or worse.'

'You never filed a complaint?' asked Cato.

'I had a word with his boss, Courtney, about three months ago. I asked her to jerk his leash.'

'And?'

'He got worse. When he's on duty, people just steer clear. Fucking RoboCop, he is. But effective at his job, I'll give him that.'

'How do you mean?' said Cato.

'If it's social cleansing he's after, it's working. There's some parts of town have become no-go areas. Too dangerous to be in on your own.'

'You mentioned bashings.'

'We've had three reports in the last month of sly kicks and punches in backstreets when nobody's around. Threats.'

'Threats?' said Cato.

'If they didn't leave town he'd come looking for them after hours, with his mates.'

Expediting the matter, as Neil the souvenir shopman might say. 'I'd like to talk to these people, the ones who've been assaulted.'

'Don't fancy your chances, they tend to avoid people like you. But I'll see what I can do.'

'Why didn't you mention this at our last meeting? Why the anonymous dob call?'

Sonya snorted. 'You kidding? His dad's a cop. Who's going to touch him?'

'Why didn't we know that?' said DI Pavlou when Cato gave her the update.

'Why would we? Parentage doesn't show up on criminal records. The questioning of him so far has been about whether he could help us with our enquiries. "Who's your daddy?" didn't come into it.'

'So what's your thinking?'

'I think he warrants a deeper background check.'

'Another interview?'

Cato shook his head. 'Not at this stage. The allegations of harassment and violence are, as yet, unproven. I think we need more before we bring him in.'

'Okay. Do we know who his dad is?'

'Bill Jenkins, recently retired sergeant down in Albany. Hard man by all accounts.'

'Don't know him,' said Pavlou. 'Didn't DI Hutchens spend some time in Albany?'

'He did. I'll follow it up.'

Pavlou moved on. 'What about Rottie Man, Wayne Bradley. The missing six minutes?'

'Yep, we should check it out.'

'Okay,' she said. 'But low-key this time, a couple of juniors clearing up loose ends. No TRG, no dramas. Put the local team on it.'

'I'll send out Thornton and Hassan.' A nod of approval. 'And I had a word with the mayor about keeping things nice. He's on side. Still to talk to his rival though. Left a message.'

'Great. How are you getting on with Amy?'

'So far, so good,' said Cato.

'And life in Major Crime?'

'So far, so good.' Cato said goodbye to Pavlou and paid Hutchens a visit.

'Bill Jenkins?' said Hutchens, looking up from his latest tweet. 'Grumpy bastard, old school, hard as nails.'

'Keep in touch?'

'Why would I? He's a country bumpkin and I'm a city sophisticate. Worlds apart.'

'Did you ever meet his family; the son?'

A shake of the head. 'Albany was my two-year penance for alleged misdeeds. Head down, bum up, do my time and don't get involved with the locals. It served me well.'

'So you can't help.' Cato tried but failed to hide his irritation.

'Snooty lot in Major Crime, aren't you?' said Hutchens. 'Figure everybody's at your beck and call.' He scribbled a number on a post-it. 'Wendy, the office manager down there, knows everybody's business and makes it her own. Great voice. Could make a few bucks on one of those chat lines if she wanted.'

Cato thanked him and returned to his outpost to phone Wendy.

'Mick Hutchens? Gorgeous man, bedroom eyes. Pity about the beer gut.' She did indeed have a very sultry voice. 'How's he going?'

'Not so much of a beer gut these days.' Wendy seemed pleased to hear that. They exchanged more small talk and Cato got to the point.

'Bill Jenkins?' she said. 'What's your interest?' Cato explained that his primary interest was the son. 'Johnny? So he's up in Perth now is he?'

'Fremantle to be exact. He's a ranger with the council.'

'Is this about those murders that were on the news?' Cato confirmed as much. 'And you think Johnny's involved?'

'Just making some enquiries.'

'Have you spoken to Bill about this?'

'Not yet, but I intend to.'

'Good luck, he had a stroke. Poor bastard can't talk very well these days. Not that he was Mr Chatty before that.'

'So,' said Cato. 'Johnny Jenkins?'

'Chip off the old block,' said Wendy. 'Doesn't suffer fools. Temper on him like you wouldn't believe. That's probably why he let the old man down as well.'

'What?'

'Everybody thought he'd follow his dad into the Job but he got chucked out of the Academy for losing his rag. Old Bill was spittin' about it for months.'


Cato dropped by Chris Thornton's desk to put him on to the Academy follow up. He and Hassan were mapping out the remains of their day. The visit to Wayne Bradley had yielded little. According to Deb

Hassan, when challenged about his missing six GPS minutes on the night of victim two's murder, Bradley had simply shrugged.

'Musta taken a piss or something.'

'For six minutes?' Hassan had pressed.

'Big bladder.' An ugly leer. 'Big everything.'

'That must be why you're such a huge success in life,' yawned Hassan.

'So that's your story,' Thornton had said. 'Six minutes to take a piss?'

'Nah, mate, one for the piss, maybe three more for a smoke and the other two to kill that sheila. Just jokin'. You finished?'

'No,' said Hassan. 'Map it out for me, the timeline.'

A shake of the head. 'Like I said, piss, smoke and on my way. The smoke was a spliff, took a while to roll it 'cause I was a bit pissed. Medicinal, for the disability and that.'

'Did you see or hear anybody out and about? Anything unusual?'

'Yeah, there was this axe murderer covered in blood. Asked me for a toke on the J, but I told him to fuck off and take his axe with him.'

'You're a laugh a minute, Wayne,' Hassan had said on her way out.

'Time to cut him loose, boss?' Thornton said now.

Cato nodded. 'Good enough for me, he's a dropkick and I don't see him doing this. Let's not waste any more time on him.' He now wanted as much background dirt on Jackboot John as possible. 'Anything from the Academy files, his career history from leaving school in Albany, anything, okay?'

'Yep.' Thornton focused on his screen and started tapping away. 'How's life in the fast lane?'

'A riot,' said Cato.

'Thinking of staying there?'

'I'm just focused on the job at hand.'

'That's what the pollies and the sport stars say before they jump ship.'

'Would you miss me?'

'You've got better personal hygiene manners than the new bloke. I swear I know every millimetre of his sinuses by sound alone.'

On cue there was a snort from two partitions down. 'That you, Kwong?'

'Paddy, keeping busy?'

'Found a vets group who know Chris White. Invited me down for a lunchtime beer at the Buffs Club. Wanna come?'

'How'd you find them?'

'My wife's dad was in Vietnam. He knows that scene. Asked around for me.'

'Cool,' said Cato. 'I'm in.'

'How many Vietnam vets does it take to change a light bulb?'

'Dunno.'

'You wouldn't, man. Because you weren't there.' He cacked himself while Cato followed him out the door.


So this is where the old men from the Nash must have gone after the renos, mused Cato. The Buffalo Club was a couple of blocks further down High Street from the cop shop. Resolutely and proudly seventies drab. Or possibly fifties. Thirties? McMahon ordered a pint of Carlton Draught and bought some nuts. Cato would have been happy enough with a lime soda but Paddy shook his head.

'Need to win their trust, mate.'

Cato settled on a middie of Carlton with a dash of lemonade. 'If they kick up a fuss, tell them I'm driving.'

'It won't wash, but fingers crossed.'

The men they were meeting were both in their mid forties. Their once square jaws had been softened by beer and there was a milkiness to the eyes. They looked like mushy peas from the same pod except not as green. The tall one was Mike, the shorter one, Pete. They all shook hands and Cato sat back to let McMahon take the running.

'So you guys knew Chris White, then?'

Sombre shaking of heads and sipping of beers. 'Top bloke,' said Pete. 'Fuckin' tragedy.'

'You served together?'

'Iraq,' said Pete.

'Afghanistan,' said Mike.

'Hairy, then?' said McMahon, getting into the Spartan speech rhythm like he was born to it.

Pete's eyes narrowed. 'At times.'

Cato wasn't in the mood for another half hour of *Full Metal Jacket*. 'Why did he leave?'

Cutting to the chase? Pete and Mike looked at him like he'd just kicked the regimental mascot. So for that matter did McMahon. 'Can't fight forever,' said Mike. 'Does your head in.'

'Was he okay when he left, no PTSD, stuff like that?'

'Wouldn't know,' said Pete, looking like he absolutely did know.

'Did you see much of him after he left in ...'

'Two thousand and seven,' chipped in McMahon.

'A bit,' said Mike.

Blood from a stone, thought Cato. 'Was he working? What was he doing? How did he seem?'

'Yeah. Consultancies. Fine, considering,' said Mike.

'What kind of consultancies?'

'Security.'

'Back in the war zones?' A nod. 'How long did he do that for?'

'Coupla years, maybe three or four,' said Mike.

'Which takes us to ...'

McMahon leaned in again. 'Two thousand and eleven, thereabouts.'

'When did you last see him?'

'About three years ago?' Mike looked to Pete for confirmation.

'And how was he?'

The two men glanced at each other again. 'Not the best,' said Mike. 'Marriage on the rocks. Out of work. Behind with the mortgage. The doctor had him on some pills that were messing him up. Sad sight, to be honest.'

'Where's his wife now?'

'She and the kids followed her new bloke over to Pommie-land.' A realisation. 'She probably doesn't even know he's dead.'

'Fuck,' said Pete.

Cato couldn't have put it better himself.


Tragic as it was, it didn't get them any closer to finding the assailant. Cato made a note to follow up with Chris White's sister, Denise, to track down some contact details for the wife. He parted ways with

McMahon, who was happy to stay at the Buffs to prolong his liquid lunch. Cato grabbed a roll and a coffee on the way back to the office and phoned home in transit.

'How are you going?'

'Great!' said Sharon. 'I called some painters and they had a cancellation on a job, a bereavement or something, they can start here from Monday.'

And remove the big 'Y'. Cato was still unsettled by the morning assault. Spitting on him before the retreat? Was that the way of things nowadays? Vandalism and assault were not enough. It needed to be rounded off with a bit of humiliation.

'No prowlers this morning, then?' he said, keeping his voice light.

'Nothing,' she said. 'Just another day in paradise.' A wail in the background. 'I'd better go, duty calls.'

'Love you,' he said.

'Yeah, you too.'

Back at the office Amy was waiting, a bit miffed that he'd gone off with McMahon without telling her. 'You've been drinking.'

'Shandy. Line of duty. Anything new?'

She handed him a post-it note. 'Marilyn from the Freo Street Doctor saw the news and wants to talk. She's had all three victims across her threshold in the last six months. Want me to set up a meeting?'

He did.

DI Pavlou stalked into his work space. 'Seen this?' She slid an iPad in front of him.

'Death and the Detectives. Keystone Cops Ignore Homeless Victims.' Cato read on. 'Norman Lip?'

'Know him?'

'No.'

'Find him and kill him,' snarled Pavlou.

Cato shrugged. 'Free press. It's what our forefathers died for.'

'We've already got calls from the *West*, ABC and a couple of other TV and radio stations looking for comment.' Pavlou blew out a steadying breath. There was a strong whiff of nicotine in it. 'I'll get Police Media on it. Neutralise the little twerp.'

# 10

For several years the Freo Street Doctor, basically a large and well-equipped van staffed by volunteer medicos, had provided an essential service for Fremantle's homeless. Parked on the green opposite the railway station, or down at South Beach, it offered a free drop-in service for the treatment of lesser ailments and injuries. In the absence of the now-closed emergency department of Fremantle Hospital, previously a walk-in sanctuary for the needy, it had assumed an even more vital role.

So ended Dr Marilyn King's introduction. They'd pulled up a couple of plastic chairs on the grass outside while Marilyn's colleague attended to the trickle of clients.

'It'll get busy again soon,' said Marilyn, checking her watch. 'I can give you maybe fifteen minutes?' She prodded her glasses back up her nose and gifted them a crooked smile.

Amy recounted the names of the victims. 'You said you'd had dealings with them?'

Marilyn nodded. 'The most recent was Mr White. Chris.'

'We asked people to come forward several days ago,' said Amy. 'Why now?'

'I've just come back off two weeks leave. Ubud. My colleagues mentioned it when I returned. Said you'd announced a link between all three.'

'Why didn't they come forward?' said Amy.

Marilyn frowned. 'This service is staffed by volunteers, it doesn't run over the weekends, maybe it fell between the cracks.' She shifted her attention to Cato. 'Would you like to hear about Chris, Maureen and Dean?'

'Yes, please,' said Cato. 'Whatever you can tell us would be appreciated.'

'Theoretically I could probably make you get a court order as this stuff should be confidential but we want to stop this maniac, don't we?'

They all agreed that was a good idea.

Marilyn had some printouts in a folder on her knee. The breeze was picking up and she needed to steady them with her hand. Some pink-and-greys pecked the grass nearby. A patient clumped down the steps from inside the van with a fresh dressing on his leg. Another took his place, blinking tearily from a half-closed eye. Conjunctivitus, guessed Cato.

'Chris White dropped by about four weeks ago.'

'What was his problem?' said Amy.

A stony look. 'Society.'

Cato cleared his throat and smiled encouragingly.

Dr Marilyn relented. 'He was very wound up, his medication had run out, antidepressants. I wrote him a prescription.'

Cato asked for the precise name of the drug and the dosage, and Amy took notes. It was the same stuff Professor Mackenzie found in the corpse.

'All of the victims, all on some form of medication or other,' said Cato. 'Antidepressants, anti-anxiety, sedatives.'

Dr Marilyn studied him. 'I don't dish them out like lollies if that's what you're getting at. This country is seriously messed-up. Some people need pills to make it through the day. And I'm not just talking the homeless here.'

'Was that the usual nature of your dealings with him?' asked Cato.

'Pretty much. He once came in with a head wound after an altercation down the beach.'

'When was this?'

'Last summer. An argument over a sleeping pitch. By the look of him, I guess he won. The other guy had been in earlier the same day in much worse shape.'

'You didn't report this?' said Amy.

'Report what? A fight between two homeless people? That's a priority for you, is it?'

'Did you ever talk to Mr White?' asked Cato. 'Get to know him in any depth?'

She shook her head. 'Not really. I know he was in the army and saw some terrible stuff.'

'That's it?'

'His wife had left him. He had some family down south but they found him hard to handle. Set him adrift.'

That would account for sister Denise's caginess when they'd spoken. She may have seen him more recently than she admitted but felt guilty about not doing more to help him. And now it was too late.

Marilyn flicked through her printouts. 'Maureen Bryant. She last came in on Tuesday, twenty-second of August.'

'The day before her murder,' said Cato. 'What did she want to see you about?'

'There was nothing physical going on, in particular. I think she was just lonely, wanted a chat. Apparently she'd just become a grandmother. She hadn't even known her daughter was pregnant. Hadn't seen her in over two years.' Sadness floated across Dr Marilyn's face. 'She was the same age as me. I get to babysit my grandies every other weekend if I want. Maureen was never going to have that. She probably couldn't have coped anyway; always looking over her shoulder for that vicious husband of hers. Did you know that, statistically, blokes and their violence are the biggest single cause of homelessness? More women than men now access homeless support services.'

'Comes as no real surprise,' said Cato.

The line of patients was growing. Some voices were raised. Marilyn's colleague poked his head around the door, looking for her, harassed.

'Sorry,' said Marilyn. 'I'd better go.'

'Just quickly: Dean Pearson. What about him?'

'That's the thing,' said Marilyn. 'He wasn't really one of our regulars. But he also called in and, checking the dates with your news stories, that was just a couple of days before he died.'

'What did he want?' said Amy.

'He wanted us to leave him alone.'

'What did he mean by that?' said Cato.

'God knows. He was really uptight. Shouting, threatening. We assumed he was on something.'

'What happened?'

'He was scaring our clients and wouldn't leave. In the end we summoned one of the transit guards from over the road at the train station, and he called the police.'

'The police took Dean away?'

'No, one of the council rangers turned up, he dealt with it in the end.'

'Describe him,' said Cato. 'Did he have ID?'

'Well he was off-duty and out of uniform, but I recognised him. Jenkins, he calls himself. John Jenkins.'


By the end of the day there was quite a case building against Jackboot Johnny Jenkins, albeit circumstantial. DI Pavlou had swung into action after Cato briefed her. Now Jenkins' phone and internet use would be tapped and scoured. Also the background checks continued apace: his friends, family, colleagues, past and present. The forensics were being reviewed, with the focus now firmly on Jenkins and the DNA samples obtained from his blood-spotted tissues which Amy had swiped from the bin in the council interview room. If anything pinged they'd get an official sample from him later. Last but not least he was being dogged by an undercover team and there was a tracker bug on his car. At the first glimpse of any hard evidence, they'd be on him.

'Getting that gooch tingle, Philip?' Pavlou passed him a cuppa from the plunger on her desk. She'd re-established herself in DI Hutchens' office for the foreseeable future in the hope that this development would be decisive and resolved quickly. Hutchens had been happy to relinquish, casting a good-natured wink and thumbs-up Cato's way as he sauntered out for an early finish.

There were indeed a few butterflies in Cato's stomach but he wasn't sure if it was excitement, or fear of failure. Or maybe he was just plain tired. He lifted his cup. 'Probably the caffeine.'

'If there's anything to find, we'll find it,' Pavlou said. 'Now or later.' She checked her watch. 'Maybe you should call it a day.'

Cato was happy to. 'I'll keep my phone on.'

McMahon rapped lightly on Pavlou's open door.

'Yes, Paddy?' said Pavlou.

'It's him I'm after,' he said, nodding at Cato. 'When you've got a moment.' Cato excused himself and followed Paddy down the corridor. 'We've pulled in one of the Hammy Hill Yardies if you want a chat. If you want to smack him about we can turn the cameras off and go and have a sausage roll.'

'No need,' said Cato. 'What's he in for?'

'A string of burgs around Beaconsfield and South Freo, vandalism, assault. Usual shit.'

The young guy in the interview room was wearing a Bob Marley T-shirt and looked familiar. Cato checked the name on the paperwork. 'Tyson Garland. That you?'

No reply.

'Used to live in Willagee, got a tacker, maybe four years old by now?'

'Six. Goes to Caralee Primary. Lives with his mum. Who the fuck are you?'

Cato guessed right. Tyson had been caught in the crossfire of a gang feud a few years ago and had his teeth hammered out by some bikies. 'You're with the Yardies now?'

Tyson yawned. His new false teeth were dazzling.

McMahon handed some photos to Cato. 'Tyson's handiwork.'

Spray-painted Ys around the suburbs. Cato spread them on the table. 'If the real Yardies knew you were using their name they'd chop you up.'

He shrugged. 'So what do you want, Ching-Chong?'

'Where were you about two o'clock this morning?'

'Asleep probably.'

'Any witnesses?'

'Yeah mon, ma bitch.'

'Name?'

'Lady Gaga.'

They weren't getting anywhere with this. 'If you come around my house again I'll come looking for you.' Cato prodded the file in front of him. 'We know where you live.'

Tyson sniffed. 'Don't know what you're on about but if that's a threat then it really worked. Look at me now, bro. Shiver.'

'That's the spirit, Tysie, keep smiling.'

When Cato checked his phone, there was a message from Brian Knight, the mayor's rival. He returned the call. Knight could spare thirty minutes and how about a quick beer in the Newport? Like now. Sure, Cato had said. Knight described himself — Pierce Brosnan, only shorter and with a crooked nose.

Cato never felt comfortable in the Newport, like he was always one nudge away from a glassing. Knight was on a stool at the bar and he was pretty much as described. He had a couple of mates with him, young, gymmed-up, looked like they were wanted for questioning. They all shook hands, the mates went to the pool table and Cato ordered a lime soda.

'You're kidding,' said Knight.

'On duty.'

'What's this about then?'

'The election.'

'Pinder complaining about the devil's horns somebody drew on his posters?'

Cato appraised him. 'You'll have heard about these recent killings?'

'Yeah. Dreadful. Poor bastards.'

'My boss is hoping they don't become an election issue, we don't need the distraction.'

'Fair enough too.'

'So we can count on you?'

'Of course.'

Cato nodded towards the pool table. 'And your young friends?'

'What about them?'

'Can we count on them as well?'

One of them noticed the attention. Blew a kiss at Cato, squinted down the length of his cue and potted a ball. Knight laughed. 'Sure, mate. Good as gold.' He glugged some beer. 'You any closer to catching the prick?'

'Enquiries are progressing.'

'I'll take that as a no.'

'Your prerogative.'

A playful frown. 'You seem to have made up your mind not to like me. Something I said?'

Cato downed his drink. 'Not at all. I think we understand each other and I appreciate your cooperation.'

Knight lifted his hand to get the server's attention for a new round. 'Another one?'

'Not for me, thanks. Things to do.'

'You know the thing about Pinder and his kind is they're holding on to this idea of a Fremantle that no longer exists.'

'That right?' Cato wasn't really interested. Home beckoned.

'My mum was one of those Orange people. Sannyasins, whatever. Fucking embarrassing. Took all her money off her, left us with fuck all. Another Rolls for the Bhagwan I guess. Then she goes and dies in agony from some cancer and did they help? Did they fuck.'

'Sorry to hear that, but I'm not sure what you're getting at.'

'Community. Charity. That's all for suckers like my mum.'

'And that's your vision for Fremantle?'

Knight lifted his new beer in salute. 'The times they are a-changin'.'


Norman was woken by his phone buzzing. It was a text. A random number, nobody he recognised.

**clever clever — polly want a cracker?**

He'd been fielding crank calls and texts all day. He hadn't realised quite how many sad freaks there were out there. 'Fuck's sake.' He chucked the phone back on his bedside table in disgust.

A hand crept between his legs. 'Who's that?'

'Nobody, let's just sleep.' The hand didn't go away. Stroking, teasing. Another Tinder triumph but he really needed some kip. 'Give it a rest, honey.'

'Just a quickie? Anyway you like? Go on, please.'

The evidence was there now, he couldn't deny it.

The phone buzzed again.

**Check your email, Polly, I sent you some sexy killer pics xx**

It was him, it was fucking him!

The phone didn't do it justice, screen too small, his eyes still blurry from a night of drink and drugs. Norman scrabbled around for his iPad, it was on the floor under his jeans.

'Oh!' she smiled. 'Playtime.' She tossed her hair and arranged herself. Made her face sultry. 'How do you want me?'

He ignored her, bringing up his email. Three photos. He opened the first. A photo of the B-Shed at Freo Port. A slightly blurred moving shot taken through a window. The train, it must be, out of Freo Station. Norman recognised it at once, the site of the first murder, the young bloke. Pictures two and three followed the same pattern, blurred from a moving vehicle, a bus stop by the sailing club and, finally, the Carriage at Esplanade Park. But all of this was common knowledge. Any nutter could have taken these.

She was on all fours nudging her backside against his shoulder. 'Ready?'

Another email came in, one more photo. Ocean somewhere, from a moving car. The words, **Stay tuned**.

'Norman!'

He turned and kissed the offering. 'Yep. I'm ready.'

# 11

Wednesday, 13ᵗʰ September.

'Jenkins did nothing all night long.' DI Pavlou summarised the update to the Hermes executive committee. 'Didn't phone anyone, at least not from his known number. Surfed the internet for a while. Downloaded and watched three eps of *Game of Thrones*, illegally, but we'll let him have that, for now.' She chucked the sheet of A4 on the boardroom table. 'Ate a frozen pizza and had a beer, Boag's — according to the bin search. In bed by eleven.'

'Associates?' asked Cato. He was feeling refreshed. A good night's sleep, Ella for the first time had skipped a feed during the night. And he hadn't been kicked in the head that morning. Always a bonus. Plus he'd finally, having procrastinated for too long, had the phone call with Jane about Jake.

'If that's what he wants,' Jane had said, sulkily. 'What does Sharon say?'

'Fine. We have the space, or at least we will once the granny flat is cleared.'

'When are you thinking?'

'Maybe he can help me clear it out this weekend?'

'Okay. Probably for the best.'

Cato knew the feeling. The push–pull. Trying not to be hurt, to take it personally. 'He's growing up, probably needs some space.'

'Yeah, sure,' said Jane.

Thornton spoke up after a nod from Pavlou. 'Jenkins spends a lot of time at the gym down in South Freo. Most of his circle seems to be from there. There's a whisper of steroid use among some.'

'Roid rage? Is that what's behind this?' wondered Amy.

'The roids might feed it, but so far he's been a bit too organised for us to put it down to rage,' said Pavlou. 'Still, worth a closer look.'

'And it fits in with our profiling session a few days ago: young, fit, strong and confident,' noted Hutchens.

'The dad?' said Pavlou. 'Bill Jenkins. Any more there?'

Thornton spoke up. 'Not too good since his stroke but I've got a meeting with the big cheese at the Academy. She's going to give me the lowdown on why Jenkins Junior was booted and didn't live up to dad's expectations.'

Pavlou frowned. 'Try and lift your game with the respect and protocol while you're there, Chris. "Big cheese" won't cut it.'

Thornton ducked his head. 'Boss.'

'Let me know how it goes. Meantime we'll keep watching him.'

'How long for?' said Cato.

'A few more days at least. Maybe by then we'll have some evidence from our lines of enquiry ...'

'Or?' said Hutchens.

'Or he'll get another evil urge and we'll catch him red-handed.'

'Fingers crossed,' said Hutchens.


There was a message when Cato switched his mobile back on. Sonya Allegretta from St Mary's. He returned her call.

'He'll talk to you. Alone.'

'He' being one of John Jenkins' recent assault victims. No longer residing in Fremantle. Too scared, according to Allegretta.

'Where and when?'

'I'll pick you up and take you to him. Ten minutes, fifteen?'

They agreed on fifteen. Cato was waiting outside when she pulled up in a red Barina. The passenger seat was stuck and wouldn't retreat so Cato sat with his knees pressing hard into the glovebox. It reminded him of a Jetstar flight. 'Where are we going?'

Sonya said nothing and fired up a ciggie with the dashboard lighter. This was going to be one of those trips.

'Should I be wearing a hood or a blindfold or something?'

'Your call. Booragoon. Garden City. Hungry Jack's. His name's Lonely and he wants you to buy him a Whopper.'

'Lonely?'

She nodded. 'You'll know why when you meet him.'

'Okay,' said Cato. In the passenger footwell today's *West* lay open at an inside page with a photo of the Fremantle mayor dishing out meals yesterday at St Mary's, Sonya in the background. 'You're famous,' said Cato, fishing the paper out.

A snort. 'It's my job to be nice to people like him.'

Cato reached down between his knees and dragged the paper up into his lap.

'To be fair, he's in a difficult position,' Allegretta conceded. 'He's trying to appease local businesses and residents concerned about antisocial behaviour while not wanting to appear heartless in the face of real suffering and need. It's a very Freo dilemma.'

It echoed the views of Courtney the Boss Ranger. '*Plus ça change,*' said Cato.

'That's the thing,' said Allegretta. 'For such a progressive city there's a lot of resistance to change. People got upset about a new frigging skate park and the likely lure of undesirables. Imagine what they'd do if the council built social housing next door to them?'

Cato read out the quote from the mayor. 'Western Australia has squandered the boom. The richest state in one of the richest countries in the world and all for nothing. Homelessness and poverty in Fremantle are on the rise as a direct result of governments at both national and state level turning their backs on those in need. But the City of Fremantle is not in the business of kicking people when they're down.' He glanced at Allegretta. 'Can't fault that.'

Sonya flicked her cigarette out the window. 'Words. Worthless. Particularly when there's an election on. So if it's not the council, then who is sweeping beggars out of sight on the cappuccino strip, harassing them with security guards? Categorising them into "genuine" homeless and so-called "professional" beggars.'

'Wasn't that what the homelessness audit was about? Counting and categorising? Getting a clearer picture?'

'In principle it was a good idea, but somehow the numbers got spun to justify a policy that was already in the pipeline, regardless of the audit.' She lifted some fingers from the steering wheel and hooked them in quotes to illustrate her point. 'Do you know how many "genuine" homeless people are on the council beggars register? Less than a dozen. Do you know how many breakfasts, lunches and dinners St Mary's cooks every day for the homeless? Over two hundred. And that's just us, never mind the other agencies and charities. So are we being duped? Are those other one hundred and ninety we see every day milking the system? Of course they're not. It's bullshit, it's divide and rule, and the mayor knows it. He's pandering to the rednecks.'

'My impression of the boss over there, Courtney, is that she's not the bullying, redneck type.'

A sigh. 'Yeah, she's okay. Most of the rangers are. But it's the kind of job that can attract the Jenkinses of this world.'

Not unlike the cops, Cato mused. And it only takes one to slip through the recruitment net. 'What about the challenger, Knight. Any views on him?'

'I can't see him getting anywhere. He's not the type that goes down well in Freo. He'd be better running in the northern suburbs or out east.'

'How do you mean?'

'Raging bull. He'd be an embarrassment. Fremantle doesn't like to wear its prejudices on its sleeve. Prefers to be more subtle.'

'He seems to think otherwise.'

'He would.' Mercifully Sonya didn't need to light up any more cigarettes for the remainder of the journey; she was fuming enough already.


As usual there was a lot of money being spent in Garden City. Cato always found such places dystopian and other-worldly. Ostentatious consumption, weird lighting, no clocks. Everything and everyone on display, one way or another. This was a place where you dressed up to go shopping, even in Hungry Jack's. Lonely stuck out like a sore thumb. For a start he had several vacant seats either side of him in what was a busy fast-food joint. He had also attracted the attention of the store manager and a security guard who were no doubt inviting him to leave.

Cato introduced himself to them, discreetly offered some ID and requested a brief stay of execution.

'He's driving away the punters,' muttered the duty manager, a pimply ranga whose name badge read Liam.

'It's important,' said Cato.

'So's my daily sales target,' said Liam. 'Can't you take him somewhere else, like Maccas?'

Cato looked at Sonya who shook her head firmly.

'Whopper Meal Deal,' said Lonely, resolutely. 'With the upgrade.' He grinned at Liam. 'And make it snappy, Ginger.' A nod towards Cato. 'He's paying.'

The security guard by now had made himself scarce. Liam scowled and went back behind the counter. Cato followed him to the cash register and then returned to join Sonya and Lonely at the table. That's when it hit. Epic BO. Sonya didn't seem to notice it. Cato, meanwhile, was fighting his gag reflex. The meal arrived and Lonely dug in.

'Tell him,' said Sonya. 'Tell him about Jackboot John.'

Lonely was scrawny and malnourished. A twenty-year-old in the body of a twelve-year-old. He lifted his gaze from the meal to Cato. 'Jackboot John? Cunt,' he said, through a mouthful of fried mince.

'Specifics?' said Cato.

'Specifics?' Lonely slurped and burped on his Coke. 'Jackboot John is a cunt because he kicked me in the back in the middle of the night while I was sleeping in this old warehouse nobody wanted and minding my own business. Then he pissed on my sleeping bag and told me to get out of town or he'd put me in a wheelchair.'

'When was this?'

'July. Can't remember the date, I don't keep a diary.'

'Where was the warehouse?'

'Down near Capo D'Orlando, yacht club and that.'

Not far from where victim two, Maureen, was found. 'Any witnesses?' asked Cato.

A snort.

'How did he know where to find you?'

'Ask him. Maybe he was following me. Maybe he's made it his business to do a circuit of the known pitches.'

'Why did he have it in for you?'

Lonely polished off the last of his burger. 'What are you saying? I provoked him?'

'I'm trying to get an idea of why he picks on some people and not others.'

'He's a bully. Picks on squirts like me who he thinks can't fight back.'

That didn't fit with victim three, the ex-commando. 'Was July the last time you saw him?'

'Yeah, I got the fuck out. Don't need freaks like him on my back. Life's hard enough.'

'Where do you hang out these days?'

Lonely reached into his packet of fries. 'What's it to you?'

Cato didn't pursue it. 'Know anybody else who's had a run-in with Jenkins?'

Lonely looked at Sonya and got the nod he was waiting for. 'Yeah, Deano.'

'Dean Pearson?'

'Yeah. The one that got stabbed.'

'Dean was threatened by Jenkins?'

'Yeah, same deal: a kick in the back, piss on the bag and told to fuck off somewhere else.'

'Dean told you this?'

'Yep.'

'When?'

'About the same time as I got my marching orders. Early July.'

And by month's end, Dean Pearson was dead, thought Cato. 'But Dean decided not to leave?'

'That's right. He was going to nail the fucker. He was smarter than me, smarter than any of us. So he reckoned anyway.'

'In what way?'

'He *was* keeping a diary.'

None had been found on the body. 'Did you see it?'

Liam the duty manager was hovering.

A nod. 'He showed me his note book, a little yellow cheapo thing full of weird shit, drawings, poems, whatever. I told him it wouldn't make any difference.'

'And?'

'And I was right, wasn't I? Made no fuckin' difference at all.'

Cato was hunched up in Allegretta's Barina for the return trip when his mobile went. It took a while to release it in the cramped space. It was Thornton calling.

'On my way back from Joondy, Sarge.' The Police Academy at Joondalup in the far northern suburbs.

'And?'

'The grand fromage there turns out to be a good mate of DI Pavlou's.'

In the confines of the Barina, Cato was obliged to twist his head at a funny angle to take the call. He really wanted Thornton to get to the point, and told him so.

'Right. So Commander Fiona thought Jenkins was a loser from day one. Up himself, not a listener or a team player, and he assumed he was already going to pass because of his dad.'

'But none of that showed on the paperwork,' Cato said. 'It was all going well until his final year, according to the record.'

'Commander Fi wasn't in charge then. She was two-IC. I get the impression she and the big chief didn't see eye to eye.'

'Go on.'

'Jenkins was chucked out for bullying a fellow cadet. Unnamed female. He'd threatened her, then one day he decked her during an ethics and accountability class.'

'Ethics and accountability?'

'Yeah, it's what they teach them nowadays, every Tuesday morning before taser practice.'

'All very interesting but it still isn't evidence is it?'

'True.' There was a beep as contact was lost. Cato's phone rang again almost immediately. 'Sorry, driving through the Polly Pipe. Anyway, on my way out I rechecked the graduation date and called a mate who joined the same year. He remembered the biff very well. Great laugh. He helped drag Jenkins off her.'

'And?'

'He clearly remembers Jenkins screaming and going nuts, yelling "I'll kill you, bitch, don't think I won't" — stuff like that.'

Grist to the mill. 'Thanks, Chris. Write it up.'

'There's more.'

'I'm listening.'

'My mate reckons he spoke to the woman Jenkins decked. Asked her what it was all about. Why they didn't like each other. Turns out she'd made some crack about survival of the fittest when she passed him on a training run once. He never forgave her.'

'That's it?'

'That's it. Classic tiny dick syndrome she'd called it.'

'Stop the presses,' said Cato.

'One last thing, Jenkins' financials finally came through after a wrangle with the bank. You might want to take a look when you're back in the office.'

'Tell me.'

'Regular and modest but, as yet, unexplained payments direct into a high interest no-touchie account.'

'Who from?'

'Barbarossa Nominees. Sounds dodgy. I'll dig some more.'

'Thanks.' Cato closed the call. Felt the weight of Sonya's expectations. 'What's Lonely's story, how did he end up on the street?'

'Why do you want to know?'

'I'm interested. But if it's confidential, then no worries.'

'Put it this way, the stats on homeless young people and the link to domestic violence and sexual abuse are pretty ugly. That BO of his isn't just through lack of washing. He sees it as his protective force field.'


Allegretta dropped Cato outside the cop shop.

'So you heard what Lonely said: Jenkins threatened and assaulted both him and Deano. What are you going to do about it?'

Cato wanted to be able to say yeah, sure, Jenkins needs closer scrutiny. And he was already getting it. But she couldn't know that. 'Uncorroborated. One word against another. We'll continue our enquiries.' He thanked her and she squealed away in a huff. He paid a visit to Pavlou and updated her.

'And this Lonely kid will give us a statement to that effect?' Pavlou said.

'For the price of a Double Whopper, I reckon he'll do anything.'

'Deano's diary would be nice, wouldn't it?'

'Plus a bit of forensic, something scientific. It's all hearsay at the moment.' Cato shrugged. 'Maybe we should be talking to the father down in Albany?'

'More hearsay?'

Cato leaned against a filing cabinet. 'How's the surveillance going?'

'The bloke's a goody-two-shoes. It's like he knows he's being watched.' She gave Cato a weary smile. 'Until he makes a mistake or we strike jackpot on the forensics all we can do is build the case.'

'The bank account?'

They glanced at the printout. 'They're small amounts. Five hundred a month for the last six months, maybe it's a stipend from the Jenkins family trust.' Pavlou sighed. 'Fancy a quick trip to Albany?'

# 12

Bill Jenkins' wheelchair was parked by the window in the Southern Comfort nursing home. He had a stunning view out over King George Sound. The islands were hunched against the incoming cold front. Black clouds loomed from the south-west and a vicious wind tore the surface of the water. Cato had kissed Sharon and Ella goodbye and taken the early morning flight down from Perth. The local plods had picked him up at Albany Airport and left him at a cafe in town where he had breakfast and a windy wander along the foreshore to clear his mind. He'd waited until after nine before heading to Southern Comfort, biding his time with a call home and some reassuring noises from Sharon and Ella. He introduced himself to Bill Jenkins and offered a hand for shaking. The old man ignored it.

'Mind if I pull up a chair?' Cato didn't wait for a response.

Jenkins had a droopy left eyelid, in fact the whole left side of his face had slipped. He wore a West Coast Eagles sweatshirt that carried traces of recent meals down the front. Gravy, custard maybe, baked beans. The air in Southern Comfort was acrid with faeces and baby powder and the promise of boiled lunch. Over the tannoy, some piped music, a golden oldies radio station: Frank Ifield, 'I Remember You'.

Cato pulled out a photo and held it up. 'Hoping you might be able to tell us a few things about John. Your son?'

Bill Jenkins turned his head away and dabbed some spit from the corner of his downturned mouth. Cato had visions of DI Hutchens in the not too distant future. A young African woman approached with a tea trolley and set out a cup, saucer and biscuit on the table beside the old man, on his right side, the one that worked. Cato accepted a cup too, with thanks.

'No problem, doctor,' she said with a lovely smile. 'Would you like a biscuit?'

Cato took the career change in his stride and grabbed a custard cream. The way things were going so far, it might be the only result he would get from his visit to Albany.

Bill Jenkins munched on his Tim Tam and ignored the crumbs left perched on his paunch. With a trembling hand he lifted the teacup. 'What's he done?'

Cato almost jumped. This is what life in a nursing home is like, he realised. Routine, meals and medication interrupted by startling bursts of lucid conversation. 'He's a person of interest in an ongoing enquiry.'

'What's he fuckin' done?'

Cato told him, in as little detail as possible, about the homeless killings in Fremantle and, in general terms, the nature of the interest in John Jenkins. This could all backfire. For all he knew the old man was still sharp behind the drool, the shakes and the slippage. He could tip his son off.

'You think he's a killer?' Jenkins took a hankie and dabbed at his mouth again. Cato thought he saw the ghost of a smile there. It was certainly in the eyes, an iron glint of amusement.

'Tell me about him.'

'Useless. Weak. What else you wanna know?'

'He wanted to follow you into the Job. It didn't work out.'

'Like I said. Useless. Weak.'

'A disappointment?'

'Not to me. He's a mummy's boy. She got me to pull all those strings to get him into cop school. Wanted him to make something of his life. Me? I'd've cut the bastard loose long ago.'

Cato continued to choose his words. 'And he didn't make the grade? Didn't cut it?'

The old man looked at him. 'Think you're a bit special? Wind the old fucker up and get him to dish on his son.' He slurped some more tea. 'Try again, Chink.'

'Do you see him at all?' Cato waved a hand at the choking environment. 'Does he visit?'

'Fuck off.'

'Why did you want to cut him adrift?'

'Useless,' he said again. 'Weak.'

Cato left his business card beside Bill Jenkins' elbow. 'Enjoy the view.'

'Piss off.'


Cato strolled down the hill and parked himself in a cafe halfway along York Street, the main drag. The rain still hadn't arrived but the wind had blown the traces of the Southern Comfort home off his clothes. Out on the sound, a bulk carrier, escorted by two tugs, had nosed into the harbour ahead of the weather. It was now late morning, nearly lunchtime. Cato ordered a coffee, unable to face cooked food while the nursing home haunted his nostrils. The session with Bill Jenkins had delivered nothing. The old man's naked contempt for his son was no surprise but any detail was locked behind the stroke-ravaged face. He'd called his son a mummy's boy. Unfortunately, Cato knew from the files, mummy was dead. Mrs Jenkins had died of breast cancer three years ago. Now it was just father and son.

*I'd've cut the bastard loose long ago.*

But why?

The coffee arrived. He tried it. He'd had worse. According to the Academy records, John Jenkins had shown promise as a cadet in most areas — keen, fit, bright — but his temperament let him down.

*Useless. Weak.* The Academy profile didn't match the old man's damning assessment. John Jenkins might be a lot of things but the Academy didn't mark him as useless until that one incident. And from what Cato knew and had seen of the old man, a bad temper was in the DNA. So what had Johnny done that marked him down in the old man's eyes?

Cato called Chris Thornton. 'Do we have Jenkins' school records?'

'You really like that "troubled childhood" stuff, don't you, Sarge? What are we after now: failed tests, bullying, unrequited teenage love, torturing the animals in the science lab?'

'Just the school name will do.'

There was the tapping of a keyboard. 'Albany Senior High, it's up on Mount Clarence.' He gave Cato the address, phone number and name of the principal. 'Jenkins Junior would have been there around two thousand, two oh-one, something like that.'

Cato phoned the school and set up a meeting with the principal for late afternoon. She was really rather busy but would slot him in. Looking up, he saw a familiar face peering at him from the other side of the cafe window. He received a grin and heard the doorbell tinkle.

'White and one. You're buying.'

Tess Maguire had a few extra wisps of grey but otherwise still filled out her police uniform as well as she did the last time they'd seen each other.

'Seven, eight years is it?' said Cato, giving her a hug.

'Something like that.' She gave him the measure of her gaze and seemed to approve. 'That's not the same wedding ring you had last time.'

She was right, this one was silver, the last one gold. 'Last year; her name is Sharon, I met her in Shanghai.' Cato gave Tess the edited highlights until her coffee arrived.

'A baby too. Busy boy.' A tilt of the head. 'You seem happy, finally.'

'I am,' he conceded. 'What about you and ...'

'Melissa?'

Cato nodded, embarrassed at forgetting the name of Tess's daughter.

'She's at uni, Murdoch. Final year, on the way to becoming a primary teacher. Me?' She flicked a hand at a windy and deserted York Street. 'I transferred back to the big smoke.' Cato knew what she meant: after Hopetoun, population fifteen hundred or so, even Albany would seem like downtown Manila. Tess took a sip of coffee. 'What brings you here?'

'Job.' He filled her in on the story so far. 'Ever come across Bill Jenkins, or the son?'

She shook her head. 'Before my time. I've only been here a couple of years.'

'Feel free to ask around. Let me know if you hear anything.'

'You really think the son could be your killer?'

'Maybe. He seems spiteful enough.'

'I'll keep my ear to the ground.' Tess grimaced. 'This job.'

'Lost its shine?'

Tess took some froth onto her spoon. Licked it off. 'Not sure it ever had one. Melissa called me last night. She's on a prac at some school beside the freeway south of Perth. Had to pull a kid off another in the toilets. Trying to bugger him. Year three they are. Turns out the kid keeps moving schools every few months or so. Big brother and dad are the likely culprits, grooming another rapist in the family.' Spoon back on the saucer. 'Melissa wants to chuck it all in. Already.'

Cato said nothing. He had plenty of his own horror stories.

'Cops, teachers, nurses.' Tess grimaced. 'Sometimes I wonder if we're just dung beetles, rolling shit across this wide brown land.'

'Low blood sugar, I'm guessing. Want a lamington or something?'

'Happy days,' she said, playfully punching his upper arm. 'Sorry for the downer.' Her radio crackled and her mobile beeped simultaneously. She checked in. 'Gotta go, car crash out near Manypeaks.'

He was sad to see her go. It wasn't the lingering regret of an old flame. She was just really easy to be with, even when she was pissed off. He waved his mobile and lifted his chin at hers. 'Same number?'

'Yep. You too?' Tess zipped up her jacket against the wind. 'I'll shout the coffees next time. Good luck with your nutcase.'

She was off, a patrol car pulled up outside and she hopped in, gave him a final wave.


The principal of Albany Senior High was more relaxed than she had been earlier on the phone. Her name was Val.

'Spot fires,' she smiled. 'Helicopter parents, bad kids, grumpy staff.' Cato nodded in sympathy. Val tapped her keyboard and squinted at the computer screen. 'John Joseph Jenkins? Why the interest?'

'I'm unable to give full details but this is in connection with a major enquiry.'

'Those homeless murders. I saw you on the news, standing behind your boss.'

'Very observant. You have a good memory.'

'I'm Indian by birth, Mauritius. I notice diversity in situations where I don't usually expect it.'

Cato didn't respond. He kept his face neutral, patient, expectant.

'Access to children's confidential school records needs to be more formal than this, Sergeant Kwong. Paperwork. Protocol. You know the form.'

He shrugged. 'I was in the area. Just passing. The idea only occurred following a chat I had this morning.'

'Old Bill.' She noticed the alarm in Cato's eyes. 'Albany's a village.' She gazed at her screen again as Cato fought the temptation to lean over the desk and spin it his way. 'You'll need to get the paperwork and make it formal. Modern pedagogy is all about covering your backside. Or in this case, mine. Sorry.'

Cato sat back in his chair.

She lifted a hand. She hadn't finished. 'Either way, he was before my time. But confidentially and off the record, you might like to have a chat with Francine Riley, she was here at the time. Teaches English. She remembers him well.'

Val led him along a corridor. A short rap and she opened a door and ushered him through. 'The bloke I told you about, Fran.' She smiled a farewell to Cato.

Fran Riley was petite, nudging retirement, and looked hard as nails. She had an impressive bookshelf and a poster of Virginia Woolf on her wall. Her desk was swamped with half-marked essays. 'Tea?' There was a kettle and a spare cup on top of her filing cabinet.

Cato nodded. 'Yeah, cheers.'

She produced two teabags and a carton of UHT from a desk drawer and flicked on the kettle. As she stood, Cato noticed she had a slight deformity, the right leg shorter than the other. Polio, he guessed.

'Johnny Jenkins was a little bastard. Whatever you think he's done, you're probably right. He needs to be out of circulation. Throw away the key.'

Don't hold back, thought Cato. He accepted the proffered mug and slopped in some milk, leaving the bag stewing a bit longer. 'You taught him?'

'He wasn't the brightest of boys. Had street smarts though. Manipulative. Cunning. Took to Othello like a duck to water. I think he fancied himself as Iago. No problems with his self-esteem.'

'And?'

'You know the saying about how children can be cruel?' Cato nodded. 'Johnny had it in spades.' She tapped her deformed right leg. 'He loved this. Spak, freak, crip, fancy a dance, miss? It gave him hours of amusement.'

Cato sipped his tea and waited.

'You're thinking, pathetic old bint, couldn't cope with a bit of ribbing from a kid. Toughen up, princess. Right?'

'I wouldn't have put it in such harsh terms.'

A flint of pain and repressed fury. 'No,' she said. 'I don't suppose you would.'

'There was more, wasn't there? More than just words.'

'Just words.' She smiled grimly. 'Last week of term two. Winter, two thousand. He was in year eleven. He'd been playing up all of that period. I'd had enough. I kept him back for detention.'

Cato felt the heat of the mug radiate through his hand. Heard the ticking of the clock on her wall. A breeze fluttered the papers on her desk.

'It wasn't as if there wasn't anybody around. It was only just gone four. The cleaners were still here, other teachers, students at the homework club.' Her voice had dropped to barely more than a whisper. 'I told him to finish the work he should have been doing in class. Jesus, it was like dealing with a little kid in primary. He never argued, a lot of them come up with reasons why they can't do the detention, or they threaten you with their parents. Him? Nothing. He seemed to find it funny. It was as if it was all part of the plan.'

Sometimes it's the flimsiest, least consequential of things: a word, a look, a twitch. Cato wondered if this was one of those moments when a case turns, a door opens and the truth is revealed.

'I turned my back to write something up on the whiteboard for the following day. All of a sudden I was on the floor, my head spinning.' She barked out a short, mystified, bitter laugh. 'He'd king-hit me.' She folded her arms, trying to shield herself from the memory. 'He squatted over me. Called me a cripple.' She lifted an index finger. 'Poking me, all over. Filthy names, horrible. Finally he spat in my face and walked out.'

'The school did nothing?'

'The principal at the time was a friend of Bill Jenkins. They sorted it out between them.'

'The department didn't back you? The union?'

'It's a small town. I needed to keep working, not rock the boat. My mother had dementia, she was living with me. Needed me.'

'What about him? Jenkins. What was he like after that?'

'I had to keep teaching him until the end of that year. He acted like it had never happened.'

'But his father obviously knew about it.'

'Bill used to see me in the street. He'd stop and say hello. We'd talk about the weather usually, anything that didn't matter. It was never mentioned. But the look, every time, he knew. He knew what I wanted, an apology, an acknowledgement, and he was never going to give it to me.'

There was a message on Cato's mobile from Tess Maguire. The crash at Manypeaks wasn't as bad as first thought. If he was in town for the night did he fancy catching up for a feed? He was about to text back and decline, he hoped to get the early evening flight back to Perth. Maybe next time. The phone went off again, incoming call, unknown number.

'Kwong?' The voice was male, gruff, accusing. Could have been any of half-a-dozen people he worked with.

Cato said that yes, he was Kwong.

'Bill Jenkins.'

'What can I do for you?'

'You can stop nosing around me and my family and fuck off home.'

'I was due to leave this arvo but I've just changed my mind.'

'Don't push your luck.'

'Enjoy your dinner. They should be wheeling you in soon.'

Cato hadn't changed his mind, he still intended to be on that six-thirty flight. He just didn't like being bossed around by the poisonous old bastard. And now, having skipped lunch, with the reek of the nursing home fading, he was finally getting hungry. He checked the time, late afternoon. Should he grab something now or hold out until he got home, mid-evening? He opted for instant gratification. A southerly whipped up York Street and rain began to fall. Cato ducked into a fast-noodle joint and ordered mee goreng, parking himself at a table to read last week's *Albany Advertiser* while he waited. Five minutes later he was much the wiser about what happened in the Great Southern last week — petty crime and weather — and his noodles were ready. As he turned from the counter, two men blocked his path. One of them punched him in the face. When he fell, they kept on punching him and gave him a few kicks as well. After a minute or so it was over. The shop owner seemed to have wisely made himself scarce, but hopefully he was on the phone to the cops. Cato had had worse: he recalled a particularly thorough beating in Shanghai which seemed to go on forever. Still, he could have done without it. His face and head hurt, his lips were split, his nose throbbed and his ribs complained. The man who'd landed the first blow knelt down and breathed old cigarettes on him.

'You've still got time to make that plane, cuz. We'll drive you out there if you like.'

Cato said thanks but no thanks, and sprayed some speckles of blood on the man's shirt. 'Have you guys been following me?'

The man smiled, took Cato's mee goreng and some spare chopsticks, and left with his mate. That settled it. If Bill Jenkins wanted him gone this badly, it must be worth staying. He got to his feet and texted Tess, accepting her invitation to dinner.

The Italian restaurant was just a hundred metres further down the hill. Cato had phoned home and let Sharon know that he was staying over, and why.

'Try not to be too much of a punch bag, Phil, you don't need to impress me.' She'd wound up with an enquiry, where was he staying and had he eaten yet. Then she cursed herself for being mumsy.

'I'll grab something in town then check into a hotel. The town is deserted, there won't be a problem with vacancies.' He'd signed off saying he loved her and telling her to make sure she locked up. He was still trying to work out why he hadn't mentioned he was catching up with a colleague for dinner. A colleague and an old flame.

Cato had phoned ahead to book a hotel for the night. He also attempted to clean himself up and bought a new shirt at Target before it closed. He looked a mess and the waiter only conceded admission once Cato had flashed his ID. Tess was waiting at a window table with a glass of red by her elbow, shaking her head at his injuries.

'I can't leave you alone for five minutes.' She signalled for a second wine. 'So what happened?'

'I overstayed my welcome.'

'It's becoming a habit.'

Cato knew what she was referring to. Until today, the last time they'd seen each other was when he wandered up her front path in Hopetoun with a bloodied nose and a face scalded by close proximity to a barbecue hotplate. 'I didn't heed that warning, either.' His wine arrived and he took a slug. Stinging lip aside, it felt good. They ordered: penne carbonara for him, chicken and mushroom tortellini for her.

'So what happened since lunchtime that earned you a beating?'

Cato told her about the visit to the school and the talk with Francine Riley. About Bill Jenkins pulling strings to protect his bully son.

'Small towns,' she acknowledged. 'They can chew you up and spit you out. It's a real boys' club, even now.'

Their food arrived and they got stuck in. 'I still can't work out why he wants me out of town. All I'm learning is ancient history about his dropkick son. Evidentially, it's worthless.'

'Maybe there's still a few skeletons rattling around. Maybe he's protecting his own secrets, not his son's.'

That made sense but, much as he'd like to sour the old man's remaining days on this earth, Cato knew it wasn't the main game. The focus had to be on either nailing Johnny Jenkins, or eliminating him from their enquiries. But starting where? He'd stayed in Albany as a stubborn 'up yours' to Bill Jenkins and his goons but beyond that he didn't have a plan. The wine was going down nicely. They ordered a bottle this time and Cato changed the subject.

'So how's your love life?'

'Non-existent. There was a bloke about a year ago. A farmer. It fizzled out. Ships in the night and nothing in common.'

'Shame,' said Cato.

'And the half-dozen since him have all been duds in the sack.' There was a sparkle in her eye. 'Except maybe one.'

'So you've been celibate for what, a fortnight?'

'Give or take.' They clinked glasses. 'Married life suits you, then?'

Cato admitted that it did, very well.

'How's your boy handling it, the older one, what's his name?'

'Jake.' Cato considered the question and felt that old tightness in his chest. An intangible anxiety whenever he was reminded that Jake existed. 'He's taking it in his stride, as far as I can tell.'

'Great,' said Tess. They clinked glasses again, Cato less committed to the gesture this time. 'Speaking of old times, which we weren't, guess who I saw around town a few weeks ago.'

'Who?'

'Kerry Stevenson. She'd had a few, so it took her a while to place me.'

Cato racked his brain and finally an image swam into memory. A velour tracksuit, a curl of cigarette smoke, a voice like a hacksaw: the mother of the Disaffected Youth of Hopetoun. 'Sweet,' said Cato. 'Doing well is she? She and Keith still the life and soul of the Great Southern?' Entrepreneur and hard man Keith Stevenson had been the one who tried to flame-grill Cato's face. Cato had sent him to prison not long after.

'Apparently not,' said Tess. 'Keith died in prison. Heart attack.'

'Shame,' said Cato, insincerely.

'Kerry told me to remember her to you if I ever saw you again.'

'Really?' said Cato.

'Yeah.' Tess lifted her middle finger. 'Love from Kerry.'

'I'll drink to that.' They clinked glasses again. Dessert and coffee followed and they finished the wine. Cato rose unsteadily to his feet and claimed the bill. 'Per diems,' he said, waving away her protest.

Outside, they hugged and Cato enjoyed the smell and feel of her. He didn't want to let go. He put it down to the alcohol and the beating.

Tess detached herself with a half-smile. 'Know where you're headed?'

Cato nodded up the hill. 'A couple of hundred metres.'

'Okay, look after yourself.' A cab pulled up and Tess hopped into it. 'Sure you don't need a lift?'

He waved and blew her a drunken kiss.

The taxi pulled away and Cato set off up the hill.

Kelvin felt a tug on the line and started reeling in. The wind had picked up once the sun went down and it had turned a pleasant evening's fishing into another cold and miserable end to the day. A herring danced on the end of the line. He dislodged the hook, put his knife through the gills and lobbed the fish into the bucket. There was probably enough for a feed now. He didn't know the time but guessed at around 7.30, 8.00 maybe. He started packing up and, looking back along the jetty, saw headlights swing into the car park — their car park. No squeal of tyres or shouting, so probably not local hoons bringing extra grief. Small mercies. The vehicle parked a discreet distance from the Kombi; canoodling privacy distance maybe, or self-medicating distance.

Just south, Rockingham twinkled: the apartment blocks, the beachside mansions, everybody everywhere was settling down for a night in front of the idiot box — a bitchy food show maybe, or house makeovers turning family homes into bland show homes. He'd get Liz to fire up the two-ring burner, hopefully there was enough left in the gas bottle to see them through to the weekend. Heat some beans to have with the fish, then a cup of tea, maybe a read by the headtorch and an early night. They needed to be up at sparrow fart tomorrow before the ranger did his circuit. Then off to the chemist to pick up Liz's happy pills.

He reeled in, packed up, took one last look around. No, he hadn't forgotten anything. He set off back along the jetty, jacket flapping in the wind. The car from earlier was pulling out again, obviously deciding they didn't fancy the company. Homeless oldies in the van next door would be a real passion killer if you were after a quickie. Away it went, picking up speed heading south towards Rocky. Kelvin waved and lifted his bucket.

'Fire her up, love. Time to eat. Four fat ones.'

The words must have been blown away. There was no movement. Maybe she was snoozing. The pills did that to her, slowed her down, made her sleepy. But she seemed less anxious these days, more able. She'd never get her job back though. Those bitches in the real estate office didn't forgive or forget. Thirty-odd properties she'd been managing, their best and most consistent rental returns. That didn't matter one jot when it came down to it. They piled on the pressure for results, ticked her off when she got sick, backstabbers the lot of them. Yes, there she was, snoozing, as he'd thought. She was in the passenger seat, reclined, interior light off. He'd give her a while longer, cook the fish himself and wake her when it was ready.

He went around to the back of the Kombi and set up the two-ring. Lifting and checking the bottle, he was satisfied there'd be enough gas for a couple more days. He crouched down, staying quiet so as not to disturb her, and began gutting the catch by the light of his headtorch. It was strange though. There was a rivulet of blood running past his boots and he'd hardly cut into the herring.

# 13

Cato was woken early by the call on his mobile. His head was thick from the wine and the beating. It was DI Pavlou.

'Which do you want first, the bad news or the worse news?'

'Tell me.'

'There was another murder last night. Homeless.'

'Is that the bad or the worse?'

'It couldn't have been Jenkins. According to the guard dogs he never left home all night.'

'Ah.'

Pavlou filled him in. A woman living rough with her husband, sleeping in a campervan in a car park just north of Rockingham. Throat slit.

'The husband?'

'Was fishing on the jetty. Saw a car come and go. He found her when he got back to the van.'

'And you're happy it's not him, using the serial murders as cover?'

'There was a playing card, diamonds. He couldn't have known about that.'

'I'll get the next plane out.'

'The next one scheduled is not until this afternoon. We've hitched you a ride with a Customs plane heading this way. Be at the airport in the next forty-five minutes and phone this guy.' She gave him a number. 'Hope you enjoyed your Great Southern junket.'

Cato thought about it: beating aside, it hadn't been so bad. He ordered a cab and hopped in the shower. On the way out to Albany airport he phoned home.

'You sound morning-after-ish. Big night?' said Sharon.

'More wine than I should have,' admitted Cato.

'Drinking alone, never a good sign.' A pause. 'You were alone, weren't you?'

'Yes,' he lied. 'How about you, how's things at your end?'

'The bed's too big without you.'

'I'm on my way back.' He told her why, keeping it simple and vague so the cab driver wouldn't bust a blood vessel.

'Another? Jesus.'

'How's Ella?'

'Good, she's forgotten who you are and taken to calling the TV "Dada".'

'You know how to twist that knife, don't you?'

'Expert from way back. Get yourself home and fuck me.'

Cato promised to do his best.


The tape was still up around the car park perimeter just south of Kwinana Beach. Cato donned the paper suit and booties offered to him by one of the uniforms. DI Pavlou had recently left but Amy was there to give him an update.

'The body's gone off to the mortuary. The husband's name is Kelvin, he's being questioned by Rockingham Ds with Chris Thornton sitting in. We're following up on the car Kelvin says he saw from the jetty.'

'Make?'

'Unsure at this stage. Dark sedan.' She pointed at the houses a few hundred metres down the street. 'We're doorknocking to find out if anyone else saw or heard it.'

'Not just last night. He could have been stalking them for a few days.'

'Right,' said Amy.

Around the immediate area it was beach, light industrial units, a lunch deli and the tower-block offices and silos of the bulk-handling terminal.

'Cameras?' asked Cato.

'Nothing, apart from at the gates to the bulk terminal way over there or further back in towards Rocky central. But we're in the process of harvesting whatever there is.'

Cato had the feeling that Pavlou had probably already asked these questions and Amy seemed to be on the verge of some Gen-Y eye-rolling. He thanked her and took a stroll Duncan Goldflam's way. 'Smoking gun?'

'Already bagged it,' said Goldflam. 'Along with the perp's driving licence and signed confession.'

'Otherwise?'

'A two-metre trail of blood and some promising tyre and foot impressions: the feet are size ten and this time it looks like he was wearing Vans skate shoes.' He waved his hand at the tarmac surface of the car park. 'A layer of damp sand from that windy shower yesterday arvo. Real bonus.'

'The playing card?'

'Rolled up and sticking out of her mouth like a ciggie.'

Grotesque, thought Cato. 'What are you thinking?'

'I think matey is getting cocky and that's when they start making mistakes.'

'Fingers crossed.' Cato had rarely seen Goldflam so chipper. Across the road and down a bit, the deli was opening. Cato was ready for a coffee.

'Looks nasty,' the proprietor said, nodding in the general direction.

'Yep.' It was nearly ten, the deli was starting late. 'You missed a bit of breakfast business here this morning. My colleagues would have been all over this place.'

'Yeah, if I'd known,' she said. 'Usually nothing moves up this end until about now. Not worth me while to do breakfasts.' She was a fit-looking woman but the lines on her face suggested life had been unkind. 'Besides, there's me yoga class in the morning. Much better than getting up at five a.m. to serve bacon and egg toasties to half-a-dozen grumpy old bastards who can't string two words together. Had enough of that with my husband, God rest his obese soul.' She clacked a coffee serve into the machine. 'What can I do for you?'

Cato introduced himself and flashed his ID. 'Philip.'

'Gwenda.' She gave him a smile.

'Flat white and ...' He surveyed the rolls and sandwiches under the glass counter and decided they'd seen better days, chose a Mars bar instead.

'You'll get fat,' she said.

Cato realised he was being flirted with. Seize the day, he thought. 'Noticed anything unusual around here lately?'

'What? Like millions of cops scouring the car park, that type of thing?' Cato sipped the coffee she handed him and made an appreciative face as if it tasted okay. 'Nothing comes to mind. There's usually a few homeless kipping in their vans over there ...' The penny dropped. 'Is that what ...? Shit, mate.' She shook her head.

'How about cars hanging around?'

Gwenda squinted. Sudden life in that sad face. 'Day before last, one pulled up just outside about nine-ish, when I was opening.' She described it: black, racy, a Mazda maybe? Her brother-in-law had one just like it, only white.

'Did you see the occupant? Did they come in?'

'No, that's why I remember it. He stayed in the car, just sat there.'

'How long for?'

'Ten, fifteen minutes maybe. Then left.'

'Just sat there?' A nod. 'Making a call, looking at his phone? Anything like that?'

'Nah.'

'But you didn't get a good look at him?'

Gwenda shook her head. 'From here all I could see was about that much of his front.' She indicated with both hands a gap from nipple to belly button.

'The shirt?'

She shrugged. 'Dark. Plain, no pattern. It fitted him well.'

'How do you mean?'

A playful smile. 'He was cut, mate. Nice flat hard tummy. While I was buttering the rolls, I was thinking about his abs.' A sudden recollection. 'That's it, I saw his arms as well. Forearms. Thick like Popeye's. And hairy.'

'Young, old?'

'Young, I guess, no older than thirties anyway.'

'What makes you say that?'

'Dunno.'

'Tattoos?'

'No, it's unusual these days, isn't it? Everybody thinks they'll suddenly look cool if they have a tatt.' She grimaced. 'They're so wrong.'

Cato thanked Gwenda and told her to expect a follow-up interview on the record.

'Send someone nice,' she said. 'Like you.'


Cato and DI Pavlou watched the tape of Kelvin's interview together. The man was devastated, kept breaking into heaving sobs. It wasn't easy viewing.

'We've got to catch this bastard, Philip.'

'Yes, boss.'

Pavlou stepped out of the room to take a call on her mobile. Cato was transfixed by the man's story.

'We were living over in Brentwood, near the primary school. Liz managed real estate lettings. I was FIFO until the nickel price dropped. Ravensthorpe, know it?'

The interviewing detective had only heard of it but Cato knew it well, he'd solved a murder near there once.

Kelvin's eyes filled. 'Liz had this breakdown. Those backstabbers at the office. Until then we'd been keeping up the mortgage payments even with me out of work. We also had a bit saved for a rainy day. Then she got the chop and within six months we're in the van.' He shook his head. 'Fucking rainy every day now.'

'Kids? Family?' The detective was getting restless, as if he needed to be elsewhere. Maybe he thought this interview had already given him all he was going to get: a time frame and a possible suspect vehicle.

'We couldn't. I'm firing blanks. Family? Back in Victoria. We came over to WA for the boom and to escape those lazy, grasping dickheads on her side. Get help from them? No chance.'

Edge of frame, Chris Thornton leant in. 'So you've been living in the van what, a year?'

'Just over. The bank took back the house, it hadn't picked up much from when we bought it. After the fees and interest we got enough to buy and fit out the Kombi.'

'No prospect of work for you?'

Kelvin shook his head bitterly. 'Black mark on my record.'

The Rockingham detective picked up a sheet of paper. 'Possession and supply, marijuana. That wasn't smart was it?'

'So I was an idiot. It was fourteen years ago. And now I'm nudging fifty and the job market is tighter with the downturn. The last lot turned a blind eye but now I'm easier to ignore.'

'Shame,' said the detective, without conviction.

'Any dealings with the homeless agencies?' said Chris Thornton.

'No. Liz was proud like that. Didn't want to be seen as a charity case, to be lumped in with them, reminded of your failure every day by God-botherers and do-gooders. Didn't want to know.'

'How about you? Did you want their help? Did you talk to anyone?'

'Nah. We were approached a few times, sometimes I'd have a yarn if I was in the mood or Liz was taking a nap, but after a while we always sent them packing.' A smile. 'What Liz says, goes.'

'Remember who you yarned with?' said Thornton.

A shrug. 'Nah, after a while it all blurs.'

'Any recent contacts with anybody from the agencies? However brief? Last few days?'

'Nothing comes to mind.'

'How many people would have known you'd be there, then?'

'Only passers-by I suppose. We've been parked there for three or four days. It's a well-known hangout for folk like us.'

'But you had the place to yourself?'

'Nice change. Maybe the previous day's rain kept people away. I don't know.'

Thornton pressed but nothing came of it. A few more exchanges and they returned to the crime, the Rockingham detective running a last check to make sure he hadn't missed anything.

'Where did the car park up? The dark sedan?'

'I dunno. A few spaces away, three or four, south on the Rocky side?'

This tallied with the recovered prints. 'And you heard no conversations, greetings, whatever? Your wife must have noticed the car come in. Seen the person get out and approach her?'

'I heard nothing from where I was, a hundred metres away on the end of the jetty, maybe more.'

'And you heard nothing, no cry for help, no cry of alarm?'

Kelvin blinked away more tears. 'Nothing. She's on these pills that zonk her out, so maybe there was nothing to hear. Either way, the wind was up, a good sou'-westerly off the sea. You wouldn't hear anything, would you?'

Another victim and more medication, noted Cato. Pavlou stepped back into the room. Cato angled the laptop towards her. The Rocky detective shifted in his seat. 'Going back a bit, after you heard about the killings on the news, you didn't think to take extra precautions with your security?'

It sounded like an accusation.

'We avoided Freo. What else do you suggest? Put up in a flash hotel until you catch him?'

'No need for sarcasm, sir. We're here to help.'

Kelvin bowed his head. 'Sorry.' Even now, even here, bossed and humiliated by somebody who would never fully grasp this man's path to disaster. Kelvin looked up, tears streaming down his face. 'Why us? What did we ever do to deserve this? It's like we've fallen off the end of the fucking earth.'

The detective slipped his notes back into a folder and stood. 'I'll get you a cup of tea, mate.'

At this point Chris Thornton turned and looked at the camera with a helpless shrug.

Cato closed the laptop. 'Why didn't she make a fuss when a stranger approached her vehicle?'

Pavlou said, 'Asleep, didn't notice him, or ...'

'He wasn't a stranger?'

'All of the above.'

'So Jenkins is definitely out of the picture now?'

Pavlou filled her glass from the water fountain. 'It would seem so.'

Cato didn't want to let it go and said so.

Pavlou shook her head. 'The bloke's a prick and a bully, but if we're assuming the same man has done these four murders, then Jenkins can't be our killer. He was home all night, we were watching him. She squinted at Cato. 'We need to stay objective and focused, Philip.'

Of course she was right but he still didn't want to let it go. 'We're dropping surveillance on him?'

'Yes. Why wouldn't we? Those resources can be better used elsewhere.'

'Fair enough. Can we keep the data and communications tap on?'

'What's our rationale? You don't like him?' She swigged her water. 'It's over. Let's get back to work and find the real killer.'

'Where?' he said, exhaustion and disappointment dragging him down.

'In the detail. In the paperwork. In the evidence.' Pavlou seemed undaunted by the prospect of returning to square one. Maybe this was what leadership was all about. 'Chin up, Philip. You can do this.'

# 14

'We need to hand that over to the cops.' Betsy pushed Norman's iPad back across the desk with the tip of her polished nail. It was like Ebola had walked into the room.

'What, two texts, two emails, four photographs? It could be from any nutter out there.'

'That's for the police to decide. They can try and trace the mobile, the ISP for the emails, examine the photos. It's what they do.'

Norman shook his head. 'They'll find nothing. He'll be expecting this, he'll have left a false trail.'

'That's their lookout. It's our obligation to hand it over. If that fourth photo is of the latest murder site, you're protecting a killer by not doing so.'

Norman ran his finger along a scar on her desktop. 'So we're already in trouble. We've been sitting on this for days.'

'*You're* in trouble. *You've* been sitting on it for days.'

'It's what you told me to do. Make contact.' Fucked if he was going to let her chuck him under a bus. 'And there's a paper trail to that effect.'

'Threats don't help, Norman. I won't be bullied.'

'We need to finish what we started. If we hand this over to the cops now we'll lose him.' He tried his beseeching face. 'Two days more?'

'How do we explain the delay in handing this over to the police?'

Norman shrugged. 'We thought it was just a crank. We didn't connect photo four with victim four.' He tapped a few keys and spun the iPad back round to face her. 'Look, it could be anywhere.'

'You've cropped out the edge of the terminal silo.' She snorted. 'Pathetic. They'll spot it immediately.'

'So blame me,' he said.

'I will. Count on it.' A shake of the head. 'If this goes pear-shaped, it could ruin us, Norman.'

'Big News plays footsy with the bad guys all the time. You know that. You've got to be in it to win it.'

'But Big News can afford big lawyers.'

'What if we help trap him? Do the cops' work for them? We'll be fucking heroes.'

'What's your plan?'

'Quid pro quo. He obviously wants something from us. But he must know he needs to reciprocate.'

'Not sure psychos do reciprocation.'

'All Norman Bates really wanted was to tell people he missed his mum.'

Betsy smiled. 'Twenty-four hours, we need something of value from him if this is going to work. Hook him and reel him in. And if the shit does hit the fan, you're the one catching it. No emails, no phone calls between us from now on to suggest any collusion. Deal?'

'Deal,' he said.

She flicked her fingers in dismissal.

'Thanks,' he said. For nothing.

'Why are you doing this, Norman? It's only a story.'

Norman shrugged, suddenly self-conscious. 'My dad always talked about going the extra yard.'

'What'd he do for a living?'

'Journo. Quite well-known in his time. Got a Walkley.'

'Good for him.' She opened up her laptop. 'Tick-tock.'

Norman didn't know how the hell he would deliver but he knew the key was in the last email he'd received that morning. He'd held it back, the rabbit in his hat.

Cato had a late lunch down the street at Cafe 55. He opted for a beef pho and grabbed an abandoned *West* while he waited, perching on a stool at the counter along the wall. Somebody had already filched the cryptic — bastards, who'd do a thing like that? The headlines continued to scream impotently about the search for the serial killer and now had the tragic story of Liz and Kelvin to feed on. The mayor was still playing nice, focusing on a range of election issues and not demonising either the homeless or the police. Knight was less circumspect. He needed a bump in the polls if he was to make any headway.

'You can understand the fear and frustration,' he was saying. 'The police are running around in circles. People are sleeping rough on the streets of Fremantle and we have developers queueing up to build more houses but the mayor doesn't want to know.' On the inside pages the talk was of nuclear war, with North Korea and USA trading nasty tweets. Meanwhile in Australia, non-essential services like health, housing and education faced more slash-and-burn from the cigar-chomping Budget razor gang. The sense of entitlement had to end, they were saying. No more free lunches and taxpayer handouts unless you were a big polluter or government minister. Cato's pho arrived, he paid for it — no free lunches on his watch.

'You finished with that?' A hipster type with bold specs and sleeve tatts nodded towards the *West*.

'Help yourself.' Cato pushed it towards him.

'Cheers.'

Cato wound some noodles around his chopsticks.

'I don't think we've been introduced but I've seen you around.' The hipster handed him a business card. 'Norman Lip. Investigative journalist. *New WAve*.'

So this was the jerk who wrote the anti-police article. Cato decided not to give him the pleasure of recognition. 'Didn't punk rock die out a few decades ago?'

'*New WAve* is an online news and opinion magazine,' said Lip. 'We've been running for about eighteen months. We've already got over three thousand likes on Facebook and eight thousand following us on Twitter.'

'Good on you,' said Cato, chasing a sliver of beef through the spicy broth.

'You're working on the rough-sleeper murders.' He squinted at some notes on his smartphone. 'Sergeant Kwong, isn't it?'

'I'm on my lunchbreak, mate.' Cato picked up the business card and handed it back. 'Try talking to Police Media up in headquarters in Perth.' He nodded towards Lip's phone. 'You can google the number.'

'I hear you've got a prime suspect.' Lip checked his phone again.

'John Jenkins, a council ranger. Jackboot John they call him.'

'You hear wrong, buddy. That kind of stuff can get you sued.'

'So you won't be giving me a quote, sergeant?'

'Like I said, Police Media, Perth. They can help you get your facts straight.'

Lip saluted a farewell and left Cato to his soup.

Absorbed in his noodles, Cato didn't notice the young man pause on the way out to take a picture of him on the smartphone.


Back at the station, Amy had some news.

'We've picked up CCTV of the sedan heading south from the beach car park and turning at the corner of Weld Street. Some rich bloke along there has a camera covering his driveway. Then a woman calling her cat in the front yard on Kent Street, one street back and parallel, saw him heading south and turning left on to Victoria, heading east. Thought he was going a bit fast and she doesn't like that sort of thing.'

'Rego? Any further description?' A shake of the head. 'Anything else?'

'Not yet. Hassan was looking for you.'

Cato paid her a visit. 'Deb?'

She was chewing a Snickers bar, a can of Mother on her desk. 'Midafternoon slump,' she explained. 'It's getting earlier every day. It'll be the death of me.'

'Keep the receipts. Might be tax-deductible.'

'Something from the doorknock. We're starting to track down hotel guests from the Esplanade. A bloke down from Geraldton for some pharmacy convention says he got talking to Chris White earlier that day at the Carriage. Turns out they had the army in common.'

'How'd they get talking?'

'The guy's from Geraldton. They'll talk to anyone.' Bit sweeping, thought Cato. 'Reckons he offered our man a bed and a feed if he ever headed north. Felt sorry for him.'

'So White told this bloke his story?'

'Yep, abridged anyway. War hero, PTSD, divorce, life on the streets.'

'Anything else?'

'Jim from Geraldton was worried about him. He said White seemed to be on the verge of a crack-up, even the fact he was spilling his guts seemed to be a giveaway.' She consulted her notes. 'Men don't do that shit, not men like him. Unquote.'

It sounded like a line from the Mike and Pete Show down at the Buffalo Club.

'He reckons he gave White one of his cards and wrote a mobile number on the back for if ever he found himself in Geraldton. Gave him twenty bucks as well.'

'Neither of which were found on the body.'

'Right. White might have spent the twenty. Pathology reckons there was the remains of a curry in him.'

'I can't imagine him blowing the lot though. You can get a takeaway for ten bucks from the food hall.'

She shrugged. 'So our killer pockets the change. Not very nice but we had our suspicions about his character already.'

'And no sign of the business card on him or nearby?'

'No, I checked with Duncan. Nothing logged in the forensic haul.'

'So did White have a mobile that we don't know about? Why did Jim assume he had the means to call? Is it something else the killer pocketed?'

'I'll do some checking.'

'Okay, thanks Deb.'

'Not finished, yet. Jim got a funny text the following day. Didn't think anything of it until later, assumed it was a wrong number.'

'Yes?'

'He deleted it but it was words to the effect of "your mate missed the last post". Then a smiley face. It was only later that he got to thinking about the military connotation of the Last Post.'

The killer taunting, playing games. 'Did you organise to get his phone?'

'Yep, Geraldton plods are picking it up now. They'll send it straight down.'


Sharon finally got Ella off to sleep at around three. She had been awake since four that morning, having only had a couple of hours before that. She was stuffed. The baby exhausted her, being bright and positive for Phil exhausted her. She caught a glimpse of herself as she passed a mirror: her shoulders sagged, her feet dragged, it was like she was heading backwards through the evolutionary chart. The graceful, lithe Sharon Wang who practised tai chi daily in the parks in China seemed like another woman — an ancestor maybe. The sex-bomb who had bewitched Philip Kwong into her bed had gone AWOL. Come home and fuck me, she'd said to him. This misshapen lump with bags under her eyes and a forced smile.

Why was she putting on a brave face for him? So he didn't want this marriage to fail like the last. Who would? I'm carrying his baggage, she thought. How many times had she done that for the men in her life? Too many. How many times had she resolved to stop? Too many. She lay down on the bed, tensed for Ella waking up again. Tight from trying not to hate her. Was this what post-natal depression was? Or was she just tired and bored?

Sharon knew she was the head-over-heels type. All or nothing. She'd done it with her arsehole first husband until he ran off with one of his students while she was on duty in the Solomons. She'd once considered dumping her career and having babies with him too. Now here she was again, in at the deep end. All or nothing.

But what if this turned out to be nothing again?

Yet Phil did seem different. Less self-obsessed than most. Getting up at night, quarantining his weekends, as far as was possible, and trying really hard. Too hard? Sometimes he seemed almost needy. Staying away last night in Albany: apologetic, guarded and really, really sorry. For a moment she'd despised him for it. But maybe that was just because she was so, so tired.

Sharon started to drift finally to sleep. She gave in, embraced it. She knew she'd feel better when she woke. All these doubts and fears and resentments would be gone.

*You did well.*

*Cheers.*

They were on chat on Facebook. That morning's email had sought proof Norman could get close to the cops. The killer obviously wanted to keep one step ahead. So Norman had sent off the sneak photo he'd taken of the Chinese detective eating his noodles, plus an offer to dig into the bloke's past, stir him up. Now he wanted something in return. He was in St John's Square, where the council provided free wi-fi alfresco. The killer had made up a Facebook identity and operated with a photo of Kenny from South Park.

*Is it safe?*

*Ha-ha*, typed Norman. *Yes it is, I've not handed you over. Yet.*

*Good. What do you want?*

*Something only you would know. And a reason to believe.*

Norman studied the screen. The flashing cursor. The reply box stayed blank. The bastard had left him. Then it came through.

*Playing cards. They've known since day one.*

It didn't make sense. *Playing cards?*

*Jacks. The first was the Jack of Hearts. The last was Diamonds.*

*Meaning?*

*Look it up, you're a journo.*

Norman gave the screen the finger. He tried a new tack. *Why do you kill these people in particular? What's your point?*

Again the excruciating pause. Was Kenny teasing or just thinking?

*I'm saving them from themselves.*

*How?*

*Zzzzzzzzzz*

A ping-pong ball from the outdoor table bounced at his feet. A backpacker babe said thank you with a delicious accent and gave him a nice smile. Norman wondered if she was on Tinder. 'What's your name?' he smouldered.

'Enculez.' She returned to the table and made a wanking gesture with her hand. Her friend laughed.

Norman pretended it wasn't about him.

*Why the Chinese cop? What's he to you?*

*Later. Maybe you can do me another favour.*

No, thought Norman. Not good enough. *He thinks you are the community ranger. Is he right?*

*OMG, they killed Kenny... :(*


Jake was straight down to the gym. He'd wagged last period, some jerk wanting to motivate them about setting goals and reaching their full potential. Easy. Just get a job on the fucking mines and piss all your wages against a wall in the Pilbara. Maybe buy a jetski.

Lance was there as usual, chatting to the hottie behind the counter.

Jake leaned in and murmured into the bullish neck, 'Do you ever work?'

Lance gave him a grin. 'You can talk, schoolboy.' He flicked a farewell wave to Cheyenne and followed Jake to the weights.

'Reckon you're in with a chance with her?'

'Always, Jakey-boy.'

'Seen her boyfriend? Big bastard. I mean really big.'

'So am I.' He got Jake in a headlock. Squeezed until Jake's face went red. 'Haven't you noticed?' He rubbed his knuckles on Jake's skull and let go.

They lifted for a while, forearm curls, checking themselves and each other out in the full-length mirrors. Lance mouthed 'gorgeous' and blew Jake a kiss and they cacked themselves.

'So what'd you learn at school today?'

Jake snorted. 'They sent us a "motivational" speaker.' He curled his fingers in air quotes around the word motivational. 'The leaflet said he was an Iraqi who came here on a boat, overcame the odds, got dux of his school, made his first million by thirty and helps out the disadvantaged in his spare time.'

'Good work. He got a girlfriend?'

'Will have by the end of today. Half of my year were in his group selfie.'

Lance checked his watch. 'So why didn't you go? School's not finished yet.'

'Better things to do, but.'

'What? Hang around the gym with me and Cheyenne?'

'Yeah,' said Jake. 'Why not?'

Lance scanned the room. 'Look at this place. Me, you, fattie over there, Cheyenne Show-us-your-tits, three walls of mirrors and a truckful of lead weights.' He jabbed his forefinger into Jake's temple. 'You've got a brain. Wasting the privileges and opportunities you have, it's fucking criminal.'

'You sound like a grumpy old man,' muttered Jake.

'Yours?'

'Nah, mine wouldn't say it like that. Prefers reason and persuasion. When he's around.'

'Yeah? Tell me about him. Is he why you're angry?'

'Another time,' said Jake. 'How about some bench presses?'

'No.' There was steel in Lance's tone. 'I want to hear all about you and your old man.' He ran his finger gently along the scar on Jake's cheek. Ignored the flinch. 'Did he do this to you?'

By the end of the day Cato felt like he was treading water. A new serial murder would normally advance a case in some way. Instead this one had receded, eliminating a prime suspect who was shaping up nicely. A call from Hassan to the good Samaritan in Geraldton confirmed that White did indeed have a mobile but, as he wasn't on any telco records, it would be a bugger chasing down the number to track his movements and his calls. Cato asked instead for a trace on the mobile used to send the text to Geraldton Jim. Meanwhile Thornton's check of Barbarossa Nominees and the monthly payments into Jenkins' account had so far come to nothing; the company was hiding somewhere in a labyrinth of offshore tax dodgers. The forensic accountants could follow it up. In the meantime Cato would go home and reconnect with the stuff of life instead of death.

When he walked through the front door he could hear Ella wailing, an indignant needy bellow.

'Shut the fuck up. Please.' Sharon. Sharp, angry, exhausted.

He went in to Ella's room, to Sharon leaning over the cot. 'Hi.'

She jumped. Turned to him. Her face wore the horror and guilt of discovery. Tears pricked her eyes and she leant into his chest. Her shoulders shook.

'Bad night?'

She pressed into him. He could feel the damp of her tears through his shirt. 'Just tired. Sometimes I need to say stuff, let it out. It doesn't mean ...'

'It's okay.'

She pushed herself away, looked up. 'I wasn't apologising. I was explaining.'

'That's not what I meant.' But he wasn't sure what he did mean. He lifted Ella out of her cot for a cuddle. The crying subsided.

Sharon glared at him and went out to the kitchen. 'Tea?' She switched the kettle on, started to clear up the detritus of the day: plastic toys, baby books, half-chewed bread, squashed banana.

'Sure,' said Cato.

'How was Albany? And who did that to your face?'

Safer ground at last: the Job, the business at hand. He told her about it.

'And the latest victim?'

Cato shook his head. 'These people have already had a tough run.' He recounted Kelvin's story of the downward spiral. 'But they were hanging it together, just. Looking after each other. The simple life.' He caught a look in Sharon's eye. Envy? He felt a surge of spite. 'Then this bastard snatches it away.' Cato clicked his fingers. 'Like that.'

Sharon opened the fridge door and peered in. 'Eaten?'

'No.'

'Eggs do you?'

'Sure.' Cato's phone buzzed.

A text from Jake. ***Still on for a move this wknd?***

***Sure***, replied Cato. ***Sunday OK?***

Thumbs up and a smiley face.

'Work?' said Sharon.

'Jake,' said Cato. 'Moving in on Sunday. That still okay with you?'

'Yeah,' she said. 'No worries.'

# 15

'Johnny, Maureen and the Jack of Hearts?' Betsy looked perplexed. 'I don't get it.'

'It's a play on a Bob Dylan song title.'

'Ah,' she said. 'Retro irony. Right. But maybe a bit obscure?' She shook her head. 'Is that what they teach at Edith Cowan?'

'You want me to change it?' Norman really didn't give a fuck. Let her score her snobby points. It was the story that mattered. His story. 'How about "The Killer Speaks"?'

'Now you're talking.'

He'd spent the rest of Friday on it and into the early hours of this morning. The gist, he explained to Betsy who, for a news editor, seemed remarkably averse to reading, was that the killer had left his signature, the jack, on all of the victims and that the police should have known they were dealing with a serial killer as early as victim two: Maureen Bryant. Further, they had a prime suspect in their sights, a council employee with a violent history whose job brought him into daily contact with the homeless. But this man, Johnny Jenkins, was still in his job and still at liberty. Finally, Detective Sergeant Philip Kwong, a key figure in the investigation, was way out of his depth: leading botched raids on disabled battlers, overseeing the reckless slaughter of beloved family pets by trigger-happy paramilitaries and allowing the prime suspect to continue roaming the streets. Meanwhile those running for mayor were pussyfooting around the subject. Not prepared to show any leadership or ask the hard questions. What were they scared of?

'Fabulous,' purred Betsy.

Norman cleared his throat. 'The shit will hit the fan. The advertisers might get jumpy.'

'Are you kidding? This is classic public interest.' Betsy beamed. 'Besides, our demographic is mainly Gen Y know-it-alls and their rich, guilty Boomer parents. They like a ringside seat at a good shitfight. Gives them something to retweet about.'

'Run it, then?'

'Sure, darling. Just pass it in front of Carmen first.'

Carmen the Lawyer. Fuck. 'Sure,' said Norman, pasting on a smile.

He didn't have time to argue. He needed to get over to River View to keep his weekly appointment with Naomi. Today it felt like one of those 'shoulds'. She was the only person, the only thing, that ever made him feel guilty, responsible. She tried not to, he knew. Abusing him, taking the piss, acting like she didn't need him. Acting tough. But sometimes backing out of her room he saw that light go out of her eyes and knew it was his doing.

As he walked into her room, he saw that same look now and offered her his good-to-see-you grin.

'Took your time.'

'Yeah, sorry.' A pause. 'Hang on, no I'm not. I don't usually get here until the afternoon. I'm early.'

'I'm blessed. Fitting me in before something more interesting?'

'Fuck, you're in a bad mood. What's up?'

'I'm a thirty-four-year-old cripple in a home full of demented eighty-year-olds. Sometimes it gets to me.' She grabbed her ciggies and lighter from the bedside table. 'Let's go. Anyway, where you been?'

'Had a meeting with Betsy.'

'I read your piece. Nice one. You're improving with age.'

'Duck off.'

'No really. No dangling participles. Terse, pacy, feisty. Dad would have been proud.'

'Ease up, sis.'

Once again, they found themselves down at the riverside cafe, a breeze blowing off the water.

'The usual?' Norman said.

'May as well.' She lit up while he rearranged the furniture like he did every Saturday and went to order the drinks. 'Did it work?' she asked on his return.

'What?'

'The vampire. Did he get in touch?'

Norman couldn't hide his smile of satisfaction. 'Yep. We're in contact.'

'Wow.' She looked impressed and horrified at the same time. 'And?'

'It's definitely him. He knows stuff the cops haven't released.'

'Sure it's not the cops toying with you?'

A frown. He hadn't thought of that. 'No, I'm pretty sure it's him.'

'So what does he want from you?'

'Nothing. Yet.'

'What's your price?'

'Price?'

An impatient suck on the straw. 'What do you want from him and how much are you prepared to pay?'

'I don't have the money to pay him.'

'I'm speaking metaphorically, Normie.'

'Oh.'

'So? How far are you prepared to go for your Devil's Walkley? '

'Fuck, sis. Why do you always have to take a dump in my dinner?'

She smiled. 'You haven't really thought this through, have you?'

'Easy to criticise; you doing any writing?' It was intended to wound, to stop her probing, finding fault. And he could tell by the hardening of her mouth that it worked. He immediately felt like shit.

'It'd take forever, two fingers of one good hand? Yeah, right.'

'Sorry, sis. I'm a jerk.'

She sniffed. 'The only jerk I've got.'

Naomi was the smarter of the two and the one with the real writing talent. The one who should have been the star. Norman conceded he didn't know where to start or when to quit. 'You should do it anyway. Write that book. Dictate it to someone.' He paused, a nervous, hopeful shine in his eyes. 'Or we could collaborate?'

Naomi drained her Coke. 'Don't be stupid.' She stubbed out her cigarette and lifted her chin defiantly. Neither of them was in a hurry to rescue the mood.

He looked out on the wind-whipped river. 'You don't think much of me, do you?'

'Oh, drop it.'

'What do you think I haven't *thought through*?'

'Dad played peek-a-boo with the premier for his scoop and people understand that, they get it, they forgive it. This guy you're dealing with — I don't know, it's a line I wouldn't cross.'

'Neither would I.'

'But you are. He's using you, and you're letting yourself be used.'

'Take after Mum, then, don't I? They reckon co-dependence takes a few generations to get flushed out.'

'Sounds like you won't take advice from anyone.'

'I know what I'm doing, sis. Don't worry.'

Her lighter clicked on the end of another ciggie. 'Take me back to Happy Valley.'

Cato had woken to a kiss and a cuppa from Sharon. After a tense and monosyllabic previous evening they'd gone to bed. They'd lain awake, spooned together, lost in their own thoughts and Cato had finally drifted to sleep. Coaxed awake in the middle of the night, Sharon had ridden him with a hunger and urgency he hadn't experienced since ... since Ella was born.

It was Saturday and, with the loss of momentum on the case, there was no real need to head into work. Emergency calls aside, the weekend was his. 'What do you want to do today?'

'What? Anything? You're not working?'

'Nah.'

They agreed a family picnic would be nice. Cato wanted to show her a favourite spot from when Jake was little. It was up in the hills, in John Forrest National Park. While Sharon readied Ella and assembled the monumental logistical supplies that go with an eight-month-old, Cato put together a Greek salad and slipped a bottle of red into the basket. They'd pick up a roast chook along the way. Sharon looked happy, like her old self, as they loaded the Volvo and Ella gurgled her approval. Cato glanced at the 'Y' on the gable wall, remembering something about painters coming soon.

'Monday,' confirmed Sharon.

On arrival they spread a rug out on a flat expanse of rock overlooking Hovea Falls, Cato dimly aware that a couple of years ago a body from DI Hutchens' past was dug up not far from here. Such was the life of a cop: where others saw a nice picnic spot, he saw a notorious dump site. There were splashes of colour as kangaroo paw and cornflowers poked their heads through the foliage. While Ella rolled around on the rug, fascinated by a group of kids nearby playing in the shallow brook, Cato and Sharon nibbled on dolmades and sipped shiraz.

'Are you happy?' she asked him.

He leaned over and kissed her. 'Blissfully.'

'Really? Why?'

A simple enough question but it threw him. Cato sensed a trap. He gestured at the space between them. 'You. Me. Us.' He caressed baby Ella's tummy. 'Everything.'

'What is it about all of this that makes you so happy?'

A cloud scudded across the sun. The breeze picked up, snatching at the edge of the rug. 'My life feels whole, complete. I love you. I love Ella. I'd be lost without you.'

'Would you?' Her face still wore the hint of a smile. Open. Honest. But there was a challenge behind the words all the same.

'How about you?' said Cato. 'Are you happy?'

'Sometimes,' she said. 'Usually.' She sipped her wine, pulled a face. 'I'd better leave this. Ella will give me hell for it later.'

'What's missing?' said Cato.

Sharon shrugged. 'Maybe I need to do a course at TAFE or something. How to be a Housewife and Mother.'

'I could go part-time, take some leave, share the load.'

She shook her head and smiled. Drained her wine glass anyway. 'Ignore me. I'm just tired. The moon's in the wrong place. It'll pass.'

'Felt like this for long?' It sounded accusatory and he tried to hide it behind a smile. 'I never knew.'

'And you the detective.' She leaned over and snogged him. It felt like he was being silenced. 'Fancy a walk?'

They wound their way along to the disused Swan View railway

tunnel. Sharon was keen to walk through it. They pushed Ella's stroller over the uneven ground and the darkness enveloped them.

'Spooky,' said Sharon, her voice dropping to a whisper. 'Cool.'

Damp clung to the walls and daylight receded behind them. Cato recalled a school visit here as part of a week-long camp. 'Apparently the narrow design and the steep approach made it almost lethal for the locomotive crews. They'd slow down to a crawl and the smoke and fumes couldn't escape. Asphyxiation was a major issue. So they abandoned it.'

'Choked to death by an uphill slog and confined spaces,' said Sharon. She hooked her arm into his. 'Well, there you go.'


Driving back down Greenmount Hill, the distant Perth city skyline was shrouded in haze. Ella was asleep in her capsule in the back seat. Sharon had her hand resting lightly on Cato's thigh as he drove.

'We're going to be okay,' she said. 'Sometimes I just voice things. I'm adjusting.' She squeezed his leg and grinned. 'From Federal Agent to Supermum wasn't as smooth as I anticipated.'

'Is it worth talking to the GP or the clinic?'

She shook her head firmly. 'I don't need diagnosing or medicating. Sometimes I get a bit bored and antsy and sick of baby talk and being alone. I'll get over it.'

'Your leave finishes in another month. Maybe we shouldn't extend it again.'

'Maybe,' she said.

Cato's phone went. It was DI Pavlou.

'We have a problem.'

Norman Lip, the pushy journo, had been at it again. This time it was personal, with Cato being named and shamed as incompetent and out of his depth. 'Christ.'

Sharon was looking at him. Worried.

'There's even a photo of you, eating noodles and reading the newspaper. The caption says "Money Pho Nothing". He doesn't like you, does he?'

'I guess not.'

'There's more,' said Pavlou. 'He knows about the playing cards.'

'How would he know that?'

'Investigations leak. It's a good excuse to kick the bastard's door down and find out.'

'Count me in,' said Cato.

Norman Lip lived in a two-storey townhouse in South Fremantle on Rockingham Road where it joins the coast road. It was a row of new-builds behind an abandoned pub. From the second-storey back window of Norman's place you could just glimpse the Indian Ocean if you stood on tiptoe and craned your neck.

'Nice view,' said Cato, doing just that.

'Arsehole,' said Norman. His voice was muffled because there was a uniformed policeman kneeling on his back and pushing his face into the rug while a colleague handcuffed him.

Cato pointed out a phone, a laptop and an iPad. 'We'll need those.'

'No worries,' said Chris Thornton. 'I'll organise a receipt.'

'Nazis,' said Norman.

'Do you have your house keys, sir?' Cato waved a hand around the place. 'We can lock up when we leave. It might be a couple of hours before you get back. Wouldn't want to leave a nice place like this unsecured.'

There was a muffled grunt from the rug.

'Beg pardon, sir?'

'Lawyer.'

'All in good time, sir.' He gestured for the uniforms to lift Norman up. 'Off we go.'

Back at the station, Cato had the phones and computers sent over to IT but given that it was a skeleton weekend roster nothing much was expected to happen before Monday. No hurry, he'd said. DI Pavlou was on her way. As head of the investigation she was most concerned by the allegations in Lip's article and the apparent disclosure of sensitive information. All this, Cato explained to Norman Lip's lawyer, a woman called Carmen.

'This is way over the top, mate.'

Cato liked her, there was a playful spark in her eyes. 'DI Pavlou should be with us in the next quarter of an hour. Can I get you coffee, tea, water?' She shook her head. 'Norman, anything for you?'

'Mr Lip to you. And the answer's no.'

'Of course, sir. My apologies.'

Pavlou walked through the door. Cato did the introductions. Pavlou had a whiff of cigarettes and barely controlled fury about her. 'Your article in *New WAve*, Mr Lip. While you have the right to criticise our efforts, we would have appreciated the opportunity to put the record straight before you published.'

'I asked him ...' a nod towards Cato. 'And he told me to get lost.'

'That's not true, Norman. I advised you to speak to Police Media.'

A staying hand from Pavlou. 'However, the primary issue of concern for us is the disclosure of sensitive information which could hinder our investigation.' Pavlou leaned in. 'Where did you get your information from, Mr Lip?'

'A confidential source.'

'Who?'

Carmen put her pen down. 'My client is a professional journalist, doing his job. He is prepared to cooperate in whatever way he can but disclosure of sources is not one of them.'

Pavlou ignored her. 'Mr Lip, has this information been supplied to you by a serving police officer or a civilian connected to the enquiry?'

Nothing.

She tried another tack. 'Are you, then, in contact with the person who may be responsible for the murders of four people?'

A momentary hesitation and an eyelid flicker. The ghost of a smile.

Jesus, he really was.

# 16

Once it became evident that Norman Lip was indeed in contact with the murderer, or at least someone who claimed he was, it was game on. Norman's phone, laptop and iPad went to the top of the queue and the techos tore them apart over the weekend, following whatever trail existed. Predictably, the ISP of the suspect email account was an obscure one in Romania and the SIM for the text was a pre-paid purchased using false identification. Thus began the long slog of tracking them down to an end user but the likelihood of a result was remote. It made Cato think of those trains grinding into the dark Swan View tunnel and those crews choking in the blackness. But the contact also revealed a number of things about this man who claimed he was the killer. First, he wanted to engage in a game, he was an egotist and a trickster, hence his calling card — the Knave. Not unusual in a sociopath but often the cause of their downfall as ego eventually outweighed caution — for only by being caught could the world know just how brilliant they'd been. Second, he'd targeted Cato. He'd steered Norman Lip towards him with a specific request for a photo. Was Cato his randomly chosen victim? Or was it something more personal? That was what energised him that Monday morning.

Norman was staying silent. All they'd gathered so far was gleaned from the emails and texts. DI Pavlou had summoned Norman's employer, Betsy Spencer, for a severe dressing down and a bit of arm-twisting. If Norman didn't start cooperating, *New WAve* was going to be hung out to dry for playing with people's lives and cosying up to a murderer. Cato suspected, from the lawyer's demeanour, that they'd already thought this through before deciding to publish, and that both

Betsy and Norman were made of sterner stuff than Pavlou anticipated. But he'd be happy to be proved wrong.

So why did the killer have a thing about Cato? The answer to that was, hopefully, the key to the killer's identity. How many toes had Cato trodden on during the course of his career? Find a football stadium and fill it. How many of those were potentially homicidal? Maybe half. So Cato came up with an alternative idea.

'I could try talking to him, direct. I could be Norman for a while.'

Pavlou liked it. Cato's first text on Norman's phone read: **Like the story?**

No reply. That had been on Saturday evening. And still nothing for the rest of the weekend. In the meantime there'd been an analysis of whatever cell site information they could gather. Predictably the killer was using the number sparingly, for less than a minute at a time, then removing the SIM and battery until the next occasion. And it hadn't been used at all before that first SMS to Norman Lip. They'd managed to pinpoint his location when he'd made that first contact. He must have been sitting right outside Norman's place at the time. Since then there'd been a blip in the area of Monument Hill in central Fremantle and down at Fisherman's Wharf.

Sunday had passed in a blur. Cato had snatched a couple of hours in the afternoon to clear out the granny flat and help Jake move in. It hadn't been the big father–son bonding exercise that Cato hoped and it was his own fault. He'd been distracted, head in the enquiry, and conversation was stilted at best.

'You and Sharon still okay with this?' Jake had asked at one point, face steeled for rejection.

'Absolutely.'

'It's not permanent. Just some breathing space from Mum and Simon. A few months maybe. Or even just weeks. Whatever.'

'Not an issue, mate. You're always welcome. This is your home, right?'

'Right.' A tentative smile. 'Really appreciate this, Dad.'

'My pleasure.' An incoming buzz on Cato's phone. 'Might need to head back into the office this evening. Few developments on the case.'

'No probs, I'll cook something up, give you and Sharon a break.'

'Thanks, mate.' Cato had tamped down his anxiety about yet again being a crap dad. It was just really bad timing. The new lead and everything.

Sharon was bright and breezy around Jake, but sending Cato daggers as he headed back into the cop shop. 'Hurry home, sweetie. We miss you already.'

And thus the weekend had slipped away.

On Monday morning, DI Hutchens strolled past Cato's desk and hooked a beckoning finger in the air without breaking stride. 'Come, come.'

Cato followed. 'What?'

'Fancy a cappuccino or something?'

Code for let's get out of here.

'Okay.' Cato, a man of habit, headed straight over the road but Hutchens wanted to go further afield. They ended up on the Strip at Gino's.

'Latte, half-strength, skimmed milk.' Hutchens' new heart-care regime.

Cato brought the coffees back to the table. Outside, the denizens were settling into their usual spots. Buses scraped by on South Terrace. People out and about. Kids in strollers, dogs on leads, phones in hands. Coffee and petrol fumes. Another weekday morning in Freo. 'So?'

'So I see you got your name in the papers again.'

The mainstream press had picked up Norman's scurrilous musings and reprinted them wholesale. They'd tutted at Norman's irresponsible journalism but enjoyed the free ride anyway.

'You might get me back on the local desk sooner than you expected.'

'That's what I thought but it seems the Velvet Hammer is sticking by you. For now.'

'Must be my aftershave.'

'So any ideas who's got it in for you?'

'None. Could be anyone. Could also be a friend or a relative of anyone. Might be a whole queue of people.' Something tugged at a synapse and evaporated. 'Did you have something special in mind or just a catch-up on gossip?'

Hutchens looked around the cafe; he suddenly seemed out of focus. Lost. 'I'm retiring at the end of next month. Thirty years is up.' He found a grim smile. 'You're the first to know. After Marjorie of course.'

'I'm honoured.'

'Don't be. I'm just taking care of business, clearing my desk, so to speak.'

Cato felt unexpectedly sad at the idea. 'So what is it you're telling me?'

'Any obligation you've felt to stick by me since the heart attack ...'

'And Mundine.' The avenging angel who took to Hutchens' head with a cricket bat.

'Yeah, him as well.' Hutchens licked the froth off his spoon. 'I'm saying you're free. Fly, my pretty. This time, if Pavlou tempts you into Major Crime for the long haul, take it. It's where you belong.'

'Do I have any say in this?'

'Sure, you can dig your heels in and rise through the ranks to end up a tweeting desk jockey like me.'

'Point taken.' Cato drank some coffee, wondered if Hutchens' drink was as tepid as his. At this rate they'd sink them and be out in a minute or two.

'Paddy McMahon is dead wood. She wants him out of her squad permanently, so the vacancy will be there. It's only a matter of whether Golly-gosh Amy gets her secondment extended, or whether you get the post.'

'I'm not the competitive type.'

'My arse, you're not. You love being right, admit it.'

'Never. Then you'd win.'

'Just do what you've always done, and leave the rest to me.'

'I've been down that path before. Usually leads to quicksand.'

'Trust me.' Hutchens smiled and pushed his cup away from him. 'Thanks for the latte. Next one's my shout.'

Cato clapped a hand on his boss's shoulder as they passed on to the street. He couldn't think of any words to accompany it.

'Save the man-love for the leaving do, mate,' muttered Hutchens, looking straight ahead.


The painters turned up a little later than they'd promised but it wasn't as if Sharon had places to go. The boss, Steve, a stocky Pommie bloke in his thirties, had nipped around the previous Friday to check out what needed doing and agree a price: it wasn't just a blanking out of the 'Y' graffiti. With a job cancellation they now had a week-long window during which they could do a quick makeover of the exterior, weather permitting, on the understanding that anything left unfinished during that time would not be their responsibility. Sharon could live with that, the forecast was for clear skies all week.

There were two of them. While the younger one unloaded the ute, Steve finalised details with Sharon. He frowned at the graffiti.

'Little buggers, eh? I blame the parents.'

Sharon smiled and nodded, bouncing Ella who was beginning to wriggle in her arms.

'You don't get this crap in Singapore, do you? Bloody cane, that's what.' He checked an incoming text. 'That's where you're from, right?'

'Bendigo,' said Sharon.

'Right,' he said. 'I need to go and check another job. The lad here'll look after you.'

The lad turned from what he'd been doing and gave her a wave. She recognised him. He came over and offered his hand. 'Nat.'

'The walking track down at South Beach?'

'That's right. You remembered me?'

'Yeah,' said Sharon. Only because I thought you were a bit of a creep.

Steve told them he'd be back by about noon and turned to Nat. 'And remember what I said about keeping the radio down. Not all of us want to listen to that shite. You got me?'

A big grin. 'Aye, no worries, Steve.' Nat turned to Sharon and the squirming Ella. 'I'll let you get back to it, then.' He reached up and tickled Ella on the chin. 'Looks like she needs a feed.'

Sharon left him to it, vaguely rattled, as if she'd just been told what to do.


Chris Thornton was waiting for Cato when he returned.

'Got something for you.' He plugged a thumb drive into Cato's desktop. 'After the Rockingham murder, I got one of the civvies to review the CCTV for the other incidents with a new focus now on dark sedans.' He brought a video up on the screen and tapped play.

'Where and when?' said Cato.

'Essex Street, the night of the murder of Chris White in the park. These cameras are on the walls of the Department of Transport building over the road from the Esplanade Hotel.' A couple of cars were in view, angle-parked. A third one appears, a dark sedan, the driver kills the lights and engine, gets out and heads out of frame, east away from the park. Thornton froze the frame. 'Hoodie and baseball cap and bowed head. He doesn't want to be recognised.'

'You've got a suspicious mind,' said Cato. 'Rego plate?'

Thornton rewound to the car pulling into the parking bay. Froze. 'He's covered it with reflective film — like those sunnies that perverts wear. Popular trick with Boy Racers and Doughnut Kings.'

'And what time is this?'

'Eleven that evening. He comes back fifteen minutes later with a takeaway coffee, and leaves.'

'So we have a dodgy hoon in a hoodie, but he's well outside the time frame.'

'That's what we all thought and it's probably why he didn't get the full treatment first time round. But look at this. Four-thirty a.m.'

Same cameras, same parking spots. Nothing happens in the bays covered by the camera. But across the road in the high left corner of the video a car pulls into a space a few bays nearer the park. Only the wheels and lower back edge of the car are visible. Dark colour but the rego plate is out of sight.

'Could be anybody,' said Cato.

'Look at the tow bar.' There was a fluoro green tennis ball stuck on to it. Thornton rewound to the earlier footage of the sedan reversing out of the bay and leaving several hours earlier. He froze the frame: a tow bar with a fluoro ball on it. 'They're not uncommon but I'm loving the coincidence.' They returned to the later footage recorded in the middle of the night.

'He's not getting out,' said Cato.

'He stays there for an hour and a quarter and then leaves just before it gets light.'

'We're there by then,' said Cato. 'The jogger had called it in by just after five-thirty.'

'The first response crew. Uniforms.' Thornton froze the frame. 'You can see the police lights reflected on his windscreen.'

'Send it to the geeks to see if they can enhance it.' Cato nudged him. 'Nice one.'

'Cheers.'

'The other scenes, does he return to them too?'

'We're looking into it. Keep you posted.'

'Anything from the bean counters on Barbarossa Nominees?'

'Nothing yet. But I did speak to the Perth Ds about that factory fire in City West and they're convinced the deaths were more by accident than design. It was essentially an insurance job. I've put it all on the case database for you to look at when you're ready.'

Thornton excused himself. A picture was building in Cato's mind of the figure caught on CCTV. An egotist who couldn't resist being there to see the response to his handiwork, like an actor or writer impatient for their first reviews. Gwenda the deli owner described seeing a set of tight abs and muscled arms like Popeye's. A narcissist. Aren't they all, thought Cato. But he was beginning to glimpse an ego that could be the undoing of the killer.

## 17

Sharon was breastfeeding Ella when she noticed Nat smiling at her through the kitchen window. He was waving his phone at her and mouthing 'Steve'. She summoned him in and covered her breasts before he arrived. He handed her the phone.

'Something's come up on this other job,' said Steve with traffic noise behind him. 'We used Antique White and we really should have got Stowe White. Fucked if I can see the difference. 'Scuse the French, love.'

Sharon was sleepy. She wanted to drift off and join Ella in her nap. A potentially blissful couple of hours before Jake got home from school. 'That's fine,' she smothered a yawn. 'Nat seems to be going along okay.'

'I might have to leave you with him for the day. We'll get an early start tomorrow to make up and I'll put an extra lad on.'

'No worries.' She handed the phone back to Nat and signalled her intention to put the baby to bed.

He winked in reply and put the phone to his ear. 'Yep. Aye boss, no worries.'

To Sharon's mind it sounded like Nat was aping his boss's northern English accent, taking the piss. Cocky as. She pulled the curtains over in Ella's room to dim the light and laid her in her cot. Her daughter was so beautiful. Sharon fought the urge of further self-recrimination for her harsh words. She kissed Ella lightly on the brow and breathed in her smell.

'Sweet.'

Sharon turned.

Nat was standing in the bedroom doorway with two mugs in his hand. 'Thought you might like a cuppa?'

This was too much, really. 'Nat, thanks for the tea. Very nice of you.

But I'd appreciate it if you could not wander around my house as if you ...'

'Live here? Own the place?' He took a sip. 'Yeah, sorry. A servant needs to know his place, eh?'

'I didn't mean it like that, it's just I like my personal space. My privacy.'

'Just a cup of tea, missus. No offence meant.'

This wasn't going well. She lifted her mug and drank from it. 'Thanks. Sorry, I'm a bit tired.'

Nat winked. 'Probably time for a nice lie down.' He waved his mug and nodded over his shoulder. 'I better get back to it.'

'Right.' She headed for the door, Nat seemed to take a moment too long to move out of her way. She found herself flushing, aware of the heat emanating from him. Aware of the hardness of his body. Weird and wrong.

Nat whistled *hi-ho, hi-ho* as he sauntered out of Sharon's kitchen to his work.


Cato was heartened by Chris Thornton's lead on the CCTV footage. Now he sat down to review the forensics, the interviews, CCTV, tele-communications, looking for that detail where Pavlou had said they'd eventually find the killer. Forensics first: on at least three out of the four occasions the killer must have been splashed by the blood of his victims. There'd been two stabbings and a stomping along with the less messy strangling. But each time any residual blood trail had ended within a five metre radius of the body. The killer must have changed into clean clothes and shoes and gone his merry way. Was he toting a backpack with the spare gear? Did he put the bloody gear into it after changing? Should they be widening the perimeter for street bin searches? Was there a partner or other family member out there wondering what the hell turned the laundry pink?

Cato examined the scene photos: young Dean on his back, a huge dark stain covering the front of his torso, the playing card protruding from the zipper of his jeans. Maureen Bryant, face down in the bus shelter, ligature coiled on her back. No blood here except from the scratches and grazes on her face, neck and hands. Chris White, curled into a ball, kicked into kingdom come. Once again the blood trail disappearing after the five-metre radius. Finally Liz Murray in a beachside car park, a single deep slash across her throat and a spray of arterial crimson across the dashboard and windscreen of the Kombi, the killer hopping into his car and taking any residual traces with him. Cato flicked through the reports of earlier crime scenes to check if there were more unusual or seemingly random objects which together, over four murders, might make some kind of sense. Down at the wharf for murder number one: cigarette ends, cans, bottles, a used condom — not so far linked to Dean Pearson — an instant noodle packet, lolly papers, chewing gum. Maureen Bryant: more cigarette ends and discarded cans and bottles, lolly papers, chewing gum, an empty jar of Dijon mustard. Mustard? That was the thing about South Fremantle beachgoers — their eclectic detritus of VB cans and sauvignon blanc bottles, Doritos packets and hummus tubs. In any case, each forensically examined and showing no apparent link to the victims.

The interviews. People queuing up to point the finger at Johnny Jenkins, the council ranger with a history of violence and a known antipathy towards the homeless — or anyone weak and vulnerable for that matter. But he had an alibi for murder number four — the police had him under surveillance. Interviews with those who knew the victims and attested to their dire straits and sad lives. People in the vicinity of the murder scenes who, for the most part, saw and heard nothing — except a dark sedan going a bit fast down a residential street in Rockingham and a set of tight abs and muscled arms in a parked car a few days earlier. Guests at the Esplanade Hotel, still being tracked down, but so far sleeping through everything.

CCTV. The dark sedan in Rockingham and in Essex Street for murders three and four. A fluoro tennis ball wedged on to a tow bar. Wayne Bradley's turbo ute in the vicinity of murders two and three, and a GPS marker on his satnav putting him within fifty metres of Maureen Bryant, within an hour or so of her death. For six long minutes, enough to tighten a rope around a neck and keep it there until the thrashing stops. But he had an alibi in a brothel for Chris White's murder, plus a physical improbability of besting an ex-commando. Or maybe Wayne was part of a tag team?

No, this was a loner. Had to be.

Telecommunications. A pushy journo playing footsy with a killer. Cato wondered if he'd get a reply to his SMS purporting to be Norman Lip.

**Like the story?**

Lip's mobile, a number specially set up for possible contact with the killer and quarantined from his daily use. Cato had it now, he looked at it sitting on his desk, willed it to light up and make contact. Nothing. An active GSM trace on the number the killer had used; all matey had to do was turn on his phone and leave it on until they came knocking at his door. But that wasn't going to happen. A trace on the mobile number used to send the text to the Geraldton Samaritan: triangulation tracking had it in White's possession the night he died. The phone had been reported stolen a week earlier — the property of a CBC year twelve student. Until then the texts and calls had been from a teenage universe. For that final week there'd been much less traffic: questions from two unknown and untraced mobiles — **how you going? Need anything? Found a pitch?** And White's terse replies *fine*, *no thanks*, *yep*. The last one the evening he died — **Keep well, mate.** To which White had replied **Always**. A relationship of sorts with the killer.

Cato scoured the details until his vision blurred and a headache threatened. He wondered if he should get his eyes tested, get some specs. He was that age now, after all. He wondered about Sharon. Was she post-natally depressed or just plain tired? She was vehemently resistant to taking it any further and he wasn't game to push back. Yet.

Lunchtime came and went, he ate a sandwich at his desk and plied himself with coffee. Amy Trimboli fed him updates as they filtered through. More interviews with hotel guests. A woman from Adelaide, in town for the pharmaceuticals conference, had finally made contact, having been on the road pretty much since the murder of Chris White.

'Her husband reckons she's at some kind of conference or junket every other week. Nice work if you can get it,' said Amy.

'Anything of interest?'

'She slept like a baby, she reckons. Heard and saw nothing.'

'Tick her off, file her away,' said Cato.

Pharmaceuticals. A recurrent theme. Society pill-popping its way to oblivion. He opened up Thornton's résumé of the factory fire. Photos of the crime scene, description of the property, fire investigator's report, detectives' reports, post-mortems. The factory — long abandoned, asbestos ridden, graffiti and rubbish strewn — had become home to three men, ages ranging from twenty-ish to sixty-ish. All that remained of them was charred meat. Dental records and other clues gave them names and a history with police, welfare and charity groups. The factory site was part of a larger block of land adjoining the railway line between City West and Perth Central and slated for redevelopment. The developer, a controversial figure with links to organised crime and bikie groups, had been caught up in a long-running feud with rivals and ex-business partners which involved tit-for-tat arson attacks on each others' cars and properties. This factory fire seemed to bring the feud to an end and the development finally went ahead. The homeless victims were seen as collateral damage. According to the file, Gangs — the Organised Crime squad — had taken an interest for a while but didn't pursue the matter once the skirmishes settled down.

Cato made some more notes and dashed off some follow-up queries for Thornton. The detail. It was in there somewhere.

By the end of the afternoon, Sharon had managed to grab a power nap and, with a giggling, playful Ella tugging at her hair, she felt refreshed and even able to compliment Nat on his progress with the painting.

'It's great, the "Y"'s gone.' She handed him a mug of coffee and settled on the front verandah couch while Nat leaned against the porch upright.

'The what?' said Nat.

'The "Y". The graffiti.' Sharon found herself unaccountably blushing.

He took a sip, eyes dancing with amusement. 'Right. No worries.'

'How long have you been doing this, the painting?' Honestly, at times she felt like she was sixteen. For fuck's sake.

'Not long. A year or so.'

His singlet was damp with perspiration, she was aware of his hard nipples pushing against the fabric. Aware of her own, tender, bursting with milk. She focused on Ella. 'So it's the front fence and porch tomorrow. Right?'

'Right.'

'Steve said you'll be here earlier. Any idea what time?'

Nat shrugged. 'Seven-ish maybe? Okay with you?'

'Sure.'

'Husband an early riser is he?'

'It varies.' She gave Ella a peck on the brow. 'Either way, *she* sets the timetable these days.'

'I bet.' He cricked his neck, boxer style. 'Must drive you nuts sometimes. Just you and the bub, baby talk and that.' He lifted his mug in salutation. 'Take my hat off to you.'

'I'm happy enough.' She didn't mean it to sound defensive.

'Yeah, I can see that.' Nat drained his coffee and put the mug back on the tray. 'Thanks for this.'

'No problem. Tomorrow then.'

He hoisted his backpack and jangled his car keys. 'See you.' The broad shoulders and tight bum danced down the steps to the front gate.

Sharon hugged Ella closer, whispering into her ear. 'Mummy's going ga-ga.'


Jake was glad he didn't have to go home. Home being where Mum lived, where he'd spent most of his life. She would be there cooing at the twins and trying to seem interested in his day. Simon would fix that false smile on his face and say 'Hey dude' and disappear into his 'studio' to play his fucking banjo. There was another letter from school that would have arrived by now: 'Jacob is distracting his fellow students and can't be arsed to do his human biol homework'. And Steph had been told to keep away from him. Bad influence, his parents reckoned. What a joke, he thought, it's your darling boy who raids your wallet for his coke habit. But Steph was always good at playing the game, saying what he knew they wanted to hear. Jake? He could never keep up the act for long, it made his face ache, made him want to punch the wall. So he was running out of mates, running out of chances at school, running out of places he felt ... what? At home in?

Would he ever feel like calling Dad's place 'home'? This morning he was gone before Jake got out of bed. Sharon had tried to be nice but that was just it: she had to try. She'd even offered to make him a packed lunch for school. Seriously. He'd ducked out the side gate while the painters were having a smoko. Ghosted out without anybody noticing him. He was getting good at that. No, he couldn't go home and face Sharon and Ella just yet: they were just another reminder that he no longer belonged anywhere. Better to get back later when Dad would be around and trade lame jokes about nothing much. Jake's eyes blurred. None of them knew him, knew the real him. Maybe he should go to the gym. Lift some metal. Talk to Lance. Lance was a laugh but shit, he scared him too. That interrogation about Dad, intense but.

*You're not going to take control over your own life until you wrest it from others.*

Wrest. Like something from *Game of Thrones*. He'd looked it up, it meant 'take by force'. Where did Lance get to hear words like that? But he was right. Dad was the key to what he was feeling. Mum and Simon and the twins didn't really come into it. Dad was the one who'd walked out on him, obsessed by that fucking job. Dad who'd come back into his life a few years ago and wanted to play happy families. Sucked in. Dad who'd walked out on him a second time with Shanghai Sharon and was too busy with his new baby now. Dad who'd given him this fucking stupid munted Chinese face and Frankenstein scar. Dad, desperate to believe everything was fine with his darling boy, needing reassurance like he was the one who was the kid. So why move in with him? One last chance, thought Jake. One last chance to prove yourself. See if you can work out the mystery of your son.

*You can do it, Jakey-boy. You can lift those big weights. You're in charge.*

Lance. What a laugh. Like one of those self-help gurus. But ripped.

Jake checked his phone. This time of day the gym would be quiet. No contest. A text came through.

**Hey faggot come and help me get hard**

Jake grinned. Speak of the devil.


Norman Lip wasn't going to give up that easily. He'd put himself on the line for this scoop. Now he'd stepped over it and there was no going back. He was the one who'd had the initiative, the sheer audacity, to make direct contact with the killer. The cops — what were they doing?

Having a bowl of soup down at the cafe and filling out the crossword, that's what. In situations like this you can choose to crash and burn, or to crash through. So the cops had his phone and his laptop and his iPad, but he'd backed everything up in the cloud and on a thumb drive. Half an hour in the Apple shop had replaced the hardware. And he had the ace up his sleeve — or was it a jack?

He swiped his thumb through Tinder until he found her, the persona the killer had created — Jacqui, twenty-one, commerce student and fitness trainer, Belmont. Pouting selfie and pushed-up tits. Big-eyed blonde. Just his type.

*Can we meet?*

Jacqui must have been waiting for his word.

*Pushy boy, how do I know you're not a pervert?*

*You don't.* A pause. The killer would know now not to use Norman's number or email any more. He would be appreciative. Norman wanted his quid pro quo. *Trust me.*

*I think I do. You've got kind eyes.*

Norman chuckled. The fucker was funny, and good at this. He played the Tinder Tease Bimbo perfectly. *So how about it? You know you want to.*

*Do you love me?*

*You know I do.*

*Prove it.*

*I already did.*

*I want more.*

Bitch. Norman was getting sick of being jerked around by people. Betsy. Detective Chow Mein. Now this. *Quid pro quo.*

*Oh I love French, such a romantic language.*

Norman laughed again, in spite of himself. Play the long game. *What do you want?*

*A token.*

*What kind?*

*A big one. A sacrifice.*

Cato's phone buzzed. He checked the time, just after midnight. It was Amy. 'Queensgate multistorey. Another rough-sleeper attack.'

'Dead?'

'No, but in a bad shape. Ambulance on its way.'

Cato was there in ten. The ambulance still hadn't arrived.

'Lot on,' said a uniform. 'Crash on the freeway, multiple casualties.' A crackle on his radio. 'ETA two minutes.'

Amy was crouched over a figure huddled in a shop doorway opposite the old police station. Another couple of uniforms in attendance. 'I can't believe this,' she muttered. 'A hospital just around the corner but nobody to help. Ridiculous.'

'They're coming,' said Cato. He edged closer. 'Bad?'

'Not as bad as we thought at first. Lot of blood but it seems superficial.' She shrugged. 'I'm no expert.'

'Details?'

'Name's Rob, said some bloke started attacking him for no reason.'

'How come you're here?'

'Out with friends. Saw the commotion and came over.' She registered his look as he caught a whiff of her breath. 'Two glasses of white wine. Don't worry, I'm still sober and able to do my job.'

The ambulance pulled up, and Amy and Cato stepped back as they got to work. A groan and some murmuring. The ambo turned his head to Amy. 'He said the bloke is still in there.'

'Who? Where?'

'Cunt that did this,' said Rob through smashed lips. 'He's in the car park.'

'How do you know?'

'I can see where the cars come out. Nothing came out yet.'

Cato got the attending officers to block the exit with their vehicles and summon reinforcements, including TRG. 'We need people on the pedestrian exits too. He might have already left by the one round the corner.'

'Doubt it,' said a uniform. 'We've had somebody on that since we arrived.' He radioed up and got it confirmed by his colleague.

'So let's go in,' said Cato.

Amy lifted her head. 'Shouldn't we wait?'

'I'll make a start, send the TRG in when they get here. There's too many ways for him to slip out, over roofs or whatever.'

'I'm coming too,' said Amy. She turned to the uniform. 'Wait here, we need all the exits covered.'

'Want this?' he offered his Glock to Amy. Along with his taser and capsicum spray.

'Thanks.' She shoved the spray in her jeans pocket, checked the gun, and gave him back the taser. 'Haven't got enough hands or big enough pockets. These should be enough.'

Cato had retrieved his own gun from the glove box in the Volvo along with a torch. 'Let's go.'

They took the lift to the top level, staying together, gradually working their way back down. Nothing on the top floor, or on the next one below. Winds eddied in the concrete battlements, cans rolled and fast-food wrappings skittered. There was salt in the air from the ocean breeze. They edged down the ramp to the next level. They could smell it now, smoke. Not from a cigarette, from a joint. A cough and a scrape, the hawking of phlegm. Cato and Amy readied their guns.

Over towards the far corner a blue haze roiled out of the open window of a black 4WD. Cato signalled for Amy to go around and approach from the other angle. A flurry of sparks as the joint was flicked out the window. The whirr as the window was rolled up. The engine purred into action and the car brake lights came on as it started to reverse out of the space. Cato ran forward, gun levelled.

'Stop. Police. Out of the car, now.'

Nothing. The car accelerated backwards, sending Amy sprawling. She yelped in pain. Cato fired two shots through the front passenger window, the one nearest him. Then two more in the front and back tyres on his side. The car screeched to a halt and the driver door opened.

'Fuck, man. Stop. Don't shoot!'

'Face down on the ground, now. Hands behind your head.'

He did as he was told. Amy limped into sight, and Cato was relieved to see she wasn't badly hurt. 'We forgot handcuffs.'

'I'll phone for backup,' said Amy. 'Meantime, he needs to be subdued.' She knelt down with her phone to her ear, summoning reinforcements while she emptied her capsicum spray into the prisoner's face. 'That's for running over my foot,' she said after wrapping up her call.

Cato recognised the prisoner now. He was one of Brian Knight's pool-playing young cronies, the one who'd blown Cato the kiss.

# 18

His name was Aaron Knight, he wasn't just a crony of Brian's, he was his son. Nineteen years old and lawyered up.

'Yep, that's him,' Rob had said. 'Just attacked me for no reason.'

It started well but began to fizzle out quite quickly.

'He wanted a smoke off me,' said Aaron, dabbing the remnants of the pepper spray from around his inflamed eyes. 'Wouldn't leave me alone. Whining loser, even grabbed my arm. Nobody does that.'

'And you beat the crap out of him for that?' said Cato.

'My client has explained his actions,' said 'Hooray' Henry Hurley QC. 'And he has confirmed his whereabouts for those other matters.' Matters meaning murders. 'All of them can be verified.' A shuffling of papers in preparation for leaving. 'And we will be filing a complaint over the excessive force used on my client.'

'What about my foot?' said Amy to Aaron. 'Aren't you going to say sorry?'

'Didn't see you. Shouldna crept up on me like that. Scared me.'

With no forensics and plenty of alibis keeping him out of the frame, they were obliged to release Aaron into the custody of his amused father. But they would be pressing assault charges for the injuries to Rob.

'Chip off the old block,' said Brian Knight, leading his son out the door. 'No patience for bludgers.'

Back to square one.

Cato had made it home just after four. A few hours later he'd woken up thinking about Tess Maguire and DI Hutchens. Not in a funny way. Both had said something recently, knowingly or unknowingly, that had briefly buzzed in his cortex like a mozzie on valium.

*So any ideas who's got it in for you?*

Join the queue, thought Cato. It was in the job description to piss people off and make enemies. But ninety-nine per cent of them were too drug-addled or stupid to ever follow through on their threats. This current targeting of him, using a journalist, was not your average junkie with a grudge. This required thought, tactics, people skills. It was a cut above. In some ways Cato would have preferred the wrong end of a baseball bat to this. In those few hours of sleep he'd tossed and turned in a half-sleeping, half-waking nether world where shadows threatened to disembowel him, oily hoods were dragged over his head, children laughed at his distress. Twice he'd woken with a start, unsure if he'd cried out or said something he shouldn't. At some point Sharon had gone to feed Ella and he found them both sound asleep on the couch in the lounge room.

'What's eating you?' she'd mumbled over the rim of her coffee mug, eyes still gummy with sleep.

'Work, as always.' He'd briefly related his midnight adventures in the car park but she didn't need the gory details, she had enough to contend with. He'd changed the subject. 'The painters made a good start.'

'Yeah.' A yawn. 'Figured I'd get on to Holloway today, see where I stand.' Holloway, her boss in the Australian Federal Police office in Perth. 'Maybe there's a desk job-share I can do, to ease myself back in.' She'd met his gaze. 'Also I could google nannies?'

'Good idea.'

But if it was such a good idea why did he feel this creeping sadness and dread? Maybe he too was just overtired. Their parting kiss that morning had felt perfunctory. A scene of domestic ennui as they went their separate ways for the day. So who could have it in for him and had the wherewithal to do something about it? Somebody who favoured the subtlety of manipulation and character assassination over the immediate satisfaction of a blunt instrument?

The only people who came to mind were either locked up or dead. Bikie gangs? Vietnamese drug lords? They didn't usually do subtle.

Amy Trimboli delivered a coffee to his desk. 'You look like you need this.'

'Cheers. How's the foot?'

'Good. No worries. You can get the next round in. I have it black with one.' She leaned against an adjacent desk. 'So are you looking at a permanent move over to Major Crime?'

Cato studied his laptop screen. 'Nothing's ever permanent.'

'You know what I mean. Paddy seems to be enjoying life in the slow lane and I don't think the boss is in a hurry to bring him back.'

'Slow lane?'

'Your old job.'

She had a way with words. 'Why do you ask?'

Amy nodded to herself. 'I reckon you'd be good in this gig. More brains and sensitivity, that's what we need. Not too much, just, you know.'

'I'll bear that in mind. Bit of grunt and testosterone now and then, you reckon? Within reason.'

'Yeah. Think you can manage it?'

'I'll give it my best shot.'

Another frown. 'So you are thinking of making it permanent?'

'That's known as entrapment. I can see you'll go far, Amy.'

A nod. 'Hurdles, glass ceilings and all,' she said.


Norman Lip had a meeting arranged with the council ranger, John Jenkins. He'd pitched the idea of an article entitled 'Primed Suspect' — how it feels to be unjustly targeted by the cops. 'Jacqui' reckoned Jenkins would be a good source of bile for another tilt at the cops. What are you playing at, Norman wondered. Is this personal or just another tactic? Anyway Ranger Jenkins had specified Hungry Jack's on the Strip. Classy guy.

'Fries with that?' Jenkins was smirking down at Norman's bacon and egg wrap. They'd just caught the last of the breakfast menu.

Norman stood and offered a hand for shaking. 'What can I get you?'

'Give it ten minutes and you can get me a Whopper meal if you like.' He slid into the booth, the furniture creaking in resistance. 'You wanted to talk.'

Norman once again outlined the theme of his next article for *New WAve*.

'"Primed Suspect". I like it.'

You would, thought Norman. It's all about you. They went through the story so far: the interviews with the police, the antipathy, the checking up on him behind his back, the smears and dobbings. The surveillance: it hadn't been hard to spot them hanging out in that car over the road all day.

'Amateurs! Don't think I don't know how to deal with dicks like that.'

'Really?' said Norman. 'How?'

A finger tap to the nose was the only reply.

Norman had dodged up to the counter in the midst of the whingeing and self-aggrandisement and brought the bastard his junk food.

'Even went down to Albany and talked to some bitter old bitch who used to teach me. Pathetic.' He shook his head and snatched at his bag of fries. 'Bothered my poor old dad in the nursing home. No shame.'

Norman oozed sympathy. 'Sounds personal, like a vendetta.'

'Fucking right. The Chink cop, Kwong. Took a dislike to me from day one and made his mind up.'

'Why the antipathy?'

'The what?'

'Why didn't he like you?'

A sneer. 'He's mates with one of the tramps. Must be one of his charity cases. Do-gooding loser.'

'Name? The tramp, I mean.'

'Barry. Noongar bloke. Fucking foul potty-mouth on him. Always in court for his bad language.'

Norman checked Jenkins for irony. No, not a trace of self-awareness about the miserable cunt.

'Sells the *Big Issue* to the bleeding hearts. Little bloke. Podgy.'

The session rambled on and finally Jenkins finished his meal and his rant. Norman grinned. 'Your shout next time. Maybe we can go to Maccas, make it a Happy Meal for a change.'

Jenkins didn't get it. 'So when are you printing it?'

'It's online actually. It'll probably go live at the end of the week. I've got your mobile, I'll let you know.'

'Cheers.' Jenkins glared at a couple of young blokes who seemed to know him and they avoided his gaze. Then he left and the place seemed momentarily brighter.

Norman had what he needed. Some bile to feed to the gorgeous monster known as Jacqui.

Cato looked hard at Chris Thornton's desktop screen. It was a frozen image from the camera keeping watch over the long-term bays where people parked before hopping on the Rottnest ferry for a few days on the island oasis that seemed increasingly the preserve of western suburb postcodes. Cato recalled overhearing a conversation outside the bakery there one day about the dearth of good wines in the supermarket bottle shop and he knew there and then that the people's paradise had lost its way.

According to the time code it was just after 10.30 p.m. About fifty metres off-screen Dean Pearson, victim number one, dead from multiple stab wounds, was about to be discovered by a security guard doing his rounds.

'I can't see our sedan anywhere,' said Cato. 'It's all 4WDs and Vote Green stickers.'

'Right enough, but check out the Landcruiser second from left.'

Cato saw it. A black one, not unlike Aaron Knight's. 'The number-plate is obscured, same fashion as our sedan, reflective sunnies style.'

'And here.' Thornton nudged the footage on a few minutes. 'See that?' He toggled it again, back and forth. A shadow in the car, moving. Getting comfortable. 'Coincidence?'

'Apparently the jury is still out on the science of Coincidence Denial. I like to keep an open mind.'

'And he likes to watch.'

'So do you it seems,' said Cato, taking in Thornton's bleary eyes.

The lad had been in since daybreak, fretting, obsessing. 'Once again, off to the techs. You need a break, Chris? A power nap?'

Thornton dug a can of Red Bull out of his drawer. 'I'll be good.'

'The locations,' said Cato. 'See a pattern?'

'Rough-sleeper pitches?' said Thornton.

Cato tapped the screen. 'Dean's surrounded by fancy four-wheel drives. Maureen was found adjacent to the sailing club. Rich and poor, haves and have-nots.'

'Where do the Esplanade and Rockingham victims fit into that?'

They didn't. Cato ceded the point, patted Thornton's shoulder and returned to his desk. While he'd been away, his phone registered two missed calls and an SMS. There was a hang-up message from Jake. Cato realised they had hardly spoken since the move into the granny flat: early starts and late finishes, and anything he had in reserve he gave to Sharon and Ella. A voice message from Sharon: could he bring some milk home with him. A sound in the background, radio playing and some male voices. A laugh. Finally, a text from an unknown number. He opened it. A photo taken from out on the street through the window of a restaurant: Cato and Tess Maguire, heads close, in intimate conversation across a dinner table in Albany. Another beep, incoming from the same number, Cato and Tess embracing outside the restaurant.

# 19

Sharon was enjoying the company. It was blokey talk, sure, and flirty but it was nice to be at the centre of some attention. Some different attention. Even Ella seemed to be enjoying herself. The house had a different energy with the young fellas chatting to her and each other effortlessly instead of through the fog of exhaustion and emotional baggage that enveloped her usual day. Ella was gurgling away and giving off her cheeky surprised smiles. For all Sharon knew, she was doing the same. It was like being slightly tipsy. Guilt-tinged tipsy. Her mobile buzzed. An SMS from a number she didn't recognise. She opened it. At first she couldn't make out what it was and she was ready to delete, assuming a wrong number or spam. Then she looked closer. Enlarged the screen with her fingertips. Yes, it was Phil. In a restaurant. With a woman. Not Sharon. There was even a helpful date and time stamp in the corner. Last Thursday night at 9.38 p.m. When he was in Albany. A second buzz, another incoming: Phil and the woman in an embrace. And an accompanying caption — *I'm sure he can explain this*.

'Are you okay?' It was Nat, prising a lid off a paint tin out on the patio.

No, I'm not okay. I'm scared and angry. 'Fine,' she said. She made the call.

'Yes?' Phil sounded distant. Busted.

'Tell me about Albany.'

'Albany?'

She turned away from the patio door, hissing into the phone. 'Tell me.'

A sigh. 'You got a photo sent to you?'

'Yes. Two of them.'

'I'll explain when I get home.'

'Now.'

'It's not what you think.'

'What am I thinking?'

'Sharon ...' Some shuffling, a hand covering the mouthpiece, muffled voices in the background. 'Something's come up. I need to deal with it. There's nothing to worry about, somebody is trying to stir things up. I'll tell you when I get home.'

'It better be good.' She severed the connection.


Cato looked at his phone: a lump of kryptonite in his hand, seeping poison into his life. Somebody was out to destroy him. Slowly. Eroding his sense of self and the people he held dear. He knew it now. This wouldn't end here. There would be a corrosive drip-feed of malice. Over and over.

'Sarge?' Amy Trimboli was jangling car keys in the air.

He gave her a nod, pocketed his phone and followed her out the door. Sonya from St Mary's had found them a known associate of Dean Pearson's. The bloke had made himself scarce, so scarce that people were wondering if he was dead somewhere. But now he was back.

'His name's Mac.'

'I know,' said Cato. 'He's on the Deano database with an urgent find note attached to him.'

Amy gave him a sideways glance. 'Right. Something troubling you, boss?'

'No.' He sighed. 'What's the urgency? Why do we need to rush down there?'

'Sonya's not sure how long she can persuade him to hang around.'

'Send some uniforms to arrest him.'

Amy snapped out a laugh. 'Sorry. It's just, I don't expect that kind of talk from you, Sarge.'

'So. The urgency?'

'Sonya said it would be really worth your while. But she wouldn't say why.'

Sonya and Mac were waiting for them in a private room at St Mary's. Mac looked somewhere in his early to mid sixties. Grizzly as. His real name was Graham McDonald according to Sonya but he'd been dubbed

Mac due to his country of origin and his almost impenetrable Scottish accent, even though he'd been here forty-odd years.

Cato offered a hand. 'Thanks for making time.'

'Where've you been?' said Amy, not offering hers.

Mac looked at her like she was an exotic and possibly dangerous species. 'Who's yer pal?' he said to Cato.

'Amy,' said Cato. 'Say hello to Mac, Amy.'

'Hello, Mac,' said Amy.

'All the same,' said Cato. 'Where *have* you been?'

'Around and about.'

'Specifically?'

'Kununurra.'

'That's a long way.'

'Top of the fuckin' state. Wasn't going to hang around here, was I?'

'Why not?'

'With that mad bastard on the loose, after what he did to Deano?'

'Which mad bastard?'

'Fuckin' Jackboot Johnny.'

'He's been eliminated from our enquiries. He's got an alibi.'

'Really?' said Mac and Sonya together.

Amy gave Cato a funny look. He'd given away more information than he should have. Thing is, he knew that, and didn't give a stuff. 'Yep.' He cast a warning glance Sonya's way. 'So, right now I can't be arsed to pursue your Jenkins vendetta. Amy here will be happy to take a full statement from you, Mr McDonald. We'll take you back to the station now.'

'No way. You don't get me in those places.'

A warning growl from Cato. 'I can arrest you for hindering an investigation.'

'Filth, you're all the same. Just stormtroopers for the evil bastards running this country. Sorry I'm no' agile and innovative enough to prosper in yer brave new world but some fuckin' accountant wrote me out of my job fifteen years ago and the computer won't give me a pension cause I keep on giving it the wrong answers. Now I'm what you might call a self-funded retiree.' He reached down for his backpack.

Cato assumed the bloke was about to do a runner. He didn't

want to arrest him but he wasn't in the mood to calm things down. He cast a glance at Amy, they both knew what was coming.

'For goodness sake,' said Sonya. 'Mac, give it to him.'

'That's what I'm doin', ya bunch of dozy bastards.' He pulled a battered, dog-eared notebook out of his backpack and tossed it on the desk. 'Deano's notebook. He gave it to me for safekeeping. The afternoon just before he died. Total rubbish if you ask me, mad as a James Joyce novel.' He snorted. 'Aye, us working classes can read impenetrable claptrap too.' A tear leaked from the bloodshot eyes. 'You're still not getting me in that fuckin' cop shop.'

Cato used a pen to edge the book closer while Amy dug out some rubber gloves. 'I think we can work something out, mate.'

Norman found Barry Potty-mouth by midafternoon. He was sitting on a bench under the olive trees outside Gino's. Norman slid in beside him.

'Who are you?' said Barry, pleased to have the company.

'Norman.'

'Got a job?'

'Yeah, I'm a … writer.' It sounded less threatening than reporter. Or so he hoped.

'Another one?' said Barry. 'Fucking heaps of the bastards up and down here. Drink coffee all day long and talk about themselves non-stop. Never see them writing though.'

'Probably doing research, or having meetings.'

'Yeah, must be.' Barry looked at him. 'Run out of money for your coffee, have you? Don't ask me, I'm skint.'

'Actually,' said Norman 'I was going to offer to buy you one.'

Barry shook his head. 'Hate the stuff. Makes me teeth brown and smells like the hostel on a hot day.'

'Tea?'

'Now you're talking.' He stood up and shuffled over to an outside table at the cafe. 'Research is it?'

'Yep.'

'So the poncy waiters can't tell me to fuck off then, can they?'

'That's right,' said Norman.

'Sweet. Earl Grey, please. And one of those Florentines while you're at it.'

Cato made it home by late afternoon. He'd left it to Amy to take a statement from Mac and arrange for the diary to be copied over at forensics. He should have been excited by the development. Instead, all he could think about was Sharon, that photo, and the cracks opening up in their relationship. They were already there, he knew it now, before the external pressure began to be applied.

'Who is she?' Sharon was sitting at the kitchen table, nursing Ella. The painters had gone and Jake wasn't home yet.

'Tess Maguire. She's in the Job. We worked a case on the south coast a few years ago.'

'Looked her up, did you? Trip down memory lane?'

'No. It was a chance meeting. I was in a coffee shop earlier in the day, she walked by.'

Sharon prodded the phone, photo on display. 'Looks like you two get on well.'

'We do. Did. We used to be an item, a long time ago.'

She looked at him. Twisted the phone around and used her fingers to zoom the photo. 'Really?' She smiled, tears pricking her eyes. 'Did you fuck her while you were down there? Old times' sake?'

'No.'

She switched Ella to the other breast. 'Did you want to?'

'No.' He reached out a hand across the table but she withdrew hers. 'I wouldn't. You are all I want.'

'You look happy, the two of you. Maybe you should get back together.'

'Sharon.'

'You fucking prick. Out on a romantic dinner with your ex, while I'm stuck here like Mrs Shit-for-Brains playing wifey and milking machine. How did that happen? How did my life end up like this?'

'I'm sorry.'

'What for?'

'That you're so ... unhappy.'

'Unhappy? I'm trying not to be, Phil.' Her voice cracked. 'I'm trying really hard.' She flicked the phone towards the centre of the table. 'And now this.'

'Nothing happened, Sharon. Believe me. I love you, I love Ella. I wouldn't do anything to risk that.'

'Yeah?' She shook her head. 'Who sent this? Who's trying to stir us up?'

'I don't know.'

Ella was asleep in her arms. 'Find the bastard and do something about it.' Sharon stood and padded out towards the bedroom. 'But make us all some dinner first.'


Jake was on his way out of the gym when Lance caught up with him.

'Need a lift, Jakey?'

'Nah, the bus'll be here soon.'

'Buses are for losers.' He zapped the locks on a white ute. 'Hop in.'

Jake slung his bag in the footwell and slid in. 'Nice. Yours?'

'No, it's my girlfriend's. My little yellow Clio's in at the mechanic's.'

'Jerk.' Jake grinned. 'I hate the early evening sesh in there. Can't move for lardarses.'

Lance put the ute into gear and gunned out of the parking bay. He squeezed Jake's thigh, left his hand resting there. 'Where to?' Jake gave him his dad's address in White Gum Valley. 'I thought you lived in East Fremantle?'

Jake explained about moving from his mum's place to his dad's.

'Staying there long?'

'Don't know.'

'So you've made it up with Daddy, then?'

'Never really fell out. We don't talk enough to fall out.'

'Letting things fester. That's the spirit.'

Lance's hand still hadn't moved. Jake shifted in his seat. 'Where do you live?'

The hand lifted back to the wheel, a smile on Lance's face. 'Got a place over in Spearwood. Share with some Filipino bloke who's always out working long hours for shit money. Suits me. Place of my own most of the time but he pays half. Sweet as.'

'What's your job?' asked Jake.

'This and that. Bouncer work, mainly.' He lifted a bicep and kissed it. 'Hired muscle.'

Jake laughed. 'Keep busy?'

'Yeah, yeah. Flat out.' They pulled up in a quiet, dark street. 'This yours?'

Lights on. Both cars in the driveway. Dad home early for a change. 'Yep, home sweet home.'

'See you, Jakey-boy. Make sure you get your homework done.'

'Fuck off.'

'Now, now.' He waggled a finger at the house and put on an admonishing adult's voice. 'You shouldn't take this stuff for granted, sonny. You'll miss it when it's gone.'


Cato had just finished loading the dishwasher when Jake walked in. Sharon was getting Ella down to sleep. The chores were a good distraction from their shared misery. Cato mustered a smile for his son.

'Had a good day?'

'Yeah, s'pose so. You?'

'Yeah, the usual, psychos and that.'

'Sharon and Ella?'

'Down the hall, getting ready for bed. You eaten?'

Jake hadn't. Cato emptied some leftovers from a container onto a plate and put it in the microwave.

'I could've done that,' said Jake. 'Thanks.'

'No worries.'

A muffled goodnight from Sharon down the hall.

'Everything okay?' said Jake in a near whisper.

'Yep.'

'If it's a problem, me being here, I can go back to Mum's.'

'No problem, mate. It's all good.'

Jake shook his head. 'Doesn't seem like it.'

'Not everything is about you, mate.'

Jake looked stung. The microwave dinged and he went to empty it.

'You'll need this.' Cato handed him a tea towel. 'Hot plate.'

'Thanks.'

A sigh. Sharon. Jake. They all needed him and he was letting them down — bringing his work home across the threshold. History repeating itself. 'Sorry, things are a bit mad right now.'

Jake blew on his hot food. Ate a forkful. Didn't meet Cato's eye. 'No worries.'

# 20

Cato hadn't slept well, again. He and Sharon had eaten a wordless dinner, busied themselves with chores, made lists for the following day and retired to bed, turning away from each other and hugging the edge. Add that to the tense exchange with Jake, and Cato was miserable as hell. Over breakfast there'd been the hint of a thaw.

'If there is someone out to destroy us we're going to have to stay strong.' Sharon wiped some toast crumbs from her lips. Ella was rolling around on the rug, getting ready to crawl, fascinated by a saucepan lid. 'You need to find out who it is and why they're doing it. Stop them.'

'I'll try.'

'Can we trace the number that sent it?'

'So far it's our private business, not a criminal enquiry.'

'Private?' she snorted. A warning glance. 'No more secrets, no more surprises.'

'Right.' He was clearing the kitchen table, acting like everything was normal. 'What have you got on today?'

'Painters. Ella. And a Skype call with Holloway. There could be an opening from January.'

'Really?'

'Long service leave, fill in. Intelligence analyst desk job.'

'Great.'

'And I'll be inviting a few possible nannies around for a chat. Do you want to be in on that?'

He'd smiled. 'I trust you.'

'There's a difference between trusting someone and taking them for granted.'

It would be a slow thaw.

Cato headed out to work, leaving Sharon to her TO DO lists. At the office he opened up his emails — mainly circulars, stats requests and meeting reminders. But there was also a scanned copy of Deano's notebook awaiting his attention, along with an analysis of Norman Lip's telecommunications and internet habits. On balance, Cato thought the journal might be a more illuminating and uplifting read. It didn't look promising though: pages and pages of childish Pokémon-style drawings of dragons and monsters, interspersed with prose, some lucid, lots not, some with a designated date, some just large scrawled capitals — LEAVE ME ALONE! He went straight to the last dated entry. The morning of the day of Dean's murder.

*Got an hour outside Katmandu before JJ turned up. I hate him — brain of a dog turd + thinks the uniform saves his miserable life. Jerk. Collected $12-60 + having a Whoppa at HJs — right now! Mac gets the rest cos I still owe him. So where to tonight? Esplanade? Duxton? Home with Daddy + new Mummy whose young enough to be my sister? No, I need to sleep somewhere quiet. Not easy when all the noise is in my head.*

Drawings: a burger, a figure sleeping peacefully with a smile on his face and ZZZs coming out of his head. Cato tried to ignore the tightness in his chest. It was not hard to imagine these could be Jake's words and pictures. He skipped a few pages to the next coherent entry.

*The pills don't help. If I'm not zonked out I'm freaked out. Am I being followed? Who wants to stalk a loser like me? JJ? Sad barstad but I'd know if it was him. Wouldn't I?*

So Deano had been rattled about something, someone. More drawings. Shadows and silhouettes against buildings. Cato flicked back to the beginning. The first entry back in late summer. Had there been another diary or journal before this? It seemed not. Early days and Dean still more or less compos mentis before the medication kicked in.

*Happy New Year! My first resolution is off to a flying start and Dear Diary it's you! Deano's Dero Memoirs. A Tale of Two Cities — my Freo and everyone else's. Dero Freo — I like that. Maybe it'll make me famous, be a best seller, a movie, and I get to live in a mansion by the beach. I woke up with that same ocean view this morning but those dicks in the South Beach apartmts paid over a million for theirs. Open my eyes and there's some mongrel taking a dump about a metre from my head. Rank. Did the owner come over with a yellow bag and pick it up? Fuck no, it's only my bedroom. Then she wanders over to the kiosk where dogs are welcome and there's a bowl of water waiting for Stinkyarse and the punters look at me like I'm the one that just pissed on their leg.*

Cato was interrupted by a cough from Amy Trimboli. 'I sent the transcript and video file of Mac's interview through to you. Did you get it?'

He closed the diary screen and opened his inbox. 'Yep. It's there.'

'Something came up. I asked him who else, apart from the ranger Jenkins, had been around acting strange or whatever.'

'And?'

'He mentioned a car cruising the area in the days before Dean died.'

'What kind?'

'A fooking Toorak tractor, he called it.'

'That was the worst Scottish accent I've ever heard. Don't give up the day job. Get Chris Thornton onto it, he's got a car thing running and he needs to know.'

'Will do.' She turned away. 'The boss called. She wants you to ring her.'

'What about?'

'I don't know.'

He rang Pavlou.

'I've had a complaint about you.'

'Who? What about?'

'Bill Jenkins. And he's brought in some heavy weights up the food chain. He reckons you're a bully.'

This from a man who arranged to have him beaten up in a noodle house. 'And?'

'I've got bigger friends even further up the food chain. I'll sort it. But watch your back, okay?'

'Okay.'

Maybe Pavlou as a boss wouldn't be the worst thing in the world. Was Bill Jenkins behind the photo of him and Tess? Possibly. If so, how did he get hold of his and Sharon's private numbers? Not beyond the capabilities of an ex-cop with connections. But a beating, and now this? It was an overreaction to Cato's enquiries. Was the person behind the photo the same one driving the character assassination of Cato via Norman Lip's articles? What on earth connected Lip and Jenkins? Whatever it was that Jenkins wanted to keep a lid on, Cato was now even more determined to lift it.


Sharon had been feeling penned in all morning. She'd left Nat and his mate to get on with the job and strapped Ella into the baby capsule in the car.

'Out for long?' Nat wanted to know.

What the fuck is it to you? 'No. Why?'

He shrugged. 'Just asking.'

She gave him an answer in spite of herself. 'A couple of hours.'

She'd driven out to the end of South Mole and sat looking out to sea while Ella snored softly in the back. She'd fought the urge to cry, breathing deeply to steady herself. It was a panicked, claustrophobic feeling: chest tight, searching for air. Phil wasn't having an affair, or even a fling, she believed that. But he wasn't sharing that happiness he had in the photo with her. Where had the fun gone? The life? The energy? She glanced in the rear-view at Ella. Did you suck it up, all eight kilos of you? She'd shopped, roaming the aisles of the IGA in a daze, buying some items she didn't really need. Mumnesia or disintegrating marriage? On her return she found Nat painting exterior window frames and his colleague scraping down the side gate.

'Need a hand with those shopping bags?' said Nat.

'Thanks.' Going up the steps into the house with a sleepy Ella in her arms she caught a leer pass between Nat and his mate. Pathetic. 'Just put them in the kitchen,' she said. 'I'll sort it once I've put her down.'

'No worries.'

She lowered Ella into the cot and sat nearby in the nursing chair waiting for her to fully drop off.

There was a crash from the kitchen: breaking glass or crockery. Ella woke up and began mewling. Sharon felt like doing the same. She went out to see what had happened. Nat was on all fours picking shards of glass from a slop of marmalade. Why had she bought that? She hated fucking marmalade. He looked up. 'Sorry.'

'Leave it,' she said. She grabbed the dustpan and brush and took over. Nat stood aside as she crouched down. 'I'll take care of this if you want to get back to what you were doing.'

'The baby's crying,' Nat said.

'I know, I can hear it.'

'Maybe ...'

'Maybe mind your own business, okay?'

'Sure,' he muttered, walking away. Under his breath she clearly heard the word: bitch.

'What did you say?'

'Switch. I was talking to Davo. Time to switch jobs.'

'I don't think so.'

He turned. Open-handed, non-confrontational. 'I'll leave you to it, then.'

Sharon let it go. Ella was bellowing, there were bigger fish to fry.

Norman Lip's phone and browsing history showed no apparent direct connection between him and Bill Jenkins, but as recently as yesterday, according to his online diary, Lip had met Jenkins Junior, the ranger, at Hungry Jack's for about an hour. Given that he was writing about the murders, then it wasn't beyond reason that he would want to talk to the man who, until recently, had been the prime suspect. Was there more to it than that? Pavlou had said watch your back. But this seeming vendetta wasn't tangible enough to warrant official enquiry. Cato would be obliged to watch his back on his own time, for now.

The telecommunications profile also gave Cato his first chuckle of the day. There was the expected: news websites, a lot of Twitter. Lip even followed the Fremantle Police tweets, DI Hutchens would be happy. He liked music, movies and food — he was a hipster after all, and he followed the soccer Bundesliga in Germany. He was also an avid, in fact downright promiscuous, user of the dating site Tinder. But what really tickled Cato was that Norman took himself very seriously and had aspirations towards the high arts. He regularly dropped in on publisher submission pages, latest news, contacts and the opportunities sections of writing agency websites, and made regular 'How to Write' purchases from online booksellers in addition to classic novels. It looked like he was really into Hemingway and Orwell at the moment, mixed in with some Hunter S. Thompson. Lip wanted to make his mark, to go down in history as a man of his times. Fair enough, thought Cato, it's nice to aim high. Lip could have taken the shortcut to immortality and auditioned for a reality TV dating or cooking show. Maybe there was hope for him yet.

His phone buzzed. Cato reached for it, but it wasn't his that was ringing. At the same time a tech from Computer Crime, the people monitoring the communications, came through his door. They'd set up an outpost in Fremantle with a direct feed to the nerve centre in Perth. She nodded towards the other phone dancing on Cato's desk, Norman Lip's hotline to the killer. An SMS had come in. Cato opened it.

*Sorry, I missed you.*

By four days? Cato texted back. *No probs. Like the article?*

*Yes, thanks.*

So what now, genius?

'Keep talking,' said the tech, whose lanyard read Imogen. 'We need to get a fix on him.'

*What now?* texted Cato, in the absence of inspiration.

'He's gone,' said Imogen. 'Battery and SIM card out.' She studied her portable screen a moment longer. 'The signal came from White Gum Valley. South Street area.'

They could send some patrol units up there for a look and a drive-by but Cato knew it would be a waste of time. A doorknock? Excuse me, madam, did you notice a bloke on a phone near here about ten minutes ago? Cato couldn't dismiss it, killers had been caught on the basis of less. He put out the call for a drive-by patrol.

The hotline buzzed once more. A different caller.

*I'll be in touch sooner than you think.*

And then he was gone again.

At the end of the day Pavlou called another case conference. Duncan Goldflam had nothing new to report, his forensic flotsam and jetsam was still being analysed. Deb Hassan had provided a summary of doorknock and canvassing interviews, and all guests at the Esplanade had now been tracked and provided absolutely nothing of value. Chris Thornton had gone home sick late in the afternoon. Exhausted and run-down, Cato surmised. So he summed up recent developments: cars with obscured regos parked near to the murder scenes, Dean's diary and the brief contact with the killer.

*I'll be in touch sooner than you think.*

'Sounds like a threat to me,' said Pavlou.

That had been Cato's thinking too. 'Lining up number five?'

'But there's no more jacks left,' said Hutchens.

'Maybe their only purpose was to let us know early on that this was a serial.' Amy Trimboli wiped her glasses on the bottom of her shirt.

'What makes you say that, Amy?' Pavlou obviously liked the idea. Cato found himself feeling slightly miffed, like he'd bought into the rivalry.

Amy shrugged. 'Just a thought.'

Something else occurred to Cato. It had pricked him while he was reviewing the case notes but he hadn't grasped what it was. Now he saw it. 'He's building to something.'

'Explain,' said Pavlou.

Cato stood by the whiteboard, tapping the photos in turn. 'Murder one, the victim is lying down, probably asleep, and stabbed before he wakes. Through the sleeping bag at first. Number two, he shares a goonie with her in the bus shelter before killing her. More risky, she's alert, albeit pissed, there's likely to be passing traffic. He's testing his nerve. Number three he takes on someone as big and tough as himself, if not more so. But most likely asleep at the time, zonked out on medication. Number four, early evening with the hubby only a hundred metres away on the jetty.'

'He's using them as practice?' Pavlou seemed unconvinced.

Cato lifted his shoulders. 'He might still have a thing about homeless people and that should remain the focus of our efforts. But ...'

'If he's building to something, it would have to be pretty bad,' said Hutchens.

Pavlou tapped her chin with the whiteboard marker. 'He definitely wants to be caught, doesn't he? It's just a matter of when. He wants the world to know about him and what he's done.'

'Hope you're right,' said Hutchens.

'Maybe we should bring people in off the streets, as a precaution?' said Cato.

'How many's that — one hundred, two hundred, three?' said Pavlou. 'And there's the people camping in their cars. And the people in temporary accommodation, hostels or what have you, that might want to go out for a walk.'

'Or broadcast an alert, something, anything.' Cato knew what was coming.

Nothing.

'Raise the threat from yellow to red you mean?' said Pavlou, almost with pity.

'If there was an imminent terror attack we would, wouldn't we?'

'Exactly, and in both cases it would be just as meaningless until the deed was done.' Pavlou relented. 'I suppose we could put the word around the agencies, heightened vigilance, keep loved ones close, keep the doors open, et cetera.'

Cato knew it would have to do. The meeting wound up and they headed home for the day. Cato felt a hand on his shoulder.

'You can't save them all, mate.' It was Hutchens. He seemed increasingly to Cato like the spare bolt left over after the IKEA shelves have been put together. Probably had a purpose but the shelves still functioned pretty well without it.

'How's the retirement plans?'

'Taking shape. Marj is looking at either a cruise down the Rhine or a fortnight in Fiji.'

'You invited?'

'Yep. On balance I think I prefer Fiji. Trouble with cruises is, if you don't like the company, you're fucking trapped with the bastards.'

Cato nodded glumly. 'Bit like the office really.'


En route home Cato remembered the missed call from Jake — this morning? Yesterday? He'd seen him since, surely? That disastrous encounter in the kitchen. He returned the call anyway.

'Yeah?'

'You rang.'

'That was yesterday.'

'Sorry, been busy.' Cato tried to stay bright, to counterbalance the low energy he perceived in his son's voice. 'Anything special?'

'Nah.'

'I'm sorry I was a bit grumpy last night. Work and stuff. Everything okay?'

'Yep, you said that at the time.'

'Jake, if you want to talk about something let's talk. I'm not a mind-reader. It doesn't have to be now, it can be whenever you like. But I haven't got the time or energy for guessing games.'

'Make an appointment, you mean?'

'Jake.'

'Forget it.'

Jake hung up. Cato chucked the phone on the passenger seat and pulled into his driveway. Steeled himself for more happy families inside.

That evening after Jake came home, he stayed in the granny flat while Cato and Sharon circled each other warily, shielded by chores and Ella. If anything, Sharon seemed even more on edge.

'How'd it go with Holloway?' asked Cato.

The Skype call had been late that afternoon after the painters left. 'Good. I can start back in the New Year and work four half-days and a full on Wednesdays.'

'Wednesdays?'

'Favourite day for meetings and bringing cake in.' She bit her lip and looked away. 'I think I've found a nanny. Good references. Julie. She's a Pom but she seems nice enough all the same.'

'Great,' said Cato.

'I'll get her over to meet Ella in the next day or two. See how they get on.'

'Good idea. How old is she?'

'Strange question.'

'Just wondering, I don't know, whatever.' Every word seemed potentially a booby trap.

'Thirtyish.' A smile twisted her lips. 'Not your type.'

'What's my type?' He tried a twinkle in return.

'Me. And don't forget it.'

'I won't.' He changed the subject while it was still on safer ground. 'The painters seem to be doing a good job.'

'Yeah, but there's one that gives me the shits.'

'What way?'

'It's like he thinks he lives here. Overfamiliar, personal comments. Stuff like that. Fancies himself.'

'You're blushing.'

'He's got a nice bod. I'd probably have ravished him by now if he wasn't such a creep.'

'Thank God he's a creep.'

'Jealous?'

'Yes.'

'Good.' Sharon scrabbled around, searching for something in her wallet. 'Julie's phone number, I must have left it in the car.' She went to get it and Cato busied himself with Ella's full and disgusting nappy. 'Shit,' she said on her return.

Cato couldn't have put it better himself. 'What's up?'

'Some bastard's taken a key to the side of my car. Scratch from one end to the other.'

'Insurance'll cover it. Worse things happen at sea.' He surveyed the contents of the nappy. 'Or perhaps not.'

# 21

*A sad story, that woman by the beach. I suppose they all are. But it's like the government says, there's two kinds of people in this world — lifters and leaners. My old man had no time for all that weepy-weepy do-gooder shit. I've been there, lived cheek by jowl with the stinking, whining, useless, weak bastards. One morning in Forrest Square I was dozing in a shop doorway when suddenly I'm soaking all over. Piss? No, a hosepipe. A cleaning contractor, and two cops laughing behind him.*

*'Sorry, mate,' he said. 'Didn't see you there.'*

*The cops' hands are on their tasers, ready to rock and roll.*

*I grin. 'Not a problem. I needed a wash. Have a good day.'*

*I found the cleaner a few days later, on his own this time, and kicked him into a coma. I heard he came out of it but he doesn't walk or talk too good any more.*

*You're thinking, why do I pick on them if I've lived that life?*

*Who says it's about revenge? Maybe it's about mercy.*

*Fuck knows. And who cares? Society doesn't, obviously. What you never had, you never miss. Everywhere people are dying horrible deaths every day. Heads chopped off by crazies in Iraq and Syria. Washed away by big waves. Big-eyed babies starving in some tent in Africa. Thousands. Day in, day out. Flies on the windscreen, that's all we are. But flies who worry about what's round the corner, thinking we can dodge it. Taking pills to help us live long enough to get demented. And still we end up as dust. All of us. The best you can do is kick a few goals, my old man would say. Enjoy the game. Maybe get a few good hits in first before they bring you down.*

*Or give yourself a project.*

*And I can see him now. My new project. Pushing his trolley up the cereal aisle to get his Rice Bubbles. Wittering away in a world of his own. The hostel is just around the corner, maybe five minutes walk. I've already traced the route. Now I'm mapping the routine. He's regular as clockwork: dinner on the dot at six before a little wander across the park to the groyne at South Beach to see what's biting tonight. They seem to know him. Share a joke. Same one every time, I bet. Routines are good. We all need that sense of the familiar so we can feel safe and secure.*

# 22

Norman Lip woke with a bad feeling. He'd got to sleep late after filing his 'Primed Suspect' piece for Betsy and the lawyer to check. He'd worked miracles turning that miserable bully Jenkins into a victim.

*John Jenkins understands life as a battler. His widowed father is confined to a wheelchair in a nursing home in Albany. Ravaged by a stroke after many years of service to the community, the retired police officer is a continuing source of pride and inspiration to his son.*

*'My old man taught me the difference between right and wrong and it's something I carry with me every day.'*

*As a Community Safety Officer in Fremantle, Jenkins is at the sharp end of the homelessness crisis besetting the port city, and understands all too well the vulnerability of people who have slipped through society's safety net.*

*'We're failing as a society if we can't look after and protect those most in need.'*

*But now he finds himself the subject of baseless allegations manufactured by investigators from Task Force Hermes, principally Detective Sergeant Philip Kwong. Jenkins is shocked and hurt to have been named as a suspect in the horrific serial killings.*

*'It's outrageous. It's like there's a personal vendetta against me and all I want is to try and do the best job I can.'*

*But this isn't the first time that Sergeant Kwong has been connected with manufacturing evidence against innocent citizens ...*

Betsy had loved the backstory on the cop, kicked into Stock Squad for framing some poor bastard ten years ago. She'd sent Norman a text at 3.00 a.m.

*Ripper, mate. Beauty!*

She must be doing an Ocker Conversation class at TAFE. Anyway it would be going live later today once Carmen the Lawyer had okayed it. So why the bad feeling? Despite several attempts to chat on Tinder, Jacqui was ignoring him. The quid pro quo just wasn't happening. All take, no give. Norman decided it was time to start playing hardball.

*Hey J, time we got together*

Nothing.

*A boy can only be patient for so long :(*

Zip.

*Sigh, looks like I'll have to find someone who really appreciates me :(*

Dots. Jacqui typing a reply. *Thought u were my BFF?*

*QPQ*

*????*

*What do I get?*

*Whole lotta love xxx*

*Not enough, need facetime*

*I'm shy*

Norman rolled his eyes. *Time & place or I swipe left*

The dots again. Thinking time. Did Norman imagine it or did those thinking dots seem angry?

*Give me your address*

Norman had the feeling Jacqui already knew where he lived but, for the purposes of a possibly monitored conversation, he gave it again.

*Look 4wd to it, what time?*

*Don't fret bad boy, L8r :)*

Norman felt better. He'd taken the initiative, turned the game around and made it his. Time for a shower, coffee and a kick-arse day.


Driving past Monument Hill onto High Street, Cato took a call on his mobile. The number was vaguely familiar and the voice even more so. They agreed to meet ten minutes hence at the Roasting Warehouse on South Terrace. The forecourt of the former petrol station turned coffee barn was full with dogs and Freo folk basking in the sun. Cato recognised a few faces and exchanged some waves and nods. His assignation had secured a table and had the coffees waiting. Cato stretched out a hand.

'John. How's things?'

'As well as.' They shook. Farmer John, so-called by Cato because of his stocky farmboy build and demeanour, operated in the shadowy twilight zone of police undercover operations. He was a consummate corporate politician and devotee of the dark arts. He was also de facto widower to Cato's erstwhile colleague, Lara Sumich, stabbed to death in the departure hall at Shanghai airport. These days he seemed incomplete, a little wasted, probably using work to try and bury his stubborn grief.

'You rang?' said Cato.

'What's your interest in Swan Lake?'

'Well, once you've heard the overture, you pretty much get the drift; after that it's all feathers.'

'Very funny.'

'Maybe you can explain while I enjoy my coffee and the vibe,' Cato said, glad he'd made John smile.

'It's a luxury housing and retail development in City West, helmed by Goran Abramovic. The subject of no end of litigation, sabotage, intimidation, you name it. Now the jewel in the crown of a Post-Dullsville Perth.'

'Ah.'

'So?'

'I'm more interested in what it was before. When the swan was still an ugly duckling.' Cato explained about the fire in the abandoned warehouse and the deaths of three homeless people.

'You think it's related to your enquiry?'

'I wouldn't be checking if I didn't.'

Farmer John sipped his coffee and cast an eye over the clientele. 'There's a lot of work gone into trapping Goran. The Feds, the ACC, us: lot of money, lot of man hours. We'd hate to see it stuffed up.'

'Are you telling me to get lost?'

'That development of his is washing a shipload of drug and human trafficking money. It's our business, not yours.'

'Am I right to be interested in him for my case? Go nosing around his affairs?'

'No. Tell you what, how about I chuck you a bone and you go searching elsewhere?'

'I'm not interested in wasting time. We've got a mad axe murderer out there. Media frothing at the mouth. Pollies getting nervous. They're not interested in your drug pusher and his shelf companies, they've got Hannibal Lecter on their doorstep. The public aren't going to like being sidelined and put in danger by a departmental turf dispute.'

Farmer John appraised him. 'You've toughened up. I'm impressed.'

'I'm patronised. Where's this going?'

'That building and the site it's on didn't come into Goran's portfolio until about three months after the fire. True, he'd shown interest in it before then, but it wasn't legally his until later.'

'So?'

'So you might want to look at the previous owners. The ones who sold him it after they'd cashed in their insurance payout, doubled their money.' He slid a sheet of paper across the table.

Cato spun it his way and took a look. 'Barbarossa Nominees?'


Cato set Thornton the task of tracking down the names, the real people behind Barbarossa Nominees. And he filled Pavlou in on developments.

'Johnny Jenkins isn't off the hook yet. This links him with the deaths of more homeless people.'

'Tenuously.'

'Money still going into his account from the same mob who owned that property. Maybe he's on a retainer from them to do some social cleansing to sweeten their property speculation.'

'But he's got an alibi. Us.'

'That needs testing. We can't ignore this, boss.'

She agreed to reallocate some resources back onto Jenkins and his supposed alibi, have the Arson Squad take a look at him too. 'You sure we're not being blindsided by the spooks just to keep us out of their hair? Maybe this Goran bloke is worth a look?'

Farmer John was slippery, no doubt, but Cato didn't see him wasting their time when there was a killer at large. A line had to be drawn somewhere and, since Lara's death, Cato had faith that John knew which side of it he was on. He said as much.

'Hope you're right.' Pavlou left him to it.

Cato sat at his desk wondering who was next. And when. He couldn't shake the feeling that the killer knew he was no longer communicating with Norman Lip on that number. That he knew exactly who he was dealing with. And that he was, once again, a few steps ahead of the game. There was a ring-around in progress asking the various agencies dealing with the homeless to be particularly vigilant and to encourage their clients to stay off the streets and/or stay together. It was laughable and very sad and it didn't take long for the media to get wind of it. Cato's phone rang. A journo from the local ABC station.

'Has there been a threat made by the killer? Are you expecting another victim soon?'

'You should be addressing your questions to Police Media. Do you want their number?'

'So that's a yes?'

'I think heightened vigilance by everybody at the moment is probably a good idea.'

'Is the killer about to strike again? Yes or no?'

'We want people to be alert, not alarmed. Sensationalism and speculation don't help the situation.'

'I'll take that as a yes.'

'Are you recording this?'

Then Norman Lip's latest article went into circulation. Poor Jackboot Johnny Jenkins the 'Primed Suspect' and Cato's history as a framer of innocent folk. DI Pavlou rang his extension.

'My office. Now.' Cato did as he was told. 'Your career prospects with Major Crime just took a nosedive. Somebody seems to want to do you, slowly.'

'Yep.'

'Any ideas who?'

'Apart from Bill Jenkins, no.'

'I've got somebody digging into that. Hopefully we'll find something to neutralise him. Or arrange for his wheelchair to go over the Gap with the old bastard in it.'

Albany's Gap wasn't as well-known as Sydney's but would fit the same purpose. A couple of hundred metres of sheer cliff ending in rocks, froth and foam. Cato felt like flying back down south to do the deed himself.

'Maybe you should be less visible for a few days?'

'I'm trying,' said Cato. 'Happy to.' A few days at home with Sharon and Ella might be timely. Or it could add to the nightmare.

Pavlou tapped her computer screen. 'This bloke needs a good shake.'

'Lip? I thought we'd already done that.'

'I've got Police Media applying the heavies to his boss.'

'Might help,' said Cato. 'But I think he thrives on the challenge of him against the world.' He thought again about Lip's browsing history and his aspirations. 'Maybe we should be nice to him, invite him into the fold, corrupt him with kindness.'

Pavlou appraised him. 'Maybe you're cut out for Major Crime after all.'


'Norman? G'day, it's Philip Kwong here. Fremantle Detectives.'

'Aren't you with Major Crime now?'

A short bark of laughter. 'Right again, I forgot.'

Norman waited for the blast, for the threats, the story was live by now. 'What can I do for you?'

'It's more what I might be able to do for you.'

'Come again?'

'I think we got off on the wrong foot. Pressure of the job, you begin to develop a siege mentality.'

'Right.'

'In the end we're all on the same side. We all want to stop this mad bastard from hurting anybody else. Right?'

'Right.'

'So we're figuring we need to look at what unites us, rather than divides us. Look at how we might cooperate, for a win-win situation.'

'Win-win,' said Norman. 'Sounds good. What do you have in mind?'

'How about a catch-up and we can meditate on the possibilities. Maybe I can shout you lunch?'

'All these offers. Must be my lucky day.'

'Really?'

'Yeah. Let's make it Mosman's down by the river. One o'clock, okay?'

'The old Mead's? Classy.'

And expensive, thought Norman. This is going to cost you.


*All these offers. Must be my lucky day.*

Sometimes Normie-boy, you can get a bit too cocky. Cato called Imogen and requested an update on Lip's telecommunications history. She brought it through ten minutes later.

'What are you looking for?'

Cato scanned the print-out. 'No unusual call numbers?'

She ran a glittery fingernail down the list. 'Only yours. The others are his editor, their lawyer, his sister.'

'Internet? Emails?'

'A few emails from his editor discussing deadlines and other issues around the latest article.' She paused and cast him a sympathetic look. 'You saw it, I guess?'

'Yep,' said Cato.

'Wanker,' said Imogen.

'So no invitations to drinks, or parties, or meetings in the last twenty-four hours or so?'

'No, why?'

*All these offers. Must be my lucky day.*

Cato told her.

'Maybe he's referring to Tinder. Looks like he's a bit of a root rat.'

They checked it out. 'Jacqui seems to be flavour of the month but she's playing hard to get.'

'Until this morning,' Imogen pointed out.

'He finally got lucky.' They studied the picture of Jacqui and her profile. 'Commerce student and fitness instructor. Nice combination.'

'Big eyes, big everything. Nice combination all over, if you like that sort of thing.'

'Norman clearly does. He's practically on bended knee to her.' Cato scrolled back through the conversations. 'She has him wrapped around her little finger.'

'It happens.'

'But look at his previous conversations with other Tinder partners.

He's bossing them all. Setting the time and place. Why the change in persona?'

'Maybe she's special?'

They scanned through the photos of earlier Norman conquests. 'Can't see what's so special. Going off previous form he should have lost patience after the first couple of exchanges and moved on to someone who would play the game his way.'

'Look at this one,' said Imogen, referring back to the exchanges with Jacqui.

**What do you want?**

**A token.**

**What kind?**

**A big one. A sacrifice.**

Cato grew cold.

Imogen pursed her lips. 'Want me to look into Jacqui?'

'Please,' said Cato. 'Maybe it's just a kinky *Fifty Shades* thing. Or maybe it's more.' He pointed out the arrangement for a rendezvous that night at Norman's. 'Either way, he'll be needing a chaperone.'

Cato was glad Pavlou pre-approved expenses on this one. Lip was deliberately ordering the most expensive dishes on the menu. When it came to the wine list, Cato had to put his foot down; Norman's finger was hovering over a bottle worth Cato's weekly wage.

'I'm driving, I'll stick with water. I can recommend a glass of the Marlborough pinot.' The warning glance said fourteen bucks is your lot.

'Sure, sounds great.' Norman smiled. They had a window table against a backdrop of a shimmering flat river occasionally rippled by a passing gin palace. A pod of dolphins cracked the surface. Shags sunned themselves on the rocks by the shore. At adjoining tables, deals were being done and assignations arranged. There was flirting and loose talk. 'So tell me about this win-win,' Norman said.

'What would be a win for you?'

Norman's pinot gris arrived with a smile and an iris flare from the waitress. Obviously she went for the style-magazine version of mannered masculinity: groomed yet wild, geeky yet blokey, casually intense, real yet false. She gave Cato his bubbly water as an afterthought. Cato realised he'd reached that age of invisibility in the eyes of a certain generation. It was mildly alarming yet somehow comforting at the same time.

'The story nobody else can get, the story they all covet.'

'The killer. All to yourself.'

'Interview with a vampire.' Norman sipped his pinot. 'Not bad.'

Cato wanted to reach across the table and squeeze Norman's throat and explain that feeding the delusions of the narcissistic prick who was causing all this misery was a shallow and immoral pursuit. But he didn't. 'What do you think he'll tell you? What's his big revelation about the human condition?'

'I doubt he has one. But look at Lee Harvey Oswald, Mark Chapman, John Hinckley Jr, they were all boring nobodies. Zapruder was just a guy with a camera in the right place at the right time. But all of them, their names live on.'

'Is that the kind of immortality you want? Piggybacked on to an atrocity?'

A thoughtful look over the pinot. 'This is interesting. I never expected you to be so clever, so ... deep.'

Supercilious little bastard. 'Or look at Truman Capote as another example.' Cato sipped his bubbly water. 'He wasn't there by accident. He made the deliberate decision to insinuate himself into a horrific murder investigation and examine it in some depth. And he comes up with the most well-known true crime book out there, perhaps the original and best. It made his name as a bestselling man of letters.' Still morally compromised, thought Cato, but we won't go there just now.

'Whoa. Intellectual overload. You sure you're a cop?'

The entrees arrived. Seared scallops for Norman, duck for Cato. 'I read stuff on my days off. And I went to uni.' Maybe he was going too fast for Norman. Maybe the intellectual and literary aspirations were beyond him and he really was just a shallow pretentious tosser after all. 'Everything now is about fleeting associations with fame. People crave it and seize it like it's an entitlement. These days Zapruder would probably miss the president's assassination because he'd be too busy taking a selfie.'

Norman laughed. 'Can I use that?'

'Be my guest.' It was strange. Cato felt flirtatious. 'But you look at the issues around these murders in Freo: homelessness, a country run by vindictive class warriors, an increasingly affluent society grappling with its sense of identity and occasionally troubled when reminded of those we're leaving behind.' Cato could almost see Norman's dream click into gear. He was already up there collecting his literary award. 'Which do you want to be? The loser who got the banal me-me-me interview from the sad sicko? Or the dude who forensically examined what was going on socially and culturally, and completely nailed it?'

Lip put down his glass and steepled his fingers like a deep thinker might do. 'What do you propose?'

# 23

Midafternoon, Cato parked down by the Round House and walked back up High Street towards the cop shop. Two hours with Norman Lip had left him feeling seedy, like he'd been caught coming out of a peep show. But Lip did seem to have taken the bait. The strategy had been worked out between himself, Pavlou and Headline Hannah from the Media Unit, and signed off by top brass. In return for easing up on the damaging attack articles and writing more constructive pieces to help win hearts and minds, Norman was to be given limited but exclusive access to the investigation. Embedded with Cato on an 'as needs' basis — maybe that's why he was feeling seedy — Lip was the last person he wanted to share an embedment with. Once the investigation was concluded and the killer caught, Norman would also be privy to the process of preparing the case for trial. Weave that level of access and detail in and out of an insightful dissection of society and bingo, Cato told him, you've got a masterpiece. All you need is a bit of insight and dissecting ability. The sting was in the 'as needs' clause — in effect the investigation team would keep Norman out of the loop for anything important and just throw him scraps when they felt like it. One twerp, neutralised — as Pavlou had put it.

'Will your editor buy the new angle?' Cato had asked.

'She'll bite my hand off,' grinned Norman. 'Catch ya later, Cato.'

Over dessert and a glass of botrytis, Cato had shared the story of his nickname with Norman. An article of faith, Pavlou had urged him. An offering. He'll love it. And indeed he had. But it felt like a betrayal or a cheapening. The nickname was designed by Anglo colleagues to put Cato in his place. It was an act of disempowerment of him by them. Taking back ownership of it had been his statement of re-empowerment. And now he was bartering it away, for what? To appease and embellish the ego of a moron like Lip.

'A moron who can lead us to the killer and stop his distracting attack articles,' Pavlou had reminded him. 'Win-win. It was your idea after all.'

True. But he hadn't anticipated how grubby it would make him feel.

'Sergeant!'

It was Barry, resplendent in a T-shirt depicting Elvis and Darth Vader shaking hands and posing for the camera. Cato nodded a greeting. 'Cool shirt.'

'Got it from the Salvos. I do some of the bin sorting. Get an early pick.'

'Beaut,' said Cato, as Barry fell into step beside him. 'Where you off to, how've you been?'

'Too many questions,' said Barry. 'A man's entitled to his fuckin' privacy.'

'Sorry.'

'Just jokin'. The answer's nowhere special and not bad. How about you?'

'Back to work and been worse,' said Cato.

Barry sighed. 'I love this time of year. Djilba.'

'Yeah? Why?'

'Season of love, baby. It's more fuckin' peaceful. Warm days. Cool nights. Before it all kicks off.'

'Yeah, you're right.' They were outside Record Finder, the hard chords of Dire Straits' 'Money for Nothing' drifting out. Next door, the cafe was deserted, a waiter flicked the table with a cloth and gave them an enquiring look. 'Cup of tea?' said Cato. 'I'm buying.'

Barry nodded, sombre, like he was doing Cato a favour. 'Don't mind if I do. Earl Grey, please.'

Cato placed the order and they took an outside table. After abasing himself before Norman Lip, Cato felt curiously energised in Barry's company.

'What do you want, then?' said Barry.

'Nothing. Just fancied a cuppa. Not holding you up, am I?'

'S'pose not.' Barry dragged a newspaper over from the adjacent table. The front page blared about the murderer in their midst. 'Found him yet?'

'Who?'

'Who d'you fuckin' think? Harold Holt? The serial killer. Fuckwit.'

Their teas arrived. 'Enjoy,' said Cato, wondering if foul-mouthed-Barry-Time was really what he needed after all. Dire Straits had been replaced by Roger Miller, 'King of the Road'.

Barry took a sip. 'Very nice. Thank you. So you gunna answer my question?'

'No, we haven't found him.'

'Whatcha been doin' all this time?'

'This and that,' said Cato. 'Trying our best.'

'Really?'

'Yeah.'

Barry frowned. 'I detect a lack of urgency, detective. I reckon you lot won't pull your fingers out unless Bad Boy Bubby kills somebody respectable by mistake.'

'That's not true,' said Cato. But it sounded lame.

Barry prodded the paper. 'People find it all a bit uncomfortable. A shame. But not enough are thinking fuck, that could be me, or my brother, son, auntie whatever. They don't have that fear. With those Claremont killings they were afraid, he was killing their kind. Respectable, nice girls.'

'Didn't help them solve it any quicker, though. Did it?'

'True. Still, it would be nice. You know, you hear people around town and there's more than a few think he's doing everyone a favour.'

They chitchatted a bit more, Cato trying to steer Barry away from shoptalk but never quite succeeding. Finally he drained his tea. 'Well I better get back to it or we'll never catch him.'

'That'd be good.' Barry nodded towards the record shop, Roger Miller wrapping up his finger-clicking hymn to freedom-loving hobos. 'Love that song. Cheers for the tea. Second one this week.'

'Second cuppa in a whole week?'

'Earl Grey. Cut above.' He winked. 'Like me.' He sauntered off, whistling 'King of the Road'.

Cato gave him a wave. 'Stay cool, Barry.'

Sharon would be glad to see the back of the painters. Steve reckoned they'd be finished by tomorrow and that was fine by her. Nat and his buddy had stuffed around for most of the day and their work was turning sloppy, particularly Nat's. She made a point of letting Steve know it while the boys were outside having an undeserved coffee break on the back patio.

'There are drips on the windows and verandah, smudges on door frames, uneven strokes. Rubbish left lying around. It's like someone else took over the job. It was going well up to now.'

Steve carried out a rudimentary inspection of the work and it obviously met his not very high standards. 'We don't usually get complaints. And no shortage of work.' He squinted at her, scratched his ear with a pencil. 'Nat mentioned you'd had words yesterday. He's apologised for the breakage and is happy to reimburse. Accidents happen. The lads are doing their best.'

'The breakage is not an issue. Really.' It's his weird, intrusive, controlling manner. Instead she said, 'But I would appreciate a bit more focus on the quality of the work.'

'We'll do our best, ma'am.' Was it her or had he just made her feel like some stuck-up bitch perfectionist? He smiled and made his departure. 'As always, the customer is king. Or queen, as they say.' The Yorkshire accent was piled on to turn it into a joke but she knew its intent. The flyscreen door slid open. 'Nat here'll fix things up, missus. However long it takes.'

Sharon thought she saw the ghost of a smirk on Nat's face but she let the matter drop. Julie, the prospective nanny, was due any moment now and Ella had to be awake, fed, happy and putting her best foot forward. Sharon set about making it happen.

The doorbell rang while Sharon was in the middle of changing Ella's nappy.

'Want me to get that?' said Nat.

Shit. 'Yes, please. Ta.'

'No worries.'

There was a murmured exchange at the front door and footsteps back along the hall. A cheery wave from a plump blonde with a nose stud. 'Hiya.'

Nat gave Sharon a wink and a grin in passing. 'Cuppa tea, love?' he said to Julie, mimicking the accent.

'Aye, great, thanks,' said Julie. 'Lovely house.'

'T'is in't it?' said Nat.

'You tekkin the mickey?'

'Nay, lass.'

But he was and she didn't seem to mind. Sharon heard them chatting away while she finished with Ella. Occasional giggles. 'Cheeky monkey,' she heard Julie say.

Sharon took over and encouraged Nat on his way. For all his cockiness and intrusive manner, he'd broken the ice and set Julie at ease, and that was a good thing. She and Ella got on like a house on fire and Sharon signed Julie up for a few hours twice a week, effective from Monday, and gradually building from then. She wanted a good transition period to make sure everything was fine before she went back to work.

'He's a card,' said Julie on her way out, nodding in the direction of Nat.

'Yes,' said Sharon. 'Never a dull moment.'

'I bet. He can park his blundies under my bed any time.'

'I'll pretend I didn't hear that. See you Monday.'

Cato couldn't get Jacqui out of his mind.

**What do you want?**

**A token.**

**What kind?**

**A big one. A sacrifice.**

Then within the next twenty-four hours the SMS direct from the killer to Norman's phone in response to Cato's planted message.

**I'll be in touch sooner than you think.**

Cato re-checked the log, the timeline, the sequence of events. In between those two messages, Lip had been in touch with Jackboot Johnny Jenkins, ostensibly to research and write his 'Primed Suspect' article. So what if all three were connected? What if the killer was Jacqui, a Tinder persona created especially as a communication backup? Jacqui wants Norman to bring her a sacrifice. Norman then pays Jenkins a visit. Next thing the killer hints at another imminent victim. Were Jacqui and Jenkins one and the same? Had Jenkins really been where the surveillance team thought he was for murder number four? Maybe he had an accomplice? The tie-in with the City West factory fire, however tenuous, left him well and truly in the running.

Or was Jenkins in fact the next target? Not homeless, but working closely with them. Also stealing the limelight as the 'Primed Suspect' — a rival, if you like. Cato had to admit it, Jenkins being victim number five wasn't the worst result he could imagine.

Or. But. Maybe. The language of straw-clutching. This was all wild speculation based on little more than coincidence and a perceived anomaly in Norman's mode of communication. Cocky egocentric hipster one minute, Jacqui's gimp the next. He called IT Imogen.

'Any news on Jacqui?'

'Her IP address used to register with Tinder is a proxy channelled through a VPN in Hong Kong.'

'Meaning?'

'Think the cyber equivalent of a Panama-registered rust bucket wandering the seven seas. Not entirely untraceable, given time. But certainly playing hard to get.'

'Not what you'd expect from a twenty-one-year-old commerce student and fitness instructor whose hobbies include clubbing, getting blazed and meeting people.'

Imogen chuckled. 'I hadn't realised you were paying so much attention to her profile.'

'She's supposedly meeting Norman tonight at his place.'

'The ball's in your court then, isn't it?'

Thornton meanwhile had sent through his latest delvings on Barbarossa Nominees. The names behind the shelf company remained elusive at this stage but he had found something interesting. A number of the buildings and blocks of land they had interests in were adjacent to the murder scenes down at the port, along Marine Terrace and across the road from Esplanade Park where the marine repair businesses were housed. Thornton had mapped them and then overlaid them with the published plans for Freo 2020.

'Neat, huh?' he'd grinned.

They were all in zones earmarked for exciting new future developments. The council was back in play and so was their employee, Jackboot Johnny Jenkins.

Cato ran his theories past DI Pavlou.

An irritated shake of the head at the idea of Jenkins being Jacqui aka the killer. 'He was definitely home that night for number four. We had two teams watching front and back. I've grilled them again and they insist, not a peep.' Cato wondered if they really would own up to the Velvet Hammer if they had stuffed up in some way. 'As to whether Jenkins is candidate for victim number five...' she shrugged. 'Maybe we'll get two for the price of one and Jacqui will rid us of both him and Lip all in one night.'

'But?' said Cato.

'But you're right. Tempting as it is, we have this damn duty of care thing to consider. Let's sit outside Norman's for the night, two cars with backup on standby, and wait for Jacqui. If it does turn out to be Jenkins, the vodkas are on me.'

'Do we still give Jenkins protection in the event it's not him?'

'Yes, I'll have somebody ring him and either advise him to get out of town for a while or be put up in a hotel by us for the foreseeable.'

'But if it's him, doesn't that tip him off?'

'We'll find a way of phrasing it as a general perceived threat. No specifics. Either way, he gets watched as a suspect and protected as a citizen.'

Cato shook his head, grimly. 'Pity we can't do this for all the rough sleepers too.'

'S'pose so. Can you sort the surveillance on Norman?'

'Sure.'

Another late one. Cato called Sharon and explained.

'No worries. I'll see you when I see you.' She put Ella on the phone for a goodnight goo-goo-ga-ga. 'Stay safe, okay?'

He promised he would.

The wind had picked up by mid-evening and pinned a plastic bag to Norman Lip's front gate. It was the only action so far. Cato and

Amy Trimboli were in one car over the road from Lip's place, Chris Thornton and Deb Hassan in the other, down the street and tucked into the private driveway of an Airbnb house specially booked for the night. Inside, playing with iPads and drinking coffee, were half-a-dozen members of the TRG. Johnny Jenkins had accepted Pavlou's kind offer of a couple of nights in the Mandurah Atrium under the watchful eye of local detectives. He seemed to find it all a bit funny — but then if you are the killer and you've just been offered two free nights in a hotel to protect you from yourself then it does begin to get laughable. Whatever. All they needed to concentrate on tonight was Norman Lip and his assignation with the lovely Jacqui.

Amy munched on a muesli bar. 'I was on this stake-out once. A peeper in Kings Park who liked to watch couples doing it in their cars. We got him, and there was all this night-vision shit, goggles and stuff, real creepy. Then we take him home and take a look at his computer. All these crappy grainy-green shots of people humping in their Mazdas. I told him, make life easier for yourself, mate. This shit's all legally available online and in much better quality.'

'But you can't beat homemade,' said Cato.

'Give me take-out any day.' Another crunch on the wildberry bar. 'Speaking of which, is that him?'

A pizza delivery car had drawn up outside Norman's. A young bloke stepped out in a red T-shirt and a baseball cap pulled low. Gym build. Cato tapped on the in-car computer console to check Norman's latest phone and internet use — a live feed organised by Imogen. 'Can't see any references here to a takeaway order.'

'So?'

'So phone Chris and the TRG crew, alert them.'

She did so, they were avoiding the radio channel in case of eaves-droppers.

Pizza Boy opened the back door of his car and reached in for the canvas warming bag. He shoved something into it.

'Did you see what that was?'

'I could be wrong,' said Amy, 'but it looked like a tyre lever to me.' She checked her Glock. 'Should we bell Norman, get him to keep the door locked?'

'Too late,' said Cato. 'He's already opened it.'

Norman had spent the rest of the day since his long lunch with Cato wondering if he could have his cake and eat it. Reining in the attack articles was no problem, they were probably running out of steam anyway. And Betsy would be in a lather at the idea of exclusive behind-the-scenes access to the investigation, so a shift in editorial stance wouldn't faze her. The only problem was Jacqui, who would chuck the mother of all tanties when Norman confessed that he'd found someone else. But stuff it. It was Jacqui who was expecting all the quo without giving any quid back. Ultimatum time, Jacqui. Give me my interview with the vampire or I go and get a big wooden stake and join Cato's team.

The doorbell went. Norman jumped up and checked himself in the mirror, then stopped. Jacqui isn't real, you idiot. She's probably a middle-aged accountant with a dungeon in the suburbs and a grievance against his mother. He opened the door to a pizza delivery boy built like a brick shithouse.

'I think you've got the wrong house, mate.'

The pizza boy opened his warmer bag and reached in.

Then all hell broke loose.

Boy and pizzas disappeared under a rugby scrum as he was jumped by three, maybe four, blokes. There was yelling, swearing and the unmistakeable sounds of flesh and bone colliding. One of the blokes looked up out of the scrum. It was Cato.

'Get back inside and lock the door. Now.'

Norman did as he was told.


'What's your name?'

'Josh.' Pizza Boy snivelled and produced some ID.

Cato hadn't expected someone so big and muscly to cry so easily. 'Who sent you?'

'The boss, Tracey. Order for number six. Hawaiian deep crust, added anchovies, and a garlic bread.'

'This is number four.'

'Yeah? Shit. Sorry.'

'What's with the tyre lever?'

'Sometimes you get jumped for the cash. Or the pizza. Happened to my mate in Hammy Hill.'

'Would you have used it?'

'Didn't get the chance.'

The TRG had dispersed back to where they came from. The Hawaiian was a sloppy mess on Norman's doorstep and the garlic bread was bent at an unnatural angle. Cato handed Josh his baseball cap. Apart from a very red face and dishevelled hair, the boy looked like he would live. 'You okay?'

'S'pose.'

Cato handed over his business card. 'If your boss wants to know what happened, get her to ring me.' He slipped him twenty bucks. 'For the broken pizza.'

'It's twenty-two fifty including the garlic bread.'

Cato made up the difference.

A head appeared around the door at number six. 'Is that my pizza?'

Josh snapped into action. 'Coming right up, mate, new one on its way.' He thumbed over his shoulder at Cato. 'Blame these guys.'

Cato rang Norman's doorbell. 'Who is it?'

Like he didn't already know. 'Me.' The door opened. Cato walked in, Amy following. 'So, Norman,' he said. 'Tell me about Jacqui.'


Barry had treated himself to fish and chips from the shop near South Beach. He unpacked them sitting on the rocks at the end of the southern groyne that marked the border with Cockburn. The sun was an orange flare on the horizon and the sea had turned purple. Seagulls wheeled and squawked.

'Getting any?' he said to the bloke with his rod in the water and a beanie with a headtorch.

'Nah.'

'Best to buy them,' chuckled Barry. He lifted the package in the bloke's direction. 'Chip?'

'Nah, mate, cheers. I've eaten.'

Bucket of steroids by the look of him. They reckoned they stunted your dick and, in this guy's case, your conversation. 'You local?'

'Good as. Ask a lot of questions, dontcha?'

'Sorry,' said Barry. And under his breath, 'Miserable cunt.'

'Say something?'

'Why would I?' said Barry. He hid 'cocksucker' under a cough.

The uncompanionable silence settled in. Barry ate his fish and fuckin' chips and fuckface dangled his bastard rod. The wind was cutting through Barry's thin jacket. Windcheater, my arse. He crumpled up his wrappings.

'Well, nice talking to you.' Not.

'Yeah,' said the bloke.

Barry set off across the grass leading to the railway line. Then he was in Wilson Park, five minutes from home. He checked his watch. If he hurried he'd catch the beginning of that new crime show on SBS, with all the subtitles, nudity and, best of all, the swearing. It cheered him up. He felt a hand on his shoulder and turned.

'Oh,' he smiled. 'It's you.'

# 24

Cato knew what it would be about even before he answered the phone.

'Back of Missy Moos, South and Harbour,' said Chris Thornton.

He had to ask anyway. 'It's him?'

'Yes. Sorry.'

'Twenty minutes.' He checked the time on his phone. Five-thirty, half-grey dawn and twittering birds outside. He rolled over and pecked Sharon on the cheek. 'Gotta go.'

She opened an eye. 'Bye.'

Norman had come clean. Yes, Tinder was a way for him to maintain contact with the killer who'd assumed the persona of Jacqui. Yes, the killer seemed to have developed a real fixation on Cato.

'This is personal isn't it?' Norman had said with widening eyes and growing realisation. 'The whole thing. It's about you and him.'

If it wasn't before, it is now.

What was the meeting with Jenkins about? A tip-off from the killer that he was worth talking to. Why? Norman didn't know. There was obviously personal animosity between Cato and Jenkins. Jenkins had mentioned that Kwong seemed to be mates with this loser called Barry, wanted to stick up for him, take sides. Yes, said Norman, I talked to Barry as well. Passed it all on to Jacqui, via yet more pay-as-you-go mobiles and the cloud.

Cato could have quite happily shot Norman there and then. 'You know what you've done, don't you?'

'What? I just thought he was gathering info for his smear campaign. You don't mean ...'

Cato had turned to Amy. 'Put the word out. We need to find

202

Barry and bring him in. All available units. High priority.' He gave a description and possible leads, *Big Issue*, St Mary's. He turned back to Norman, shook his head. 'What a piece of work. I'll make sure you're remembered for this, don't worry.'

'So is our deal still on?' asked Norman.

There had been no sign of Barry over the next few hours. He hadn't come back to the hostel in South Fremantle and wasn't at any of his known haunts. Cato had returned home well after midnight and waited for the call that must surely come. When he pulled into Harbour Road the white tent was already up in the car park behind Missy Moos. Was it just coincidence that this was the street he'd lived in until he met Sharon? Cato didn't know but, either way, it was too late for Barry.

Thornton greeted Cato with a paper suit, mask, gloves and booties. 'The body was found by an early morning dog walker. That's him over there.'

A little old man with a little old dog. Deb Hassan was taking notes.

Cato zipped the suit up. 'How did he die?'

'Head smashed in with a house brick.'

'Christ.'

'Duncan's in the tent. Wants a word.'

Cato stepped under the flap. He took in the wreck of what was once Barry Newman's head. Cato had never asked him his second name all those times they'd talked but he knew it now, courtesy of what had become a murder investigation. 'Oh, Barry,' he said, quietly.

'Friend of yours?' Duncan Goldflam still had room for sympathy in this terrible job of his.

'Recent acquaintance,' said Cato. But it didn't feel like that.

'Sorry.' Duncan stood up, his head brushing the roof of the tent. 'Main things to note. Brick dust and fragments in the wounds. No calling card.' He didn't need one, thought Cato, the choice of victim said it all. 'And he didn't die here. Not enough blood or trace patterns consistent with how he died.'

Thornton lifted the flap. He must have overheard. 'I think I might be able to help you with that. It looks like we've found the brick.'

A fitness bootcamper over on Wilson Park had stubbed her toe on it in the half-light of dawn while doing a circuit. The brick had been covered in blood.

At that moment the mobile in Cato's pocket throbbed. It was Norman's mobile, the hotline to the killer. Cato checked the incoming message, a photo of a bloodied and dead Barry. A caption: *For you xxx, Jacqui.*

Cato wanted to stamp the phone into smithereens. But he didn't. This thin sliver of communication, this torment, was just about all he had to hold onto.

DI Pavlou ran the meeting. Cato knew he had a dangerous and unstable look in his eye but right now Pavlou undoubtedly needed cold, clear focus from him and everybody else. They'd gone through the early forensics. Goldflam saw evidence of sloppiness in the decision to relocate the body.

'This bloke now has a car with trace evidence to worry about. He's creating more problems for himself. That's good for us.'

Was he saying that to make Cato feel better? Probably not. Goldflam didn't waste words like that. Thornton was coordinating intel on Barry's known movements and associates to build a picture that might eventually reveal the killer. Hassan was running doorknocks and had a team canvassing the area for any possible witnesses to anything unusual during the time frame. And Trimboli was reviewing the spreadsheets looking for points of connection between the victims. But if the killer was simply using the victims to send a message, then was Cato himself that point of connection? It was crazy. Why kill all the others; why not just get to the point?

Pavlou, accompanied by an old hand named Schultz back from long service leave, led him to a quiet room. 'This looks like the mother of all grudges, Philip. Have any idea who might be behind it? How many people could you have pissed off this badly?'

'Difficult to say. Some people blow things all out of proportion.'

Pavlou pursed her lips. 'You're going all passive-aggressive on me again. We're in this together. You know that, don't you?'

Cato closed his eyes and expelled a breath. 'If I had even half an inkling, I'd be out there chasing them down.'

'Wood for the trees, Philip. You've got a lot on your plate.' A pause. 'Maybe I've added to it by bringing you into the squad before you're ready.'

Oh, fuck off. 'Yeah, maybe you have.' He needed to be free of this. He needed time and space. Can I have a few days off to gather my thoughts in the middle of a massive murder investigation please? 'The only violently vindictive bastards that come to mind right now are Jenkins and Son. I don't know what they've got to do with this but they're in the picture somewhere. And Junior has links to some of the victims.'

'We can't pull them in on the strength of that. Jenkins Junior now has a second alibi, again us, sitting on him all night at the Mandurah Atrium. As for the dad, I've told you I've already got somebody discreetly on Bill Jenkins down in Albany.'

'Bill Jenkins doesn't respond to discreet. Who is it?'

'Senior Sergeant Tess Maguire. She's an outsider. Not part of the old boys' club. Know her?'

'Yes,' said Cato. You know I do.

'As for Johnny Jenkins, admittedly he pointed Norman towards Barry. He needs another talking to, if only to formally close the book on him. Or throw it at him, either way.'

'I'm happy to do it.'

'I think not. Schultzy here can run it. That right, Schultzy?'

'Sure,' he said. 'Maybe Cato can brief me.'

'Maybe I can watch?' said Cato.

Pavlou didn't see a problem with that.


Sergeant Schultz and Amy Trimboli did the honours with John Jenkins. Cato had only one bit of advice. 'Wind him up as tight as he'll go, I reckon he's got daddy issues, see where that gets you.' He also had a side word with Schultz who he knew to be less of a Pavlou brown-noser. 'Check his alibi for murder four.'

'I thought we were it?'

'Maybe someone fucked up and is not telling.'

'That would reflect badly on those leading this investigation, surely?'

'Yes,' said Cato. 'It would. I also want to know about those payments into his account.'

'No probs,' said Schultz.

Having made himself a coffee, Cato settled back and watched it all on the video link.

'Mr Jenkins.' Schultzy was legendary; he was one of those blokes with a treasure trove of war stories to share around the barbie. He could have you crying with laughter after a few beers. The crims loved him because he looked, acted and talked like them. They thought they were on the same wavelength, always good for a joke. They didn't realise he was a Judas goat. He could cheerily lead them up the steps to the courthouse for a ten-stretch. And if he did, they'd still thank him for the laugh along the way. But the smile was missing this morning. 'Thanks for your time today. Much appreciated.'

Jenkins checked his watch. 'This take long?'

'Things to do, places to be?'

'Something like that.'

Amy Trimboli did her bit. 'You'll leave when we're ready, Mr Jenkins.'

Schultzy winked at Johnny. 'There's your answer, mate, but we'll try our best.'

'Bit young and pretty for bad cop, aren't you?' said Jenkins to Amy.

Schultz sat back and flapped his tie. 'Watch your manners, mate. This is a modern workplace.'

'So what is it you want? Do I need a lawyer here or what?'

Amy didn't lift her eyes from her notepad. 'Not unless you've done something wrong, Mr Jenkins.' She looked up. 'Have you?'

'You had a meeting with this journo bloke.' Schultz glanced at the file. 'Norman Lisp.'

'Lip,' Amy corrected him.

'Right. What was that about?'

'What's it to you?'

Schultz pulled out a photo of Lip from the file. Bushranger beard, glasses and checked shirt. 'Conrad Cool here reckons you discussed a bloke who was found dead this morning. Murdered.'

'Who?' The media hadn't released a name yet.

'Barry Newman,' said Amy. 'You know him, I believe.'

'Fucking hell.'

'Heard you and him had a bit of biff recently,' said Schultz. 'Apparently he landed one on you?'

'No way,' said Jenkins. 'You're not pinning this on me. I want a lawyer.'

'Relax mate, we don't think it was you.' He looked askance at Amy. 'Do we, Constable Trimboli?'

She shook her head dismissively. 'Nah.' A pause. 'Probably not.'

'So what's this about?'

Schultz leaned forward across the table. 'We need your help.'

'I didn't do it. Don't know anybody who did.'

'That's the thing, you see. We know you have an alibi for the fourth murder, because we were watching you.'

Just a microsecond, but there it was. The hint of a smirk, the brightening of the eyes. The alibi wasn't all it seemed.

Schultz had picked it too, lifting his head to the video camera as if framing his next thought but Cato saw a stare meant for him. 'But you keep really bad company, John. It gets us to thinking about aiding and abetting, or even job-sharing.'

'Fuck off.' Jenkins stood to leave.

'Maybe you and the man from the souvenir shop,' suggested Amy. 'We know you're on each other's speed dials and you both don't like tramps and beggars.'

Schultz studied the paperwork. 'Neil Foster? Is he the one paying the money into your account? Is he Barbarossa Nominees?'

'You really have been giving me a going-over haven't you? Want to check my stools? I need to take a shit.'

'Five hundred bucks a month. Pin money. What does he get for that?'

'Woof,' said Jenkins. 'That's the sound of a dog under the wrong tree.'

'So enlighten us.' Schultz leaned forward. 'Who's this Barbarossa Nominees?'

'None of your business.'

'It is when the property they own gets burned down with three homeless people inside.'

A widening of the eyes. 'Call me when you can prove any of this. Until then, see ya.'

'I worked with your dad, back in the day.' Schultz folded his arms. 'Tough old sod, wasn't he?'

Here it comes, thought Cato. Enjoying the theatre.

'Still is,' said Jenkins.

'We were out on a job when he got that call from the Academy.'

'Yeah?' Jenkins was flushed. He was still standing, awkward, but compelled to hear Schultz out. 'Don't tell me, he was very disappointed. I've heard this one before.'

'Disappointed? No. In fact he laughed, thought it was a huge joke. "They're chucking the runt out," he said.'

'Sergeant,' said Amy.

'Don't interrupt, Constable.' Schulz turned back to Jenkins. 'Is that why you pick on the weak and vulnerable, Johnny? Too close to home? Daddy thinks you're just like them.'

'Is this being recorded?'

'Oops. Sorry. Forgot.'

'Fuck you,' said Jenkins.

'You have something in common with the killer. You hate the homeless. Only difference is, he's got the balls to really do something about it.' From the adjoining room, Cato winced. 'You? You piss on their sleeping bags. Weak. Useless. Just like your old man said.'

'Finished?'

'Yeah, I think so. For now.' He turned to Amy. 'Constable?'

'Nothing more from me, Sarge.'

'We will, of course, be passing on the relevant findings of our investigation to your superiors and encouraging them to hold an internal enquiry into certain allegations of harassment and abuse. And we will continue to look into you and your associates.'

Amy lifted a finger. 'Oh, I forgot. You can expect a visit from the Arson Squad any day now.'

'Blah, blah, blah.' Jenkins walked out.

Schultz turned to the camera, speaking directly to Cato. 'Well, that went well, eh?'

# 25

Norman Lip could see it all turning to shit. The morning news about the body was bad enough — all the channels, all the news sites, social media, all going ape. But now he'd just put the phone down on Betsy.

'I made the wrong call on this, Norman. I trusted you and I was wrong. It was a regrettable lapse of judgement. I'm going to have to let you go.'

It was like she was reading a statement prepared by Carmen the Lawyer. Regrettable lapse of judgement? Well, yeah. Obviously the cops had sent in the heavies from HQ to turn the screws. By the sounds of it, a few side calls had also been made to advertisers. A pincer movement. He checked his watch. It wasn't even ten o'clock and his day looked like a write-off. He chucked a pod in the espresso machine and flicked the switch. His phone beeped again. Shit. A message waiting for him on Tinder.

*Miss me?*

*Fuck off.*

*Oooh, spanky spanky.*

Norman closed his phone and chucked it on the kitchen table. The coffee machine hissed at him. He filled a cup and went out to his balcony. Wind whipped from the south-west, carrying with it the tang of the aluminium refinery down at Rockingham. The smell in his nostrils was bitter, the coffee was bitter, his whole damn life. The phone again.

*You need to find a way to release all that anger.*

This guy was a serious nut job but he didn't want to let Norman go. Why?

The realisation hit him like a faceful of ice-cold, citrus fairy dust. Jacqui needed him for something. He hadn't finished yet.

*What do you want?*

*You. Only you xxx*

*Pricktease, you say you'll meet me but you never do. Now YOU need to prove yourself to ME.*

*So masterful.* A pause, some thinking dots. Would he know by now that this too was being monitored? *Somewhere romantic. How about the Big Wheel in Esplanade Park?*

No worries, thought Norman. *Tonight. 8pm.*

*It's a date xxx*

Either Jacqui wasn't aware that the Tinder account was being monitored, or he was one cool, crazy bastard. Either way Norman was buzzing once again.

It was the last thing Cato needed. A call from Jake's school to come and attend a meeting with the principal. Like now.

'Is this really that urgent?'

'It's you or the police,' the deputy principal had said, without a trace of irony.

Apparently Jane had her phone switched off and Simon didn't want to know. And why should he? Cato breathed deeply as he pulled up in the car park at John Curtin Senior High. What now?

When Cato was shown into the principal's office he found a dishevelled and red-faced Jake, eyes blazing. Beside him the phys ed teacher in a Springboks rugby top and a name badge, Pieter de Voss: calm, alert, perhaps a little amused.

'What's going on?' Cato addressed the question to Jake.

No answer.

'Take a seat, Mr Kwong.' The principal reminded him of DI Pavlou, another Velvet Hammer. 'Sorry to have called you away from your job,' a glance towards Jake, 'but sometimes necessity prevails.'

'No problem.' Cato took the seat offered, it was on the other side of Mr de Voss, whose job seemed to be to hem Jake in to a corner. So there they sat: Jake by the wall, de Voss, then Cato. Across the desk the principal straightened her stapler and pens. 'What's he done?' The number of times Cato must have heard that from the parent of some recidivist ratbag.

'Assaulted a fellow student and a teacher.'

Cato turned to Jake. 'What's this all about?'

Nothing. No reply.

'There was some kind of argument during recess, a fight started, and when Mr de Voss intervened, he too was assaulted.'

Mr de Voss rolled up a leg of his tracky pants and showed everyone the blossoming bruise and split skin on his shin. 'Stings a bit, by crikey.'

'Jake and the other student have refused to explain what the argument was about but, whatever the reason, it's no excuse for violence, Mr Kwong.'

'Absolutely,' said Cato.

'Jacob will have to stay away from school. It's an automatic suspension for two weeks.'

'Right.'

'And once we've had time to consider the matter further, we'll be in touch.'

'Sure. And the other kid?'

'Same. His parents have already collected him.'

'Hurt?'

'A bloody nose. His parents are lawyers so they might want to pursue the matter.'

Jake was sent to collect his bag and Cato shook hands with the principal and Mr de Voss and apologised for his son's behaviour.

'Worse things happen on the rugby field,' shrugged de Voss. 'But he's usually a good kid, at least until this academic year, anyway. Funny, they usually grow out of that year nine stuff in year nine. By year eleven they settle down.' A rueful smile. 'Late developer, eh?'

In the car Cato couldn't get a word out of Jake. 'I thought you'd turned a corner. What happened?'

Nothing again.

'Jake?'

'You really want to know?'

'Yes, of course I do.'

'Some dick read about you in the papers, being useless, being corrupt, not caring about the homeless murders. Started giving me shit about it.'

Cato sighed. 'I'm sorry you're getting that kind of grief, but violence solves nothing. At school anyway. You know the rules, mate.'

'Family is family. You do whatever is right.' Jake turned and looked at his dad. 'Whatever the cost.'

Cato pulled up outside Jane's house in East Freo. 'Why are you dropping me here?' said Jake. 'I live with you now, remember?'

Cato sighed. He'd forgotten, and this seemed like the automatic, the right place to come to. 'We're under a lot of pressure right now, Sharon and me. This investigation, it's ...'

Jake's eyes filled. 'I get it.'

'It's just for a few days, mate. Until the dust settles. We'll work this out, okay?'

'Sure, Dad.'

'Jake, is there anything else going on? You seem so ... angry.'

He grabbed his bag from the back seat. 'Don't worry about it. You've got enough on your plate.'

'Jake ...' Cato's phone buzzed, he glanced at the screen, an urgent summons. When he looked up again Jake was heading up the front path.

'Jake, I'll call you tonight. Okay?'

'Bye, Dad,' he said without turning.


Back in the office, IT Imogen showed Cato the Tinder readout. The assignation between Lip and Jacqui: time, place, everything.

'We've got him.' She studied Cato's unimpressed face. 'Haven't we?'

'Show it to Pavlou, she's in charge.' He mustered a smile. 'Good work.'

'But you don't believe it?'

'I don't believe much of anything right now. But it won't harm for us to be there.' He thought of something else. 'I'll pay Norman a visit. He'll be expecting our call.'

'Sure,' said Imogen.

Cato took off alone. Chris, Deb and Amy would be tied up doing the donkey work on victim five. Victim five: Barry Newman, aged forty-two, born in Coolbellup. Parents both deceased. Younger brother, Bruce, had Down syndrome and lived in special care accommodation in Palmyra. In recent years Barry had worked as a community newspaper deliverer, a shelf-stacker at Woolworths and IGA and, latterly, as a *Big*

*Issue* seller. The hostel where he lived was only temporary and he would have had to move on once his six months was up. He wasn't homeless the way most people imagine it — a bundle of rags in a doorway. He just didn't have anywhere permanent that he could call home. And victim five was well-liked, an eternal optimist with a potty-mouth, and not a bad bone in his body.

Norman answered after the third knock. Cato had rung ahead to check he'd be home.

'Jeez, mate,' said Norman. 'Terrible news.'

Cato ignored him. 'Jacqui has been in touch. You've set up a meeting.'

'Tonight,' Norman confirmed. 'The park.'

'Does he know we're on to the Tinder thing?'

'I don't think so, I don't know.'

'Were you planning to tell us?'

'S'pose so, but you're listening in anyway. Right?'

Cato nodded. 'Why's he still talking to you?'

An affronted smart as if Cato had slapped him. 'I'm obviously still of some use to him.'

'So he's not finished.'

'Not by a long chalk.'

'What makes you say that?'

'Well we're surmising he's got a thing about you, right?' Norman offered a coffee from his shiny machine. Cato accepted. 'Barry brings it closer to home. But until he's hurt you directly, the job's not done. Is it?'

Cato couldn't fault the logic. Sometimes the simplest truths seem the hardest to fathom.


Esplanade Park was crawling with cops. Admittedly, the uniformed ones were out of sight in plain vans: the TRG ninjas, armed to the teeth and waiting for the word. DI Pavlou wanted in too. She was in a car with Schultzy angle-parked opposite Joe's Fish Shack facing the big ferris wheel, which was lit up with garish purple highlights. Cato and Amy had a table outside Little Creatures. Half of the evening revellers within a hundred metre radius were WA's finest. Even the sullen young guy with the nose stud collecting the money in the Big Wheel booth was, until this afternoon, a probationary constable wondering when he might get a taste of some proper action. Now he knew. The clip-on nose stud was his idea.

Schultzy had taken Cato aside for a quiet word before they all took up their positions.

'I did some discreet enquiries on the Jenkins surveillance team.'

'And?'

'Car two, out back, they're an item. Apparently they're known for snatching quickies whenever they can. Odds on they were too busy sucking each others tonsils to take much notice of what Jenkins might be doing.'

'Did you front them with it?'

'He denied everything but she's married and I know her hubby. He's in the Job. She fessed up if I promised to keep schtum.'

'Will you? Pavlou needs to know.'

Schultz broke for a second while a colleague passed close by. 'I promised I wouldn't tell, but what you do is your business. My opinion? Jenkins hasn't got the wherewithal to pull off the stuff this guy is doing. His alibi might be shaky again for number four, maybe he nipped out for a beer just to prove to himself that he's a smartypants, but I don't see him being your man. Especially for number five, we were watching him then too and lightning doesn't strike twice.'

'Famous last words? He might still have a partner.'

Schultz patted Cato's shoulder. 'I'll leave it with you.'

Approaching zero hour, Cato and Amy downed their drinks and took a leisurely stroll towards the big wheel. The queue was short. They stood back admiring the lights, enjoying the air. It was a balmy spring night, quiet for a Friday, and it was already dark. The genuine punters looked like tourists who perhaps didn't know any better — money to burn to go up high and see not very much. But it could be romantic if you were in the mood. Did Jacqui really not know the Tinder account was compromised? Would it all really be this simple? There was nowhere to go once you stepped into the gondola. No escape. Was Norman in danger? Possibly. Was anybody unduly concerned? Not really and he'd signed a liability waiver so all good, the lawyers could argue the rest later. Lip had been briefed: act normal and obey all instructions, be they from Jacqui or the TRG. Norman hovered near the booth, he'd had a late Tinder request to pre-buy two tickets. But who in the queue was Jacqui? The decision was made to allow the assignation to proceed. Go too early and jump on the wrong person, and all was lost. Best to be sure — the person who caught Norman's eye and joined him in the gondola had to be Jacqui. They'd just bring them back down again to a nice warm reception.

Norman was wired for sound so they could tell what was happening in the gondola, and contribute it to the weight of evidence. Lip was encouraged to use his journalistic skills to ask questions that would deliver useful answers. But where was Jacqui? The wheel was slowing to disgorge the previous handful of punters. It was 8.00 p.m. Was this another time-wasting, resource-wasting stunt? The queue shuffled forward, an affluent-looking baby boomer couple in matching sweatshirts. Cato had seen the same shirts around town today, there was a cruise ship in. And a young Japanese or Korean couple, rugged up and immersed in each other. And then there was Norman. The boomer cruisers stepped into their gondola and were swept up a notch to allow the young couple to step into theirs. It was Norman's turn next. The gondola glided in and he handed over his tickets. Looking around and shrugging his shoulders, Johnny-No-Mates stepped into the gondola. At the last minute a figure emerged from the shadows of the Norfolk pines and ran up, baseball cap and hooded jacket, waving. Cato tensed. He knew everyone else must have too.

A muffled cry. 'Wait, wait.'

The latecomer skipped into Norman's gondola and up it went.


Their earpieces were linked to the van monitoring the conversation in the gondola.

There was silence. Some rustling. A polite cough. All the time the car drifting upwards.

'You must be Norman.' Slightly breathless, perhaps from the last-minute dash. Or a fey affectation.

'Jacqui, I presume,' said Norman. 'But what's your real name?'

'Jacqui will do.' A sniff. 'Nice view, eh? I can see my house from here.'

'Which one?'

'That'd be telling.'

'You're not what I imagined.'

'Meaning?'

Norman hmmmed. 'You don't seem dangerous.'

A chortle. 'Yeah, well. You get that.' A pause. 'So, here I am. What now?'

'I want to know why you're doing this.'

The gondola would be descending soon. They could slow it, stop it, seize it. A crackle through the earpiece to that effect from Pavlou.

'One more circuit,' said Cato. 'Let's hear him out.'

Pavlou assented.

'What? Meeting you?' replied Jacqui.

'Don't piss about. The murders. What's it all about?'

'Murders? Dude, I don't know what you mean.'

The thing is, realised Cato, Jacqui sounded fair dinkum. 'Bring it down,' he sighed.

The TRG surrounded the gondola as it came to rest. The safest course of action, under the circumstances, was to leave the other punters in theirs until Norman and Jacqui were off the scene. Jacqui was pressed face down onto the ground and handcuffed.

'Fuck man, what is this?'

DI Pavlou crouched down by his head. 'Who are you?'

'Kyle. Kyle Surma. I'm at WAAPA. Third year drama.' His man bun was coming loose under the stress of the encounter.

'What are you doing here, Kyle?'

'This guy put an ad on Gumtree. Paid me two hundred bucks to call myself Jacqui and deliver a message to Norman Lip.'

'What was the message?' said Cato.

'It's in my pocket. The envelope. I was about to hand it over to him.'

A TRG man extracted it, passed it over. There was a photo inside of Sharon pushing Ella in her pram, right outside their home.

# 26

'What day was this?' He showed her the picture. 'Any idea?'

Under any other circumstances this could have been a nice family Saturday morning. The house was theirs again. The painters had pretty much finished: a couple of window frames needed touching up but there was no need to get them back in for that. Even the parting had been more or less back on even keel. Nat returned to his charming and helpful self, cleaned up some of his handiwork, and Steve knocked two hundred bucks off the bill for the unfinished windows plus a further ten per cent discount for cash payment. The black economy, backbone of the nation. Ella had slept through all night. Phil's recent long days and absences had made Sharon's heart grow fonder. They'd even had a delicious early morning bonk. A slow, sensuous, tender affair. Phil looming over her, a softness in his eyes. At first she'd mistaken it for fear. But that had dissolved. Until she woke this morning and realised she hadn't been mistaken at all.

She studied the photo. It had been taken through a car window across the road and a little way down the street from where they lived. 'Recent, I think.' She prodded the picture. 'I only got that top about a fortnight ago.' She gave it further thought. 'Last week, I reckon. Tuesday.' They both squinted at the calendar on the kitchen wall. 'The nineteenth.' Ella gave a squeal of delight. She was bouncing in her Jolly Jumper in the kitchen doorway.

'Same day I got my head kicked in by the graffiti guy.'

'Connected, you think?'

'Who knows?' He shrugged. 'Don't suppose you got a car description and rego?'

'Sure, I log all comings and goings in the area as a matter of course.' She shook her head. 'Any busybodies in the street who might have?'

'The bloke a few doors up is a saddo curtain-twitcher. I'll ask him.'

'Getting Ella out of the house is a major military campaign. Nothing would have happened before at least nine-thirty.'

'And it looks like you're going, rather than coming, so definitely early rather than late.'

Sharon found herself enjoying the exchange. Shared cop stuff. Pity it related to a probable threat on their lives. 'So where to from here? Do I need to be an American Mom and start packin'?'

'Wouldn't hurt.' He reached his hand out, folded it over hers. 'Or you could go away for a while until we've caught the bastard.'

'How long? A week? A month? What if you don't find him?'

'He'll come looking for us by the sound of things.'

Ella seemed to be tiring of the Jolly Jumper. Sharon lifted her to freedom. 'It's settled then.'


Cato was at work by 8.30 a.m. On his way he'd knocked on the door of the curtain-twitcher, but there had been no answer. He'd catch him later. Overnight there had been some progress: a wakeful resident in the townhouses over the road from Missy Moos had looked out of her window and seen a car parked behind the burger joint in the early hours. A dark sedan. No signs of people or movement though. Earlier in the evening, around 8.30, a dog walker had seen two blokes, arms around each other's shoulders, stumbling across Wilson Park heading south-east towards the South Fremantle McMansions. One bloke big and well-built, the other was shorter, stocky, podgy even. Drunk, he assumed. They were chatting amiably enough.

'Barry knew his killer?' Cato wondered aloud.

'Or he'll gas with anybody who seems friendly,' suggested Pavlou. 'Or it wasn't even them.'

'But if it was, and Barry was killed in the park, then where was the car and what happened between then and dumping the body at Missy Moos some four or five hours later?'

'He drove around with Barry in the boot. Or parked up somewhere for a while.'

'Risky,' said Cato.

'Murder tends to be.'

Finally a glimpse on CCTV outside a South Terrace bike shop — a dark sedan leaving the area, turning left into Douro Road and heading east. The tow bar cushioned by a fluoro green tennis ball and the rego plate obscured. The time was 1.16 a.m.

'Chris Thornton is chasing more CCTV along any variations on the route from there.' Pavlou was twitchy, she needed a cigarette. 'Join me outside?'

Cato skipped across the road and brought them both back a coffee while Pavlou took her nicotine fix. She looked worried. 'How's the family?'

'Good.'

'Do you want me to make arrangements for accommodation somewhere? Bali maybe?'

'Not practical. We're staying put.'

'I don't think that's a good idea.'

Cato shrugged. 'As Sharon said, this could drag on and on. We might never catch him.'

'What do you think?'

'If he's really fixated on us for whatever reason then he's going to come and find us.'

'I like your commitment and work ethic, but there's really no need to use your own family as bait for a serial killer.'

'That's pretty much what I said to Sharon.' Cato drained his coffee. 'Feel free to have a marked car parked outside as a deterrence. Otherwise, unless you have a specific task in mind I'm going to devote my day to working out who this killer might be.'


So who *did* hate him this much? Cato left his computer closed and sat there with a biro and note pad. Names, any names, just make a start. So far he had Jenkins father and son, recent converts to the 'Get Cato' club and both carried murderous spite in their veins. Who else? He'd shot a man once, turned him quadriplegic, a gangster with connections and a vengeful brother in prison. Cato added them both to the list. Brothers and fathers and sons, the age-old story. Ever since the Old Testament, revenge — a game the whole family can play. Who else? He'd helped frame a man once, putting him away for ten years for something he didn't do. That would quicken the blood. Another name on the list. Who else? There were so many he'd put away for shorter sentences or hadn't physically harmed or fitted up. It wasn't inconceivable that someone could develop a lethal grudge over a twelve-month stretch for selling drugs or king-hitting a stranger or stealing a truckload of power tools. If so, then the list would be longer than the Doomsday Book. No, this had to be somebody whose life he had substantially altered, whose dreams he had shattered. But who?

Cato checked the time: nearly half-eleven. He opened up his computer and logged into the case database. If Barry's death and dumping behind Missy Moos was a direct message to Cato, was there something about the other deaths he was missing? He trawled through the lists and photos from the crime scenes. There was the usual detritus but what about those strange items that didn't immediately fit, that you wouldn't normally expect? Like an empty mustard jar near Maureen Bryant. Cato brought up the photo: Dijonnaise, it said on the label. He was none the wiser. The wharf where Dean Pearson was found: bottles, cans, cigarette ends, a used condom. It bore no traces of Dean, inside or out, according to the labs. What else? The noodle packet, Master Kong Spicy Beef, Chinese style. Traces of said noodles had been found in Dean's stomach contents so it explained the packet crumpled up under his makeshift pillow of spare clothes crammed into a shopping bag. Nothing of consequence from the Rockingham car park. If there were any messages in any of this, they were more cryptic than those crosswords Cato tackled most days.

Meanwhile Chris Thornton was building a picture of where the dark sedan went after it left South Fremantle in the early hours. Another CCTV camera at a fast-food outlet had picked it up on Rockingham Road at the junction with Phoenix Road, turning left and heading further east and south. Nothing after that. Thornton was now following up on the rego plates of other cars picked up not far behind the sedan, tracing the owners to see what they remembered about where it went. The car was already out there on the police Twitter and Facebook feeds from Thornton's earlier work — *#HaveYouSeenThisCar*: a nondescript dark sedan with a fluoro tennis ball on the tow bar. A remarkable number of people claimed they had. That would be followed up, filtering out the genuine from the mistaken, mad and malicious. Maybe the killer was parked outside Cato's home right now, sharpening his axe for Sharon and Ella. He gave her a call.

'Everything okay?'

'Yep, the washing's on, Ella's just filled her nappy and I've sent the toyboy home after fucking his brains out. You?'

Cato smiled. 'Just wondering if you need me to get anything on the way home. Milk? Bread? A Glock and a box of bullets?'

'Some more nappies would be good. When are you due home?'

'Mid-arvo maybe? Everything is kind of in hand here, the wheels are turning well enough without me.'

'So why are you there?'

'I'm making a list of anybody who hates me.'

'How's it going?'

'Mercifully short but maybe I'm deluding myself.'

'Keep on the right side of me and it will stay short. See you when I see you. Wait ... what's that noise?' Cato's heart jumped in his mouth. 'Just joking,' said Sharon. 'Thought it might get you home quicker.'


Norman Lip was idly flipping through his Tinder gallery. Maybe a bit of release was what he needed. There were two messages waiting for him, from Jacqui, but he didn't want to play. He was aware that even right now his thumb swipes were probably being monitored. It felt strange. Would Big Brother approve or disapprove of his choices? It was like having a heavy breather wanking in your wardrobe with an eye glued to the keyhole. Maybe he could write a piece on it. Oh, yes, that's right, he was unemployed. Still, the idea of the wanker in the wardrobe strangely titillated him. It added a degree of urgency to his thumb swipes. In the end though, he succumbed. What did Jacqui want now?

**Sorry. Forgive me?**

He opened the second one.

**I don't want to lose you.**

He deleted both and went back to his thumb swipes. He avoided the overly pouty selfies and the arm-squeeze cleavage, fearing a clash of egos with his own. Finally he came across Zoe from Applecross — likes: clubs, good food, cool music, real men, passion.

*Do you like jazz?* she'd asked.

Fucking hate it actually. *Biensur!*

*What?*

*Yes.*

After a couple more exchanges he had a date that night at Creatures NextDoor. He admired his reflection in the phone screen; he hadn't lost his touch. His eyes strayed to his notebook: leather-bound, he'd found it in a street market in Surabaya, it was like his own Joseph Conrad moment. It cost him just four bucks to feel like a writer. Except it was a transitory feeling, and the book was barely touched. He was incapable of writing even the first line of the great Australian novel. Or word for that matter. There were no notes of interesting conversations he'd overheard. Why would there be? He was too busy talking over them. Nor were there any musings on the universal condition of the human soul. With the right shirt and kitchen gadget, you could just look like you know that shit. No attempts to lyrically capture that fall of light at a certain time of day on the water or through the trees. He'd already snapped it on his iPhone so job done. He was a fraud. Wait. He suddenly realised he was doing deep self-awareness. That was kinda cool.

But there *was* something in that notebook, a scribbled note on page one. The night he'd bedded that woman from Adelaide, the woman from Big Pharma over for a conference. That view from her hotel window. The man who would be Jacqui, sitting in a dark car watching the police go about their work. Lip had known this time would come. Half a rear rego plate glimpsed in a weird play of light — it had been covered in that reflective film the hoons liked to use but it had curled and partly peeled away. All he needed to do was hand the information over to the cops and they'd have their man. Yeah, okay, so maybe if he was a good guy he should have passed this over to them straight away, but what would that have meant for him? Big fat nothing. They'd made an offer for him to be part of the action then almost as soon withdrawn it: like it was his fault the dero died. But now he needed to trace this plate, find the killer himself and deliver him up. Wouldn't that be the mother of all scoops?

While waiting for lunch, pasta at a joint down the street and around the corner on Mouat, Cato brought up Dean's journal on his iPad. A cold Wednesday in late July and a few days left to live.

*Fuck that was a cold night. Shiver shiver shiver + Jenkins piss up my nose. Too many crazies around here + old blokes sobbing or high. One shouting sorry, sorry, sorry over + over. Some war he was in some family he killed. No angel to tuck him in say night night my love sweet dreams*

More Pokémon-style drawings. A winged dragon breathing fire. A man with a sad face and tears.

*Over this shit. Maybe I could make it up with Dad + go to uni + be a good boy. Thing is I could be perfect + he still wont want me around. That bloke reading the paper at the cafe over the road. No hurries no worries. What a life.*

Cato's pasta arrived and he dug in. Was the crazy, sobbing army vet Chris White? Was the bloke reading the paper in the cafe stalking Dean? Or were they both nobodies in the legion of passers-by and fellow travellers in Dean's doomed life? Family again emerging as a theme, Dean not fitting into his. Feeling abandoned by his father. Significant, or just the universal stuff of life? Trying to find clues in this diary seemed as big a task as tracing back through his own history. But the same killer was lurking somewhere in those shared shadows.

Jake felt like punching someone again. Anyone. Simon had made some snide comment about a shitty chore that needed doing. The word 'freeloader' was in there somewhere. Jake had told him to get fucked and get a life.

Mum. 'Tone it down in front of the twins, guys.'

Simon. 'I'm not the one using profanities. Don't say "guys" when you mean "Jake".'

Mum to Jake. 'Can you do those jobs sometime this morning, love? Keep the peace?'

She was meant to say, 'Back off Simon, Jake is my son, he's my family, he lives here as long as he wants.' But she didn't. Instead she said, 'Maybe empty the bins before you go out, sweetie?'

He didn't.

And he left his bedroom light on.

And the tap dripping in the bathroom.

And squeezed the toothpaste tube at the top.

And didn't bother picking his towel up off the floor.

Or washing his breakfast dishes.

He hopped off the bus and walked across the car park to the gym entrance. A car pulled up alongside him.

'Hop in, sexy. We're goin' for a drive.'

Jake cheered up just at the sight of Lance's face. He slung his bag in the back and climbed in. 'You'll get fat if you keep piking out on your seshes.'

Lance slapped his tight midriff and dragged Jake's hand across onto it. 'I am already. Feel that. Jelly.'

'Disgusting.' Jake pulled his hand away, laughing, flushed. 'Where we going, then?'

'You'll see.' Lance plugged his iPod in and found some tunes. Retro stuff, seventies rock.

'What's this crap?'

'Philistine.' Lance cranked up the volume. 'Aussie rock, maaaate! The best.'

Batshit crazy. Jake soaked it up. They were heading east on Leach Highway: fast food, fuel and furnishings. The old guy from way back was singing about how most people he knew thought he was crazy. Yep, that was right up Lance's street. 'What you been up to, then?'

'This and that. How's life with Daddy?'

'Shit. They don't want me around either. Went back home.'

'Home?'

'Mum's. I got suspended from school for decking a dick.'

'Good work!' They bumped fists. 'And how did Mummy take it?'

'Doesn't know yet but I know what it'll be.' Jake screwed up his face and put on a prissy voice. 'We're very disappointed with you, Jacob. What's going on?'

'You know what you need?'

'Tell me.'

'Sex and drugs and rock'n'roll.' He shuffled his iPod and a song came on with those very same words. Lance made it blast. The song was bad, so bad, but funny as. He reached over and snapped open the glove box. Handed Jake a tin box. 'Check that out.'

Three fat spliffs.

'Help yourself,' said Lance.

Jake lit up. The suburbs slid by and on they drove. Soon they were climbing into the hills. In the wing mirror Jake could see behind him a low blanket of grey-brown smog hovering over the city beneath an explosion of blue sky. He checked the clock on the dashboard.

'When will we be heading back?' said Jake.

'What for?' said Lance. 'It's Saturday. No school. No work. Your parents suck and homework's a waste of fuckin' time. Right?'

Jake nodded. Convincing himself. 'Right.' He got out his phone. 'I'll just text them and let them know I'm out for the day. See me when they see me.'

Lance took the phone out of Jake's hand and tossed it in the back seat. 'No need for that. You're your own man now. Right?' He turned and gave him a grin. 'Right?'

'Right,' said Jake.


While he waited for his contact to get back to him, Norman rushed over to keep his weekly appointment with Naomi. She was in good spirits, hair brushed, and wearing her 'I'm With Stupid' T-shirt.

'Let's just stay here and get a cuppa from the kitchen.'

'What, with all those oldies you hate so much?'

'You can wheel me out to the Rose Garden where they leave the demented ones. Nobody will believe them if they dob me in for smoking.'

And there they sat for a solid hour and a half, drinking tea made from cheap, weak bags and exchanging a whole bunch of childhood memories that Norman hadn't realised he'd forgotten. Some were happy, and they cacked themselves. Some, not so.

'D'you reckon Mum knew about Dad's affairs?'

'Course she did, Normie. He didn't try to hide it.'

'Arsehole.'

'She's well out of it now. Both of them are. No need for us to worry any more.'

'Pity she took the coward's way out. You might not have to be in here now.'

'What? You reckon it was her duty to look after me? You're a fucking judgemental, Neanderthal prick sometimes, Norman.'

'Yeah, well.'

'Yeah, well nothing. I don't need anyone. Don't need Mum, don't need you.'

'Yes, you do.' He grinned. 'You're useless without me. Admit it.'

'Right, this one hour a week is all I live for. That tiny window of irreplaceable family warmth you slot between Tinder hook-ups and editorial deadlines. The intellectual stimulation. Speaking of which, what's with you and Mephisto?'

'Who?'

'Google it, you ignoramus. The devil you're dealing with.'

'Oh, him. He's got too big for his boots. Time the tables were turned.' He'd decided to keep his sacking to himself. No need to burden her with that.

A shadow across her face. 'Watch yourself with this, alright? Have you got an exit strategy?'

'Don't worry, sis. All under control.' He lifted his chin at her T-shirt. 'You only wear that when you've had a really good day. So tell me,' he smiled. 'Who is he?'

Naomi blushed. A rare thing indeed. 'This new volunteer carer. Wheels us here, there and everywhere. Cups of tea. Chats. He's spent a lot of time with me this week. Probably 'cause I'm better looking and smarter than everybody else here. And about forty years younger.'

'Spoken like a true Lip.'

'He was here this morning pressing his firm tummy against my shoulders while he brushed my hair. I'm hoping to persuade him to change my nappy next time he visits.'

'Sis!'

A dirty laugh. 'Got to take your chances when they come, mate.'

Norman's phone beeped. He checked it. 'Gotta go, sis.'

She reached up for a goodbye hug. Not like her. But it felt nice anyway. 'Take care, Normie. You hear?'


People Who Hate Me, Part Two. After lunch Cato returned to his list. He'd trodden on some toes in China — a billionaire and his family put before a firing squad after he helped entrap them on trumped-up corruption charges. Still, they had it coming, they were behind the murder of his colleague. An up-and-coming gangster left floating in a river in Shanghai. Again, not undeservedly. Did those people have friends or relatives with a score to settle? In both cases he was aware of their extraordinarily long reach and resourcefulness but he remained unconvinced.

Nudging four o'clock, he decided to call it a day. He picked up disposable nappies on the way home and dropped by the curtain-twitching neighbour up the street to see if he recalled a serial killer photographing Cato's house recently. The man was underemployed, too young to retire, too old to be bossed around. He wore a diarrhoea-coloured Neil Young T-shirt and nervously scratched his untidy grey facial fuzz. He wasn't used to talking to his neighbours, only watching them.

'Frank.' The bloke offered a hand for shaking.

'Phil,' Cato obliged and then explained himself. 'So, do you recall seeing anything unusual that day?'

'Come through,' said Frank. 'I'll just check the calendar.'

Cato was led up a dingy hallway that needed airing, back to a surprisingly bright kitchen and a view on to a well-kept, verdant backyard. 'Nice place,' said Cato.

'Yeah,' said Frank. 'Thanks.' He took the calendar down off the wall: Huts of Australia. September was somewhere in Tasmania beside a tarn. 'What day did you say?' Cato told him. Frank traced a finger along, tongue poking out between his lips. 'Tuesday.'

'Yep.'

'You had the cops around later in the day. Vandalism. That big "Y" on your gable end.'

'That's right.'

Frank nodded, consulted a notebook. 'A young bloke popped something in your mailbox not long after you went to work, around seven-fifteen.'

'Description?'

'Fit. Full of himself.' His finger traced a line down the page. 'And there was a car parked just over the road for an hour or so, eight-thirty to nine-forty. Pointing the wrong way.'

'Colour? Make?'

'Dark blue. Mazda.'

'Did you get the rego?'

Frank gave him a sideways glance. 'Reckon I'm a snooping busybody or something?'

'Hoping you are,' said Cato.

'Nice to be appreciated for a change.' He gave Cato the rego number.

'Notice anything about the car or the occupant?'

'No, not really, he stayed inside, I got the impression of a young'un though.'

'Why?'

'He was playing crap music.'

This was getting too good to be true. Cato's blood quickened. 'Could it have been the same person as earlier, the one who put something in the mailbox?'

'Who knows? Maybe.'

'Anything else? Did he get out of the car?'

'Nope, he stuck his phone out the window and snapped a couple off, just as your wife was taking the tacker for a stroll. Then he left.'


'It must have been Nat.'

'Nat?'

'The painter boy,' said Sharon. 'The description fits. Gym bod, cocky as.' She rummaged among the detritus on the kitchen counter beside the phone and dug out the business card that had been dropped in the letterbox that day.

Cato phoned through the car rego number for Thornton to check. No mention of any Nat. 'David Samuels, an address in Yangebup.' Cato wrote it down. 'What do you want to do about it, boss?'

They could get the ninjas round there and kick his door in. 'Give me a sec, I'll call you back. Meantime send his licence details through to me, his pic, I need to see it.'

He conferred with Sharon. What was her impression? This was a bloke who'd given her the shits while he was working here in their house. She shrugged. 'Maybe the kid just saw the police activity, saw the graffiti and lined himself up some work.'

Or he did the graffiti himself and was there the following day, first in, best dressed. 'The photographs?' said Cato.

'Evidence for his boss. Get in quick, kind of thing?'

'But?'

She chewed on her lip. 'He's worth a conversation. I'd met him on the beach walking track before that. Again, personal space was not his strong point. He likes to be in control. Put that together with this, and you could interpret it as stalking.'

Cato got on the phone to DI Pavlou and brought her up to date.

'No record?'

'Nothing. He's clean. We've been trying to get hold of his employer, bloke called Steve Nichols, but no reply. Neighbour says he often takes the family out on his boat on the weekends.' An incoming call from Thornton. He asked Pavlou to hold.

Thornton was breathless, excited. 'David Samuels is on our list of volunteers working for an NGO connected with the homeless.'

'We've already talked to him?'

'Not yet. He was always out when we called. We left messages on his mobile. He was on the action list for the coming week.' Thornton felt the need to defend himself. 'It was a big list, boss. And with no previous he wasn't high on it.'

Cato got back to Pavlou.

'Let's bring him in,' she said.


It was a plain brick place in Yangebup, a few kilometres inland south-east of Fremantle, with a driveway sloping down from the road: an anywhere suburban house of the 1970s with neglected rosebushes in the front yard and a patchy lawn that needed mowing. Beyond the cordon, the neighbours stood casually interested, battlers for the most part, saving up for a bigger house in a better suburb. They smoked and chatted to each other, lifted their phones to get a selfie with the TRG armoured truck in the background. The driveway was empty and it looked like there was nobody home.

Cato, Pavlou and Thornton were kitted up in Kevlar and ready to go in behind the TRG. Samuels wasn't answering his phone. Nor was his housemate Ferdinand Navarro, an electrician in Australia on a 457 visa, three months off the plane from Manila. The licence photo of Samuels hadn't registered with Sharon.

'Sure?' asked Cato. 'That's not Nat?'

'Pretty sure.'

'False ID?'

'Or different person,' she'd said.

The TRG gave the all clear and the detectives moved in, fanning out around the house. The kitchen was sparse, fridge all but empty except for basics of milk and marge and a few eggs and vegies, sliced white in the bread box, washing up stacked on the draining rack. In the lounge room, a wide-screen TV and remote, and a three-piece facing it. Basketball and boxing DVDs on a shelf. Navarro's room had a photo of him and his family on a bedside table: a smiling wife and three daughters. They looked a nice enough bunch. Some clothes hanging in a wardrobe, an empty suitcase pushed under the bed. It felt like a room that hadn't been lived in for a while. Cato hoped there was nothing sinister behind that. Samuel's room: queen single, made up, polyester blue and white striped doona. Clothes in drawers and on hangers. Bland casuals, no distinctive character. All to be bagged and tested by forensics. Work boots, size ten Steel Blues. No family photographs, no books or music to give any indication of personality. A blank canvas.

'Let's leave the detail to Duncan and his crew,' said Pavlou.

They retreated from the house. Beyond the cordon, two news crews had materialised and a helicopter hovered overhead. Thornton was dispatched back to the station to collate everything there was on David Samuels. A squad meeting would be held an hour hence. His description, the car's description and rego were already in circulation.

This man, if it was the same one, had spent the last week or so in Cato's house with his wife and child. He racked his brains for a memory of the name and what he might have done to incur the man's wrath. Samuels. Who the hell was this vengeful and dangerous human being who had made threats to Sharon and Ella? And why, given the opportunity, had he not already followed through?

'He's twenty-two years old. Works as an odd-jobber, hotel doorman, builder's labourer, you name it. Volunteers with a religious charity, Street Angels, they help the homeless as long as they're prepared to endure some fire and brimstone with their cup of soup.'

Thornton had been busy. He'd pinned a copy of the licence photo of David Samuels up on the board. Cato studied it. A young, strong and fresh face, firm jaw, gym neck. Sculpted facial hair and more than a hint of vanity. The gallery of rogues he'd put away was a large one and this face was as vaguely familiar as any of them.

'No previous,' said Thornton. 'Not a peep across all states.'

So how had he crossed paths with Cato? Where did the grudge come from? 'Family? Associates?' he said out loud.

'Parents are dead, according to a form he filled out when he signed up with Street Angels. But they don't have the manpower to check on their employees or volunteers. Plenty of faith in the Lord though.'

'School records?' asked Cato.

'Nothing. We're still chasing it.'

'Birth certificate?'

'Same. I know what you're thinking. Is David Samuels even his real name?'

Pavlou stepped up. 'Thanks Chris, keep digging.' She actioned Deb Hassan and Amy Trimboli to talk to the painting boss to see if Nat and Samuels were the same man, get a photo of Nat if there was one. She met Cato's eye, tapped the photo of Samuels. 'Ring any bells?'

Cato shook his head.

Duncan Goldflam and his team would be scraping the Yangebup house. Thornton and his data wranglers would be looking for traces of Samuels on any records anywhere. IT Imogen was tracking phones and internet accounts linked to David Samuels, aka Jacqui. Doors were being knocked, CCTV collated and mobile patrols were on the lookout. Once again, Cato felt surplus to requirements even though he was central to what all this was about. Pavlou closed the meeting and pulled Cato aside.

'Samuels has declared his hand. We're on to him. It's only a matter of time.'

'Boss.'

'But we both know that makes him more erratic, unpredictable now. Fair chance he'll come looking for you. Time to come inside, Philip.'

She was right. They organised for a car to go and fetch Sharon and Ella and they'd all be put up in a secured hotel for the foreseeable.

'Shit,' said Sharon when he phoned her with the news. 'I'd just got Ella down for a sleep.'

'Sorry,' he said. 'We're close now, a matter of hours, has to be.'

'Gives me the creeps knowing he was here all that time.' A doorbell in the background. 'That must be the patrol car,' said Sharon. 'So who is he? What's he got to do with us?'

'I don't know,' said Cato.


Norman Lip had tried the number he'd been given: a friend of a friend of a bikie who had a pet cop who did computer searches for a price. He'd used a street payphone to avoid the monitoring. Real Woodward and Bernstein stuff. After a brief exchange, where they agreed an amount, he was provided with a name and address. He'd gone down there on his Vespa, seen the police vehicles and the cordon. He wondered how they'd got their breakthrough. He'd seen the Chinese detective, Cato Kwong, beyond the cordon. Norman felt frustration and shame in equal parts. Each time he thought he was on a win, it was snatched away. He texted to cancel his evening date with Zoe the Jazz Lover as things were getting interesting and he wanted to stay in the game. As soon as he finished, his phone beeped: a message from an unknown number. It was a photo of some bloke, bleeding, a plastic supermarket bag over his head. Norman seized the initiative.

**Hi Dave, whats your point?**

A pause. **I knew you'd get there in the end**

**I joined the good guys**

**Oh no!**

Norman closed his phone. He wondered, bleakly, who the bloke was in the photo. His phone went again.

**I want to confess**

Norman ignored him. Enough. This had to stop.

*It's all over They will have me soon This is your last chance*

Norman thought about it. Career up the spout and this mad prick-teasing fucker was all he had to show for it. And now, clearly, another victim had been lined up.

*No more, I'm finished with you, I hope they catch you soon crackpot*

A few seconds later another photograph came through from another number. No words this time. But his blood ran cold all the same.

Sharon went to answer the door. The bell rang again and woke Ella who gave a little mewl of complaint.

'Coming!'

She opened up. It was Nat. 'Hi,' he said. 'Can I come in?'

She closed the door on him but his foot was in the gap. Sharon pulled it open and slammed it back on his ankle as hard as she could.

'Ow, fuck! No need for that. I only want to talk.'

She ran down the corridor into Ella's room and pushed whatever furniture she could find against the door. Ella was bellowing by now. Sharon quick-dialled Cato's number. 'He's here!'

'Samuels?'

'Yes, Nat, him. He's in the house.' The door handle turned. 'Oh god.'

Nat's voice. 'I just want to talk to you, Sharon ...'

'I'm nearly there,' said Cato down the phone. Engine noise and sirens in the background. 'Hold on.'

'Sharon.' Nat pushed against the barricade. 'Don't be scared. It's just me.' Another shove. Stronger, more determined. Sharon struggled to keep the chest of drawers from toppling. 'There's no need for this. Really.'

'The police are on their way. Give yourself up, now,' she hissed.

'Police?'

There was loud thumping in the hallway, voices, orders, crashing sounds. After a while a calm voice, female. 'You can come out now.'

Nat was lying on his stomach, hands cuffed behind his back. The knee of a male constable on his neck. 'Get them off me!'

'You put your business card in my mailbox. You did the graffiti. You took photos of me and my child. Who the fuck are you?'

'Photos?'

At that moment, Cato came through the door, ready to kill.

The female uniform got in his way. 'Everything's under control, sir. We have him.' She explained that they had received instructions to pick up Sharon and Ella and interrupted what seemed to be a home invasion.

'Home invasion?' said Nat, face squashed against the floorboards. 'This is ...'

'This is going to take some explaining,' said Sharon, gesturing for the knee hold to be eased. 'So start now.'

# 27

They were on the top floor of a short-stay apartment block overlooking the river at North Fremantle. Two uniforms posted outside the door and a vanload more in the car park downstairs. Sun setting through the railway bridge, massive dock cranes in silhouette. Ella was fractious and wouldn't settle; Cato and Sharon were much the same.

'How long do we have to do this for?'

Cato chucked a half-eaten slice of delivery pizza back onto the cardboard box. 'Not long, I hope.' But he didn't have a clue and they both knew it.

Nat was just Nat. A cocky creep who kept himself in fairly constant casual painting jobs by doing the odd bit of graffiti, then dropping a business card in his victim's mailbox, like a volunteer firefighter taking to arson to keep himself busy. The jury was out on whether Steve the Boss was in on the scam or not. In this case, though, Nat insisted, he hadn't done this particular spray-painting, he'd just noticed it in passing and saw an opportunity. So what was he doing this time on Sharon's doorstep? He had called round ostensibly to pick up an iPod he'd left behind but it was clear he'd also developed a fixation on Sharon and had fantasies that she might reciprocate. He had a fetish for what he described as 'bored older housewives' and claimed a fifty-fifty strike rate.

'Ugh,' said Sharon.

True, Nat shared the same gym-honed physique as Samuels but his was not the photo on the driver's licence. Certain. Fact.

Meanwhile Samuels' Filipino housemate Ferdinand Navarro had finally been located. He was alive and well. He'd been down south fishing with some compatriots, phone turned off. Detectives were now grilling him to find out as much as they could about David Samuels.

'Nice guy,' was the gist of it. 'Funny. Good at sharing the bills.'

There'd been a brief flurry of excitement when they learned that Samuels and Norman Lip had been in contact in the last few hours operating from yet another in his supply of pay-as-you-go mobiles: a photo of the probable next victim, another poor homeless person with a bag over his head and the revelation that Norman Lip already knew the name of the killer.

*Hi Dave, whats your point?*

'We ran a check,' said Chris Thornton. 'Somebody else looked him up on the vehicle rego database earlier today: a DC from Bunbury. Not the first time he's done this kind of thing apparently. He's getting a good talking to as we speak. Might need to show due cause why he shouldn't be out on his arse.'

And an assignation had been arranged.

*I want to confess ... It's all over ... They will have me soon ...*

'Norman has gone AWOL,' confirmed DI Pavlou. 'We kicked his door in but he's off chasing his big scoop.'

It didn't need to be said: Norman Lip was probably a dead man. Nobody seemed overly concerned at the prospect.

David Samuels, once again one step ahead, and playing with them. But who the hell was David Samuels and who was that doomed bloke with a bag over his head? Another photo had been sent to Lip from a different number. No message. It was a picture of a woman in a wheelchair, smiling up at the camera. Chris Thornton had done some homework: apparently it was Lip's sister looking well and happy. Not apparently germane to the enquiry.

'If all of this is about you, why does he have to hurt other people?' Sharon detached Ella, asleep at last, from her nipple. 'Not that I want him to cut to the chase or anything.'

'Maybe they're to keep his furnace burning.'

'He's building to his big finish and you're it.' She shuddered. 'He knows you're watching and listening and he's laying out the trail.' Sharon gave him a warning glare. 'And don't you even think about following it.'

'No danger.' Cato took another bite of cold pizza. His phone thrummed on the carpet. It was Jane, his ex.

'Is Jake with you?'

'No.'

Jane tutted. 'He's not answering his phone. He does this.'

'Anything happened in particular?' said Cato, feeling guilty for neglecting to call and discuss the school incident with her.

An almost audible bristling at the other end of the line. 'Nothing out of the ordinary. He and Simon had words. It's a weekly occurrence these days. Stormed out just before lunch.'

'Did the school contact you?'

'I had a letter about him not doing his homework and being a disruptive influence.'

'Nothing about him being suspended? The fight?'

A sigh. 'No.'

Obviously Jake hadn't mentioned it either. Cato explained, apologising along the way for his own neglect. 'I was going to call you, and him. Talk about everything that's going on. Work out what's for the best, for him. Us.'

'I was wondering why he was back home so soon. No word from him, you, anyone.'

'Been busy, it's madness here. The enquiry. All that.'

'Yeah,' said Jane. She'd heard it all before, Cato's lame excuses for lax fatherhood. 'That might explain Jake's brittleness the last twenty-four hours. He's been a real pain lately. I just can't get through.'

'He's probably gone to a mate's for a big whinge and he'll be back when he's hungry.'

'That's the thing. His mates rang for him, wondered where he was.'

Cato checked the time. Jake had been off the radar for about six or seven hours and it wasn't the first time he'd done this in his teenagerdom. Still a little early to be getting worried? 'How about we give it another hour or two?'

'Okay. You're probably right.' A pause, drawing perhaps on her reserves of grace and civility. 'How's the family?'

The other one, he thought. The one that's not you, me and Jake. He wondered if that was also going through her mind. 'Good. Sleep is a distant memory but I wouldn't be dead for quids. How about the twins?'

'Same. But double.'

'Simon?'

'Seems to have discovered his inner grumpy old man these last few months. Bit disappointing really.'

'Chin up,' said Cato, strangely cheered. 'Let me know when Jake appears.'

He didn't have to wait long. Jane phoned back half an hour later. 'Got a text. He's sleeping over at a mate's, guy from the gym.' She sounded relieved.

'Great,' said Cato. 'We can all sleep easy, then.'


Norman had tried phoning Naomi — no answer. Then he'd phoned the care home.

'Isn't she with you?' they said.

'I wouldn't be phoning you otherwise.'

'David told us you were all catching up for dinner and he'd bring her back after that.'

David. The new volunteer carer. 'Did you ever check David's references, you fucking morons?'

He'd found a payphone at his local deli and dialled the most recent mobile number, the one that sent her photo — wearing the same shirt he'd seen her in this morning: I'm with Stupid. The pic had been taken by her new carer mate at River View.

'Hi, Normie.'

'How did you find her?'

'You need to check your rear-view more often.'

'You don't need to threaten her. She's not part of this. Please.'

*Watch yourself with this, alright? Have you got an exit strategy?*

'Trust me. She'll be fine as long as you do what you're told.'

# 28

*Blood stains the greasy frayed carpet. Traffic roaring by on the highway. I'm floating high above it all, looking down on this sorry world we've created: a trail of ants carrying food and other debris to and from the colony. Looking down on the pulsing city squeezing blood along its arteries. Looking down through a microscope zooming in on the dark clusters of cancer cells reproducing, re-forming, multiplying. Down on the rot and dieback in the forest undergrowth, eating away at the core of life, light and goodness. Down on the swamp, the microbes and the belching gases sucking and oozing.*

*Blow out some smoke. Good shit this.*

*I read. I observe. People don't get that about me. They see muscles, they see casual worker, they see a kid who fucked up at school and never had a hope of going to uni. They see cashed-up bogan. Yobbo. They expect the least, the worst, not much.*

*I pull the bag off his head and take another photo. Switch on a table lamp to help illuminate the scene. I'm good at this. In another life I might have been a film or theatre director. An artist. I watch movies and TV. I play video games. I understand production values, presentation, all that shit. Pride in your work. I don't need to spend three years on campus with a bunch of wankers to prove myself. The old man never did. He used his brain, his fists. School of life.*

*He gave it everything he had. Put himself on the line. For me.*

*'Presentation?' he'd say. 'Yeah, sure. There's a difference between having your tea and having people round for dinner. People like to think they're getting value for money. Suck them in and suck them dry. The toffs have been doing that for years and we're as good as any of them. That right, son?'*

*Yes, Dad. This is the least I can do. The worst. Not much. But enough.*

# 29

It was just after midnight when Cato woke to his phone buzzing. Norman Lip.

'What do you want?'

'I need to talk to you. I tried knocking at your door. You're not at home.'

'Neither are you. We checked. Where's Samuels, are you with him?'

'No. We really need to talk, you and me.'

Sharon stirred. She looked fragile, exhausted. 'I'm not interested in any more of your games,' said Cato. 'If you've got information pass it over to Crimestoppers.'

'Samuels wants to meet you.'

'Tell him I'll be ready and waiting. In my office. Monday morning. Tomorrow. Whatever.'

'Tonight.'

'Get lost. This is another stunt, he's playing you, Norman.' Cato closed his phone and sank back into bed.

A minute later the phone went again, an SMS this time. He angrily snatched the phone up with the intention of turning it off completely. But of course he had to check. A photo. The supermarket bag had been removed from the head of Samuel's probable next victim.

It was Jake.

An icy stillness at his core. Cato had been focused on his immediate family. Sharon, Ella, himself. It had never occurred to him that his son could be in danger. He rang Norman.

'Looks like it's still his game and his rules, huh?' said Lip.

The gist was that they had been summoned: Samuels wanted

Norman to bring Cato to him. A choked sob. 'He's got my sister. Naomi.' That other photo of the woman in the wheelchair. Not so innocent after all. 'So we've got no choice. Have we?'

'Jesus, what a mess. This better not be another trick.'

A sigh. 'I'm just the messenger boy. Tell me where you are.' Cato did. 'I'll be there in half an hour, wait outside.'

There was a lot to do. After telling Sharon what was going on, he phoned DI Pavlou to bring her up to speed but she'd already been alerted by IT monitoring of the latest exchange. Then he let Jane know what had happened to their son.

'You? It's all about you?' An anguished cry. 'It always fucking was.'

'I'll find him. I promise.'

'Shove your fucking promises.'

And she was gone. Cato looked at the image in his hand. Was Jake still alive? The photo looked bloody and discouraging but something told him that this wasn't a lifeless body, just an unconscious one. What told him? The straw he so desperately clutched.

'I have to go,' said Cato, 'Lip will be here any minute.'

'Uh-uh,' said Sharon, shaking her head. 'No way.'

'Jake's my son. What would you do?'

'And what about us?' Sharon said.

Both questions that neither could answer.

They were interrupted by a knock at the door. Thornton. 'Norman's got his marching orders from Samuels.'

A simple text message. **Head for the hills.**

Pavlou's head appeared behind Thornton's. 'Ready? We've got a convoy in place. Choppers, the lot. More to follow in due course.' She offered him a bulletproof vest. 'You'll need this.'

Cato strapped it on and picked up his Glock from the kitchen counter. Swept up in the tidal rush of fate and wondering still how he might change its course. He could hear Ella mumbling gaily in her cot. His chest ready to burst.

'Phil,' said Sharon. He turned. 'Be careful.'

Then he walked outside as Lip pulled into the car park.

Despite Norman's protests, his Bayswater Rental Corolla had been fitted with a GPS tracking device and was now on Roe Highway being escorted discreetly by two cars of plain-clothes TRG plus a van full of their ninja-suited colleagues two vehicles back. The chopper also kept a respectful distance. All of this was being monitored on live audio and video feeds direct to DI Pavlou and some other brass back at Freo cop shop. Cato was driving, Norman Lip in the passenger seat, cradling his phone. Something about him — cold, reckless. Past caring. A strange half-smile on his lips. At a time like this?

'Something funny?' said Cato.

'Just like TV.'

'You got what you wanted.'

'What's that?'

'Starring role.'

They left Roe and crawled up Greenmount Hill. Headlights flashed by. Lip nodded towards the cars in front. 'He's not going to buy this, is he? The escorts. He's too clever for that.'

'Or too arrogant. The jails are full of blokes who thought they were smarter than us.'

'But so far he is, isn't he?'

'So far,' conceded Cato.

'And you haven't worked out yet why he's targeting you.'

'No.'

'We could change the game,' Lip said.

'This isn't a game.'

'You know what I mean. He's making all the running. It's a game for him.'

'A game that your sister and my son have no part in. We need to stay tight on this, Norman.'

'This car's got a tracker, right?'

'Yes.'

'And the chopper, everybody, watching us all the way.'

'Yep.'

'Everybody's attention is on us here, in the hills.'

'And?'

Norman slotted his phone in the hands-free cradle, took a gun out of his jacket pocket and wedged it into the gap under Cato's armpit where the Kevlar straps joined. 'How about you make them all go away?'


'I have him.'

Yep, Norman had changed the game.

The support convoy and chopper had peeled away on request once the situation was confirmed by Cato. There was still the tracker on the car and he was in the process of disabling it. With the gun in the back of Cato's neck, Norman was on the phone to Samuels. They must have worked this out beforehand. Gambling, rightly so, on the belief that nobody would be checking Norman for a gun. Why would they?

'Where did you get it?' Cato had asked.

'It was left in my mailbox.' No prizes for guessing who by. 'Went on YouTube to work out how to use it. Borrowed a girlfriend's computer so you couldn't look over my shoulder.'

Norman had brought along a spare phone too, and Samuels was on to what must have been his sixth or seventh SIM card by now. Once he'd told the escort to leave, Cato's phone had been chucked out the car window back on Greenmount Hill, along with his Glock. Now they were parked in some bush in John Forrest National Park while Cato dismantled the tracker. It was 1.30 a.m. and clouds covered the moon. Trees rustled in the breeze, strange animal and bird sounds and scratchings. The smell of gum, mould and fox piss.

'Done,' Cato said.

'Right,' said Norman in response to something from Samuels on the other end of the phone.

Cato felt strangely calm. He at least knew now that this was not another stunt. He really was about to be delivered up to Samuels. So was Jake still alive? Would Samuels give him back in return for his real prize?

Norman took the tracking device off Cato, dropped it to the ground and stamped on it. Then he chucked it into the bush. He gestured back to the car. 'Get in.' Norman went in the back seat this time, keeping the gun pressed against Cato's neck. 'Drive back out towards Great Eastern. Keep the lights off.'

By now the UCs in their utes and battered Datsuns would be waiting to take up the chase. They'd have had a signal from the tracker right up until the last moment. Until about five minutes ago they knew where Cato was. With only a few roads in and out of John Forrest, the exits would be covered.

'What did he promise you?'

No reply.

'This doesn't guarantee her safety. You know that.'

'No,' Norman said. 'But doing nothing guarantees she'll die.' The track forked. 'Take the right.'

'Where are we going?'

'You'll see.' Norman prodded him. 'Left here.'

It was a narrow, unsealed track. Back through more bush. They weren't going out to the highway after all. 'We'll get bogged in the sand.'

'No, we won't. Keep driving.'

Tree branches scraped the side of the Corolla and the ruts got deep and uneven. The gun barrel poked painfully into his neck and Cato hoped Norman's finger was clear of the trigger. 'Brought your pen and paper?'

'What?'

'What did you call it? Interview with the vampire. The big scoop?'

'Don't start.'

'Gave up on the hard story, I see. The dissection of society, this bloke's fixation on the homeless and what that says about us as a nation. Easier to just let him control it, eh? Give you his media release to cut and paste.' Cato snorted. 'You're just a hack like all the rest.'

The gun dug into his ear. 'Please, mate. Just shut up. You don't know me. Don't even begin to try.'

'What's to know? You're a gullible fool, Norman. We're your only chance right now. Yours and Naomi's.'

'And what? You'd go in and rescue her? Where? How?' Norman moaned. 'We all know what he can do.'

'He'll kill you as well. You do know that, don't you?'

'I'm out of options.'

'No, you're not. There's still time to pull back from this.'

'No. There isn't. I stuffed up. Now I'm just doing what I need to do.'

A space opened up and they were back on a sealed surface. Ahead some parking bays, it seemed familiar. 'Pull in over there,' Norman said, and Cato started to get out of the car. 'Stay where you are.'

So they sat in the dark in a parking bay somewhere in John Forrest National Park. After a few minutes, some distance away in the gloom, a light flashed. Three times.

They were being summoned.


'Where the fuck is he?' DI Hutchens had taken the call from Deb Hassan just after 3.00 a.m.

'We don't know, boss. Somewhere in John Forrest.'

It was a place that sent shudders down his spine. A place where a body had been found some years back. A body many believed he had put there. 'And Pavlou sits back and lets it happen?'

'Didn't sound like there was much choice.'

'There's always a choice. Give me fifteen.' He dressed and had another turn on the dunny. It was all salads these days, nothing for the guts to get a good grip on.

'Off out, love?' said Marjorie, sitting up in bed and reaching for her specs and her Kobo. She was looking better on the diet regime than him. The curves had re-formed. Her eyes were bright. Him? He just looked like he had cancer. 'Try not to get bashed with a cricket bat again. I really don't want to spend my dotage spooning porridge into a fuckwit. Stay safe.'

'Stay sexy.' He kissed her and left.

Deb Hassan had taken a risk bringing him into the loop. DI Pavlou wouldn't appreciate people going behind her back. Besides, apart from the huff and puff, what would he have done differently? Cato, Cato, Cato, he thought. Once more unto the breach.

'We're a bit busy here, Mick,' said Pavlou when he entered the operations room. The other brass barely spared him a glance.

'I'll keep quiet.' He found himself a chair in the corner, out of their way but giving him a view of the video feed.

'Mick.' A note of warning.

'Cato's a mate.'

Pavlou turned back to the screen, aerials from the chopper, thermal camera tracking through John Forrest National Park, four blobs

of colour in the top left. She spoke into her headset. 'Is that them?'
Crackle and static and affirmative. She consulted a map on an adjacent
screen. 'He's waiting for them at the entrance to the old Swan View rail
tunnel.' She looked again at the thermal images. 'At least the boy's still
alive. There's four warm bodies.'

'No news is good news,' said Hutchens.

A frozen look from Pavlou. She started issuing orders through her
headset. 'Get people into position ready to move in and cover each end
of the tunnel if that's where they're headed. But hold back for now,
wait for my word.'

Hutchens watched the two blobs moving towards the static others.
Like a virus under a miscroscope. A man with a lethal grudge against
Cato. Hutchens was pretty familiar with Cato's career and couldn't
think of anyone this crazy who wasn't already dead or in prison. Crazy,
yet also patient. Patient enough to play long, drawn-out games. Crazy
enough to kill others purely as a message, like a post on Twitter for
fuck's sake.

Twitter.

A memory stirred. Those trolls who'd been taking the piss out of
him the last few weeks. One in particular, Special K: a troll for all
seasons. Never quite on topic. Often using the hashtag *FriendorFoe?*
Hutchens excused himself, to the obvious relief of Pavlou, and went
to his office. He opened up his desktop, logged on and reviewed his
posts for the past fortnight. There he was, Special K, following him; his
profile picture was a cartoon character — the Roadrunner — his profile
ran to three words — Bat Shit Crazy.

An innocuous post from Hutchens about locking and leaving
valuables in your car.

Special K. **Bad people out there. Lost something special down
Rocky yesterday :( #FriendorFoe**

Hutchens checked the date of the post: the day after the murder of
the woman in the Rockingham car park.

Earlier Hutchens posts. **LPT3 coming your way with a warrant
sometime soon #drugsarebad**

Special K. **Man am hearin ya. Crazy druggies kept me awake all
last night #slaythosedragons #FriendorFoe**

The day after the late-night death of Maureen Bryant, addicted to prescription painkillers and antidepressants.

So on and so forth: semi-cryptic tweets from Special K lining up with the recent deaths of homeless around Fremantle. Coincidence? Maybe, maybe not. But what did this do to help Cato walking into that disused railway tunnel up in the hills?

'No further,' Norman said.

Cato stopped. He estimated he was about fifty metres away from the intermittently flashing torch.

The gun scraped the back of his neck. 'What makes you think you've got a say in this?'

'So shoot me. Go on.'

'Don't think I won't.'

There was a humming, whining noise. Like a distant pump. Above him. That couldn't be right. 'Thing is,' said Cato, 'that's exactly what I think. You're a jerk but you're not a bad person. This isn't you. You're out of your depth, Norman. Give me the gun and let me deal with this. That's your best chance of getting your sister back safe.'

'No. He'll win. He always does.' A nudge, a sniffle. 'Keep walking.'

'No.'

'Last warning.'

Cato stood his ground. 'Stop talking about it. Do something.'

Norman came around and stood facing Cato. He lifted the gun to eye level. 'Don't push me.'

A muffled voice from ahead. 'What's happening?'

Eyes adjusted to the gloom, Cato now knew where he was. The Swan View rail tunnel was just ahead. This was where he, Sharon and Ella had come for their family picnic, what, a week ago? Was Samuels already on their trail then, following them? 'Nothing, Samuels. Where's my son?'

'Jake?' A throaty chuckle, strangely familiar. 'He's with me. Waiting for you.'

'I don't believe you.'

'You don't have any option.' The voice still muffled, not just by distance. A hood?

'Prove he's fine. I don't go a step further until then.'

'Normie?'

'Norman won't do anything, mate. He hasn't got the ticker.'

The gun clicked, Norman's finger curled on the trigger. The wind blew through the trees and a bird screeched somewhere.

'Is that right, Norman?' said the voice.

'Besides,' said Cato quickly, not ready yet to test his intuition, 'he would be denying you your pleasure.'

'Norman?' said the voice. 'Think about Naomi. She needs you. Don't let her down.'

Norman stepped forward. Pressed the barrel hard into Cato's forehead. 'Move.'

'No.'

Norman hesitated, shook his head and lowered the gun.

Then he whipped Cato across the temple with it.


Cato used to have this mate at primary school: Ben, a good-natured, outgoing, knockabout kid. He was everything Cato wasn't and he sometimes wondered how they'd become friends. He lived up the street and both his parents were profoundly deaf and dumb, although nowadays you wouldn't use those words. Ben wasn't hearing impaired and he grew up bridging both worlds. He was fluent in sign language and lip-reading by the time he was at school with Cato, five or six years old. One day they'd been playing with some toy cars and trucks on the floor of the kitchen in Cato's house, sun blazing through the window, and Mum chopping vegies at the counter. She was wearing stilettos, ready to go out and meet somebody as soon as Cato's sister got back from high school to babysit him. She'd stepped back from the counter to open the cupboard door beneath and her high heel sliced at the edge of Ben's hand, drawing a spurt of blood. Mum didn't notice what she'd done and Ben didn't cry out or make a noise even though you could see in his eyes that it had really, really hurt.

Years later, when they were teenagers, Cato had asked Ben why he never cried out when he was in so much pain that day.

'What's the point?' he'd said. 'My folks couldn't hear me.'

When Cato opened his blood-gummed eyes he saw his son Jake twisting in the soft breeze that blew through the dark tunnel, illuminated by a torch strategically placed, like a stage light. There was a rope around his neck and his hands were bound behind him. He was on tiptoe on the edge of an upturned milkcrate, trying not to fall. Cato scrambled to his feet, noticing only now that his own hands were also bound behind him. He rushed forward as Jake toppled.

# 30

Cato got to the last page of *The Lorax*, went back to the front and started again. From despair and destruction to a glimpse of hope and back again to despair. Over and over. He had read it countless times in the last fortnight. Out loud. Like he used to do at bedtime. The machines beeped, the respirator hissed and Jake stayed sleeping.

*Family is family. You do whatever feels right at the time ... whatever the cost.*

A slideshow played in Cato's head: Jake as a toddler taking his first three steps before collapsing onto his bum with a delighted cackle, blowing out two candles on an ice-cream and Smarties birthday cake, first day at school dwarfed in oversized shorts, polo shirt and sunhat, leaping off Cato's shoulder into the sea at South Beach, all the birthdays Cato missed as his career took off and he later caught up on video, Jake at eleven with a nail gun pressed into his cheek by a gangster who'd paid them a home visit.

He could see now that night in the kitchen just a few weeks ago: Jake on one side of the table, brave and smiling and saying what he knew they wanted to hear, and Cato and his new happy family on the other. Jacob Kwong fitted the victim profile perfectly: he was one of society's orphans, left behind while everyone else moved on and tried not to think too much about him because he reminded them of their failings. He didn't need to be curled up in a shop doorway or shuffling in the soup queue to be one of the lost. David Samuels had spotted him a mile off. Spotted that need and preyed upon it.

When the reinforcements had arrived, triggered into action by the audio and images from a surveillance drone (that humming noise Cato had heard), they'd found Cato, hands bound, desperately using his back and shoulders to try to support the suspended weight of his son. Jake was hanging from a rusty hook in the wall of the tunnel and had lost supply of oxygen to the brain when his carotid was crushed by the fall. He might or might not come out of the coma, he may or may not be seriously brain-damaged. All they could do was wait and hope. Why had Samuels not killed him and/or Cato? Probably his theatrics had been interrupted by the drone and the reinforcements. The kicked-away milkcrate catching on a loose brick leaving the slimmest of purchases for a few moments before Jake lost his balance.

One thing they did know was that Norman Lip was dead with a bullet in the head — according to the drone recording it had been delivered straight away without any overtures. Norman didn't even have time to enquire after his sister. Bang, you're dead. His shooting had spurred the TRG into action. David Samuels had evaporated, leaving no trace but plenty of casualties. It turned out Pavlou's team had been working from an outdated plan of the tunnel. A later one showed an escape chute with a ladder climbing to a trapdoor and the outside world. Installed after the asphyxiation tragedy way back in the day but never used once the decision was made to abandon the tunnel and the railway line. How Samuels knew about it was anyone's guess — maybe he'd researched it in a school project, maybe he'd come across it in a recce. A thick thermal blanket held over his head was enough to fool the heat-imaging camera on the chopper for long enough for him to melt into the confusing camouflage of the hills suburbs.

Samuels — there he sat in the centre of the murder board in the Major Incident Room. Cato had gone in one day last week and stood and stared at the photograph, the one from Samuels' driver's licence.

'Cato, mate, you shouldn't be here.' DI Hutchens had steered him into his office and closed the door behind them.

'Neither should you. I thought you were retiring?'

'Deferred for three months.' He'd waved his fingers at the space between them. 'Need a steady hand on the tiller.'

'Samuels?'

'Still no sign. Go home, mate. Or the hospital. Be with Jake. Be with Sharon and the bub. They need you.'

'No phone trace, nothing?'

'Leave it to us, Cato. You can't be here, you know you can't.'

Cato had nodded. 'Right.'

A nurse popped her head around the door. 'Everything okay?'

'Yeah, thanks. Doctor around?'

'Here she is now. I'll ask her if she has time for a word.'

'Great.'

The doctor was about fifteen years old with red hair tied up in a bun. 'Mr Kwong?'

'Any news from the tests?'

A shake of the head. 'Nothing significant.'

'How long will this go on for?'

'Hard to say, could be days, could be months. Wish I could be more helpful.' She smiled sympathetically. 'Sorry. I'm needed elsewhere.'

'Sure,' said Cato. 'Thanks.' He better get going himself. Jane was due in for her shift in ten minutes. He tried to avoid crossing paths with her these days.

Senior Sergeant Tess Maguire sat in a gloop-stained armchair in the Southern Comfort nursing home in Albany and studied the dozing Bill Jenkins. She could smell cleaning fluid, cabbage and faeces, and that, combined with the excessive heat from the radiators, left her in no mood to hang around. She jabbed him awake.

'Oi, Billy. It's me again.'

Jenkins wiped some drool from his chin with a cardigan sleeve and focused his droopy eyes on her. 'What?'

'You lied to me.'

'Did I?'

Rain pounded the window, blurring the view of King George Sound. Still, she'd prefer to be out there in the driving rain than here in this suffocating stink hole with the likes of Bill Jenkins.

'You said you had nothing to hide from Detective Sergeant Kwong and that you had nothing to do with him getting bashed.'

'And?'

'You didn't want him nosing into all those rackets you were running when you were in the job, the ones you still get a cut from today.'

She lifted her chin at the surroundings. 'Helps pay for your bed here, I expect.'

An amused glint in his eyes. 'Rackets?'

'Drugs. Cheap illegal labour on the farms. Escort services.'

'Been on the turps, have you? Heard you had a taste for it, after that walloping you got up north.'

He'd been checking up on her too. 'Good try, Billy. Those blokes you got to do the bashing, they run the backpacker hostels where you keep your slaves. I've closed them down and set a few government departments on them. I might even give them a bad review on TripAdvisor too.'

The amusement slipped away, from glint to flint. 'People get upset when the boat's rocked. Small towns. Everybody knows everybody's business but usually minds their own.'

'Yeah, yeah, you know where I live. And I know where to find you, too. So don't even think about it, Billy boy.'

He didn't look too fazed; if anything there was the hint of relief. It wasn't just the rackets and the corruption he'd been hiding. What else then?

Cato sat down at Fishing Boat Harbour at a table outside Cicerello's. A smattering of tourists battled strengthening winds to keep their fish and chip lunches from flying away and the seagulls exploited the chaos to full effect. He couldn't go home. Sharon wanted something from him that he'd lost: love, hope, belief, reason. Ella reminded him of baby Jake looking up with innocent, wondering, trustful eyes. She reminded him of promises he'd disastrously failed to keep. The tourists, Poms by the sound of them, at the adjoining table finally gave up and abandoned their food to the wind and the gleeful squabbling gulls.

'Australia? Huh. What happened to the fooking sunshine then?'

They'd left a *West* behind and Cato grabbed it before the south-westerly took it. Fremantle mayoral candidate Brian Knight had been photographed on a long lens onboard a gin palace belonging to a well-known property developer with his fingers in the port city 2020 pie. There was some incriminating email contact and bank deposits too. Naughty. Less than a week from election day, it wasn't a good look. The crossword. Nine across. *Idle boots upset family bonds.* Five and four. He knew he'd be sent packing from the office, that he had returned way too early. But he needed the job and the trappings of it if he was to hunt down David Samuels. He didn't want to waste any time. But he was also needed at Jake's bedside. Wasn't he? He had to be there when, if, Jake woke up. Days, weeks, months from now. Years? *Idle boots upset family bonds.* 'Upset' means anagram. Cato clicked his biro. Idle boots — blood ties. Family again, a universal and recurrent theme. One, he was sure, that was the key behind all this. The morning after the Swan View tunnel incident, the police had found Norman Lip's sister, Naomi. The one in the photo SMSed to Norman just twelve hours before he was killed. She was alive and unharmed, if somewhat dehydrated. She'd been given a moderate dose of sedatives and left asleep in her wheelchair, parked in a storeroom of the River View care home. Naomi had another photo to show them: a selfie with her and one of the new volunteer carers, David Samuels. Why was she allowed to live? Maybe Samuels drew a line at the wheelchair-bound. Maybe she was destined to die but he was interrupted, or he had eyes on a bigger prize. She'd apologised for her brother's role in the tragedy. It wasn't like him, she said. He was there for her every week — rain or shine. Cato had wanted to pay her a visit when he heard. Wanted to go there and tell her all about her narcissistic imbecile of a brother and how he was glad the bastard was dead. He'd wanted to pour all his anger out on some poor woman in a wheelchair in a nursing home. It took all his will to stay away. Blood ties. The things you do for love.

She's lost it, Hutchens realised with grim satisfaction but also a little shiver of awe. DI Pavlou really has lost it.

'Something to say, Mick?'

He shook his head. 'I'm as stumped as everybody else.' Hutchens shared a wink with Schultzy who'd been drafted in to take up Cato's workload.

They were at Freo cop shop in the big meeting room on the top floor: the one where the old bank directors would have made their decisions about whose farm to repossess, whose mortgage to call in, which boat to buy for the coming summer. The body count was growing and David Samuels was nowhere to be found. The top brass were taking a long hard look at DI Sandra Pavlou's fitness for the task at hand. This was a high-profile case attracting media attention, nationally and even from overseas, with the BBC and *The Guardian* pontificating on the meta-meaning of the homelessness killings to this affluent sun-drenched land of lotus eaters. Locally there was the ongoing tabloid and shock-jock hysteria. Only *New WAve* was striking a sombre note in the wake of their former star writer's demise and milking the publicity for all it was worth. A lot of money and resources had gone into the investigation and the news just kept getting worse. Pavlou's pallor verged on grey: sleepless nights, too much coffee and too many cigarettes. She made Hutchens feel downright chipper.

'Chris?' She looked across at Thornton. 'Give me something, anything.'

He ran a hand through his crew cut. 'Samuels doesn't show up on any government records, state or federal, except for his driver's licence and car rego. He has a bank account which hasn't been touched the last two weeks; his pub bouncer work was cash in hand so it doesn't look like he was paying any taxes.'

'And that would hardly be enough to run the car and pay his rent.'

'Or his gym membership and steroids,' chipped in Amy Trimboli. Following up on the text message about Jake's planned sleepover with a mate from the gym it turned out that that was where Samuels had honed in on him. Shown the licence photo, the receptionist, Cheyenne, had confirmed it was him and talked dreamily about 'Lance' Samuels: his body, his jokes. Cheyenne had been flattered to learn that it was her picture on Tinder purporting to be Jacqui.

'So he's got another source of income, and neither Lance nor David Samuels is his real name.' Pavlou flicked her gaze back to Thornton. 'Anything else?'

A nod. 'Not directly related to the business at hand, we did get word from the forensic bean counters re Jenkins.'

'Father or son?' said Hutchens.

'Both. One of the three directors of Barbarossa Nominees is Bill Jenkins, two others are associates in Albany, also retired police officers. The fourth is an accountant-turned-property speculator linked to at least four insurance frauds. And who, coincidentally, according to my contact in Fraud, has been subsidising the election coffers of mayoral candidate Brian Knight.'

Amy looked up from her notepad. 'So Bill's paying pocket money to his son to clear hobos out of any old factories he's interested in?'

'That's one theory.'

'Accepting pennies from your old man in the nursing home.' Schultzy shook his head. 'No wonder Bill thinks he's useless and weak.'

'Not so useless that Bill stops giving him the work,' observed Hutchens.

'S'pose it keeps it in the family,' Schultz conceded.

'Not just that,' said Thornton. 'Jenkins Senior had his son down as a tax mule.'

'Tax mule?' said Pavlou.

'Instead of going through Customs with a kilo of smack up your arse, you help a rich rellie hide money from the tax office instead.' All eyes turned to Hutchens. 'Marjorie specialises in this stuff.'

Thornton nodded his agreement. 'The notional payment from Barbarossa Nominees could be in exchange for financial services rendered.'

'Speculation.' Pavlou checked the clock on the wall. 'The factory fire in City West?'

'Arson Squad can't link Jenkins Junior or Senior to it except coincidentally,' said Thornton. 'They're putting it on the backburner, so to speak.'

Pavlou, irritated, turned her attention back to Hutchens. 'Nothing more on this Special K character, Mick?'

Hutchens shrugged. 'The geeks have been on it.' IT Imogen shifted in her chair and gave him a frown. 'But the trail goes via Romania or some fucking place, Timbuktu, whatever.'

'But if it was him ...'

'Trolling us, he's got too much time on his hands and bucketloads of bile to spill.'

'It's the zeitgeist,' muttered Pavlou. 'Sign of the times.'

'Ghost,' said Thornton. 'Literally ghost or spirit of the times.'

She glared at him. 'I've been to uni too, sonny.'

Ghost of the times, thought Hutchens. Who you gonna call?

From down the street, Cato watched and waited for the nanny to arrive before venturing home again. Julie's presence would be a neutralising buffer, nothing intense would happen while she was around. Not on the surface anyway. They could all assume some kind of normality, however strained and abnormal, for a short while at least.

'You're back!' Sharon looked up from her laptop, came over and hugged him. Nuzzling into him and kissing his neck. He did the same back to her. At the kitchen counter Julie spooned some food into Ella and they both smiled at him. 'How's Jake today?' said Sharon.

'Same.'

'Who's with him now?'

'Jane was due in a few minutes after I left.'

'What about work? Any news?'

'Not needed on the thin blue line. What's happening around here?'

'Nothing much,' said Sharon. 'Coffee?'

'Sure.' They manoeuvred around each other to the kitchen where the kettle was flicked on. Like tiptoeing through a minefield. 'Any news from your work?' asked Cato.

'Still set to start first Monday in January.'

'Great.' He took the coffee Sharon handed him. Turned to the nanny. 'How's things with you, Julie?'

'Aye, great thanks. Me and Ella are getting on really well, aren't we, love?' An appreciative lip bubble from Ella. Silence swooped in and the job of spooning food into the baby's mouth suddenly required intense concentration.

'Maybe we should go away for a while, even just a long weekend, if you're not needed at work and before I start mine?' Sharon sipped her coffee. 'Down south, or over east, maybe?'

'Something happened?'

'No, nothing. It's just ...' Sharon's eyes teared up, she lifted her palms in a helpless gesture and Cato saw the misery her life too had become. And he had nothing to offer. It took all he had just to hold himself together.

'Yeah,' he said. 'Great. But there's Jake, you know?'

'Right, of course.'

Cato's phone buzzed, a message from Hutchens.

*Fancy a coffee?*

He downed the one he had in his hand and texted back.

*Sure*

Cato lifted his phone, a thin smile of both regret and relief. 'Duty calls.'

Sharon's nod seemed to hold that same mix of regret and relief. That's probably how their marriage would end.

'Pavlou doesn't want you anywhere near the investigation. She thinks you'll go pop and make a mess in the office.'

'Understandable.' They were sitting in the courtyard cafe in the Freo Arts Centre. The place used to be a lunatic asylum, haunted still by the ghosts of the sad and demented.

'Officially I'm inclined to agree with her. You *would* go pop sitting in the office following procedure and protocol at a time like this when what you really want to do is ...'

'Find the bastard and kill him.'

'Exactly.' Hutchens munched on a chocolate brownie which surely wasn't part of the new health regime. 'I can only begin to guess how you might be feeling.'

'Don't try.'

'No, you're right. Me? I'd want blood, sure. But I'm me and you're you. I'm not sure what the outcome is going to be and I don't like the idea of you wasting your life in prison for the few seconds of pleasure in killing the prick.' A sip of coffee. 'Still, there's some creative energy to be harnessed here, an opportunity to think and act outside the usual confines, and I've seen what you're like with the bit between your teeth.'

'So?'

'So, I'm going to feed you tidbits and set you running.'

'That's going to get you in trouble.'

'Who cares? I'm three months off retirement.'

'You might lose your pension.'

'Fuck that, salted plenty away from bribery and corruption over the years.' Hutchens finished off his brownie. 'Joke.'

'No promises from my end.'

A nod. 'You must be hurting real bad right now but Jake needs you, and Sharon and Ella are the best things that ever happened to you, mate. Don't throw them away.'

Cato's vision blurred. 'I know.'

Back to the hospital for the early evening shift. He'd texted Jane to say he was running a few minutes late. No need to wait. It hadn't worked, she was sitting in an armchair in Jake's room. She looked tired. Grey was creeping into her hair. For the briefest of moments he thought they were still married.

'Didn't expect you to be here, thought you had the twins to wrangle?'

'Simon's taking care of it.'

Cato nodded towards Jake. 'Any changes?'

'Nothing.' Jane folded her arms. 'What happened to you, Phil?'

'What?'

'A long time ago there was this bloke I fell in love with. Funny, warm, smart. Brave.'

'Brave?'

'Not any more. You've been avoiding me.' She lifted her chin towards Jake. 'That's our son lying over there. We made him. Together.'

Cato sighed. 'I failed him.'

'Hmmm?' She stood up, gestured for them both to step out of the room. 'He might be hearing this.' Outside, leaning against Jake's door, Jane met his eye. 'You were saying?'

'Jake.' Cato patted his chest. 'My job. Me, I caused all this.'

A nod. 'Yep. It definitely wouldn't have happened if I hadn't known you. I would never have had Jake in the first place and now he wouldn't be lying here in ICU.'

'Sorry.'

'Are you? That job is eating you alive and you let it. All that fun and warmth, that courage. Us. You let it consume all of us. You, me, Jake.'

'Sorry. I don't know what else to say.'

'That's it? You've finished?' She straightened up. 'Thanks.'

'I just ...'

'Just what? Just wanted to let me know how sad you are? Well guess what, I'm sad too. But it's all about you, isn't it? It always is, always has been. You were never around because of your job, your cases, your responsibilities. Now this. Your son, your shame, your guilt. Nobody understands you because you're so fucking special.'

Cato didn't move. Tears rolled down his face.

'Cry them, Phil. Cry them all out. You fucked up on being his father and maybe I fucked up on being his mum, especially lately. But at least let's learn from our mistakes.' Jane shook her head. 'You can't undo what's been done and your part in that. But when you've finished crying, get on with finding the bastard that did this to Jake. It's probably the one useful thing you can do, the one thing you're good at. You owe us all that.'

# 31

Cato woke before dawn and went out driving. Rain had blown in from down south and the wipers on his old Volvo struggled with the unseasonal deluge. Wind shook the trees and power lines and anybody with any sense was still under their doonas. He found himself down at the wharf near where the first victim, Dean Pearson, had been found with a multitude of stab wounds.

He took out his iPad with the scan of Dean's Dero Diary and read the entry that had jolted him awake in the early hours. In July, about three weeks before his death, Dean had been musing, in his own sweet way, on the nature of altruism.

*Give me a kick off Jackboot Johnny any day over a dollar off that woman who thinks I'm her fault. Feels guilty about us, unclean unseen. Puh-lease, get a life! You don't know me — don't know my family — where I came from. I'm not here because people voted the wrong way in the election. I'm just fucking here + thats that. Keep your dollar. Go + bleed your heart over somebody else or DO SOMETHING!*

In more big caps, BOO HOO! Then a scrawled picture of a Pokémon dragon holding a dagger dripping with blood. Some expletives. Skip forward to the next block of prose.

*Not all do-gooders are wankers or soft touches. Even godbotherers can be a good laugh. That dude cracking funnies + taking the piss — breath of fresh air.*

Blink and you'd miss it. No names. Only a passing reference. God-bothering do-gooder. Samuels from the Street Angels, always good for a laugh, cracking funnies. Angels. Cato scrolled back, looked at them again. Maybe, maybe not. What if all those winged dragons were really badly-drawn angels breathing hellfire sermons? Who are you, David Samuels, and what made you so lethally mad? What made you focus on the homeless? On my son?

Cato checked the time on the dashboard, still way too early for the Street Angels office to be open. But being Fremantle, there was no shortage of coffee shops to greet the early worms. Another flashback. Early morning shifts looking after Jake while Jane caught up on sleep. A drive down to North Mole to watch ships coming and going or check out the buckets of the anglers. Then off to the coffee shop, the staff aleady knowing Jake's preference for a babycino. Jane shaking her head if she went in with him later in the day to find the staff and her little boy chatting like old friends.

Cato's eyes blurred. Everything reminded him, tore at him.


Sharon had heard Phil get up and go, and chose to pretend she was still asleep. But as soon as his car rolled out the driveway she got up and sat staring at the calendar on the wall as her tea went cold. They needed to break the circuit. Maybe she should take Ella over east and visit the folks for a week or two? No, that would fix nothing. Maybe she should slap Phil out of his grief and self-recrimination and remind him he still had a family to think about. Harsh but true. But perhaps too early. There was a fine line between too early and too late. When was the right moment? A bit after they decided to switch off Jake's machines? Or maybe hang in there in the hope Jake woke up and everyone could live happily ever after. It could be a while. She was lost. It wasn't something she was used to, having an unsolvable problem. She was a results girl, a go-getter. Sure-thing-Sharon. Now she'd fallen in love with this impossible, lovely man and brought their baby into the world and, seemingly, lost control over her life. And, of course, there was Samuels, who had fixated on and looked like destroying this family. In some ways he represented the kind of problem she was used to — a bad guy. Find him, stop him and lock him up. Phil's self-loathing grief was another matter altogether.

First things first.

Find out who Samuels really is. Transnational identity theft was one of the things the AFP was good at and she knew exactly the right people to talk to. She checked the clock on the wall, nine-thirty in Canberra, they should have started work by now. Time to make a few calls.

After coffee and scrambled eggs down at South Beach kiosk, with the weather keeping the dogs and their owners mercifully at bay, Cato popped his head around the door of Street Angels, a former Point Street townhouse turned into offices. Outside a 4WD was parked. It looked to Cato like it could have been the one spotted on CCTV down by the port the night Dean Pearson died. Cato relished the first feeling of calm and focus he'd felt in a long time. Last night Jane had torn a strip off him but had also made a deal.

'I'll sit in with Jake full-time, take your shifts, sleep here if I have to. I've got somebody who can keep the consultancy ticking over and Simon's got the twins under control. You might feel warmer and fuzzier reading *The Lorax* to him but it doesn't help track down this Samuels bastard.'

'There's a few dozen cops already on the case.'

'None of them with your level of motivation.' She smiled sadly. 'Besides, I can tell Jake's getting bored with you. He's ready for *Yertle the Turtle* now.'

Jane knew him too well.

There was a poster on the Street Angels office wall: an Aryan-looking woman offering solace to a homeless waif straight out of Oliver Twist — *Street Angels*, read the caption, *Heaven Sent*. By the window a clean-cut bloke, mid thirties, looked up from his computer screen and pushed his wire frame specs back up his nose.

'Yes?'

Cato introduced himself and stated his business.

The ID received only the most cursory of glances. 'I've already been interviewed by your colleagues.' He seemed a tad cold and defensive for an angel. 'Samuels was an impostor, an aberration. We've reviewed and tightened our recruiting procedures since then.'

Cato fought the urge to punch the man into silence. Instead he smiled reassuringly. 'A routine follow-up. Samuels still hasn't been apprehended and we need to review all lines of enquiry.' Another smile from Cato. 'Your name again?'

'Giles. Giles Strachan.'

'How well do you know Samuels?'

'Did. He's no longer with us. And no, not very.'

'What records do you have relating to him in your system?'

'As I said to your colleague ...'

'Let's pretend my colleague never came here, and start afresh. A new morning has broken.' Cato tapped the top of the man's Acer. 'What do you have on Samuels?'

Giles' lips pursed. 'An address and a scan of his driver's licence.'

'That's it? You took him on on the strength of that?'

'As I said, we have since tightened our recruiting procedures.'

Cato shook his head. 'What was his speciality?'

'How do you mean?'

'Soup kitchen? Driver? Clothes sorter? What?'

'He turned his hand to most things as I recall. Particularly diligent when we were doing the audit for the council.'

'In what way?'

'He went out to all the known pitches. Got to know the rough sleepers. Made sure they were counted in the audit. Brought us some new converts ... clients,' he added, seemingly as an afterthought.

That accounted for Samuels' solid knowledge of who was where and how to find them. And why they might not have been so surprised by his presence in those moments just before they died.

'Did he say why he'd come to Street Angels, of all the organisations he might have chosen?' Apart from their obvious lack of recruitment vetting diligence.

'He'd had dealings with us previously, I think.'

'What dealings?'

'This is all second-hand, we've just been talking among ourselves. I didn't know him well myself. But somebody mentioned he might have been a client of ours a few years back.'

'Homeless, you mean?'

'I guess so.'

'How many years back? One, two, three?'

A shrug. Strachan rummaged in a drawer and pulled out an envelope. 'But he wasn't just a nobody who walked in off the street. One of our volunteer supervisors dropped this by last week, she'd forgotten to put it into the system. A reference.'

'Reference?'

'A character reference, from a pastor in New Zealand.'

'Did you pass this on to the officer who interviewed you?'

'I thought this was a new start, a new morning breaking?' Giles said, prissily.

'Did you?'

'At the time of the original visit I wasn't aware of it. As I said, the volunteer only brought it in at the end of last week.'

'And you didn't think to phone the officer concerned?'

'I mislaid her card.' And wanted us all to go away and not come back, thought Cato. He clicked his fingers in a gimme gesture. Giles shook his head. 'It's confidential.'

'This is a murder investigation.' Cato took the envelope from Giles and slipped it into his pocket. 'Need a receipt?'

'No, I suppose not.'

'Anything else you can tell me about Samuels?'

'As I said, I never had any significant dealings with him, directly. I remember him at some of our meetings and congregations.'

'Why?'

'Pardon?'

'Why did you remember him?'

'He was a striking physical presence. One of the women referred to him as a real Christian Soldier.'

'Got that wrong, didn't she?' Or maybe not. Cato stood to leave and handed Giles a business card. 'Don't mislay this one. Anything else, call me. My mobile and home numbers are on the back.'

Giles studied the card. 'Kwong. Are you ...' Realisation dawned on him and his face radiated pity. 'I'm so sorry about your son.'

'Don't bother.'


Back in the car with the wind buffeting the side panels, Cato read the character reference for Samuels. It was dated two years earlier and signed by Pastor Dennis Nelson of the Pinedale Pentecostal Congregation in Marlborough, South Island.

*To Whom It May Concern.*
*I have known David Lance Samuels for many years as a member of this congregation. He is a fine, upstanding young man blessed with a strong Christian spirit and work ethic. He is respectful to his elders and respected by his peers. He mixes well in a range of social situations and, I believe, would be an asset to any organisation whose aim is to do good work in the community and spread the word of God.*

David Lance Samuels seemed to have been a long-standing member of the local community, odds-on Kiwi born and bred. The one in the rail tunnel didn't seem to have the accent although very little was said at the time. Was this reference for somebody else? The real Samuels? There was a telephone number on the letterhead but when Cato rang it he got a disconnected tone. He googled the Pinedale Pentecostal Congregation and, through salacious reports in the local media, he learned that it had since disbanded and Pastor Nelson had eloped with the church funds and a parishioner and was believed to be hiding somewhere on the North Island. There was a quote from a local police officer and a number to ring if anybody had any useful information. Cato rang it.

'Nick Chester, Havelock Police.'

Cato introduced himself and stated his business.

'Oh aye, aye, I remember that one.'

The accent was familiar to Cato, he'd heard something similar many years ago in Hopetoun: the crazy Pom from northern England, wreaking havoc across the years and across the world. 'Anything you can tell me?'

'Well the vicar still hasn't been found but the woman he ran off with came back a month later. Mary, lovely lass, farm girl through and through.'

'David Lance Samuels?'

'Ah, well there's the thing you see. Davey was reported missing by his folks a good eighteen months ago.'

'Missing from New Zealand?'

'Nah, nah, he was in Kalgoorlie by then, working on the mines like all the other Kiwis.'

'Was this reported to Australian police?'

'Probably but let's see.' A few clicks on the keyboard. 'Aye, Kalgoorlie Police notified on ...' and he gave a date.

'No trace?'

'Thin air, mate. Poor lad's probably down a mineshaft. Give us a yell if he shows up, eh?'


Mick Hutchens decided it was time to reacquaint himself with Special K. He had a number of community messages that needed to be sent out this morning on Twitter: car thefts, shoplifters, drive safely in the bad weather, etcetera. Normally he tasked them to a civilian or a junior officer whose leash needed jerking, but today he wanted to be more hands on. Photos of Samuels and 'Have you seen this man?' were already circulating on the police Twitter and Facebook feeds but there was no harm in adding to them. And if you wanted it to go wider than the usual busybodies and saddos who followed them you had to jazz it up a bit.

**Have you seen this man? Wanted for serious offences Male 20–25 Dodgy facial hair, built like Buzz Lightyear #closinginBuzz**

The favourites and retweets were coming thick and fast, at this rate he'd be trending by lunchtime. Mick Hutchens, a fucking viral sensation. It wasn't long before someone tipped off his superiors. An incoming call from an assistant commissioner.

'Hutchens, what are you up to? The Commissioner thinks you're taking the piss out of her initiative.'

'Perish the thought, sir.'

'So stop. Now.'

'Trust me on this one, sir. It's a matter of operational imperative that we let it run.' He explained himself further. 'If it fails you can kick me out, if it succeeds the boss looks like the dog's bollocks and she'll be getting interviewed by the BBC, CNN, you name it.'

'Not sure she wants to look like dog's bollocks.' The AC grunted. 'One hour. I'll let her know to stop biting the carpet until then.'

'How about lunchtime?'

A chuckle. 'You're a fucking riot, Hutchens. We're going to miss you.'

Cato's next call was to Kalgoorlie police to see what they had on the missing person David Lance Samuels. The woman on the other end of the phone had a smoker's voice as she clacked the keyboard.

'Worked at one of those small mines out near Laverton.' She gave a name and Cato noted it along with contact details. 'Didn't show up for work one Monday. Apparently he was one of those bible-bashers — he didn't grog and whore his wages away.'

'No sightings?'

'Nothing. He'd opened a bank account here in Kal and there were regular transfers back to another one in NZ but that stopped after he went missing.'

Cato heard the hesitation in her voice. 'But?'

'But it was cleared out over the first weekend, cash withdrawals to the max. The bank didn't get onto it until the Monday.'

'That wasn't being monitored?'

'It was only after a week that his folks notified the NZ police who called us. Before that he was just assumed to have gone out bush, camping, detox from Sodom, whatever. By the time we were called in the money had gone.'

'ATM cameras?'

'Inconclusive: hoodie, bowed head, you know how it goes.'

'So foul play is suspected.'

'S'pose so.'

'But not a priority?'

'The Ds here looked into it but it went nowhere and there's plenty else to do. Kal's a big town with lots of bad people. Bikies, you name it.'

'Yeah,' said Cato, who'd used up his sympathy for defensive overstretched people a long time ago. 'Cheers.'

In Kalgoorlie or Laverton or somewhere over that way, David Lance Samuels crossed paths with the man who would assume his identity, kill him and others, and try to kill Jacob Kwong. Phone calls and internet searches weren't enough. Cato needed to be out there, nosing around.

Hutchens got what he wanted around eleven-thirty: a love heart from Special K and a thread into the conversation.

*Dude! You are the Man! Like my dads shirt said #oldguysrock*

So, Special K saw him as part of the game. **Who are you calling old?**

**Camera never lies, big guy. Famous as! Page 7 in the Freo Gazette.**

Just last week. The Media Unit had set it up: the human face of warmth and local experience behind the Commissioner's new social media strategy. Constable fucking Care for the twenty-first century. People used to be scared of me, thought Hutchens, now they troll me. With impunity. Not any more.

**David Samuels, wanted for questioning. Male, big, loves his dad, desperate to impress #whosyourdaddyBuzz?**

Straight back from Special K.

*not nice :( :( :( :( :(*

A call from the AC again. 'Enough, Mick. Pull it down. The boss is having kittens. She's getting calls from the nerd desks at the newspapers and she doesn't have a clue what they're on about. She hates being behind the eight ball.'

Hutchens beamed. 'No worries, sir.'

'Anyway since when did you become an expert in this shit?'

'I like to rise to any challenge presented to me, sir.'

'We'll see you at your leaving do, Hutchens. Make sure you leave.'

The daddy thing seemed to wind Samuels up. Was 'daddy' somebody Cato had put away in the last few years? Or was he the person who made Samuels tick? Drove him to murder? Where to start. The mental hospitals, the orphanages, where? Hutchens shook his head and logged off.


That evening some semblance of normality briefly returned to the household. Sharon had been surprised when Phil came home enthused about the idea of getting away for a while for some quality family time. A light had come back into his eyes, a fizz of energy had returned to their connection, they'd even had sex for the first time in a while. They had slung the camping gear into his Volvo for an early getaway. Camping wasn't quite what she'd had in mind, particularly in this weather. She'd been thinking a B&B in Margaret River maybe, or a weekend in Melbourne, maybe pop down to see Dad in Bendigo. But he'd assured her the forecast was for things to improve.

'Laverton?' she'd asked. 'Where's that, what's there?'

A shrug and a smile. 'We'll never, never know if we never, never go.'

# 32

The clouds, wind and rain stayed with them for three hundred and seventy kilometres east into the Big Empty until just before Southern Cross, then sunshine took over. Cato felt guilty about his subterfuge with the camping trip and his real intentions about Laverton, but he wasn't game to leave Sharon and Ella on their own in Fremantle and he feared the consequences of telling the truth. Why? Sharon was meant to be his new soulmate. No more lies or secrets, she'd said. And, by taking Sharon and Ella with him, was he actually putting them both in more danger? Had he learned nothing from his experience with Jake? Maybe not. All he knew was that he wanted to keep them close.

'Penny for them?' Sharon said.

Ella was snoozing in the capsule in the back and he'd thought Sharon had also been catching up after a restless night. 'Thinking maybe we should pull in soon for some coffee and food?'

'Sure. You looked deeper in thought than that though.'

'Yeah, well.'

He thought he detected a flint of anger or frustration there before she smiled and said, 'So tell me about Laverton.'

'It's an old mining town.'

'Like Bendigo?'

'Smaller and without the vibrancy and culture.'

'So why are we going there?'

'Beautiful countryside surrounding it.' Although, for the life of him, he hadn't a clue where it might be.

'Bushman Phil, huh?'

He smiled. 'Got it in one.'

Her hand slid over his thigh. 'It's nice to get acquainted again.'

'Yep,' he said. 'It is.'

She leaned her head on his shoulder. 'We'll get through this, love.'

'Yeah.' A road train roared past, a crosswind buffeting the Volvo and sending a jolt through Cato's jangled nerves. Up ahead lay the Southern Cross townsite. Cato smothered a yawn. 'Time for some caffeine.'

Tess Maguire found herself thinking about Cato. Through news media she'd read and heard about what had happened to his son and could only begin to imagine what Cato must be feeling. Her calls to him had gone unanswered and, to her shame, there was a degree of relief there. Besides, now he had that new woman in his life to share the burden, Tess no longer had any claim over him. Perhaps she never had; after all it was a good twelve or more years since they had been an item. Her visits to Bill Jenkins had been her way of helping in whatever small way she could: put the evil old bastard back in his box and give Cato one less thing to worry about. A call from his colleague, Chris Thornton, had wrapped up the last thing old Bill had been holding back. She'd paid him one more visit.

'Three people burned to death so you can double your investment? What a piece of work you are.'

Eyes glued to the view out the window. Voice barely a whisper. 'Accidents will happen.'

'And Johnny-boy continuing the good work for you in Fremantle. Moving people on. What do they call it, vacant possession?'

'You done?'

'No brainer for him, he gets to bully vulnerable people and get paid, by you and the council. Win-win.'

'Need to piss.'

'Use your bag. Why keep on employing him if you think he's so weak and useless?'

'His mum loved him.'

'Nice to be able to still help the kids out, isn't it? They'll always be our babies, come what may. Unconditional love.'

'Get lost and don't bother me here anymore or I'll have you up for harassment.'

'My pleasure, you vicious old bastard.'

It was getting close to lunchtime and the main drag in Albany was bustling. The rain had moved on and the miscreants were strangely inactive. She'd pulled over a couple of speeders, served some warrants, caught up on her reports and allocated some uniform support to a drug raid set for tomorrow. She thought she might even go along herself to keep her hand in. She had one more warrant to serve and then she'd call it a day. She was on the early shift, so this and a bit of paper-shuffling back at the office would take her through to two o'clock and home time. She climbed the hill to Mount Clarence and pulled into the driveway of a dilapidated weatherboard house. The front lawn could have done with a mowing and the rubbish needed to be taken out. A ute sat on three wheels in the driveway, fourth one propped up on bricks. The blinds were still drawn, the Eureka flag in the window along with an empty tinnie of rum and Coke. She knocked on the front door and some flakes of paint drifted down. It was like being in a bogan snow dome.

A hacking cough and the door opened to reveal bleary eyes and Bundaberg breath.

'Travis Grant?' said Tess.

'Yeah, who's askin'?'

Tess looked down at her uniform; no, she hadn't forgotten to put it on. 'Police.' She handed him an envelope and held a clipboard his way for a signature of receipt. 'Warrant. You failed to appear before the magistrate last week and didn't give any excuse. Be there day after tomorrow or we'll come and arrest you.'

He shrugged. 'Okay,' and signed the form.

He seemed familiar, and the name too, but then so did all the Albany dropkicks after a while. 'Where've I seen you before, Travis?'

'Dunno.'

Travis was Shane Warne before the strawberry milkshake and botox diet. The cigarettes and beergut glory days when he could rip through the England top batting order before lunchtime and his hangover had even cleared. Have a pie and a smoke and go out and do it again in the afternoon. Then it came to her, a dusty road on the outskirts of Hopetoun, the Stop–Go sign man working for the mine, directing the traffic and the 457 visa workers on the chain gang. She clicked her fingers in recognition. 'Western Minerals, Hopetoun.'

He grinned. 'Good job, that. Money coming out of my ears. Chicks too.' He peered closely at her. 'I didn't ...?'

'No, you didn't. Not my type, mate.' She lifted her chin at the decrepit state of him and his house. 'What happened?'

'Job folded after the mine closed and the boss went to prison.' He frowned. 'String of bad luck, you know?'

Tess nodded. 'Shame.' She pointed at the envelope in his hands. 'Be there day after tomorrow, ten on the dot, or we'll come and get you.'


Half an hour before sunset they set up camp at a site just outside of Laverton. It had minimal facilities, a drop dunny and that was it. The landscape was unimpressive, some red dirt and low scrub and flies by the thousand.

'Are we staying here long?' asked Sharon. 'Only I'm still waiting to be impressed by the natural splendour of outback WA.'

'Wait until the stars come out,' said Cato, swatting the blowies from his face. 'Glorious.'

Sharon was rummaging around in the car, searching for insect repellent and a protective net for Ella. That's when she found the Glock. She hoisted it. 'Was this really necessary?'

A shrug. 'Samuels is out there, he hasn't gone away and he probably hasn't finished.'

'Fair enough.' She watched him tightening the guy ropes and inspecting the pegs. 'Why are we here, Phil? Truth. Now.'

He sighed in surrender. Then he told her about his enquiries with Street Angels, the reference from the pastor in New Zealand, and the real David Lance Samuels going missing from his job at a Laverton mine.

'So this isn't quality family time. It's the Job.'

'Yes. Sorry.'

'Stop fucking saying sorry.' She stepped up close to him. 'I'm a cop too, remember? I can do this shit and I can do it with you. You need to trust me, share it with me. If we can't do that then what's the point of us?'

He nodded. 'The Dragonfly mine is about ten ks down the road from here. That's where the real Samuels worked before he disappeared. Tomorrow I want to try and talk to somebody about who he associated with, who he might have met, who took his name.'

'Okay,' said Sharon. Ella was getting fractious and hungry. 'Dinner, and then you can show me these glorious stars of yours.'

'Great.' A smile of relief that the interrogation was over, then a clouding and sudden alertness.

'What?'

'A reflection, something glinted in the sun on that hill over there.'

They both looked over that way. Studied the red dirt landscape for a few moments more. 'Nothing,' said Sharon. 'Probably somebody else out for a romantic camping trip in outback WA. Just waiting for that fabulous night sky to kick in.' Sharon laid the gun back in its resting place. 'This better be good.'

It was.

Cato and Sharon lay on their backs in their swags and stared at the millions of pinpricks of light above them and the cloudy path of the Milky Way.

'It's beautiful,' she said. 'Incredible.'

Satellites orbited, stars flickered and died in front of them, and Cato's chest felt ready to burst. He recalled evenings in the backyard in Fremantle trying to pick out the constellations from a book from Jake's school library but the light pollution of a city made it slim pickings. The Southern Cross was usually the best they could ever manage. And Mars. So Cato would make up constellations to compensate.

'See over there,' said Cato. 'Spottus the Dog.'

'Doesn't exist, Dad. It's not in the book.'

'I can see Uranus from here.'

'Yuk.' A giggle and a nudge.

The sky blurred.

They both drifted off to sleep.

# 33

The manager of the Dragonfly mine was the hard, sinewy, unyielding type. If he hadn't been managing a pit he would have been running the young thugs on his remand wing and scaring everybody, screws included, shitless. If the man had been thirty years younger Cato would have had him top of the list for throwing David Lance Samuels down a mineshaft and stealing his identity. But perhaps you shouldn't judge a book by its cover.

'Bob,' he said. 'Bob Peake. Can I see that ID of yours again?' Cato obliged. 'Kwong. Chinese. They own this place. Some consortium in bloody Shanghai. They'll run the world soon, I reckon.'

Yeah, thought Cato. Met your type before. 'What do you mine here?'

'Lithium. For the batteries for all those gadgets we can't get enough of. The Chinks especially. No offence.'

No offence. People seemed to be saying it more and more these days. It had long since lost its currency. People no longer gave a damn whether they were being offensive or not because free speech gave everybody the right to be a bigot and that was high on the list of national priorities, right up there with slashing welfare. So, was Dragonfly on the list of assets owned by the Shanghai entrepreneur Cato had helped bring down? His mind was grasping at any possible clues from his past. No. Stay focused. 'David Lance Samuels, young Kiwi bloke, worked here before he went missing. Remember him?'

'Yeah, he stuck out like a sore thumb. Bible-basher. Didn't fit in with the pisspot degenerates we usually have on the payroll.'

'Did that cause any problems? The religion? Anyone take offence?' That word again.

'Nah. They take the mickey but nobody fights over theology around here.' An afterthought. 'Depending on the religion, I suppose.'

'Godforsaken place to come and work, for a fella like him, I mean.'

A shrug. 'Kiwis. Their economy's fucked. Need the money, don't they?'

Something jagged in Cato's memory. 'Where did Samuels come from?'

'New Zealand, like I said.'

'What I meant was, where did the company find him? I did a check on the website and there wasn't much in the way of situations vacant. Does Dragonfly hire directly or subcontract all that?'

'Does it matter?'

'I'll decide that.'

A shrug. 'Subcontractors.'

'Any in particular? Names?'

'Different ones.'

'Names?'

'Give me your email and I'll send them through. Need to check with them first.'

'No, you don't.'

'Yes.' A locking of eyes. 'I do.'

Cato changed tack. 'Anybody he connected with, any pals?'

'Not that I noticed but I'm not the pastoral care type anyway. Shift's end, I'm in my donga watching a video or sleeping.'

'The weekend he disappeared, what do you remember about that?'

'I told the cops already. The Kalgoorlie ones.'

'Tell me.'

Bob checked the time on his mobile, spun it absent-mindedly on the desk. 'He was heading south to do some fishing. He had five days off. He didn't come back. I gave it a few days in case he'd just gone on a bender.'

'Then what?'

'I told my superiors.'

'And?'

'Left it with them. They must have sat on it as well and done nothing because it wasn't until two or three days later the Kal cops come calling. His folks in Kiwi-land had reported him missing.'

'What did they find out? The Kal cops?'

'Are you checking up on them or something?'

Cato levelled his gaze at Peake. 'Just tell me and I'll be gone, soon as you like.'

Bob squinted back. 'Ute never found, Samuels never found, no sightings, nothing.'

'Did he go fishing a lot?'

'Most leave periods he'd be off. Gun it via Norseman and you can be on the south coast in four or five hours.'

'Anything else?' Cato handed him a business card with his mobile and email contacts on it.

'He was a good fisherman, always brought back a big feed and shared it around.' A pause. 'He was a good kid. I hope you find out what happened to him.'

When Cato got back to the campsite Sharon and Ella weren't there. There was nothing apparently amiss, no sign of a struggle or violence. And he couldn't see the BabyBjorn, so odds-on Sharon had just gone exploring. Still. He studied the ground. At the northern corner, her footsteps, deepened by the weight of Ella, disappeared as sand gave way to bush. He wondered how far she'd gone. Thought it might have been more considerate of her to at least leave him a note.

'Sharon?' he called. 'I'm back.'

No answer. Breeze rustling the low scrub and something scurrying in the undergrowth. A flash from a distant low hill. Binoculars? Was there someone out there?

'Shaz?' He found himself following the trail. The buzzing of the flies seemed suddenly louder in his ears. Senses on high alert. 'You there?'

A rabbit broke from cover and bounded away in front of him. Cato tried to picture whether they were on the right or wrong side of the rabbit-proof fence. And what the hell that mattered anyway.

'Sharon?' His call was louder, a shout. Surely she couldn't have gone so far that she couldn't hear him. He looked around, behind him. He could no longer see their campsite or her footprints. Was she lost? Was he lost?

Retrace steps. That was the sensible thing and she'd realise that too.

Wait by the car. They'll come. Relax.

Flies worried at his face. He waved them away. Surprised to find his gun was in his hand. When did that happen? 'Sharon?'

His voice cracked, his chest tightened, vision swam. He was finding it hard to breathe. He sat down in the red dust and started sobbing.


Mick Hutchens was treating Deb Hassan and Chris Thornton to lunch and they were suspicious as hell.

'Go for your life,' he beamed. 'My shout.'

He'd brought them well away from downtown Freo to the Left Bank down by the river. It was a good place to go if you didn't want to risk colleagues passing by and wondering what the hell you were up to. They had a window table near a group of rowdy real estate types readying to carve up the coastline once again. The noise of their wine-soaked bravado suited Hutchens' purposes very well.

'So,' he said, dipping his sourdough into a dish of EVOO, 'what's the Velvet Hammer got you on these days?'

'Going through Sarge's old cases and cross-referencing them with recent prisoner releases.' Thornton dabbed his bread into the oil and left a drip trail across the tablecloth on the way to his mouth.

'You?' Hutchens turned to Hassan.

'Still interviewing other clients at the gym Samuels attended.'

Out the window, a pelican launched itself from a jetty post and glided low across the water before lifting onto an identical post a hundred metres away. Probably escaping the guffaws of the housing developers. Hutchens took a sip of shiraz. 'Waste of time, isn't it?'

Neither nodded, neither shook their head. Hassan's Greek salad arrived and she suddenly found it very interesting.

'Cato deserves better,' said Hutchens. 'And we are going to do whatever we can to help him.'

'Yeah?' said Thornton. 'How?'

'You can narrow your search down to Cato's cases where I've been actively involved, not just as supervising officer.' He elaborated on the killer's fixation with Cato and, more recently, him. 'He recognises me, made me part of his agenda too. And it's not ex-cons we're looking at, it's the son of a con who is either still inside or perhaps has died in the last year or two.' Thornton was taking notes on his iPhone. 'And look for the letter K.'

'K?'

'It's special, it has some meaning to the killer.' The bill was being presented to the rowdy realtors, rolled up and tossed on the floor contemptuously by one who chucked his credit card onto the waiter's tray. Wanker. 'And follow the money,' said Hutchens. 'Samuels couldn't do what he did on casual doorman's wages. Where's the money coming from?' Hutchens surveyed his newly arrived fish and chips and attacked with relish, jabbing a chip in the direction of Hassan. 'Drop the gym buddies. Get back to that homeless charity where Samuels worked and roast them. They took the fucker into their flock and I want to know why. You don't just walk off the streets these days and say let me loose on your waifs and strays. You're meant to have clearances, references whatever.'

'What about Pavlou?' Thornton toppled his seafood stack.

'Leave her to me.'

Hassan pushed her salad away and stole a forkful of Hutchens' chips. 'Why are we here? The cloak and dagger? The lunchtime treat?'

'Because,' he said, fencing her fork away with his, 'we're not going to tell Pavlou. We're going to find this bastard and then I'm going to kill him.'

'I know you mean well, boss. But I don't think we're allowed to.'

'Leave that to me to worry about, Deb. That's why I assume the burden of leadership.'


Sharon had taken over the driving. Ella was asleep in the back and Phil had mercifully dropped off in the front beside her. She was worried about him. Very worried. They had packed up the camping gear and were now heading south to the coast. A bank of black cloud loomed on the horizon and it seemed as if the long straight road ahead was pulling them into a mass of darkness. After so many years in the thriving concrete beehive of Beijing, the empty highways of the Western Australian outback were as alien to her as a moonscape. Even growing up in country Victoria, things had never seemed quite as stark and extreme as this: huge, beautiful and terrifying. Wandering through the bush near the campsite with Ella strapped to her, Sharon had been in awe of the otherness of the place: the scrubby trees, the hard, dry, dark red earth, the sharp blue sky, the low hum and click of insects. Shattered by the heartbreaking sound and sight of Phil weeping, curled up on the ground like a whipped child.

She looked at him asleep now: mouth slightly open, snoring softly, an anxious frown still creasing his forehead. Would they ever get to the other side of this? They were approaching the town of Norseman and her phone beeped. She checked it, a message from her AFP contact, and some names. The names meant nothing to her.

'Where are we?'

'Norseman. Sleep well?'

'Yeah, good thanks.' He nodded towards the phone. 'Anything interesting?'

'Nah,' she said. 'Just work.'

Why hadn't she passed the names on to him? Was she afraid he might do something even more terrible if he knew? Bring down yet more disaster on them? Secrets. Lies. She was doing exactly what she'd chastised him for. They were as bad as each other. She would enquire further. Firm it up, narrow it down, and send it all through to Phil's colleagues to be dealt with properly. Sharon checked the rear-vision. Just the one car, way back in the distance. Ahead of them, the storm.

Hutchens had prised Deb Hassan out of DI Pavlou's grasp fairly easily by offering Morose McMahon back as temporary compensation and claiming a spike in the city workload needed the kind of local knowledge that Deb had in spades. What she'd been doing for Pavlou's team was donkey work after all, to which McMahon was well suited. Chris Thornton was another matter: he had a gift for background research which went beyond the soulless world of metadata, bytes and beeps inhabited by the geeks in IT. Thornton was able to draw a story from it all. If they weren't careful, the lad would be press-ganged by Pavlou into Major Crime for good. Same old story, just like the Dockers, spend years grooming a good player then sell him to another team to kick goals there instead.

'Just widen your search parameters, she won't care — she's too busy looking for a career-saving exit strategy.'

'I've noticed that about management.' Thornton tapped his keyboard. 'I'm watching and learning.'

'Good lad. If you're lucky, you'll get through to retirement like me with a warm glow of satisfaction from decades of selfless giving to the community.'

'That warm glow might come in handy in winter. You'll probably lose your pension after they find out you've killed Samuels.'

'You and Cato. Everybody's worried about my pension. No need, the missus is a financial planner, we'll be living off other people's life savings, we'll be fine.'

Thornton swung his screen around to give Hutchens a better view. 'Five names, a couple of K's in there too, any of them mean anything?'

Hutchens frowned. 'Only five? Thought I'd made a lot more enemies than that over the years. Bit fucking disappointed, actually.'


Bob Peake had finished for the day and was ready to pop a tinnie and chuck on a video. He was on his way past the casual dongas where the blokes hot-bedded between shifts much to the disgust of the union but the Chinese owners didn't give a fuck about that. Chinese, they don't let up once they've got the bit between their teeth. Like that cop this morning, he wasn't going away any time soon. Fair enough, he was only doing his job but you don't need people sticking their noses in where they're not wanted, who knows what they'll find.

He poked his head around the door of Samuels' old donga, well used by others since the Kal cops had taken a quick look through but not deemed it worthy of the crime-scene treatment. He'd been relieved that the Chink hadn't requested the same: maybe not as sharp as he appeared, or maybe he'd be back any day now with reinforcements. The dark patch low on the wall was still there, blindingly obvious if you knew what you were looking for. It seemed to Peake that the bleachy metallic smell was still there too but imagination is a powerful thing, plays tricks like you wouldn't believe.

The air stirred and a shadow crossed behind him. He turned.

'Oh,' he said. 'It's you.'

Deb Hassan knocked on Hutchens' door late afternoon. 'Finally got hold of that bloke from Street Angels, he's a hard man to nail down, never in the office and never answers his phone or emails.'

Hutchens lifted his eyes from his laptop and nodded, impatient.

'He said Cato was in there a couple of days ago. Took some letter away with him that none of us knew about.'

'Letter?'

'A character reference for a David Lance Samuels. Some volunteer supervisor had it at home and only dropped it in the office in the last few days.'

'Gist?'

'Some pastor in New Zealand reckoned Samuels was a nice bloke.'

'New fucking Zealand? Where's this going, Deb?'

'Cato's house is empty and he's not answering his phone. The neighbourhood watch bloke up the street saw them packing and leaving for what looked like a camping trip. Maybe we should be tracking Sarge's phone, see where he's headed. Might be something, might be nothing.'

'Funny time to go off camping. Your son in intensive care.' Hutchens' eyes flicked back to the computer screen. 'Kal cops are trending. Something big going on over there.'


They reached Esperance as the sun was setting. Anglers were out on the long jetty, wrapped up tight against the biting wind. The rain clouds stayed out over the Southern Ocean, procrastinating about whether or not to make landfall, turning the water gunmetal grey in the meantime. Cato couldn't be bothered putting up the tent in these conditions and booked them into a motel unit on the seafront instead.

He remembered his last time here: blood and baby formula spilt across the back seat of an old green Landrover. The man whose life he'd ended on the salt flats out at Lake King. As the kilometres had ticked down from Norseman to here, his suspicion had grown as to who it was that he was dealing with. Peake's discomfort with some of the questioning fuelled Cato's speculation. Things still didn't make full sense: the face he'd seen on the driving licence photo didn't just bear the transformations of boy to man, it was as if a mask was in place, concealing the original identity. The ages didn't match but they were going off the age on Samuels' ID, not the real age of the person they were looking for.

'Phil?' Sharon emerged from the bathroom wrapped in a towel, hair glistening around her bare shoulders as she dried it with a second towel. Behind her on the muted TV, a news flash: pictures streamed live from a helicopter hovering over a patch of red dust and sheds in the outback, police wrapping tape around trees, forensics moving in, a white tent, flashing lights on an ambulance. A banner headline sliding across the bottom of the screen. BREAKING. MAN CRITICAL AFTER VICIOUS ASSUALT AT LAVERTON MINE SITE. Then there was a photo of Bob Peake, the mine manager. 'Phil, if we're extending this trip I really need to get some more undies.'

Cato looked at his wife, and at his daughter snoozing in the capsule. They were his world. Nobody was going to take them from him, he would die to ensure it. He clasped Sharon in a tight embrace, breathing her in.

'Sure. How about tomorrow?' He flicked the TV off with the remote. 'Let's go and eat.'

Cato knew he wasn't far behind the man who claimed to be David Lance Samuels. But it was clear that Samuels wasn't far behind him either.

# 34

You must be close to guessing by now. Yes, it's wise to ditch the tent and get a more solid shell around you. The weather's coming in and these southern storms can cause havoc. One time I was out in the boat with my old man and we were fishing in deep water, off the edge of the shelf. It was beautiful and calm, the ocean looked like you could have walked on it. We must have pulled in a year's worth of fish that day and my arms were sore as. Finally he said enough is enough, time to head home.

And the motor wouldn't start. Nothing. No power, no juice, no radio. Nothing.

Then these clouds came from nowhere and within half an hour it was pissing down and blowing a gale. And we were up and down like a cork in a spa, taking water into the engine compartment. Dad stayed calm, taking shit apart, going hmmm and putting it back together again. I was getting spewy and saying sorry to God for being such a little bastard but would he please just let the motor start so we could get the fuck out of there.

And Dad put his arm around my shoulder and said, 'Doesn't look too good right now, does it?'

Well, no.

'What do you think we should do, son?'

Cry. Drink all the beer even though I'm only ten. Shout help. 'Send up a flare?'

He clapped me on the back. 'Fucking genius.'

'Activate the EPIRB?'

'Guru. My oath.'

'Try again with the engine?'

'I can die happy. My son is not an idiot.'

*And he tried again. And the boat started. And I withdrew my apology to God. Later he told me that the engine was fine. He was just checking on how useless I really was. The message was: think things through and keep your options open. Stay calm when the storm closes in.*

# 35

Tess Maguire couldn't believe that Travis Grant would push his luck this far. At five minutes past ten, the magistrate had looked up from his paperwork to find that Grant wasn't in court as summoned. He'd looked at Tess over the rim of his spectacles as if Grant's recidivism was her fault.

'Can somebody go and find Mr Grant and bring him here? Today, please.'

So Tess was back again, knocking on the shabby door of that Mount Clarence shack. 'Travis, open up, it's the police and you're in trouble.'

Another hacking cough from inside and the door juddering in the jamb. 'What?'

Tess lodged her foot in the gap, put her weight against the door and grabbed the neck of his T-shirt. 'You're coming with me.'

'Hang on, me clothes!' Tess glanced downwards and grimaced. He was naked from the waist down. What had possessed him to answer the door like that?

'Jocks, strides, shoes. Ten seconds.' She unclipped her taser. 'I'm counting.'

'Fuck's sake.'

'Three, four, five ...'

'No need for this shit, I've got rights.'

'Seven, eight ...'

'I'm coming. Take it easy.'

She put him in the front passenger seat rather than the cage. He was pathetic, not dangerous. 'Why'd you make me do this, Travis? You knew you had to be in court by ten.'

'Yeah, tomorrow.'

'Tomorrow is Saturday. It was today you had to be there.'

'Today? Where'd Thursday go?'

God knows. 'How'd you fall so low, Travis? I don't recall you being such a loser.'

'Are you allowed to speak to me like that?'

'Harden up. If you have a problem, tell it to the magistrate. He doesn't like being taken for granted either. Odds on he'll lock you up.'

'Shit. That's not fair.'

'Life sucks. Get over it.'

Travis lifted his T-shirt to reveal a pale, blubbery belly.

Tess growled. 'What are you doing now?'

'You wanted to know why I'm a loser?' Another centimeter higher and there was an ugly purple scar running horizontally under his man boobs. 'That mad fucker Stevenson did this. Said he was going to cut my heart out. I was in hospital for a month while they tucked my intestines and shit back in. Still have post-dramatic stress syndrome and that.'

'Traumatic.'

'Yeah, it fuckin' was.'

She searched for the Stevenson boy's name in her memory. 'Why'd Kane do that to you?'

'Kane? Nah, he'd been dead a week by then. It was that psycho brother of his. Scariest fourteen-year-old you could meet. Fuckin' werewolf man, I tell ya. Rabid.'

'Jai?'

'That's the cunt.'

Tess was aware of a chill creeping through her insides. 'Where is he now?'

'Dead, I hope.'

'He didn't do time for stabbing you?'

'You joking? I'm not a snitch. Specially not where he's concerned.'

'Last I heard he was in boarding school in Esperance?'

'He was expelled the same year he went for me. Bad year for that family, daddy carked it in prison, Kane dead in a car crash, and that wasn't my fault just 'cause he was coming home from my place pissed, you can't blame me.'

'What about the mum?'

'Well you'd imagine Kerry'd be a bit upset wouldn't you? Hubby and first-born dead and your only remaining child the devil's spawn.'

'Was she?'

He pulled his T-shirt back down. 'Took it in her stride, I think.'


Tess dropped Travis off in the care of the Court Custody Officer and went back to the office to look up Kerry Stevenson, mother of the devil's spawn. If Jai, who must be eighteen or nineteen by now, was behind all this mayhem, then maybe Kerry had some idea where he might be. Jai Stevenson. They'd had a nickname for him — the Disaffected Youth of Hopetoun. She recalled the siege in their Hopetoun house, the police officer he'd shot and the tense stand-off before they could get help. An eleven-year-old child totally lacking in remorse, who seemed to have no understanding of right and wrong. She'd tasered him once; she'd obviously used the wrong weapon.

According to the driving licence records, Kerry Stevenson was living in a Homeswest unit on the outskirts of Albany one street back from the busy highway to the north. It was a drab, ugly area of light industrial units and fast-food outlets and the road to her home was covered in broken glass and burnout tyre marks. The Fast and the Furious lived out here, and Tess could see their point. She rapped on a buckled screen door that bore the scars of previous jemmy attempts.

'Anyone home?'

'Who's askin'?'

There was a window open and Tess could smell cigarette smoke through the gap. 'Tess Maguire, Albany police. Can I come in?'

'Why?'

'I need to talk to you. Open up so I don't have to go away and fetch the big blokes with the battering ram.'

'Haven't seen him.'

'Who?'

'Jai. That's who you're after, isn't it?'

'How do you know?'

'Saw that Chinese cop on the news. His boy got hurt. Bloke with a grudge, they said. That'd be my Jai, I thought.'

'Open the door, I don't want to have this conversation through a window.'

'No wuckers.' A heave, some padding of feet on lino, and the snick of a latch.

Tess followed her back into the gloom, wrinkling her nose at the cigarette fug. 'Maybe we could sit out the back?'

'If you want. I'd offer you tea or coffee or something but I can't be arsed.'

They took their seats on the underused, unloved plastic patio furniture. 'Any idea where Jai is now?' Tess scraped some cigarette butts away with her shoe and pushed the ashtray nearer to Kerry. Jai's mum hadn't changed that much, still favoured velour trackies and sweat tops, eyes jaundiced by fags and bad food.

'No.'

'When did you last hear from him?'

'About six months ago.'

'Where was he then?'

'Perth, he got in with some Christian youth club.' Cue quote fingers. 'Said he'd been "saved", "seen the light".' A snort and a cascade of smoke.

'You didn't believe him.'

'Why would I? He uses people, says what they want to hear, then guts them when they're not lookin'. I should fuckin' know. Christianity? Fuck that. He's having everybody on.'

'And he'd been expelled from boarding school when he was what, fourteen? Round about the time his dad died.'

'Just after. They kicked him out when we stopped paying the fees. He went to the local high school here for a while — well, he was enrolled but never went much.'

'You sold the place in Hopetoun?'

'Bank took it. All Keith left us was his debts.'

'Where did you live?'

'With my sister but she kicked me out after three months 'cause she's a selfish, ungrateful bitch. A mate put me up for a while until the department gave me this place.'

'Where was Jai all this time? With you?'

'Fuck knows. He didn't want to live in other people's houses. Didn't want their charity.' She lifted her chin at the grim surroundings as she blew out some smoke. 'Wasn't ever going to live in a shithole like this.'

'He lived on the streets? With friends? Rellies?'

'No. Who'd want him as a house guest?'

'So on the streets then?'

'S'pose so.'

'From the age of fourteen? How long for?'

'How should I know? I'd hear from him maybe once or twice a year. Usually he'd come round if he needed something. Had a few break-ins here during that time; 'spect they were him.'

Homeless at fourteen. Quite possibly for at least a couple of years. In some people that might foster empathy, in others a steely resourcefulness. Jai? Tess could imagine that for him it would also help develop a lethal grudge. Especially if you already had psychopathic tendencies. 'So apart from tapping you for cash, how could Jai cover his expenses all that time?'

She shrugged. 'Maybe bashed a granny or two, or sold his arse.' A rasping chuckle. 'Maybe he found a sugar mummy or daddy.'

Sugar daddy.

'Keith didn't leave him anything? Some stash in a foreign trust fund or something? Maybe matured when he hit eighteen. Wasn't Jai his favourite?'

A narrowing of the eyes. 'You might be onto something there.' Kerry furiously stabbed her cigarette into the ashtray. 'Bastard. Typical, and here's me, the love of his fucking life, left penniless. Arsehole.'

'And you have no idea at all where Jai is now?'

'Nah.'

'It didn't occur to you to phone the cops when you saw that stuff on the news and guessed Jai might be behind it?'

'Nah, sorry.'

Tess's hand hovered over her taser before she reached into a pocket and found a business card. She wrote her mobile and home number on the back. 'If he gets in touch, call me, immediately.'

'Oh, okay, sure officer.'

Tess leaned down close to Kerry. 'I mean it. You've bred a killer.' She waved her fingers at the bleak decor. 'You reckon your life is shit now? Try spending a few years in Bandyup as an accessory to murder. One way or another I'll make it my job to make the rest of your life hell.'

Kerry sucked on her cigarette, the aim was for cool defiance but she couldn't quite pull it off. There was a memory stirring there. 'Don't I know you from somewhere? I've seen you around town in the last few months, haven't I? You're that cow from Hopetoun.'

'Yes,' said Tess. 'Remember me now? I'm the mad bitch who tasered your little boy for no good reason. There's no telling what I'm capable of.'

Cato had no real idea where to start. The trail had led him south to Esperance, maybe somewhere along this coast the real Samuels had met his nemesis and failed to return from his fateful fishing trip. But it was a lot of coastline and countless good fishing spots. The man who'd set Cato on this trail, mine manager Bob Peake, was now in a coma. According to the news updates he'd been bludgeoned and left for dead. With one shift on duty and another sleeping, there had been no useful witnesses. Security at the mine site was non-existent, it wasn't that kind of place.

Sharon had handed Ella over while she went to Target in search of undies. They were at a window seat in a cafe on the main drag and Ella was shaking something colourful and plastic while Cato sipped at a tepid flat white, eyeing all passers-by in case they were the man he was after. His phone went. Caller ID Tess Maguire.

'It's Jai ...'

'Stevenson,' said Cato. 'How do you know?' She told him. It made absolute sense and no sense at all. 'I've seen his photo. Even accounting for the change from boy to man there was little or no resemblance to the kid I remember.'

'Maybe he had surgery. Where are you and how do you know it's him?'

'Esperance.' He told her about the trail from Street Angels to the Laverton mine and the attack on Bob Peake. 'I was going off not much more than gut feeling and geographical coincidence. Until you rang.'

'So he's following you. Go to the Esperance cop shop and don't leave until I get there.'

'There's no need ...'

'Don't be a bloody idiot, you know already what he's capable of. Just do it.'

'I ...'

'I'll call them and tell them to expect you. See you in about four or five hours.'

She signed off and almost immediately there was an incoming message on Cato's mobile. From Jane: ***Jake has woken up.***

# 36

By late morning, Cato had put Sharon and Ella on the next plane out to Perth where they would be met by colleagues and taken to safe accommodation. After he saw what was on her phone, his mind was made up. Under the guise of the undies shopping expedition to Target, she'd checked her emails again. Her AFP colleagues in Canberra had not only narrowed it down to this one name, Jai Stevenson, but they'd also connected him to two credit cards and three bank accounts: a dormant one in the name of David Lance Samuels and an active one in the Stevenson name, plus a further one based offshore known under the title SaS Family Trust. Cato recalled that SaS was also the name of the labour hire subcontracting firm run by the Stevensons. Was that what Peake was getting antsy about? Did they have connections into Dragonfly mine? At around about the time the last cash withdrawal was made from the Samuels account, a similar cash amount was deposited in Jai Stevenson's personal account. Otherwise there were regular transfers from the substantial offshore trust to top up Stevenson's personal stash and the credit cards. The most recent activity on the Stevenson account had been two ATM withdrawals in two days, Kalgoorlie and then Esperance, earlier this morning.

Stevenson was nearby. Cato wasn't taking any more risks.

'You should be coming with us.' Sharon was angry and worried. 'You know that.'

Cato wanted to be on that plane with his family, but he also wanted to end this. Jane had reassured him the vital signs were good but that Jake was still asleep more than he was awake. 'If this

295

bastard is so close, go after him. Stop him. Jake is going to be fine. He'll be here when you get back.' A pause. 'Just make sure you do come back, that's all.'

He'd stayed with Sharon and Ella all the way to the gate and watched them cross the tarmac. He'd also kept a close eye on their fellow passengers. Jai Stevenson, to the best of Cato's knowledge, was not on that plane to Perth. Sharon, with Ella asleep in the sling, had turned at the top of the steps, giving him a look before disappearing into the gloom of the aircraft. The plane taxied and took off and Cato followed it with his eyes until it flew into the clouds.

'Que pasa?'

Cato turned. It was Hutchens, minus the usual suit and tie, clad instead in jeans and windcheater. He was clutching a holdall. 'What are you doing here?'

'I came in on the early morning flight.' He thumbed over his shoulder. 'Been sitting in the cafe behind a newspaper until they'd gone.'

'News doesn't travel that fast. You've known something for a few hours at least?'

'Deb and Chris have been helping me out. Deb talked to the homeless charity and worked out you'd gone to Laverton. Then that bloke got attacked at the mine, it was on the news. Finally Chris Thornton dug up some names from your past and I joined the dots with this Special K nutter that's been trolling me.'

'Special K?'

'Keith, Kane, Kerry, Kwong — take your pick. That Stevenson kid from the Hopetoun job a few years ago. All the special Ks in his life, special either because he loved or hated them. I never met him but I remember you telling me you thought he did the killing his dad took the fall for. And daddy died five years ago in prison.'

'Five? He's taken a while to latch on to me.'

'Not sure you've been a priority until now.' Hutchens swapped the holdall from one hand to another. 'How about we jump in your car and talk there? This thing's heavy. Long story short, we did a trace on your mobile, found out where you were and so here I am.'

They headed for the car park. 'Pavlou in on this?' said Cato, reaching into a pocket for the keys.

'No. Not yet.' Hutchens checked his watch. 'Deb's due to tell her about now.' As if on cue his mobile buzzed. He scanned the screen and waggled it at Cato with a grin before switching it off.

'Appreciate the company and the concern, but you needn't have.'

'Fuck's sake, mate.' Hutchens unzipped the holdall and reached inside for something before slinging it on the back seat. He ratcheted the Glock. 'Give me one more bit of fun before I retire.'


Tess Maguire got a call from Cato as she was driving through Ravensthorpe, still two hours or so from Esperance.

'We think he's in the mine manager's car from Laverton, a silver Prado. It's missing from the crime scene, although he might have swapped it for something else since then. But that's what we're looking for, and we've got a chopper and spotter plane out too. Where are you?'

'I'm in Ravy.' A pause. Tess knew they were both thinking the same thing. This was going to end where it all began: Hopetoun, just fifty kilometres down the road from where she was. 'I'll wait here, make some calls.' Maybe if Stevenson was headed that way, then she would be the only thing stopping him. The light was fading and there were spots of rain on her windshield. She could see through the pub windows a handful of hardened drinkers at the bar: men whose determination was matched only by their nihilism and potential for brutality. At home, wives would be enjoying the brief respite and dogs would be cowering, waiting for the next kick. Tess had suffered firsthand from men, violence and alcohol – a mundane reality in Australia. She was sick of it.

She called Kerry Stevenson.

'You again.'

'That place you had in Hopetoun, that the bank took. Anybody living there now?'

'How the fuck would I know?'

'Jai been in touch since we spoke?'

'Yeah, he sent me flowers and a card and apologised for missing Mother's Day.'

'Some time in the next twenty-four hours your ratbag son is

going to die. Who knows? Maybe I'll be the one that does it. Then it'll just be you to go and, to be frank, the world will be a better place.'

'Good luck with that.'

Tess closed the call and rang the Hopey officer in charge, Greg Fisher, her offsider all those years ago.

'That little kid you zapped way back when? Jeez, sis, sounds like you turned him into Frankenstein.'

'Thanks for the reminder, Greg. Anyway Frankenstein's monster had some redeeming features. This bloke doesn't have any.'

'It explains a few things.'

'Like what?'

'They've never been able to fill that house. Anybody moves in, they keep having runs of bad luck, car catches fire, dog dies, you name it. They're gone after a few months. It's been empty for a good year or so now.'


Tess had stationed herself in an unmarked car on the corner of Wilkinson Street in Hopetoun, just a few doors down from the house she'd lived in when she was the officer in charge. Across the road, on the expensive side, was the old Stevenson McMansion: dark and empty. Indeed, the whole estate was darker and emptier than usual, just a few cars in a few driveways. The new owners of the nickel mine ran it on the smell of an oily rag and, with nickel prices once again in freefall, production had been scaled back, costs and staff cut further in readiness for either the next climb out of the doldrums or yet another closure. Hopetoun was no longer boom town, it was fingers-crossed town. Still she had felt a brief spark of affection and nostalgia as she'd crossed the roundabout and smelled the salt of the wind-whipped ocean spray blowing up Veal Street.

And it was good to see Greg Fisher again. Now Senior Constable. Parts of his face and neck still bore that shiny tightness from the skin grafts after the explosion and, as predicted, he had put on some weight. But maybe that was what marriage and kids did for men.

'Four.' He proudly showed her the latest photo in his wallet. 'Ellis, two months old.' He slipped the pic back in its place, patting the wallet fondly. 'This a good idea, sis? Only this bloke's Freddy Kreuger and

I'm a bit slow and fat these days. Maybe get the ninjas in, that's what they're paid for.'

'Don't worry, mate, we're just watching and waiting. No heroics. We'll call them in when we know he's arrived. Don't want to waste their time before that, do we?'

Greg dug into his packet of chips and offered Tess some. She crammed a few into her mouth and tried to crunch quietly. Greg poured the remnant crumbs into his palm and tossed the bag on the seat behind him. 'Did I ever tell you he used to be a hero of mine, that Sergeant Kwong?'

Yes, he had told her, but she was happy to keep the conversation going. 'Was he?'

'Step Forward. They used him on the recruiting posters. I fell for it, big time, the idea that somebody who's not a whitefella can make a difference.'

'You don't believe it?'

'Idealism's good when you're young. It's hard yakka when you're older, lived a bit of the reality. Must've been called a coconut and sellout five hundred times since then.'

Tess looked at him. 'You're a good man, Greg. We need good people in this job. Don't worry, you are making a difference.'

His face lit up. 'You think that, really?'

'Yep.'

A shake of the head. 'Man, he's had it tough, that Sergeant Kwong.' Fisher dug around in the glove box until he found what he was looking for: Black & Gold party mix. 'Lolly?'

Cato now knew that Tess was headed for the empty ex-Stevenson house in Hopetoun and it was a good bet that it would be where Jai Stevenson was also headed. DI Hutchens had agreed with him that calling in the TRG too early might scare Stevenson away. The only way they could get there quickly would be by chopper, and the noise of it would tip him off and send him elsewhere.

'They could land along the coast and come in by boat.' Hutchens was fiddling with his Glock in an uncharacteristically nervous manner.

They dismissed that too. One thing Stevenson was good at was changing the game, doing the unpredictable, staying one step ahead. Commit the ninjas to tramping up the beach at Hopetoun while Stevenson rocks up somewhere else like Norseman, and you're looking at what Hutchens would call a dog's breakfast. No, best to have them on standby a short hop away in Esperance and let others do the guesswork.

Cato was getting jumpy at Hutchens checking and re-checking his pistol. 'You fired one of them recently? Up to date on your proficiency training?'

'You just point it and pull the trigger. What's to know?'

'You needn't be down here, you know. I appreciate it and everything but ...'

'Wouldn't have it any other way, mate. I know how you stood by me after that bloke whacked me with the willow.'

Cato looked sideways at him. 'Don't go taking any bullets for me. I've already got enough on my conscience.'

'I'll try not to burden you unnecessarily.' Another nervous pistol ratchet. 'I'd never have picked Stevenson from the list. Didn't have that much to do with it, even though I was nominally supervising, but he latched on to me anyway. He must have seen me in the paper taking credit for your work at the time. Maybe saw me again talking tweets in the community newspaper.'

'I still don't get the appearance thing, though. All I remember is a scrawny little kid sucking a ChupaChup.' A kid with a small scar.

Hutchens nodded confirmation. 'The hare lip. Cleft palate I think they call it now. Thornton ran his passport through the system and old credit card records and it turns out he'd paid a visit to a private hospital in Bangkok just over a year ago. Good quality plastic surgery at very reasonable rates. Marj had her facelift and tits done in a similar place two years back to celebrate me coming out of my coma.'

'I thought she was looking well.'

'A bit of extra sculpting on the nose and chin, and long sessions in the gym to change the general build. Chuck in some carefully carved facial hair to help mask the scars and hey presto, new Jai.'

'All that work for nothing.' Cato slowed as a roo bounded across the road ahead. 'I'm going to kill him.'

'Get in line,' said Hutchens. 'Privilege of rank.'

Tess saw Stevenson pull up in the driveway of the house. She nudged Greg Fisher out of his snooze.

'He's here.'

Stevenson was leaning into the back of the car. Dragging something out of the back seat. Something? Somebody. A moan. Sounded like a woman. He hoisted her onto his shoulder, fireman-style. 'Let's go,' said Tess.

'But I thought ...'

'I know we were going to wait for backup but he's got a hostage. He's not expecting us. It's our best chance.'

'Hang on ...'

She turned. 'Call it in, then watch my back. That's all I ask.' Then she was out of the car and walking as quickly and as quietly as she could up the street. Her gun drawn, forty metres to go. Thirty metres, heart hammering in her chest: do it now, just kill him, shoot him in the back. Nobody will care. Yes they would. She would. Would she? Tess bringing the Glock up into firing position. Could she get a clear shot in this dim light and not hit the hostage? 'Stop. Police.'

Stevenson froze, back towards her. The woman's blonde hair tumbling around his hip.

'Slowly, gently, put her down, then kneel on the ground, hands behind your head.'

He did nothing.

'Do as I say.'

Greg Fisher had joined her, his gun out too. Circling around to be side-on to Stevenson.

'Jai, do as I say or I will shoot you.'

'I know that voice. Taser Tess.' A chuckle. 'Brilliant! Man, that was some jolt you gave me.'

'Jai ...'

Slowly he turned around, the blonde still slumped over his shoulder, a gun pressed into her ribs. 'So what now?' he said.

Greg glanced at Tess, tightened his finger on the trigger.

'Now,' said Jai. 'Both of you throw your guns away.'

'No,' said Tess.

'You know I'll kill her.'

A dog barked a few houses down. Somebody yelled at it to shut up. Lights were coming on and front doors opening. Curious silhouettes. Tess was a police officer, Greg was a police officer. Their priority was public safety. She couldn't risk drawing the neighbours into this. 'Okay, let's all stay calm. We're going to do as you say and we don't want anybody getting hurt.'

Greg Fisher was shaking his head. 'Sarge ...'

An elderly woman, a neighbour Tess remembered from years ago, was walking towards them. 'What's going on there, everything alright?'

'No problem, Mary. Get back inside, it's cold out.'

'Is that you, Tess Maguire? Well, I'll be. How are you, dear?'

'I'll be down to talk to you in a minute, Mary. Put the kettle on.' Mary went away. Tess crouched down and placed her gun on the ground.

'Taser too,' said Stevenson. She did as she was told. Stevenson turned to Fisher. 'You as well.'

A hesitation. Greg looking at her for guidance. Tess felt an overwhelming sadness. Another mistake. Another poor judgement call. She had a flashback of the night she'd led a previous colleague into disaster in that pub up north. 'Do it, Greg. Please.'

A resigned shake of the head and he dropped his gun and taser to the ground. A tentative reaching for his wallet. Just a pat. The family photos inside.

Stevenson shot Fisher.

'No. Oh god, no.' Tess braced herself.

'Kneel.'

A tear leaked from her eye. 'Fuck you.'

He prodded the gun hard into the blonde woman's ribs again. Elicited a groan. 'Do it, or she dies.'

Tess knelt. Aware of Stevenson edging around behind her. An execution, here in the street in bloody Hopetoun. She closed her eyes. Waited. Heard him shuffling closer.

Then Tess felt a huge jolt in her chest. Knew immediately she'd been tasered. She fought to stay in control and lost. Stevenson dropped the blonde and the taser on the ground, retrieved the gun from his waistband, grabbed Tess by the ankles and dragged her into the house. The door slammed behind him.

# 37

'You need to ease up on the pedal, mate. There'll be roos all over this road. We'll be no use to anybody arse-up in a ditch.'

They'd had the call. Hopetoun. Residents reporting shots fired and officers down. Officers down: Tess Maguire and Greg Fisher. Cato had floored it the last hundred ks from Munglinup and now they were halfway down the dark, winding road from Ravensthorpe to Hopetoun. The speed Cato was going, they'd be there in ten minutes.

'TRG should be with us in fifteen. Ambulance on the way?'

'The local one's already there. And the Ravy one should be joining them about now, along with the Ravy cops.' Hutchens cleared his throat. 'Don't blame yourself, Cato. This is all down to Stevenson. All of it.'

Nice sentiments but Cato was already neck-deep in self-blame. He'd have loved to just curl up on the ground and give it all away. Instead he'd been hiding behind banter with the boss and the detail of the task at hand, keeping a lid on that bubbling cauldron of panic and despair. But once that call came in, the cold and calm returned.

Rain had come and gone several times throughout the journey and the wind had picked up. Clouds scudded across the sky, occasionally clearing and bathing them in moonlight, exposing the brooding silhouette of the Barren Ranges to the west. A big black sleeping dog that Cato had never let lie. And that's why he was here. On the outskirts of town and back in mobile range, Cato's phone lit up. Hutchens grabbed it. Showed Cato the screen.

A photo of Tess, prone on a bed.

**No need to rush, c u when we c u :)**


'Fuck that hurt.' A tearing of velcro straps on the bulletproof vest. The bullet had hit Greg square in the chest. The Kevlar had taken the brunt of it but he was winded and surprised to be alive. But what about Tess?

'Tess? Tess, you alright?'

No answer. The lights were on in the Stevenson house. Was she in there?

Flashing reds, an ambulance. A male voice. 'You okay there, Greg?'

'Stevo, where ya been?'

'The mine, bloke trapped his hand in some machine. Would've been back quicker but I had to sign something for Health and Safety.'

Greg nodded towards the house. 'Better stay back, there's a bloke with a gun just in there.'

'Fuck that, let's get you away first.'

Greg shook his head, groggy. 'Tess. You seen Tess anywhere?'

Stevo looked around, shaking his head. 'Nah, mate.' Then he saw the figure slumped by the vehicle in the driveway. Ran over. 'Someone here.' Mumbling, groaning. Indecipherable. 'It's not Tess. Lay still, love. You're gonna be okay.'

More murmuring. It turned out she was Dutch. A backpacker. Hitchhiking along the south coast. Hitching in Oz, thought Greg. Who does that since Ivan Milat? 'She okay?'

'Bit bashed about, but should be.' Stevo looked at the lit-up house. 'Maybe Tess's in there?'

Greg had already worked that out. 'We need to get a perimeter up, keep people away.'

More lights, another ambulance, more cops. Just the beginning. This would be a real circus soon enough. Greg struggled to his feet. He briefed the newly arrived Ravy cops and they set about clearing the street, arranging for the handful of residents affected to be either housed at friends or family or put up in the motel. Greg studied the house from the end of the driveway. Lights were on upstairs but nowhere else. He shuddered at the thought of what might be happening in there. Fought the urge to kick the door down and go in guns blazing. At this stage, there was a chance that Tess was still alive. If they did things his way, he might feel better but, for sure, Tess would die.

In the distance the sound of an approaching helicopter. The ninjas had arrived. Leave it to the professionals. Another car approaching the perimeter. The glare of the headlights blinded Greg but he knew that it would be Cato.


Tess came to, groggy. She was in a room, on a bed. Her head pounded and her eyes felt puffy, bruised. She'd felt herself being dragged into the house by her feet as if she was a lightweight doll. Then fists raining down on her, blacking her out. Stevenson was at the window, to one side, peering down through a gap in the curtains. He turned.

'You're awake.'

Tess shook her head softly. It hurt. 'You're going to die, you know that, don't you?'

He put his gun down on the window sill. 'Living's not all it's cracked up to be.'

'Why are you doing this?'

'All of it or just this, now?'

'Whatever.'

'You think Kwong's a good bloke. Course you do. But he killed my dad, my big brother, took away everything we had.'

'I think you've got the wrong guy.'

'No,' he said. 'I haven't. My dad was put in jail for a crime he didn't commit. Kwong has a history of doing that to people. If it hadn't been for him, my dad would have got the medical care he needed. He died alone, in the prison hospital, without any of us there.'

Little House on the bloody Prairie. 'Fairy story, Jai. You know it.'

'It's all Kwong's fault. I'm just righting a wrong.'

No point, thought Tess. No point arguing. 'Who was the woman in your car?'

'Some backpacker. Travel insurance. But when I realised who you were, I decided to upgrade.'

'Are you going to kill me?'

'Yes.'

Cato shrugged on a spare Kevlar from Hutchens' heavy holdall and checked the Glock he'd just been handed. The chopper had just landed a few blocks away in the park opposite the pub. Its light turning everything below from night to day, its roar deafening.

'He's upstairs,' said Greg. 'I saw the curtain move.'

'He'll be wanting me in there,' said Cato.

'No way,' growled Hutchens. 'Anyone got plans of the house?'

'I have.' It was DI Pavlou in combat gear, leading a squad of TRG up the road, swiping her iPad on the way.

'Who booked fucking Cirque du Soleil?' snarled Hutchens.

'Be nice, Mick.' Pavlou nodded to TRG Dave to get his squad in place.

'I know the layout of the house,' said Cato. 'I've been inside.' He knew the back patio and garden where he'd had his face singed on a barbecue hotplate. He knew the inside where he'd taken a boy's life to the brink to extract a confession from a father who turned out to be innocent and taking the fall for his killer son. Chickens coming home to roost. 'Open-plan kitchen and living area and a staircase leading to four bedrooms, bath, and toilet up top. Ensuite in the main.'

'Where they are now,' said Greg. He introduced himself to Pavlou. 'I'm one of the officers downed.' He tapped his chest. 'Kevlar.'

'Lucky boy,' said Pavlou. 'Is there a landline in there?'

Greg shook his head. 'The wire goes in but it's probably disconnected.'

Pavlou summoned TRG Dave and his tech Tristram, a baby-faced muscle man. 'Do whatever you need to do to reconnect the landline; meantime, what mobile's he on?'

'He's using this one.' Cato gave them the number from the last message he received, the photo of Tess. 'It's me he wants in there. It's not going to end any other way.'

'Bullshit,' said Pavlou and TRG Dave nodded his agreement. 'We do this by the book. Whatever the consequences.'

'Yeah?' said Cato. He ran the five metres or so to the front door of the house and threw his full weight onto it, crashing through. 'Jai?' he shouted up the stairs. 'It's me.'

Jai had dragged Tess to the top of the stairs in a headlock, holding her as his shield, gun at her ear. 'Close the door.'

One hinge was loose but most of the damage was around the latch. Cato pushed it shut. 'Can't lock it. Sorry.'

'Open it again and throw your gun, vest and phone outside. Then come up the stairs, on your knees.' Cato did as he was asked, Jai backing away with Tess the nearer Cato got to the top.

'You okay, Tess?'

She blinked, grim-faced.

'She's fine,' said Jai.

Cato studied him. 'You've changed since I last saw you.'

'At heart I'm still the same.' They retreated to the master bedroom with Cato following on his knees like an abject penitent on a pilgrimage. 'Sorry about your son.'

'No, you're not.'

A smile. 'Guess not. I did kinda like him though. Jake was a trier down at the gym.' Stevenson sighed, like he meant it. 'But so lonely and sad. He told me he felt like he'd been left behind, everybody moved on and, however hard he tried, he just couldn't catch up again.'

Cato fought it down, saw this for what it was. He couldn't let Stevenson enjoy that pain. 'Jake is recovering well. You failed. So what's the homeless thing about? Why them?'

'You don't want to talk about Jake, I understand that. He found it hard to talk about you, too. He'd given up on you, like you'd given up on him.'

'Yeah, I'd love to say you're wrong, Jai. But I can't.' Cato tilted his head. 'You have me now, let Tess go.'

'Not yet.'

'You could have killed us both by now. What are you waiting for?'

'Junk food is for chucking down. Save up for a nice steak, you want to enjoy it, don't you?'

'Besides, you're surrounded. You need something to bargain with, right?'

'Maybe. Either way I'm in charge.'

'You? You're a fuck-up. Like your dad.'

'Watch yourself,' he said softly, twisting a handful of Tess's hair and prodding the gun barrel into her cheek.

'Gun come from daddy's old contacts?' enquired Cato.

Jai shrugged. 'What about it?'

'Reckon Keith was Dad of the Year do you? Your special K? All I remember is a greedy, money-grubbing little bully. A small man with small, spiteful ideas about the world.'

The face darkened. Cato recalled that black-eyed kid playing his ultra-violent video games while the adults talked in the kitchen. The glower when he was asked to mute the noise of murder and mayhem. 'Dog-eat-dog, life's tough. All those bludgers were a waste of space. They were nothing.'

'Living on the streets at fourteen can't have been easy,' said Tess. 'Never know when somebody's going to want a piece of you.'

A snort. 'Nobody ever got it though.'

Cato picked up on the theme. 'And until then you'd grown up wanting for nothing. Must have reminded you every day of how shitty your life had turned. How your dad had failed you.'

An irritable shake of the head. 'Nah, you're wrong.'

'All of those homeless were battlers,' said Tess. 'More than you ever were, little rich boy, scabbing off daddy's trust account.'

'Only once he turned eighteen,' Cato pointed out. 'Before that he had it rough. Those years on the streets, hard when you're not used to it, eh?'

'Reckon?' said Jai. 'Got a dollar, mister? Help me with my bus fare, mate?' His face twisted. 'Pity me. Pity me.'

'And it's easier to attack them than go after the big end of town, I expect,' said Tess.

'I had to hang out with those losers, because of him.' He turned back to Cato. 'Because of what you did to my dad.'

'He was in prison for what you did. His choice. And you let him. And what a legacy he left behind ...'

Jai pointed his gun at Cato. 'Shut it.'

'... A spoilt brat, entitlement on legs.'

He pulled the trigger.


They heard the roar outside.

'We need to go in.' Hutchens took a step towards the house.

'Stop there, don't be such an idiot, Mick.' Pavlou was interrupted by a wave from TRG Dave. Stevenson had turned the mobile off but the landline was now connected by remote. 'Call him.'

They could hear the landline phone ringing, downstairs in the kitchen. It rang out, unanswered.

'The mobile's back on.'

Almost immediately Cato's phone lit up and danced in the driveway. Hutchens retrieved it, ignoring the warnings from Pavlou and TRG Dave. 'What?'

'You rang me first,' said Stevenson.

'What was the shot?'

'Your colleague, he's bleeding.'

'Dead?'

'No, I'm not finished with him yet.'

'What about the woman?'

'Same.'

'Let them both go.'

'No.'

'What do you want from us?'

'Nothing.'

'We're going to kill you, fuckface.'

'I'll be waiting.' The phone died.

Pavlou stared at him. 'You haven't done the latest hostage negotiation course have you?'

'Bit rusty, that's all.'

TRG Dave sidled up. 'I reckon you should put off retirement and come over to us. There's a balaclava with your name on it, just waiting.'

Hutchens would have laughed but he didn't have time. This was turning pear-shaped. Protocol be damned.


Mary was determined to make Greg a cup of tea and she seemed so frail and so relieved that he wasn't dead that it would be a shame to deny her.

'Milk and one, that'd be great.'

Hutchens said milk and none for him. Outside, he'd taken Fisher aside and asked his advice. Greg had an idea. 'Follow me,' he'd said. 'Fancy a cuppa?'

They had walked two doors down from the Stevenson house. Mary's was slightly more modest than the other McMansions on that side but still a palace compared to the police house Fisher now occupied directly over the road. He'd given Hutchens the background as they walked. Mary's son had installed her in there when he worked at the mine under the original owners. He had long since moved on with his young family but Mary had taken a shine to the place and stayed, rattling around in there like a contented pea in a tin.

'What on earth is going on?' Mary's tea was thick and brown and sluiced out of the spout like it had to be somewhere in a hurry. 'Is Tess going to be alright?'

'Hope so, Mary. Fingers crossed. The old Stevenson house. Remember the boy, always in trouble?' said Greg. A nod. 'Well he's back and worse, a lot worse.'

'He killed my darling Henry, I'm sure of it.'

'The tortoiseshell tom?'

'Never proven, but the whole week after Henry went missing that little bastard had a smirk on his face.' Mary wrenched open a pack of chocolate digestives and offered them out. Hutchens declined. 'They were a pain in the arse, the lot of them. And the noise! Parties every other weekend and music going all hours. It was a relief when Keith went to prison.'

Greg nodded, he remembered the parties and the complaints every following morning that he or Tess usually had to deal with. 'Next door's still empty, right?'

'Yes. There was a South African couple in there for a few months, both at the mine, but I think they found it all a bit too quiet. He got a job with some other outfit in Port Hedland and they shipped out.'

The thing about these McMansions, Greg had told Hutchens, was that while the houses were enormous the blocks were still the same size as the rest in the street. Gardens had been sacrificed for gadget space. That meant the houses were close together, barely a metre or so separating them. 'You'll have to do the honours, boss.' He'd prodded his gut. 'Too much of the good life. I won't fit through the window.'

'Mind if I use the dunny, Mary?' Hutchens pointed upstairs.

'Be my guest. There's plenty of paper.' Mary seemed a lovely woman but maybe just a touch too intimate for polite company. 'There's also the one downstairs, back there on the left.'

'I'll use the upstairs one if it's okay.' He patted his tummy. 'Had a curry last night. Came back to bite me.'

'Suit yourself. Been a bit farty myself lately.'


Squeezing out on to the window ledge, Hutchens was able to reach the window of the neighbour's house with a long stretch of his leg. Fisher had been right. The tubby git would never have got through the bathroom window. Three cheers for Marjorie's salads. He steadied himself, gripping a TV satellite dish securely mounted nearby. Once over, he bent down and stabbed his baton into the glass hoping the noise would be muffled by distance, wind and the small gap between the houses. It was a laborious process but necessary. The TRG would never have let him through their cordon and he was determined not to let Stevenson win while Pavlou dithered. Time for some fucking leadership one last time before pension day.

One more house to go. He crept through the dark empty rooms to the far side, his path illuminated here and there by pools of moonlight through windows. The next step was trickier. He couldn't smash his way into the upstairs toilet of the Stevenson house, it would be heard either by the TRG or by Stevenson himself. But when he'd looked up from outside he'd seen a skylight open higher in the roof space.

He wondered where the equivalent would be in this neighbouring house. They were no doubt built to a plan, off-the-peg, so there should be one, but there was no obvious staircase to another level. He was loathe to turn on any lights or use a torch and give himself away. He rested, tried to let his eyes accustom to the gloom. After a while he saw it, a trapdoor in the ceiling with a metal ring protruding. He opened a nearby cupboard and found what he was looking for. The pole hook that would open it and bring down the retractable ladder.

The roof space was just that — no den or bolt-hole office, just insulation batts, rat poison in old ice-cream containers and a skylight. He opened it. The Stevenson house was an extended step away across an eight-metre drop. Hutchens heard a strange humming noise, wondered if it was his tinnitus from that time the gun went off near his head.

Hutchens and the local plod had gone walkabout. God knows what they were up to. 'The guy's out of control,' said Pavlou. 'I'm going to throw the book at him.'

'Might just be settling down the neighbours,' TRG Dave offered. 'Probably best to focus on the job at hand, eh?'

'I don't need any advice from you, thanks.'

'No,' he murmured. 'I can see that.'

Pavlou was itching for a fight. 'Meaning?'

They were saved by an interruption from Tristram the Techie with his laptop. 'We've got the drone up there watching and listening.'

'And?'

Tristram stroked his fingers on the keypad. A shaky blur on the screen morphed into thermal images, two figures together and a third about a metre away — not moving.

Pavlou prodded the third static figure on the screen. 'Cato?'

'Fair bet.' TRG Dave straightened his back. A prelude to a decision. 'We know exactly where they are, we know where to go in. If Cato's been shot, he's in danger the longer we leave it. And this joker isn't going to be negotiated out of there, is he?'

Pavlou nodded. 'Better do it then.'

Tristram lifted a hand, eyes glued to his screen. 'There's a complication.'

'What?'

'The drone's picked up something else.' He turned his screen to face them. A shadowy figure stepping from the roof of the neighbour's house over to this one.

'Is that who I think it is?' growled Pavlou.

Cato felt himself drifting. The pain was excruciating but, more worrying, was the creeping numbness up his leg and the blood spreading out from his thigh and across the floor.

'I think your colleagues are worried about you,' said Stevenson. 'They'll probably make a move soon.'

'Let Tess go. This is about you and me, nobody else.'

'Wasn't always. I was just having my fun. Probably would have stopped after the jacks. Maybe the queens, kings, dunno. Then I saw you were involved. Looking for me.'

'So, like I said. Let her go.'

'Easy enough to track you down. And there was your son. Same needy look I've seen so many times before. A gift.'

Cato could steadily bleed his life away here while Jai taunted him about his son. He needed to keep the conversation going until rescue came, or a plan materialised, or a miracle occurred. Tess met his eyes. She was thinking the same thing. Planning something maybe? Distract him. 'The mine manager in Laverton. He knew what you'd done with David Samuels. Otherwise why try to kill him?'

'Try? Haven't you heard? He died.'

'Whatever. I'm right though, aren't I?'

'Bobby was an old mate of my dad's. Happy to keep the business ticking over but Dad never trusted him. A skimmer with a big mouth.'

So the Stevenson labour supply business was under new management but retaining the same old shifty rip-off practices. 'And David Samuels got wind of it? So you both took care of him. Took his ID while you were at it.'

'Two birds, one stone.'

'Keith would have been proud.'

'Yeah,' said Stevenson. 'He would.'

Cato could see something shifting in Stevenson's demeanour. A steeling, a bracing, a build to something new, something worse. He had talked himself up and he was ready.

'Let Tess go, Jai. Just you and me, okay?'

'She tasered me. Why would I? You don't get it, do you?'

Yes, he did. Jai intended to inflict maximum hurt and that meant harming those Cato loved and cared for. Before his eyes. Cato had run out of options. Failed. It was a useless waste of time and they were all going to die. 'Those people you killed. Every single one of them was a better person than you or your stinking father. You make me sick.'

'Finished?' Stevenson cocked his gun and pressed Tess into a kneeling position. 'Good. Now watch this.' He placed the barrel against the top of her skull.

'Please God, no.' Cato reached out an arm, beseeching. 'Me. Just kill me.'

Tess's eyes squeezed shut.

'So beg,' said Jai. 'Go on.'

Cato was on all fours, crawling towards them, leaving a crimson trail on the carpet. 'I'm sorry. I'm sorry for your dad. Please ... Don't.' Cato saw the look of triumph on Stevenson's face. Cato brought so low. 'Please.'

Tess and Cato looked at each other, one last time.

There was a deafening explosion.

The shot had caught Stevenson under the arm and swung him around before dropping him. Hutchens quickly took the remaining steps on the spiral staircase. He pulled out a penknife and cut the cable ties: Tess was bruised and beaten but okay. Cato was a mess and needed an ambulance quickly. Doors were banging downstairs, the TRG were on their way. Tess knew she had very little time. She took the gun off Hutchens who seemed to be momentarily surprised at what he'd done. She knelt over Jai Stevenson, he was still breathing, looking up at her with a smirk on his face.

'Maguire?' said Hutchens. 'What you doing?'

She put the Glock against Jai's head. This way would be okay, looking him in the eye.

'Nah, Tess. Not allowed.' Hutchens held out his hand. 'Give it back.'

'Let me.' Cato was sitting up, holding his hand out for her gun. 'Tess, please.'

'Fuck's sake,' said Hutchens. 'What is this? Pass the parcel?'

Tess knew how much Cato wanted to, knew how much it meant to him. But she couldn't let him. He had a family he needed to be with. She on the other hand had a daughter who was grown up and would be fine. It was the last good thing she could do for him.

'Maguire. Stop now,' said Hutchens. 'That's an order.'

'Do it, Tess.' Stevenson smiled through the bubbles of blood on his lips and teeth. 'Do it for Cato.'

He thought he could still win, manipulate her to deny Cato the coup de grâce. Maybe he was right.

'You can't, can you?' Stevenson goaded.

Sometimes, thought Tess, you just have to do what's right.

She handed the gun to Hutchens. 'Here you go.' Back to Stevenson. 'This isn't one of your dumb kiddie video games where everybody goes down in a blaze of glory. Justice? It's boring, bland, shit-drudge where you have to do what you're told. That's your life from now on, Jai.'

Hutchens checked the Glock. 'Shit, put it like that, feel like eating a bullet myself.'

'Everybody face down, hands out to the side.' The gun was eased from his grip. 'You too, Hutchens.'

The TRG secured the room then called in the backup. Cato attended to there and then by one paramedic and Stevenson by another. DI Pavlou was not far behind. Eyes blazing, she gave the signal for Hutchens and Tess to be released.

'What the fuck did you think you were doing?'

Hutchens surveyed the scene. 'Your job. Hostages safe, perpetrator in custody.'

'There are civilians out there, the media have rolled up, this whole shambles, live on TV and the internet.'

Tess stepped between Pavlou and Hutchens. 'It might look like a shambles at your end but it's all sorted in here.'

Pavlou shook her head. 'Get out of here, we'll talk later.'

Tess glanced over at Cato on the way out. He looked lost. She'd denied him what he most wanted but she wasn't sorry. And she would have to keep telling herself that, over and over.

# EPILOGUE

One Month Later.

'I want another dad.'

Cato looked up from his crossword. He'd thought his son was still asleep. Jake was home now, not in the granny flat but in the room inside next to Cato and Sharon's. An hour ago they'd returned from another gruelling physio session as Jake tried to retrain his brain into connecting properly with the leg muscles again. They both went to the same rehab place in Shenton Park. Cato was there to try and get his leg to work after the bullet had passed through muscle, tissue, tendons. Jake had been exhausted on their return, as he often was, and disappeared for a nap. Cato put the paper down and jumped up to put the kettle on. 'Any ideas who?'

'Anybody. Even Simon. You're too dangerous to be related to.' The words slurred a bit, the brain needed to reacquaint itself with his speech muscles too. All in good time, the doctors had reassured them.

'Yeah, sorry about that. Yet again.'

A munted grin. 'Relax. Just testing my joke muscles.' He slumped into an armchair and accepted a coffee. 'I prob'ly should be on a herbal or something but it all tastes like shit.'

'You're right though. I am pretty crap, as dads go.'

'Yeah. I can't half pick 'em, eh?'

'Hmmm?'

'Lance. I thought he was a mate.' Tears welled. 'Got that wrong.'

'You weren't to know.'

'No? Maybe I should have.'

It had been over a cup of shit herbal stuff last week that Jake had told him he was gay. Cato hadn't guessed or even suspected. But why should he? His mind was usually elsewhere. He thought he was okay with that, knew he should be. Yes, he was. And Sharon had gently pointed out that he had no real choice in that matter — he had to be okay with it. End of story.

'No. Anyway he's out of action now.'

A nod. 'You could've been an accountant or something. Or a musician, you should have stuck at the piano when you were a kid.'

'Not a bad thought.'

'Nah. I reckon we're jinxed you and me. I'd probably trip over your abacus, or you'd close the piano lid on my fingers by accident.'

Cato winced. 'Tradie maybe? Good money.'

Jake pointed to the nail-gun scar on his cheek. 'Nah.'

'Ballet dancer?'

A snort. 'You in tights? I'd die of embarrassment.'

Cato grinned. 'Farmer.'

'Mad cow disease.'

And so it went. When Sharon got home she found them crying with laughter and unable to explain to her what was so funny. Cato's laughter, he knew, had been forced but the tears were real enough. Come to that, maybe Jake's too.


Cato limped into Hutchens' retirement do on the top floor and the room hushed for a second until he reassured them all with a grin and a raised glass of sauvignon blanc.

'Glad you could make it.' Hutchens clinked his stubby of Rogers against the wine glass and they stood shoulder to shoulder surveying the room.

'Wouldn't miss it for the world. Needed to make sure you left the premises.'

'I think that's why most of the top brass are here too. How's the leg?'

'Might never play the piano again.'

Hutchens came around in front of him. 'Seriously, mate. How are you holding up?'

Cato took a sip of wine. 'Jake's good. He's had the equivalent of a stroke. Got to relearn how to do a few basic things, like walk and talk.

But in the long run he'll get there.' Physically anyway. The doctors had also given Jake some pills for the dark days. They seemed to be helping. Cato's GP had prescribed the same ones to him too. The ones ex-Commando Chris had been on. Cato carried them everywhere with him. Unopened. 'Sharon starts back at work in the new year.' He didn't mention that she seemed mightily relieved to be doing so. Cato now openly fearful of losing everything and unable to shake that fear off. 'Me? I'm ready to chuck it all in.'

'Resign?'

'You can only bring so much of your work home with you. This was the last straw.' Cato patted his jacket pocket. 'Got the letter here and there's an email in your successor's inbox.'

'Who'da figured Paddy McMahon for DI material? Must be really scraping the barrel.'

'Another reason I'm leaving.'

'Pity, but I can see your point.' Hutchens gestured with his bottle towards the far corner of the room. 'Pavlou will be disappointed. She was hoping that with me gone you'd head over to the Dark Side with her. Now young Trimboli will probably get your spot.'

'She's welcome.' Cato could see Amy Trimboli sticking proprietorially close to her mentor. 'It's over.'

'It'll never be over while Stevenson sits in Casuarina playing games with the justice system. You'll be living with it for another few years yet.'

Jai had survived Hutchens' bullet. Unfortunately.

'I'll cross that bridge, but at least I won't have to put up with the daily trudge through the sewer.'

Hutchens eyed him. 'I mean this as a mate. You're too good to be beaten by this. The world needs more people like you, not less. It's easy for me to say, I'm going off into the sunset and I haven't been through what you've been through.'

'No, you haven't.' Cato relented. 'Although being bashed into a coma with a cricket bat couldn't have been much fun.'

'And look at me now. Speaking of which, did you hear about Johnny Jenkins?'

'No.'

'Somebody beat the crap out of him and left him at the East Perth bus station with a one-way ticket to Albany in his pocket.'

'Any suspects?'

'Hundreds. Imogen from IT showed us a screen grab from a specially set-up Facebook page. It looks like the bus ticket was crowdfunded. He could have had a return ten times over.' Hutchens grabbed a party pie from a passing tray. 'The world is mired in lies, chaos and darkness, mate.' He dipped the pie in tomato sauce and took a bite. 'You're a bringer of truth, order and light.'

'Not any more, I've had enough.'

Hutchens shook his head. 'What would you do with your time anyway? I'm already going spare trying to get away from Marjorie and her job lists and the diets she makes us go on.'

'Enjoy my family, write my memoirs. Play the piano.'

'That's the first six months taken care of.'

Cato shrugged. 'Crosswords. Maybe I could go to uni, learn something. Do a masters or a PhD.'

Hutchens scarfed the rest of the pie. 'Fuck's sake.'


Sharon had just got Ella off to sleep and returned to her emails. She wasn't due to start back until after Christmas but already her inbox was filling with the detritus of federal bureaucracy. Was she ready for this? She had to be. Life at home with Phil was a drain on her energy. Mood swings, more often down than up. It was sucking her dry and it couldn't go on, for all of their sakes. Ella mustn't be allowed to grow up with that toxicity in her life.

If it wouldn't change then it had to end.

But she'd found Phil and Jake laughing today. Surely that was a good sign? It was a nice change but it had dried up almost immediately. She'd detected an air of hysteria, a letting off of steam. So was she the one who was toxic? Was she being too impatient, too harsh, too demanding? Maybe. She had no idea what was allowable and reasonable under these circumstances. Depression and anxiety, she suspected, is as long as a piece of string and as predictable as a meth head. Maybe by leaving and taking Ella with her it would snap him out of it, break the circuit. It wasn't too late to arrange a transfer nearer to her dad's place in Victoria. Maybe Phil could follow them over when he'd sorted himself out and they'd start life anew, rebuild from there. Or maybe her leaving would be the final straw for him, with unfathomable consequences, but Sharon couldn't allow that to shake her from doing the best thing for herself and for Ella.

Try as she might, she just couldn't persuade him that the tide really had turned and it would turn further with the passage of time. Not everybody was like Stevenson, not everybody was out to destroy Phil and take his loved ones away. Why couldn't he see that? They'd prevailed. Stevenson had lost, hadn't he? But as she studied, through blurred eyes, the vacant AFP postings around the country and idly checked flight prices and timetables, Sharon reflected that perhaps Jai Stevenson had won after all.


Wind buffeted the train to Freo as it crossed the river and slowed to the station. Cato folded the *Fremantle Gazette*: no crosswords and no news to speak of. The mayor had been voted back in and it was business as usual. Brian Knight was under investigation for certain financial irregularities and had stepped down from council pending the outcome. Fraud Squad had been called in. Cato staggered a little as he stepped onto the platform and binned the paper. He'd had more drink than he intended at Hutchens' leaving do and been brooding all the way back. Sharon was right, he was being selfish. There is a time limit on stuff like grief, shame, guilt, depression, anxiety. Those around you would never say it but it was there nevertheless. A month, a year, whatever: unspoken, arbitrary, and always too soon. Cato had climbed into his own dark cave and rolled a rock over the entrance, sealing himself off.

In the park over the road from the railway station the Freo Street Doctor was packing up the van for the night and a handful of homeless patrons had gathered at a nearby picnic table. It would be an unseasonably cold night and rain threatened. Cato wandered over, one hand in a pocket jingling the loose change. The other on his medication.

'Evenin',' said one of the men, warily. 'You alright there, mate?'

'Yeah,' said Cato. He pulled his jacket closer. 'Going to be a rough night.'

'Shit happens. Want to share my swag?' A grim chuckle. The coins rubbed in Cato's pocket. 'Keep your money, mate. We've all got our beds for the night at St Mary's. We're just having a yak before we turn in.'

'Yeah,' Cato nodded. 'Right.'

'Speak for yersel'. If he wants to give me a dollar I can use it to enhance my super fund in that offshore fuckin' tax haven.' From the back of the pack, it was a voice Cato recognised. 'Don't I know you, pal?'

'G'day, Mac.'

'Hey lads, this is the copper that caught the mad bastard that wanted us all dead.' A round of handshakes and goodonyers. Cato noticed grazes on the men's knuckles. Were they the ones who'd put Johnny Jenkins in his place? 'The diary of Deano's I gave you. That help?'

'Yeah, it did.'

'Good.' Mac slung his backpack over his shoulder and lifted his jacket collar against the cold. 'We'll be going then.'

Cato nodded but made no move to leave. It seemed wrong that after all that had happened, this life, their lives, his, should just go on as usual. The haves and the have-nots coexisting in discordant harmony. Something fundamental should have changed. But it hadn't, it wouldn't.

Mac seemed to sense his paralysis. He leaned in and spoke softly. 'You need to piss off home and spend some time with your family. Sleep off all that drink you've had.'

'Right,' said Cato. 'G'night, then.'

'Yeah, g'night, mate.'

Cato headed back over to the bus stop. Those blokes were fine, they didn't need his charity. He watched them amble off across the park. Low murmurs, a laugh. Shoulders hunched against the weather. Another day battling the elements. Like yesterday, tomorrow and the day after. People just keep on keeping on, whatever the world throws at them. And he wasn't in this alone. He had Sharon, the woman it seemed he'd been waiting for all his life, a soulmate. But he'd locked her out. He had Ella, beautiful precious Ella. And Jake. Jake needed him more than ever. To lose them would be the biggest mistake of his life and he needed to do everything he could to keep them. Shake off his crippling fears and anxieties.

Cato took the pill bottle out of his pocket, unscrewed the cap, palmed one and swallowed it. He nodded determinedly to himself, he would show them that things would get better. That he was there for them, forever. That he wasn't afraid. He shivered in the wind. His bus was approaching: a light in the darkness. Today, the first day of the long journey back.

Naomi Lip glanced out of her window at the River View care home. From wheelchair height there was little to see. Some streetlights, the shadows of trees, the occasional passing car on a quiet road. Dinner was over and she had taken her medication. They'd be coming in soon to change her nappy and put the toothpaste on her brush. She was warm, had a roof over her head and regular meals. The people here weren't so bad and she really should stop giving them a hard time. All that anger, chewing away inside her all these years. With her good hand she opened up her new laptop. Created a Word document. Her hand stroked the keys. The book that everyone said was in her. The book she probably agreed was in there. The one that Norman always wanted her to write. The one that he'd coveted in himself. This was going to take fucking years. She centred the tab and pressed the italic key. Typed the dedication:

*For my brother, Norman.*

# ACKNOWLEDGEMENTS

First on the list has to be the real-life Norman Lip who, very generously, donated a large sum to an Oxfam Quiz Night auction way back in 2014 in return for having his name in the next Cato Kwong book. He bravely agreed to my exacting conditions to be able to portray the character any damn way I chose — and for the record, to the best of my knowledge, the real Norman Lip is not a promiscuous, narcissistic imbecile. The real Norman Lip has also been very patient in waiting for Cato 4 to arrive, having been delayed by *Marlborough Man* in the meantime. Once again, thank you Norman.

I would also like to thank Freo Mayor Brad Pettitt, and Michael Piu from St Pat's Community Support Centre, who gave up their valuable time to explain to me the policies and realities of the homelessness situation both in Fremantle and generally in WA. Anything I've got right is thanks to them, anything I've got wrong is down to me. The growing gap between the haves and have-nots, and our demonisation of those left behind, continue to shame us all.

Once again many thanks to my agent Clive Newman who continues to battle on my behalf. The team at Fremantle Press who do an amazing job of promoting me here and overseas (thank you Jane and Claire) and of course my wise editor Georgia Richter.

As always none of this could happen without my beautiful wife Kath continuing to allow me the freedom to dream, to stare blankly into space and to make stuff up while she does all the real work around here.

# MORE GREAT CRIME READS FROM ALAN CARTER

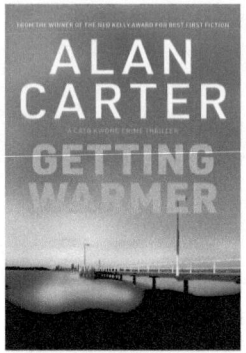

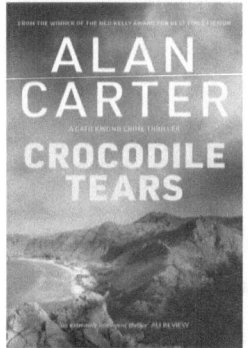

A gritty and engrossing look at crime and racism in a small Western Australian town ... a promising new talent in the field of Australian crime fiction. — *Australian Book Review*

A very strong and enjoyable read. As with all good crime fiction there are many layers to this story, genuine 'aha' moments and a very strong cast of main and supporting characters. \*\*\*\*

— *Bookseller+Publisher*

Descriptive ... witty, well researched and confident, this tale of crime in Australia's 'boom town' is a rollicking good read for those who enjoy a thrilling story. — *Minestyle Magazine*

An excellent read — let's hope we get to see more of Carter's hero, DSC Cato Kwong. — *West Australian*

ONLINE AT FREMANTLEPRESS.COM.AU

First published 2018 by
FREMANTLE PRESS

Fremantle Press Inc. trading as Fremantle Press
PO Box 158, North Fremantle, Western Australia, 6159
fremantlepress.com.au

Cover photograph by 'Slip Street', Seng Mah, venturephotography.com.au
Cover design by Nada Backovic, nadabackovic.com
and Karmen Lee, hellokarma.com

 A catalogue record for this
book is available from the
National Library of Australia

ISBN 9781925591798 (paperback)
ISBN 9781925591804 (ebook)

Fremantle Press is supported by the Western Australian State
Government through the Department of Cultural Industries, Tourism
and Sport.

Fremantle Press respectfully acknowledges the Whadjuk people of the
Noongar nation as the Traditional Owners and Custodians of the land
where we work in Walyalup.

www.ingramcontent.com/pod-product-compliance
Lightning Source LLC
Chambersburg PA
CBHW020842020726
47497CB00005B/1211